Love...
Like Snow in
Florida on a Hot
Summer Day

This book is a work of fiction. Names, characters, places, and incidents are the product of the authors' imagination or used fictitiously. Any resemblance to actual events, locales, or persons, living or dead, is coincidental. *Italics* denote places and things that are copyrighted or registered trademarks.

Copyright© 2009 by Tracy L. Darity

All rights reserved. No part of this book may be reproduced in any form or by any electronic means, including information storage, and retrieval systems, without written permission from the publisher, except by a reviewer who may quote brief passages in a review.

Teganjaz Books is a registered trademark
The Teganjaz Books colophon featuring three little girls positioned on the wording is the trademark of Tracy L. Darity

ISBN-13: 978-1-7354743-0-4

For additional copies of this book or to obtain further information, visit:
www.TracyLDarity.com
Facebook, Twitter, Goodreads – Keyword: TracyLDarity

Love... Like Snow in Florida on a Hot Summer Day

By Tracy L. Darity

 ™

Also by Tracy L. Darity

He Loves Me He Loves Me Not!

"*He Loves Me, He Loves Me Not!* is an interesting read, and many readers will reminisce about their present and past relationships - love lost and gained and, more importantly - lessons learned from each of these relationships regardless of the outcome."
Sonja of Books and Beignets Book Club

"*HE LOVES ME, HE LOVES ME NOT!* is the impressive debut from Tracy L. Darity."
Paula of The RAWSISTAZ ™ Reviewers

"*HE LOVES ME HE LOVES ME NOT!* is an awesome debut novel by Tracy Darity. This book reads like a true to life story."
Leona of UrbanFireBooks

"*He Loves Me He Loves Me Not*" was an incredible read."
Tange of OOSA Online Book Club

"When you find yourself shouting and talking to the book, you know you have found a winner."
Donnica of APOOO Book Club

Special Thanks

Angela Godwin
Tamela Gray
NaToya Jackson McMurray
Anita Reece
Juanita Caison Williams

Over a year ago, I stepped out on faith and followed my dreams of becoming a published author…*what was I thinking*. Now here I'm with my second release, and just as fearful but doubly excited about the possibilities.

I had no clue how *He Loves Me He Loves Me Not!* would be received, but every time I open an email or letter from a reader telling me how my work has touched their life, my spirit is renewed.

God has blessed me with the talent to write and craft meaningful stories, and I thank Him for this gift. I'm also thankful for great friends who believe in me, and support me, and go 110% to keep me motivated and pushing forward. Along the way, I've made new friends that I'm grateful to have in my life. Also, to all the readers out there who took a chance on unknown talent and went the extra step to send encouragement, and support words, Thank you!

Because of all of you, I'm even more convinced that this is my true calling in life, and I won't stop until I reach the top of every bestseller list out there.

So, I say thank you and ask for your continued support.

Prologue

My heart fluttered at just the thought of him. I had never known such happiness and wanted to shout it to the world, just like that white man in the *De Beers* diamond commercial, *Declaration*. He's standing on the steps of Piazza San Marco Square in Venice, Italy, professing his love for his woman. "I love this woman. I love this woman. I love this woman!"

I was so giddy with joy that I must have had a lapse in common sense. What other logical explanation would explain my sitting here telling my Grandmother about this man, about this forbidden fruit from which I'd taken a succulent bite? My Grandma Janie, the woman who began taking me to church when I was a wee bit toddler of two or three. The woman who claimed if she hadn't introduced me to God, my soul would've been lost. My Grandma Janie, the woman who loved, married, then buried her soulmate. He was a man she claims to have loved every second of every hour, of every day, of every week, of every month, of every year, sixty-three of them to be exact, that God blessed her to know him. My Grandma Janie, the woman who had taught me to be a self-respecting, Christian woman who loved the Lord and feared his wrath. So why was I shocked, hurt, even saddened when she looked me straight in my eyes, showing all the wisdom of her 89 years, and said, "Baby, God ain't gonna bless you with another woman's husband. Not today, tomorrow, not ever."

I sat straight up in my bed, gasping for air and searching my surroundings. Sometimes my dreams seem so real. Oh, how I wish I were sitting in my granny's kitchen eating her sweet potato pie and drinking iced cold sweet tea. Tea made by the power of the sun. In her backyard on a tree stump. The remnants of an oak tree we once spent our days climbing and trying to build a treehouse before the violent winds of a tropical storm downed it. Grandma Janie would always use

Sweet'n Low instead of sugar, even before the maker sold the substitute sweetener by the box. She said sugar would settle to the bottom once the tea chilled, so breaking open all those individual packets was worth it. "Sometimes you just have to do a little extra to make something you love just right," she would say.

I grab my pillow and hug it tight, smothering my sobs. It's been ten years since my granny passed peacefully in her sleep, and I still miss her as much right now as I did the day we received the call from my cousin letting us know she was gone. I look at the digital clock, and the large green numbers scream back at me. It's three a.m. Always three a.m. Too late to go back to what could have been and too early to decide which direction to go next. Three a.m., the bewitching hour that paralyzes the soul. I'm immediately reminded of a novel long ago, *Something Wicked This Way Comes,* by Ray Bradbury. We read it in middle school English class. Every time I'm awakened by a dream at three a.m., the fading memories of this book spook me. I stare out into the darkness. There's no moon and no stars to greet me. It's just me, and my dreams, and the stern admonition of my dead Granny, "Baby, God ain't gonna bless you with another woman's husband. **Not today, tomorrow, not ever."**

LOVE...

- is patient
- is kind
- is not rude
- does not envy
- will not lie
- is not self-seeking
- is not proud
- is not quick to anger
- protects
- does not boast
- does not record wrongs
- trusts
- hopes
- perseveres
- finds no joy in evil but celebrates truth
- never fails

Mya

I awoke from my dream as I had five or six nights in the past three months. Shivering, bewildered, and surprised, the dream quite lucid in my mind. I slide my trembling hand across my stomach and downward. My fingers travel through my pubic hairs and into the moistness engulfing my pulsating clitoris. I need confirmation of what I already knew would be there, the clear fluid, slick, and warm. The results of an orgasm, so earth-shattering, it awakened me from my sleep. An orgasm I only experienced from the imaginary touch of a man whose face I could not see. A man whose touch made me feel whole. The man I prayed would one day come to fruition.

The dream was always the same. I'm shopping, trying on designer shoes in an upscale department store. International Plaza is buzzing with shoppers, and he appears by my side and tells me he likes the red ones because my foot is narrow. He loves the crimson polish on my professionally pedicured toes. The crisscrossing silk straps, he says, have an air of elegance. How corny, I thought, but blush just the same. "I'm shopping for an outfit to wear to an upcoming fundraiser." I divulge. He asks if I have a date. "No" is my simple reply.

The dream then finds us in the formal wear department, and he's taking a stunning red dress from the rack. As quickly as the dream transitions from shoes to dresses, it moves from dresses to his luxurious bedroom in a waterfront condo. I'm wearing the red dress he purchased and red shoes. He opens the French doors, and we overlook the quiet of downtown's Beach Drive as we sip wine and watch the gentle waves glide to shore from Tampa Bay. We kiss, kiss, and kiss again, his cool tongue playing a dance inside my mouth. His arousal is apparent, so I step back. Embarrassed, I ask to use the restroom. He points to a door on the opposite side of the room. I excuse myself. Minutes later, I'm re-entering the bedroom, and he's in bed.

His actions are pretty presumptuous, I think. He pulls back the comforter, and in all the glory God has blessed him with, he invites me to join him. Moments later, my body trembles from the explosion of our passionate love-making. Subconsciously, I feel myself moving in the bed as my pelvis meets his thrusts. The tremor comes from deep inside of me. Sometimes it's so good I grab the sheets to absorb the wild fluttering consuming my total being.

Through it all, I can never envision his face when I awaken. My psyche is telling me he's well over six feet tall. In heels, I'm barely five feet nine inches. In my dream, I'm looking up to him when we kiss. He's a man of physical substance because he makes me feel secure in his arms. His complexion was deep dark chocolate. His nakedness against the white sheets of his bed intrigues me. It's the beauty of his blackness that draws me near so I can feel his heat.

Three weeks after my last dream, I received a call from my best friend, Angie. Angie and I met online. We belonged to a *Yahoo Group* created by an African-American woman to enlighten and enrich women of color. ForMySisters.com was a great concept, but in the end, it turned out to be nothing more than the same female relationships we women were trying to escape in our real lives. The great thing about the site is that you can press delete if you want to shut someone up, unlike personal relationships. Or, you can place them on ignore if you don't want to see their fonts. On a few occasions, you can tell that person what you thought without them calling your home or showing up at your front door. For the most part, the chances of you ever meeting one of these women is slim to none unless you wanted to.

That was the case with Angie and me. Jill Scott was coming to the *House of Blues* in Orlando. I wanted to go, but as usual, my broke friends weren't interested. A few days before the show, I started a discussion on the Yahoo group about missing out on life because of friends with limited funds. Later that day, a personal email arrived in my inbox from Angie, stating that she would go with me if I were still interested. We met for lunch the following day, traveled to Orlando that weekend, and two years later, we rarely made a move without each other.

Angie was calling to see if I wanted to attend a Celebrity Auction with her the following weekend. Although Angie is married, we often attend these types of functions together. Her husband, Bernie, works the second shift and only has weekends off once a month. As luck would have it, for me, that is, his weekend off rarely fell on a weekend when something good was taking place. Bernie took good care of his wife and wasn't the jealous type. He wanted Angie to enjoy herself even if he couldn't be there. He often stated that he loved the fact that she had befriended a woman with morals who wouldn't lead her down a destructive path.

The Celebrity Auction is a fundraiser for a non-profit organization by the name of Men About Town. Proceeds benefit recipients of their male mentoring program and provide college scholarships to deserving young men. I don't know why it's called a celebrity auction since none of the people auctioned are ever celebrities. When I think of celebrities, I think of actors, athletes, media personalities. Instead, attendees had their pick of community professionals, business owners, and the like. I was a bit disappointed. Then again, I wasn't about to shell out hundreds, even thousands of dollars for some guy I could meet for free at the local club. The packages that came with the date were nothing compared to the packages offered at a recent auction hosted by a local organization raising funds to support breast cancer awareness. The difference was black and white, literally. There are just some things White people do that Black people shouldn't imitate, and this event was clearly one of them.

As Angie and I made our way towards the exit, I spotted a familiar face in the crowd. It was someone I had admired from a distance through the years. Someone I thought was handsome, fine as hell, and not a chance in this lifetime of ever wanting to get to know me. Although I had seen him on several occasions over the years, we had never spoken to one another. For all I knew, he didn't know I existed. As we moved with the crowd, my thoughts sprang to life, and I found myself wondering if he was single, if he was straight, or if I had ever even seen him with a woman. Oh my God, he could be gay! Since reading all of author E. Lynn Harris's books, and the talk of "Down Low" brothers took on a life of its own, it's hard not to ask the question. The thought was unnerving, so I quickly moved it out of my mind. Besides, Angie was talking. She was asking me if I wanted to ride over to Harbour Island for drinks at *Jackson's*. She was driving, so I was going whether I wanted to or not.

We hung out at *Jackson's* for over an hour before we finally conceded that the night wasn't getting any better, paid our tab, and prepared to leave. Someone palmed my elbow as we made our way through the racially diverse crowd. When I turned to see who had touched me, I found myself staring into the eyes of my secret crush. There were a decent number of people at *Jackson's* tonight, so I don't know when he arrived or how long he had been here.

"Excuse me," I said after regaining my composure. He smiled a beaming smile showcasing straight white teeth framed by succulent lips. Umph, umph, umph.

"No, excuse me," he replied. "LaDamien Bryson," he offered. "Mya Blake, right?" His delivery was smooth as cream, and his tone was deep and commanding.

By now, I was sweating and feeling weak in my knees. The crowd surrounding us faded into the recesses of my mind. He guided me from the path of exiting party-goers and led me outside to the waterfront patio overlooking the bay. When my heart settled, I confirmed my identity and scanned the room for Angie. There she was, standing guard at the outside bar. Ever so discreet but keeping a watchful eye just in case, I give the subtle nod indicating I needed her to rescue me.

"So, how do you know my name?" I asked after we gave the waitress *my* drink order. Not a good sign, I thought. I hate when guys offer to buy you a drink and then indicate they don't drink. Either they are trying to get you intoxicated for apparent reasons. Or they don't care for women who drink and are putting you through one of their silly rites of passage. This is why I ask for a glass of Chardonnay.

"I know you're not going to believe this and will probably think I'm running game on you, but I've been planning this introduction ever since I saw you at The Cotton Club. Back then, it was called Grace's Place. You were with a girl named Rolsium. She and I attended the same school. About a week later, I ran into her at the mall and asked her your name." He gave me a look that said he was checking to see if I was buying his story and if he should continue. I chuckled nervously and was relieved when the barmaid handed me my wine. I quickly took a sip and looked in Angie's direction to see if she was cool with me staying a little longer. She smiled, letting me know to take my time.

"Grace's Place, there's more years than I care to remember since I've been to that club., and I was with Rolsium?" This was a shocker since I had to be in my early twenties at the time. Thinking back, I don't recall Rolsium ever telling me someone had asked about me. No need to ask her now because she would never remember.

Rolsium was my road dawg back in the day. We use to work together at a local hospital. When we turned twenty-one, we were in the club Thursday through Sunday, dragging ourselves from the club at three in the morning, home to shower and change so that we could clock in at work by six a.m. Although we hung pretty tight back in the day, we grew apart through the years as our lives moved in different directions. Still, I label her a friend and know I can call her at any time, and she will be there for me.

He blushes. "Yep, it's been a very long time."

"So, what happened? Did you ask for my number? Did you ask Roz to give me your number?" My inquiring mind wants to know.

Our conversation continues with me telling him what functions I've seen him at around town and all our missed opportunities. To say I'm in awe that he has been attracted to me all these years, and never made an attempt to meet me, is an understatement.

LaDamien tells me that he only asked Roz my name. She told him that I was seeing someone, so he didn't want to interfere. He went on to tell me he was in college at the time and home on break. It was almost five years later when he saw me again. I was at a Buccaneer football game, only four rows down from him. He says I was with a guy about six feet four, and we seemed comfortable together as we huddled in the cold watching the game.

His story is funny. "The Bucs versus the Lions, in ninety-seven, was a playoff game, if my memory serves me right. It was cold as I don't know what, and we were so high up in the stands that if we didn't huddle together, the wind would have blown us out of the stands."

"So, what happened to you, and that guy? He looked a little young for you. Then again, different things attract different people." He looks on intensely as he awaits my response.

"Nothing happened to us. He's still very much an important part of my life." My response is two-fold.

LaDamien frowns, or is it his disappointment. He tells me that he didn't mean to intrude. He wishes I had said that I was in a relationship when he first stopped me. My first thought was, is he serious. Is he upset he spent his money on the drink, or if it took a lot for him to muster up the nerve to speak to me? My answer comes when he thanks me for my time and looks nervously around to see if anyone noticed he had just gotten shot down. Before he walks off, I reach for his hand and let him know that the guy I was with is still in my life, and yes, he's younger than me. Eleven years to be exact. He does the math. "He's my nephew." My confession brings him back, and he lets out a faint laugh.

As Angie drove us back across the bay, I tell her word for word about my conversation with LaDamien. She repeats my every thought. How could a man that fine be so shy? How sweet that he's pined for me all those years. What kept him from making his move? Where would our lives be if one of us had acknowledged the other years ago? Maybe then wasn't the right time, and right now is.

Angie is silent as I replay my dream from a few weeks earlier. The red dress, the dark, handsome man, I think it's fate, but Angie isn't convinced. "The proof will be in his love-making," I joke. I will let her know if we ever get to that point. If LaDamien's love-making resembles that of the lover in my dream, I will know without a doubt God has answered my prayers.

LaDamien calls me the following day, and we are on the phone for hours. He tells me his entire life story. He's the youngest of five children and the only boy. His parents divorced when he was a toddler, and his mom sometimes struggled as a single mother. Through it all, they managed, and all are successful adults. He played sports in high school, which earned him a college scholarship. It was his goal to relocate to Houston and start a life there. As fate would have it, things didn't work out the way he planned. He had been back in the area permanently for five years. However, he teetered back and forth between here and several other cities like Houston, Miami, and Atlanta, preceding his move back.

I was intrigued by his conversation, flattered by his boyish crush, and in awe that any man could carry a torch for me all these years. He quizzed me on everything from my favorite color, a favorite song, family, friends, ex beaus, you name it, he asked it. Finally, I asked him what made him make his move the night before. LaDamien shared with me a conversation he'd had with his mother before he arrived at the fundraiser. She had admonished him for not following his dreams and settling for what was easy. She told him not to worry about her and what would happen if she wasn't here any longer. She just wanted him to promise her that he'd live life to the fullest, take chances, but most of all, be happy.

According to him, when he saw me walk into the grand ballroom of the *Hyatt Regency,* it became crystal clear what his mother had meant. It made him wonder, what if he never took a chance on getting to know me and missed out on the opportunity to know his soulmate.

A soulmate is a word with such a powerful meaning. It denotes completeness, purpose, God anointed. To connect with their true soulmate is a blessing that few people rarely experience and a gift rarely received…at least not in this day and age. The conversation took a philosophical turn. We discussed the true meaning of soulmate, destiny, and fate. We explored the paths that our lives took to get us in the same place at the same time so we could be intertwined.

As delightful as the discussion was, I viewed my watch and saw that we were approaching the four-hour mark. We needed to save something to talk about on the next call, so I steered the conversation towards closure.

"Wow, look at the time," I commented.

LaDamien got the hint. "Would you like to have lunch with me tomorrow?" he asked.

"Of course, what time?"

"Whatever is good for you, my time is pretty flexible. We can go wherever you want," he added.

We pitter-pattered around like this for another thirty minutes, not wanting the call to end. After we finalize the plans, I asked LaDamien if there's something else he wants to say. "You sound hesitant like you're pondering something."

"I am. I always want to be honest with you and never keep secrets. In my heart, I know we are meant to be together, and I'm going to do whatever it takes to give us a fair chance."

"Cool, so what is it?" I ask without hesitation, wanting to hear this man's voice deep into the night and throughout my remaining days. Then he says it. "I'm married."

LaDamien

Walking into the bedroom, I can't overlook Kim lying across the bed. There's a pint of *Haagen-Dazs'* Butter Pecan ice cream and a pack of *Oreo* Double Stuff cookies next to her. The sight repulses me. She has gained a good fifty pounds in the five years we've been married. I use to want more children with her. Still, I'm terrified that if she becomes pregnant again, she will reach a point of obesity that she will not be able to overcome.

"What are you doing? I thought we were going to visit my mom?"

It's apparent that she has no intentions of going with me. My mom lives alone in an assisted living facility. She's a resilient woman. Well into her eighties, she has suffered several mild heart attacks and the latest assault on her body, diabetes.

My eldest sister Veronica is retired from nursing and spends much of her time with our mother during the day. My other three siblings and I rotate visiting in the evenings, so she doesn't have to eat dinner alone.

Tonight, is my turn. Kim has not accompanied me much lately. Since returning to school, she has become distant and doesn't have time to focus on my needs. She's vying for the position of Vice President of Human Resources at her job. When the current VP told her in a sidebar conversation that she would be retiring in two years, Kim thought nothing of it. But as always, I had to encourage her to start preparing herself to be in contention for the position.

Kim rolls into an upright position, stuffs the lid into the empty container, and folds the *Oreo* package in half. "Karen called. She wants to go to the movies and have drinks. We're meeting at five."

It is almost impossible for me to contain the joy of knowing I will not have to come up with a lie to get out of the house without her.

She has provided me with an out, although she has seen the ticket to the Celebrity Auction. It was in the glove compartment of my *Cadillac Escalade*. The vehicle she never drives unless she feels the need to snoop. The ticket was under the owner's manual, but it was on top when I checked earlier. Her way of letting me know I'm not slick.

Kim rolls her eyes when I say I will be driving the *Lexus* coupe to visit my mother, "Might as well wash it so it will be clean for the weekend." I explain.

She doesn't say a word. Instead, she heads towards the kitchen. Grabbing the keys, I head to the garage without saying goodbye. When I return two hours later, Kim is gone. I shower, dress in my navy *Armani* suit, spray on my *Calvin Klein Obsession*, put on my *Omega* watch, and slide my wedding band into my pocket.

The visit with my mom was somewhat different. She senses that my marriage to Kim is in jeopardy. I'm assuming this is why she asked me several times if things were okay between us and if I was sure I had made the right decision in marrying Kim. She knows I'm not in love with my wife and only married her so that I wouldn't be alone. As a child, I always felt alone. Not having my dad in my life full-time added to my frustrations. My mom had to work two, sometimes three jobs, to keep up with the bills. My sisters were there until they discovered boys. Thirteen was probably the age when the feelings of abandonment began to rear their ugly head. In high school, I quelled my fears by hanging close to my teammates. I worked hard to succeed, be popular, and ensure people would want to be in my inner circle.

In college, I tried to do the same, but the transition was tough. College guys hung tough during the season, but afterward, they played catch-up with the ladies. Attracting women was never a problem; it was the drama that went along with them. If I could have said to a girl, "I just want to fuck you and not have any other attachment," and get away with it, my life would have been fine. But it wasn't because they always wanted much more. So, I tried to keep it simple by dating only women who never thought they could attract a campus athlete's attention. They were so ecstatic to be the chosen one. They did whatever I said to keep me. Most of the time, that meant looking the other way when I was seeing other women.

After graduation, I was alone again. The people I thought were my friends weren't. I couldn't count on the people I met in college for contacts and references in the real world, the real black world that is. My white counterparts were forever mentioning some college buddy who had hooked them up or turned them on to a great opportunity.

When Mya makes her entrance into the ballroom, my heart skips a beat. She's so beautiful. Why I never pursued her when I had the chance is a mystery. It makes me angry with myself for not putting my fear of rejection aside and going for what I want. This phobia of mine has cost me a lot.

Mya is wearing a form-fitting red dress. It compliments her well. She's with a female that I have seen her out with on other occasions. This leads me to wonder if she's a lesbian, if I'm a day late, and a dollar short, once again. The evening goes by slowly, and I can't keep my eyes off of her. She has a radiant smile that I love. She listens intently to the people at her table, even though she doesn't know them, which was evident by how she introduced herself and her companion to each of them. Secretly, I wish I could have heard her introduction. Did she say, "Hi, my name is Mya, and this is my friend, or my lover, or my significant other, so-and-so?" Or maybe she just gave her name, leaving the table to wonder as I'm doing now.

The guy to the left of Mya seems interested. From my visual, her interaction with him doesn't give him much hope. She smiles but doesn't appear to encourage conversation. She's polite, probably does a lot of pity dating because she doesn't want to hurt anyone. A female walks over to the table and begins talking to the guy. Mya looks relieved, and this makes me very happy.

The auction has come to an end, and I'm thrilled that Mya didn't bid on anyone, male or female. Not once did she look towards the numbered paddle used to notify the auctioneer that she's placing a bid.

As the crowd heads for the door, Mya appears to be checking me out. Tonight will be the night that I make my feelings for her known. It's time for me to pursue my happiness and stop worrying about everyone else.

The crowd was moving slowly, and I was unable to catch Mya. My hope was diminishing. Why wasn't this meant to be? Why won't God give us a chance? These questions came to the surface tonight as they have every time the opportunity to meet her has come and gone in the past.

The first time I saw Mya, I was at a nightclub in Tampa. I admired her from a distance as I did tonight. The girl she was with that night was someone I knew, so I made a mental note to get the scoop on Mya from her. Rolsium, the girl Mya was with the night before, was in the mall the following day. She gave me Mya's name but added that she was in a relationship with some Navy guy.

The second time, I'd just moved back from Miami, where I attended college and was out riding with a friend. We pulled into the parking lot of a *7-Eleven* convenience store. Several people had gathered in front of the store. To my surprise, Mya walked out the door. My heartbeat quickened. My friend hastened me to hurry and park because he saw an old friend and wanted to say hi. As I prepared to tell him about my crush on the lady leaving the store, he exclaimed, "Mya gets finer with time, wonder if she has any kids." My hopes deflated as he told me they had dated a few years back. Next was the time I spotted her at a *Tampa Bay Buccaneers* football game. She was with a guy who barely looked twenty. Mya had to be at least thirty at the time.

My last encounter was at a restaurant located in the professional complex where I have my office. I stood at the window looking out at the parking lot when she pulled up and headed towards the small eatery a few doors down. Without hesitation, I grabbed my jacket and headed over. She was standing at the counter, paying for her order. I stood next to her and said, "Hello." Before she could respond, the cashier handed her the order and bid her a good day. Mya took the order and turned to leave, sending a slight smile in my direction.

Just like that, my nerve vanished. Then the thought occurred to me that she may not even know my name. If so, had she made the connection from the sign outside, and was she impressed. Most women got turned on when they learned of my business. But Mya wasn't like most women, or so I thought. After she exited the restaurant, I waited about five minutes hoping she would make the connection and come back, but she never did. Pushing my hands deep inside my pockets, I felt the cold metal of my wedding band and cringed.

A home is a place I rarely want to be. Truth be told, I never want to go home. It's hard for me to admit, but sometimes I hate Kim and wish she was dead. My dreams are often about her dying in a car accident or getting shot during a store robbery. Each morning I awake, turn to face her side of the bed, and there she is every time.

My decision to ask her to marry me will haunt me for the rest of my life. Knowing that I'm stuck in this marriage has my disdain for her growing by the day. I will continue to despise her for accepting my offer to get married. For not leaving when I lost my job with the City, and I took my anger out on her with violent verbal assaults. For not leaving when she learned of my first affair, and the second, and the third. If things work out with Mya, Kim will finally have to get the message I've been trying to convey for years. Marrying her was a huge mistake.

Mya and her friend are at *Jackson's*. It's destiny calling. This night will not end without me making my move. They are dancing together, and my fear that she's a lesbian resurfaces. However, they aren't touching each other in a way that would lead me to believe they are anything more than girls out for a night of fun. Mya is so sexy, and there are so many men in the club. Why does she prefer to be with her friend? Maybe it was her choice. Maybe she has suffered so much hurt and disappointment at the hands of men she no longer trusts. Maybe it's too late for me. Maybe it just wasn't meant to be.

Mya brushes past me, and her touch consumes me with desire. Impulsively, I reach for her arm, and she turns to face me. She's confused by my touch. Or is it disgust? She says, "excuse me," as though she has imposed herself into my space. She isn't put off by my bold gesture, which is comforting. Moments later, we are outside, and I'm telling her how I have longed to meet her. She gives me her number, and I promise to call her the next day, which I do.

It is a humid Saturday evening. We talk for hours as I drive through the city, cross the Skyway Bridge into Bradenton, hop on 75 North, and make my way into Hillsborough County. From I-4, I travel west to I-275 across Howard Frankland Bridge back into Pinellas County, exiting at Roosevelt Boulevard, and making my way to Clearwater Beach.

Talking to Mya is so easy. She's genuinely concerned when I tell her about my mother's failing health. Her parents are getting on in age. She's worried they too could fall victim to similar illnesses brought on by unhealthy eating and lack of exercise. She's impressed as I talk about my business, and she wants to hear about my siblings and our upbringing. Mya grew up in a two-parent home, which brings out the little green monster in me. Her parents are growing old together, enjoying their retirement, spending their time volunteering, and traveling. As strong as her relationship with her parents is, she credits her Grandma for helping her become the woman that she is today. She has one sister who is much older than she is, so for the most part, she grew up feeling like an only child.

After talking to Mya, I know loving her will be easy, and I'm sure I'm making the right decision. We make plans to see each other the following day. I don't want the call to end and assume Mya feels the same way. Where she is, I want to be also—holding her through the night, making love to her, making babies with her, and making a life with her. Instead, I'm telling her that I'm married. Why did I say it? Why couldn't I wait to see what the future could hold for us? I take a deep breath. Our silence lasts for what seems like an eternity. The only sound is the waves rolling ashore onto the white sand and carrying it back to sea. Finally, I hear Mya say, "I know," and for some strange reason, my heart rejoices.

Kim

LaDamien has been different these past few days, the conspicuous signs that he has found another lover. My count stopped at four. They come and go so quickly, some for a few weeks and others for a few months. The longest was over a year. He was seeing her when he asked me to marry him. I was just getting out of a horrific relationship that left me penniless. My former lover had walked away, leaving me to clean up the mess he had made. If it wasn't bad enough that he had left me for a woman fresh out of high school, but he had wiped out our bank account in the process. Bill collectors were calling from sun up until sundown. There was no peace in my life. Slowly, I was losing it. The shame from his betrayal led me to a self-imposed exile, unable to share the true extent of my situation with anyone. My mother had warned me against shacking, saying people weren't supposed to act like they were married when they weren't.

    LaDamien showed up at the right moment. I had all but given up. He assured me that things would be all right. "First thing you need to do is get your finances in order and take care of your outstanding debts," he told me. After his pep talk, he helped me sell my house before the bank could foreclose. He also helped me work out repayment plans with my creditors. He then encouraged me to put my business degree to use. Go out on a limb, and apply for positions I never imagined I would qualify to interview for, let alone get a callback. My self-esteem rose instantly, and my desire for him shot through the roof.

    When he informed me of his decision to move to Houston, Texas, to join a friend who was doing well in real estate, I jumped at the opportunity to go with him. My friends thought I was crazy to up and quit when my career was just shifting into full swing. But they didn't know the real reason I was ready to start anew in a new place with people we didn't know. They didn't know about Faye, who was causing me to lose sleep at night and question my womanhood. I was so intent on not losing another man that I would have done anything to keep her away from LaDamien. All I knew at that point was that I needed to get him away from Faye if we stood a chance. My determination to get him away from that heifer with her obnoxious and evilness outweighed my better judgment. All reasoning went out the window. Unfortunately, my efforts were worthless. We were back in St. Petersburg in less than six months, and he and Faye picked up where they left off.

When we returned, I ended up taking a lesser paying job. I didn't care and was just happy that my employer was willing to take me back. Janice, the VP of Human Resources, was one of the many people who tried to convince me not to leave. "Let him go ahead and prepare a home for you. Once he gets settled and is sure this plan will work, then you can consider moving." But no, all I could think of was getting him out of Faye's claws.

My friend Debra was so angry with me. When I finally confided in her about Faye, she asked, "Wouldn't it have been a more straightforward solution to simply call Faye's husband and tell him his wife is screwing my man?"

That was over five years ago. LaDamien was doing odd jobs here and there, taking work wherever he could find it. I could hardly concentrate on my job for worrying if he was with Faye or looking for steady employment. Debra, and Karen, another close friend, pulled me aside for a reality check.

"What are you doing?" They asked one evening during a girl's night out. I didn't expect them to understand my connection to LaDamien what his support and concern meant to me after my break-up with Steve. They knew him, and I had dated briefly after college, but they didn't know about the occasional hook-up through the years. To me, he was intelligent and charming and such a motivator. Not to mention his skills in the bedroom or wherever the mood struck us. I believe it was the latter that drove me crazy when it came to Faye. This was the only logical explanation for this broad jeopardizing her marriage; LaDamien had to be laying it down as she'd never had it laid down before.

Debra, and Karen, both married since graduating from college, would think I was crazy for sure, so I didn't say it. Instead, I told them that I thought LaDamien, and I could have something special if he would just settle down. A month after that conversation, LaDamien asked me to marry him. He came over one evening and asked if I wanted to do it. Three days later, he picked me up for lunch, and we went to the courthouse to get a marriage license. Afterward, we drove to his place, and waiting was his sister Pamela, and her husband, along with a friend of LaDamien's who was also a minister. We were married right in his living room. It wasn't exactly what I had hoped for, but at least we were finally husband and wife.

I don't know what I thought was going to happen once we said, "I do." We weren't settled in our marriage a good two weeks when LaDamien informed me his lease was up at the end of the month, and he wasn't renewing. This revelation came so quickly. I felt I had no other choice but to go to my mother and ask her if we could temporarily live with her until we could find a place.

Going back to my mothers' home yet again was embarrassing, but this time seemed worse. After Steve left me, I moved into her waterfront home located in Boca Ciega Bay's Broadwater subdivision. It was a beautiful waterfront home she inherited mortgage-free from her deceased husband. Ralph and my mother were only together three short years before being diagnosed with brain cancer, and he died months later. I was in my sophomore year of high school when they met. Having never known my birth father, I was happy to have a male figure in my life finally. His death hurt more than I ever thought imaginable, but he took care of my mother and ensured I could go to college. My mom had already told me she disapproved of my marriage to LaDamien. She felt he was a freeloading sleaze, who manipulated women for his gain, but like most mothers, she wanted what was best for me and agreed to allow us to move in.

We were not at my mother's home a week when LaDamien stayed gone well into the early morning hours of the following day. When my mother entered the kitchen to join me for breakfast, she didn't mention the heated argument that rattled the tranquility of her home just hours earlier. I guess my humiliation was apparent, and she didn't want to make me feel any worse.

Finally, the City called to offer LaDamien a position in their Purchasing Department, and not a minute too soon. Not just because we needed the money but also because he was spending so much time with Faye. There had been numerous sightings, and people were not hesitant about letting me know. It was as if they had no concern for my feelings. Some were so undaunted, making it evident they didn't care how this gossip was affecting me, even after seeing the hurt in my eyes after sharing their news. Little did they know, I had loved LaDamien far too long and had made too many sacrifices trying to prove my love. Now that things had finally worked in my favor, I was going to do whatever I could to hold on to him and to make this marriage work.

The day I finally caught him with Faye is still vivid in my mind. It was two in the afternoon, and I was on my way to the doctor's office for my annual GYN visit. I got stopped by the red light on Martin Luther King Street and Twenty-second Avenue when a glance to my right caused my heart to skip a beat. They were in Faye's *Toyota Rav4*. She looked at me and waved as she turned right onto Twenty-second Avenue and headed east. My first inclination was to get over and follow suit, but what would I say or do when I caught up with them. She was so damn smug and arrogant, and LaDamien, well, there were no words to express how his actions made me feel. This day will forever become etched in my mind as the day I gave my husband permission to disrespect me and our marriage vows. Still, more important, it was the day I lost my dignity and self-respect. The more I think about it, the more I believe I should have followed them, and once I had them cornered, I should have called Faye's husband and told him where he could find his cheating ass wife. I also should have put LaDamien out and filed for divorce. Instead, I told my doctor to remove my IUD.

Ariel was born the following year, a beautiful baby girl. When I told LaDamien I was pregnant, he was so angry I thought he would push me down the stairs causing me to abort. Thank God my mother was there to intervene. There was no understanding of his ugly outburst. He accused me of trying to trap him, of being dishonest and manipulative for getting pregnant without his consent. I argued he gave his consent every time he entered me without a condom. For heaven's sake, we were husband and wife. We had never discussed birth control or how we felt about having children. His reaction to the news hurt like hell.

After LaDamien's bizarre reaction to the news, my mother asked if I thought things had gone on long enough. She suggested I cut my losses, that I abort my baby and my marriage. I was devastated. It was then that she told me she had decided to relocate to New York and wanted me to join her.

My mother was born and raised in Far Rockaway, New York, and now that she was retired and her husband had passed, she wanted to return home. She was afraid for me, she argued. "Something isn't right with LaDamien. Why can't you see it?" she asked with urgency. I didn't quite follow where she was going with that statement, so I argued that he was under a lot of stress. I should have told him I wanted to have a baby, that he felt like a failure because we were living in her home. He saw this as a test of his manhood. My mother shook her head and begged me to open my eyes, to see that my marriage was a mistake, and to get out as quickly as possible.

The relationship became strained after that conversation. However, my mother agreed not to move until after the baby was born. The decision seemed to infuriate LaDamien even more, and he used my mother's presence as an excuse to stay gone more than he already had been. My stress level was off the charts. Except for work, I rarely left the house. Debra and Karen joined my mother in her insistent pleas that I divorce LaDamien, and get on with my life. I was falling into a deep depression and regretted getting pregnant. What could I have possibly been thinking?

Entering my eighth month of pregnancy, I decided to ask LaDamien if he wanted a divorce. He pondered the question for several moments before asking me a question that nearly caused me to go into shock. "Are you pregnant from someone else?" My husband looked me straight in my face with no emotion whatsoever and accused me of cheating on him. Should I dignify the question with an answer or throw the lamp sitting on the end table next to me at him? It seemed like my only option at the time but instead, I screamed, "Are you fucking crazy?"

He stated calmly, "No, I think it's a fair question. What woman asks her husband for a divorce weeks before she's due to deliver. What, you did the calculations and finally realized it couldn't be mine? Or, did your lover decide to step up to the plate, and you've decided you'd rather be with him than me? Go ahead, and leave. I'm used to it. That's what everyone does. They leave me."

It just kept getting worse. Maybe my mother was on to something. Maybe LaDamien was experiencing some type of nervous breakdown. What else could explain the foolishness coming out of his mouth? He looked at me when I began to laugh. The laughter grew, and he asked if I was ridiculing him. The crazed uncontrollable laughter continued, prohibiting me from responding. LaDamien walked out with a look that seemed to be a mixture of contempt and humiliation.

Later that evening, when he returned, I was upstairs in bed. LaDamien came into the room and sat on the bed. "I'm sorry for the way I have been acting lately. You have been a good wife to me, Kim, and I owe you a debt of gratitude." He took a long pause, which frightened me. "There's something I need to tell you," he finally said.

Sitting up in the bed, I asked him to continue. "I'm afraid of fatherhood," he replied. "I am so afraid that I won't be a good father to my children. I wonder if I will abandon my kids. Then force them to grow up in the world without that male figure I so desperately needed as a child. People say girls need their fathers, but you know it's just as hard on a boy not having his dad around. No matter what, I want to always be there for my children, and knowing that it can all be taken away from me in an instant just leaves me feeling empty and helpless."

His words make no sense to me, but I assure him that nothing will make me keep our child away from him. He's this child's father, and no matter what happens between us, he will have a relationship with our daughter. I smile and let him know that I'm not going to give up on our marriage. If it doesn't work, it's because he decided it wasn't going to work. "I am in this for the long-haul, through thick and thin, sickness, and in health, no matter what comes our way."

"You're too good to me, Kim. I don't deserve you." LaDamien said when he looked into my eyes where tears were forming. I felt he needed to know I had his back no matter what. At that moment, the baby kicked. I lifted myself to my knees and guided his hand to my full belly.

"You feel that?" I asked as the life growing inside of me moved again. He smiled.

"Yes, that's our baby." For the first time in a long time, I felt the love of my husband. Things changed dramatically after that night. It's as if a new person had entered our life, in addition to our beautiful Ariel. Unfortunately, the change in LaDamien only lasted for a while.

LOVE...

- is patient
- is kind
- is not rude
- does not envy
- will not lie
- is not self-seeking
- is not quick to anger
- does not boast
- is not proud
- protects
- does not record wrongs
- trusts
- hopes
- perseveres
- finds no joy in evil but celebrates truth
- never fails

Mya

My relationship with LaDamien is like nothing I have ever experienced before. He's so kind and so attentive. A day has not gone by that we have not seen each other. Our days start together, and they end together. My phone rings each morning at six a.m. I know before looking at the caller ID that it's him. He has gone outside to retrieve the morning paper and ensure the sprinklers are working correctly. The sound of his deep sultry voice coming through the phone infuses me with energy. "Hey, did I wake you?" It has been a little over three months since we began seeing each other, and he asks the same question. Downplaying the joy he brings, I simply say, "Oh, I need to get up anyway."

On this day, we decide to meet at the gym and take a Spin class. LaDamien has often commented on his desire to lose a few pounds and get back into lightweight training. I agree that it wouldn't hurt for me to be a little more active myself. A week later, we joined Bally's Fitness Center.

As we wait for the instructor to begin class, I admire LaDamien as he chats with a gentleman on the bike next to him. He's so unbelievably sexy and has charisma seeping from his pores. He senses that I'm watching him and turns towards me, smiling. "What are you looking at?" he teases, which makes me smile like a schoolgirl with her first crush.

"You," I respond. LaDamien winks at me as the instructor dims the lights and class begins.

Ten minutes into the class, we both realize that we are seriously out of shape. LaDamien says he's ready to leave, but I urge him to continue. Fifty minutes later, we are heading out to the parking lot.

"Wow, that was something," LaDamien says as he opens the car door for me, and I agree. He suggests we stop for breakfast before he drops me off. Mindful of the time, I decline his offer. I have gotten so caught up in this relationship that I have allowed myself to get totally off track, and tardiness is becoming an issue at work.

"It's almost eight, and I wanted to make an effort to get to the office by nine today." He looks disappointed that I have chosen work over him. "Maybe we can do lunch," a consolation offer.

LaDamien is a man who's not accustomed to being turned down. We stop at the red light, and he reaches over and kisses me. Our tongues are moving in sync as he pulls me closer. A horn blows, and we realize the light has changed. When I try to pull back, his kiss intensifies. The driver of the car pulls from behind us and yells an obscenity as he speeds by. LaDamien chuckles as he leans back in his seat and drives off. He asks me again if I want to go to breakfast. This time my answer is yes.

It is ten-fifteen when I sign on to my computer. I admonish myself for being so weak and promise myself to do better. As if he has a monitor in my brain, LaDamien calls and apologizes for being so selfish and monopolizing my time. He suggests that we set a schedule that will allow us to spend time together in the mornings and still allow me to get to work on time. His thoughtfulness is appreciated. After we agree, we make plans to meet for lunch.

"LB," I begin, which is one of my pet names for LaDamien, "you know it does us no good to work out and then eat out." We have decided on *Chili's*, or shall I say I have decided. LaDamien agrees to come but quickly lets me know that it isn't his favorite place once we are seated, but he's willing to sacrifice for me.

"Well, we still have to eat, so what do you suggest?" he asks.

"We should try to eat a little healthier, maybe subs and salads." LaDamien doesn't have a problem with my suggestion and assigns me the task of coming up with a menu we can follow when I plan the schedule for our mornings. He says this with a hint of sarcasm, so I ask him if he was serious about the schedule he mentioned earlier.

"I wouldn't have said it if I wasn't serious, baby." LaDamien is very good at delegating, something I realized early in our relationship. For some reason, his authoritativeness turns me on.

During our breakfast and lunch outings, I listen to him talk about his marriage, sharing the little quirks of their relationship with me. He signs over his monthly paycheck to his wife for the bills, allowing her to do what she chooses with her money. He ensures that the vehicles are taken care of, and maintenance on the home gets done. Kim, his wife, is responsible for running their home and taking care of their daughter. It sounds fair to me until he begins to share with me things about Kim that irritates him.

His main gripe is always the lack of sex. He swears Kim has not allowed him to touch her in years. They share the same bed, and if by chance their bodies touch, they make the necessary adjustments to create more space between them. What married man doesn't make this assertion, I think to myself. Still, I don't comment one way or the other because I realize that I'm the other woman, and he's going to say whatever he feels he needs to for me to stay with him. But I do let him know that he doesn't have to put his wife down or paint a gloomy picture of her for me to stay. On most days, Kim doesn't exist in my world, so I don't want to waste my time forming an opinion.

LaDamien realizes he's going on and on about his marriage and apologizes. He asks me if I can take off on Friday and travel with him to Venice. He has to look at some property he and his partner are thinking about adding to their portfolio. This will be the third trip I have accompanied him on if I decide to go. They were only day trips, but we made the most of them. On this particular outing, we would leave by seven a.m. and return around three that afternoon. Venice was only an hour away but placed us far enough away from home to not worry about being seen. Not, not that being seen ever seemed to bother him. It felt so good to be able to hold LaDamien's hand in public, to stop and kiss because the urge hit us, or to just go to the mall or a movie and not worry. LaDamien asked why I worried so much about being with him in public. He even insinuated on more than one occasion that *I* acted as if I had a man somewhere lurking. I countered that I was being discreet, something he knew nothing about. He laughed and assured me that I had nothing to be discreet about because he loved me and didn't care who knew, not even Kim.

Friday morning, LaDamien calls and asks if I would like to head down to Naples after leaving Venice. He suggests I pack an overnight bag if it gets late, and we need to stay the night. He tells me it's not a problem when I ask how he plans to pull this off. At this point in our relationship, we have not made love. However, the intimacy we experience is impressive. LaDamien is so sensual. His kisses melt my heart literally, making me forget that we have no business being together. He's the first man I have ever dated who loves to French kiss. We can't depart without a kiss, so passion-filled that it takes my breath away. He tells me he loves my kisses because they are sincere…whatever that means. When we aren't kissing, he's touching me. Not just his hand on my hand, but his hand on my arms, on my thighs, my back, my butt. He says he loves my skin because it's so soft. He loves my scent because it's so pure.

LaDamien asked me not to wear pants when we are together, nor am I to wear closed-toe shoes. Femininity is what he craves in a woman. He loves to see *his* woman in dresses and skirts whenever possible. LaDamien also has a foot fetish. I have never dated anyone with a foot fetish before, so I'm not sure exactly what it entails. All I know is, he inspects my feet all the time, and he expects them to be soft and neatly polished at all times. Pastels and bright colors are his preference.

Staying the night, if needed, will not be a problem. Excited by the prospect of staying the night with him is an understatement. We hang up, and I begin to go through my closet, looking for something cute to wear. I decide on a crinkle white skirt and lavender top and pull out a pair of wedge-heeled, ankle wrap sandals. My toes are polished with white nail color and a yellow daisy on each big toe.

The phone rings and I look to see that it's Angie. She wants to know what I have planned for the weekend. Bernie's sister invited them to a cook-out, and she wants me to attend. The invite means they have someone they want me to meet, someone who is single and unattached. Angie sighs after I tell her I'm going out of town with LaDamien. My relationship troubles her since she's married, but I'm a grown woman capable of making decisions. Our call ends with me letting Angie know I will do my best to make it over. We hang up, both knowing I won't be there.

It is seven-thirty, and I have been ready for more than thirty minutes. LaDamien isn't picking up when I call, which frustrates me. This is a major downside to dealing with a married man. If something comes up, and he can't call you, you're left wondering what is going on. Is he okay, is he safe, has his wife learned of our plans? My fears subside when the phone rings at eight-thirty. He explains he was preparing to leave when Kim returned home to retrieve some papers. According to him, she began to meander around the house, delaying his departure with casual conversation. He swears he will be here in ten minutes, but ten minutes turns into twenty, and I decide to go to work if he isn't here by nine forty-five.

As I'm pulling out of the driveway, LaDamien turns the corner. He's apologetic as I enter his vehicle after running back inside, changing back into my outfit, and grabbing my bag.

"Why were you leaving?" he asks me.

"Because I was upset with the delays and didn't want to sit here feeling stupid if you didn't show up." My voice was a mixture of whining and frustration. He explains that Kim was acting suspicious, so he headed to the office. Once there, his secretary detained him with talk about outstanding invoices and upcoming networking events. I forget that LaDamien is a business owner and can't always follow his set schedule. I also must remember that Kim is there, and she would have to be blind, dumb, and crazy not to know her husband is having an affair.

We are only in Venice for a short time. The property is a dud. LaDamien is upset that his secretary didn't do better research on the listing before suggesting he consider it for their real estate portfolio.

"We would need to put at least sixty thousand dollars into that place to sell it, and the location is horrible. What was she thinking?" he adds.

Moments later, he's on the phone, expressing the same to his business partner, and asking him to put Wanda, their secretary, on the phone. I listen as he chews this woman out. When he hangs up, I joke that I would never work for him. He's mean. As quickly as his mood descended after seeing the property, he looks at me, and his eyes brighten. "You still want to go to Naples?" Of course, I do, so we enter I-75 and continue heading south.

In Naples, we check into the Doubletree Hotel, located on Tamiami Trail. We are only a couple of miles from the beach and a little further from downtown. Our room is a one-bedroom suite equipped with a Jacuzzi. The balcony overlooks the pool, and we have a view of the *Cocohatchee River*. We are on the top floor of the small hotel which only has three levels. After freshening up, we head out to dinner. *Maxwell's On the Bay* is our destination. One of the front desk clerks recommended it and called in our reservation. Luckily, we could get outside seating, perfect for the eighty-degree weather we're experiencing.

Midway through dinner, LaDamien asked me what I thought about him. I was sure he already knew the answer based on my constant blushing and childish giggling. He said he wanted to hear me describe it, to tell him exactly what I thought about him. Was this a trap? Was he looking for a specific answer? He told me to be honest and tell the truth. Looking into his eyes, I said what came to mind. "I think you're undeniably sexy, and you're handsome and kind. You make me feel wanted and loved, and you say things that always make me feel beautiful."

LaDamien cut me off. "That's not what I asked you to tell me. Tell me what you think about me. You know, do you think I'm a good person, bad person, do you think I'm wrong for cheating on my wife, that kind of stuff."

What a loaded question, I think to myself, but give his question deep consideration. "Well, you are a good person in that you always put the needs of others first. As for cheating on your wife, I think it's the wrong thing to do, but I don't think it makes you a bad person, a bad husband, yes, but not a bad person."

"Go on," LaDamien urges.

"I don't know what else you want me to say. You have been kind to me. No other man has done for me the things you have." Smiling, I add, "You know you have spent more money on me in the past three months than all the men I have ever dated combined? You have a great sense of humor, and I feel comfortable with you like I have known you all my life." LaDamien is rubbing my hand and looking directly into my eyes. The urge to turn away can't overpower his intense stare. He's holding me captive. Moments later, the tables turn, and he's now on the hot seat.

LaDamien takes the challenge, "I think you are a very good person. You only want to see the good in people. You want a man who is strong, intelligent and takes charge. You are struggling with this affair, but you want it to work between us, so you are willing to look the other way in hopes that I will leave my wife so we can be together."

"Will you?" I ask.

He counters, "Will I do what?"

My response is straightforward, "Will you leave your wife? Not for me, but because you aren't happy and no longer want to be with her." He tells me it's not that easy. He has a daughter to consider and his business. He tells me Kim has not lifted a finger to help him with his business, and he would instead dissolve his interest and sacrifice his hard work than give her half. LaDamien's eyes have become intense, and small lumps have formed in his temples, lumps that are now pulsating. It's apparent he has become agitated, so I try to lighten the mood by asking what he wants to do after dinner. A walk on the beach is his suggestion, and I happily agree.

We made it over to the beach in time to catch the last of the sun disappearing into the horizon. The sky, infused with a unique mixture of pinks, and purples, streaked with gold, is stunning. Custom homes and condos line the stretch of beach we are on. Nearby new construction is underway for as far as I can see. Both LaDamien, and I agreed that homes near the shore took away from the beach and made it less enjoyable. We take off our shoes and walk into the water. It's cold but revitalizing. LaDamien has yet to turn my hand loose. Our fingers are entwined since leaving the restaurant. We stop to admire a home. There we see what looks like a dolphin diving in and out of the gulf.

LaDamien stops and turns to face me. "You know I love you, right?" He has said this to me on several occasions, but tonight is the first time I feel it's coming from a place deep inside. I look into his brown eyes and let him know I'm falling in love with him, also…major faux pas on my part.

"I am not falling in love. I'm already in love, so you need to catch up." Then he lures me into a sensual kiss.

Back in our hotel room, LaDamien fills the Jacuzzi. He then comes over to me and undresses me while kissing my neck, breast, and stomach. As he kneels to remove my panties, he stops and inhales deeply. I'm nervous. I first thought I don't smell so fresh down there, but then I look at the expression on his face and know the remnants of *Victoria Secrets* Love Spell lingers. LaDamien lifts my right leg and places my foot on the side of the tub. He takes his hand and rubs my clitoris. He knows this turns me on because he has driven me crazy so many times before doing this. My vagina moistens as I anticipate his middle finger sliding inside of me. LaDamien has large hands, hands that make for great athletes. His fingers are long and thick. They feel so good when he glides them in and slides them back out. But for now, he just continues stroking me back and forth as if he's hypnotized.

When the Jacuzzi is full, he helps me in. LaDamien turns and walks away. As I sit enjoying the water as it provides a pulsating massage to my muscles, I realize LaDamien is talking to someone on the phone in the other room. I try to make out the words, but he's talking in a low tone. After several minutes, his voice gets louder, and I can make out the words, "I love you too, baby." My heart sinks. My sadness shows on my face because LaDamien enters the room and apologizes for taking so long. "Kim has called several times since dinner, and I had to call her back. Then Ariel got on the phone and wanted to tell me goodnight."

I didn't mean to be so blunt, but the words just came out. "Who did you say I love you to?" LaDamien doesn't miss a beat. He assures me he was talking to Ariel and not Kim.

He's completely nude. I swallow hard. LaDamien doesn't have a body to shame Adonis, but it's apparent that ten years ago, he did. He still has taut legs that are long and muscular. His arms have definition in them, and his pectoral muscles are still well-defined. It's only his mid-section that has begun to defy him, and now I understand why he's so adamant about working out. But it's not his torso muscles that have my full attention; it's the stiff muscle he has propped in his hand. LaDamien has been stroking it since walking into the room. When I begin to blush, his lips form into a huge smile.

We stay in the Jacuzzi until the water turns cold. We have talked, laughed, touched, caressed, and kissed. As I prepare to exit the tub, LaDamien stops me. "Turn around," he instructs me. I turn and look down at him. He lifts himself up and then leans backward on his heels. He lifts my left leg over his right shoulder, and within seconds his tongue is invading my vagina. Like his fingers, LaDamien has a long thick tongue, a tongue that moves deeper and deeper inside of me. I'm rising on my tiptoes. My right leg is growing weaker, and my hands begin to tremble as I try to brace myself. I palm the top of his head to push him back, but this only causes his movement to intensify. He's now teasing my clit with the tip of his tongue as he uses his fingers to masturbate me to orgasm. Getting out of his grip without falling is a different feat. When I'm able to compose myself, I move my leg from his shoulder and step over the side of the Jacuzzi. LaDamien is laughing as he follows me out.

"Why are you running from me?" he asks as he wraps his arms around me from behind and kisses the back of my neck. "You taste so good. I want some more."

I am still trying to recover from his oral foreplay when he directs me over to the bed. He turns me around and sets me down. LaDamien lies on top of me, and our tongues begin a new dance. "Umm, see how good you taste," he asks as he moves down to my breast. He suckles the right until I tell him the nipple is beginning to hurt, and then he turns his attention to the left. As his journey continues down my mid-section, he places his hands behind my knees and lifts them. Before long, his tongue is in action again. If I didn't know better, I would think he was trying to put his whole head inside me. He's licking and fingering me in quick motions. He's sucking my clit as he enters me with his middle finger. As my juices multiply, he inserts a second finger, and the sucking continues. I'm now moving to his strokes, and I can tell it's driving him crazy. He has removed his fingers and is taking long strokes with his tongue across my wet pussy. The sensation is overwhelming, and I'm about to orgasm. I arch my back and grab the sheets. The harder I press my bottom into the bed the faster, and harder he licks. Just as my orgasm releases, he jabs his tongue into me and sucks my juices. I lose all control and release a sound that originates from the pit of my soul.

The chance to recover or to think rationally comes and goes. LaDamien towers over me, and in one thrust, he has entered me. Bone hard, no warning, no rest, and no condom. I want to tell him to stop, to admonish him for being so reckless, and to let him know I'm not on the pill. We never discussed sex. This is ignorance on my part, especially since I knew this was where we were heading when he said he wanted to stay overnight. He feels so good inside of me, all eight inches, "Oh, you're on my spot," I moan as I rethink his length. Maybe it's ten. This man is working me over, and I love every second of it. I forget about the condom and the size of his penis. My only thoughts are on staying in sync with his movement so that I can feel every piece of him.

LaDamien is staring down at me and mumbling something about sucking and nipples. I finally figure out what he's telling me to do. I pinch his hardened nipples between my middle and index fingers and massage them with my thumb. He loves this. I feel him tighten his ass muscles as his thrusts are more defined and labored. He's gripping the sheets as I had done earlier when he was driving me over the edge with his tongue action. It's as though the work I'm doing on his nipples has left him stuck in transition, so I reach up and suck his right nipple into my mouth. I'm sucking, and teasing his right nipple with my tongue, while I continue to finger the left nipple with my thumb.

LaDamien begins to lose control. He's now the one trembling and unable to hold on. His thrusts are quickening and not as controlled as before. He's not moaning but yelling out, "Ah, oh baby, that feels good, that feels good, I'm going to cum, I'm going to cum." I feel the muscles in his penis spasm, and I know he's ejaculating. But he doesn't stop. He continues to love me as he brings his mouth down over mine. We kiss, and kiss, and kiss some more. Our tongues are moving in sync with our bodies, and I feel him growing inside me. For the next hour, I let LaDamien guide me, teach me, show me ways of love-making I never knew imaginable. His sexual appetite is insatiable. No sooner than I think he can give no more, he turns me in another position and starts sexing me again.

It is two a.m. when he climbs out of bed and takes my hand. We get into the shower, and he bathes me from head to toe. He knows I'm sore in that special place, so he takes gentle care when washing between my legs. When he's finished, he tells me to get back in the bed, and he will be there in a few minutes. As I leave the bathroom, I notice the red light blinking on his cell phone. I glance at the phone as I grab a towel off the rack. He has nine missed calls. I can't help but wonder if it's Kim.

As I lie in bed waiting for LaDamien, I begin to feel guilty. What if something has happened to his daughter? What if Kim is calling about his ailing mother or some other family emergency? How selfish of us to steal away like this. What if God is punishing us for our sins by allowing something terrible to happen back home?

The water is still running, but I can hear LaDamien's voice. He has returned the phone calls. The minutes are passing slowly. I keep my eyes on the red numbers illuminating in the darkness of the room. Sixteen, seventeen…twenty, and LaDamien awakens me. "Come here." He says as he pulls me into his arms. He had climbed back into bed, and I didn't even notice. The clock reads two thirty-five. My head is resting on his chest as he caresses my arm. I think he's about to tell me about his phone conversation. Still, instead, he begins singing an unfamiliar song to me. *Baby say what's on your mind… what's on your mind… I've been here all morning waitin' for your answer I'm waitin'*... The lyrics are nice, but I can't identify the song. LaDamien asks me if I recognize it, and I say no. He tells me it's *Say*, by Kem.

When I tell him that I've never heard of Kem, he's surprised and accuses me of not being a true lover of music. He promises to stop and buy me the CD on our way home. We spend the next thirty minutes or so talking about our favorite love songs. Well, I talked about mine while LaDamien sang verses of his. Sleep is tugging at me, and my eyelids are closing as he begins singing, *I Believe in You and Me*. He tells me this is his all-time favorite love song, and when I tell him I love the song, as well, and have *The Preacher's Wife* soundtrack, he schools me, "Whitney Houston wasn't the first one to do this song. The Four Tops recorded it long before her."

Hours later, I awaken, still lying in LaDamien's arms. He isn't asleep. I ask if everything is okay. He says he isn't ready to return home, to go back to Kim, the arguing, and the fighting. I can't imagine what it's like to live in a home full of unhappiness and discontent. Nor do I understand why anyone would settle for such a life. Lifting, I turn to face him. "What can I do to make it better?" This simple question garners a smile.

"I'm serious," I say. LaDamien lets me know that he believes me. We stay this way, me looking at him and him staring at the ceiling, for several moments. We both hear his phone vibrating on the bathroom counter. It's six-fifty. To distract me, he takes my hand and moves it to his swollen shaft. As I massage him, he closes his eyes and sighs in relief. Minutes later, I'm on top of him, riding us into a land far away, where only we reside, and Kim can't find us…a land with no rules, no wives, and no cell phones vibrating in the distance.

Kim

LaDamien's body language is yelling out that he's lying. He's talking fast as he recites the lie he's laying out to me. He's going on a business trip to meet the guy Barry he and Mark met a few months back at one of those networking events. Barry has invited them to attend a function down in Naples to expose them to some new contacts. The event will not end until late, so they'll stay the night. I know it's a lie because he has offered it to me in a gift box with a pretty bow on top. He has gone overboard to ensure I understand it's a business trip and nothing for me to worry about. Plus, he knows my quarterly business meeting is tomorrow, and I will not be able to take off or leave early to join him.

It is Friday morning, and I need to get going, but I don't want to leave because I know LaDamien is up to no good. I can't put leaving off any longer, so I say goodbye and lead Ariel out to the car. LaDamien follows us out to the garage and kisses us both goodbye. He reminds me again that he's leaving for Naples around three and will not be back until tomorrow. He's too accommodating. I'm convinced more than ever that he's lying. "Maybe we can have lunch," I suggest. He quickly shoots me down. He has to drive over to Venice to view a property. He may just continue to Naples from Venice instead of returning home. My heart aches.

After dropping Ariel off at school, I head home instead of merging on to the interstate. LaDamien's *Cadillac* Escalade is still in the garage. He has just stepped out of the shower when I reach our bedroom. "What are you doing back here?" he asks me.

The excuse I use, "I forgot the report I was working on last night. It's part of my presentation for today's meeting." I ask him more about Barry and what type of contacts he's looking to make at this function to waste time. He's becoming annoyed by my questions and continues to veer over at the clock. His cell phone, lying next to his overnight bag, is lighting up, indicating that a call is coming in. He picks the phone up and rejects the call. He then presses the end button a little longer than necessary, and the phone shuts off. LaDamien steps to me and begins running his hands along my hips, sliding my skirt up. He pushes me up against the dresser as he pulls my pantyhose, girdle, and panties down. I brace his shoulders as he enters me. He's asking me if I'm scared he's going to give my dick away. If this is why I have returned? I want to scream yes, but instead, I say, "No, I did leave my report, but I'm glad I came back."

Minutes later, we are finished, and I'm in the bathroom cleaning up. LaDamien has crawled back into bed. I exit the bathroom and redress as LaDamien watches my every move. Immediately, I become self-conscious. Although he tells me he loves every part of me, I know he's put off by my weight gain because he's always urging me to go work out with him. "Do you know where you will be staying," I ask to kill the silence between us?

"No, we'll just stop at whatever *Comfort Inn* or *Best Western* that's closest. I'm not going to spend a bunch of money for a few hours to lay my head. Depending on how Mark feels, we might just come back tonight if it isn't too late." This makes me feel better as I head out the door for the second time.

Although LaDamien made some of my anxiety subside, the feelings return when I call him later in the day, and he doesn't answer. He called around five to say hi, but his phone was off when I called him back thirty minutes later. I spend the remainder of my night calling his number and numerous hotels. Still, none have a LaDamien Bryson or Mark Goins registered. I don't know Mya's last name, so I ride by her house and get the address. The same house my beautician's cousin claims to have seen his car at many times. When I asked who lived there, he claimed not to know what I was talking about and insinuating it must be someone with a car similar to ours.

A search of the property appraiser's database has the property listed under Mya Blake. Her phone number comes up in the White Pages search engine. I enter star sixty-seven, and then the number. No answer. My heart is pounding fast, and I'm panicking. I call the same hotels back and ask for Mya Blake. They have no one by that name registered. All types of thoughts are going through my mind, preventing me from resting. What are they doing? Did he take her to the networking function? How did he introduce her? I know I could just call Sharon, Mark's wife, but what would I say to get the information without raising her suspensions. Or, I could call Mark.

The truth is, I'm too afraid to make the calls because if Mark answers his home phone, I will die. I'm pacing back and forth when the house phone rings. It's LaDamien.

"My battery died," he begins. He's lying. Instead of challenging him on it, I remain calm and keep him on the phone, letting him know how scared I was that something terrible had happened. I tell him about my meeting and ask about his day. My goal is to keep him on the phone, so I tell him about my friends and what is happening in their lives, and then I suggest we visit his mom when he returns and maybe take her to dinner. I keep talking to see if I can get any indication that there's someone with him. All I hear is the TV playing in the background. Finally, when there's nothing else to talk about, I say, "I love you." He surprises me by saying, "I love you too, baby."

For hours I toss and turn, unable to fall into a deep sleep. It's hard to get settled when LaDamien isn't here, so I decide to call him. He will be annoyed, but hopefully, he will understand how much I miss him being here. He doesn't answer. I know I should let him sleep, that I may be disturbing Mark if he is there, they are probably tired, but the more I think about it, the more I want him to wake-up, and assure me he's alone. I call four more times before I realize how silly I'm acting. If he's with someone, he wouldn't have talked so freely to me earlier. When I finally settle down and drift off, the ringing phone awakens me. It's two a.m., and LaDamien is calling to ask me if everything is okay. I tell him I was just missing him. He says okay, and tells me to get some sleep. This makes me feel better, and I take his advice. Yet, hours later, I'm catering to my suspicions and calling his number repeatedly, wondering why he can't answer the phone when I call.

LaDamien was not the same after he returned from Naples. He began spending more and more time away from home. At times it's as if Ariel and I no longer exist. His business dealings are on the rise, and most seem to require travel. I ask him if he still loves me if he still wants to be married, and he says yes. He asks why I would ask such a thing. I even go so far as to ask him about this woman named Mya that keeps popping up in conversations I have with other people.

"Rumors are going around that you are spending a lot of time with her," I say. In response, he says, she's just an acquaintance. Someone he's known for quite some time but ran into recently at a networking event. She helps him with some ideas he and Mark have about branching out into other areas to grow their business. To quell my fears, he offers to introduce us.

On the day we are to meet, LaDamien must travel to Pensacola to visit his sister. She is having trouble dealing with her teenage son. He claims Dawn has called regarding Dexter. He's becoming unruly and disrespectful. LaDamien says he wants to go visit to see what he can do to help. He invites me to tag along, and I decide to go.

We are traveling north on I-275, approaching Gainesville, when LaDamien pulls over at a rest stop. He heads to the men's room while I direct Ariel into the ladies' room. When we exit, LaDamien has made his way to the picnic area and is talking on his cell phone. We head over to where he's standing, and when he notices us, he hangs up. We stop at least three more times before we reach Pensacola, each time LaDamien wonders away to make a phone call. Each time I ask him who he's talking to, he simply states he's returning missed calls. When I inquire why his phone is off, he states he doesn't want the constant interruption.

When we arrive in Pensacola, we check into the hotel, and LaDamien suggests I get something to eat while he calls his sister to let her know we have arrived. Dawn lives in a low-income housing project and doesn't have room to house us. As I'm driving around looking for something LaDamien will like, I call and ask him what he wants to eat. His phone beeps in between rings, indicating he's on a call. LaDamien clicks over to answer. He tells me chicken, but before I hang up, I ask him if he's talking to Dawn or Dexter, and he says he called, but no one answered. His answer prompts me to ask who he was talking to when I called, and he states he was not on the phone.

At first, I was going to explain how I knew he was on the phone. On second thought, I decide not to say anything at all. We end the call after I place the order at the KFC drive-in.

I return to the room, and LaDamien isn't there, so I get Ariel settled and look for him. He's out by the pool, cell phone to his ear. Instead of calling his name, I quietly approach him from behind. He's telling the person on the other end that he will be returning earlier than he planned. His nephew isn't in town, and he sees no reason to stay an extra day. He will get some rest and get on the road by three a.m. Someone coughs, and he turns around and spots me. He closes the cell phone without saying goodbye. Again, I ask who he was talking to, and this time he says it was his sister Lynn back in St. Petersburg.

Back in the room, I ask about Dexter. LaDamien stops eating and tells me that he finally reached Dawn, and she advised him that Dexter went out of town with one of his cousins and won't be back until Sunday night.

It turns out LaDamien didn't tell Dawn or Dexter that he was coming to visit. This revelation leaves me wondering if this was all a big charade to keep me from meeting Mya. I do all I can to get him to stay the weekend, despite our not seeing his nephew. We can visit with Dawn and other family members, but as he stated to the caller on the phone, we left Pensacola around three a.m.

Shortly after eleven, we arrive in St. Pete. LaDamien didn't even bother coming inside. He dropped Ariel and me off and pretended he needed to go by his sister Veronica's house to take a look at her air conditioner. I wanted to call her and verify this but thought it would bring suspicion to the state of our marriage. Like a good wife, I went into the house and patiently waited for him to return. As usual, it was late into the night.

LaDamien

After Mya allowed me to taste her sweetness, I know I have made the biggest mistake of my life. I had no idea a woman could please me the way Mya pleases me. We have made love numerous times since returning from Naples. Every time I'm inside her, I want to bury myself there. Wherever Mya is, I want to be pleasing her beyond all comprehension. Although she has made herself available to me, I get so turned on just thinking about her that I find myself masturbating at all hours of the day.

My desire for Mya is growing with every second. I'm leaving home at all hours of the night to ride by her house. I need to subdue my fears of someone else taking what I hope belongs only to me. Like now, I'm sitting outside her house with an erection hard as a rock. I want to pick up the phone and call her to ask if I can come inside and make sweet love. No doubt, she will agree, but I don't want to risk Kim catching me here. She knows something is going on. That this affair is nothing like the others, and she even knows where Mya lives. I have seen her twice, tailing me as I left the house. The first time I was a few blocks from Mya's, the second time, I was turning on to the main street that leads to Mya's subdivision. Both times, I led Kim to the home of my oldest sister, who lives about a mile away.

For the first time, I believe Kim feels threatened that she may lose me to another woman. Mya could make me leave Kim. All she needs to do is show me that our love will be forever, that she'll be loyal to me and always put me first, and most importantly, she'll never abandon me. Kim does all these things, not because of her unconditional love for me but because she's secure in what we have. She's secure in knowing the bills get paid, and she can drive nice cars, and she can spend her money on whatever she chooses. She loves having a successful husband that she can flaunt in front of her friends and colleagues. Although Kim is secure in our relationship, I don't share her feelings because, unlike my wife, I need so much more to make me whole.

The ache in my loins is becoming unbearable, so I dial Mya's number. She answers on the second ring, and I ask her if she's alone. She's offended by the question, but I don't apologize. "Do you want to go for a ride?" She pauses then informs me it's one in the morning.

"Look out the window, I'm outside, and my dick is throbbing," Mya asks me if I need her to rub it. As she's talking, I find myself stroking my penis harder and harder, then faster. The seat is back as far as it will go, and I recline backward. I'm turned on by her telling me what she'll do to me once I'm in her bed. It's getting hotter in my car. My breathing is becoming constricted. My thoughts go to our time in Naples, we're in our hotel room, and my face is buried between Mya's legs. She tastes so good; it's as if I can taste her now. She's asking me if I'm on top or if she's on top.

"Uhm, you're on top." I want to grip her firm hips like I'm gripping my steering wheel. She's telling me to throw it back harder, and I respond by thrusting upwards. Removing one hand off the steering wheel and grabbing my rod, I ask Mya to suck it for me, and she agrees. She tells me not to push so hard but to let it ease its way down her throat. How does she know I'm pushing harder and harder with her every word? I lose control, and my juices fly. Mya asks me if I'm okay. After recovering from my explosion, I tell her "yes."

It's the first time we have phone sex. My orgasm is almost as fulfilling as when I'm between Mya's legs. It took her only four minutes to get me off, but it was satisfying, nonetheless. Reaching into the glove compartment, I pull out some wet wipes to clean up the mess I've made. Now I can go home and go to bed, satisfied and content. Mya and I talk my entire drive back to the house as if our phone sex experience never took place. I sit in the garage talking, not wanting the call to end. The kitchen light illuminates under the door as I tell Mya I love her and will meet her at the gym at seven. As soon as I enter the house, Kim kills my mood.

Kim has finally asked about Mya. Who is she, and what she means to me? I tell her that Mya is an old acquaintance that I ran into recently. She works in marketing and thinks she can help take the business to the next level. To calm her down, I offer to introduce her to Mya, lying about a planned lunch with Mya, and Mark, on Friday that she can attend. Hopefully, this will put her insecurities to rest. Of course, I had no intentions of introducing Kim to Mya. Instead, I tell Kim the night before that we need to go to Pensacola to visit my sister and nephew.

Dawn *has* called several times to tell me that Dexter, her son, is becoming a handful. Dawn is a single parent. According to her, Dexter has taken up with the wrong crowd. I have promised to visit, but that was before Mya and I went to Naples. Since that trip, I have not wanted to be away from her more than the required time needed to be home. If I could take Mya to Pensacola with me, I would have been there already. But I know Kim wouldn't understand why she couldn't go. So, I decided to kill two birds with one stone and avoid explaining why Mya can't meet us for lunch while checking on Dexter to figure out what is going on with him.

Things don't turn out the way I planned. I didn't get a chance to see or talk to Mya after deciding to make the trip. I turned off my phone, and I don't turn it back on until we are at a rest stop near Gainesville. I have numerous messages, and several are from Mya. She's concerned that something is wrong, so I give her a call to let her know I'm okay. As soon as she answers the phone, Kim approaches, so I hang up and turn the phone off again because I know Mya will call me back. We stop several times before reaching Pensacola. Each time I call Mya back. Kim is becoming suspicious. After we get to the hotel, I send Kim to get dinner, giving me a chance to speak with Mya. I miss Mya intensely. It probably wouldn't be so bad had I seen her before I left, but it has now been more than a day since we last saw each other, and I can't stand it. Dawn and Dexter will have to wait. Instead of calling to let them know we are here, I decided to get some sleep so we can head back home. Mya is all I can think of, and I want to see her, touch her, and make love to her. I don't know how long this can last. Kim has to know that I'm in love with someone else. She has to know, but the question is how long she will tolerate it.

LOVE...

- is patient
- is kind
- is not rude
- does not envy
- is not self-seeking
- will not lie
- is not proud
- is not quick to anger
- protects
- does not boast
- does not record wrongs
- trusts
- hopes
- perseveres
- finds no joy in evil but celebrates truth
- never fails

Mya

LaDamien and I sit at the red light at the intersection of Thirty-fourth Street and Fifty-fourth Avenue. We have just left the *IHOP* and are heading back to my place. It's a beautiful Friday morning, and he's trying his best to talk me into calling off for the day. *The Steve Harvey Morning Show* is on, and they are doing "Freedom Friday."

Freedom Fridays is a segment on the show, whereas Steve and his crew pick a theme and then play their favorite songs centered on the theme. It becomes a sort of competition to see who picks the best songs, and listeners get to call in and voice their opinions. Music-wise, it's the best day to listen to the show. Depending on the theme, some great oldies get played. Steve is such a trip. Sometimes before he plays a song, he reads the lyrics and tells the listeners what the artist meant while writing it. Today's theme is great party songs. Nephew Tommy selects Chuck Brown's *Woody Woodpecker*. LaDamien turns up the volume and is in another zone just like that. We reach my home, and he reaches over and kisses my lips. He doesn't mention my taking the day off, and I quickly exit the vehicle. I turn around to wave, and he has rolled the window down, tapping his hand on the outside of the door to the funky beat of E.U.'s *Doing the Butt*. He tells me to go inside, and he will call me later. I know he just wants to look at *my* butt.

My calls to him go unanswered for the remainder of the day. He annoys me so much when he does this, so I decide that if he doesn't call me, I'm not going to call him. It's Monday before I hear from him again. I answer the phone all nonchalantly as we have just spoken hours earlier. He tells me he's outside, and he wants me to open the door for him. Once inside, he asks me who I spent my weekend with. A chuckle escapes me as I let him know the only time I left the house was when Angie and I went to the mall. He seems not to believe me, but I'm smart enough to know it's a deflection to keep me from asking him why I have not heard from him since he dropped me off on Friday. He plays this silly game until he thinks he's in the clear, and then I ask, "So what did you and the family do this weekend?" For a second, his temples pulsate but subside as quickly as it started.

"Kim had a conference to attend in Orlando last week, so we decided to send for my nephew. I drove over with him and Ariel so we could go to *Disney World*."

I'm crushed. He never mentioned Kim was out of town last week, and he never mentioned his nephew coming or this trip. Then I noted how he said, "we decided" it was the first time he spoke of him and his wife as a couple who did things together as a couple. This revelation not only alarmed me, but the comment pierced my soul. The emotions confused me, and I didn't particularly appreciate how it felt. LaDamien looked at me, not with concern that his words hurt me, but as if he dared me to question him any further.

"Why didn't you tell me? Why did you have me sitting here all weekend wondering what was going on?" His demeanor didn't frighten me. It just agitated me.

He replied, "You know I'm married, right? Sometimes I have to do things with my family, with my daughter that includes my wife?" he corrected.

He didn't get it. Of course, I understood those things. What I didn't understand was why it was such a big secret. He shares everything else with me, so why was this event such a big secret? And why did he feel the need to keep me in the dark? The more I tried to get him to see my point, the deeper he shoved the invisible knife into my heart. Finally, I told him I had to get ready for work because I had an early meeting.

It was about two in the afternoon when I looked up, and the security guard was standing at my desk. In his hand was a beautiful bouquet. A smile made its home on my face. After the guard walked away, I took out the card and read the simple message imprinted on it, "Just because..." No signature, just a manufactured card in a plain white envelope. Minutes later, my desk phone rang, and LaDamien's number appeared on the caller ID. Immediately, I thanked him for the flowers. He was pleased with himself, and just like that, the events of the weekend and our earlier conversation were a distant memory.

Two weeks passed, and LaDamien stated out of the blue that if he wanted to be bored half to death, he would just sit at home with Kim.

"Sorry for being such a bore. What do you suggest? Being with someone's husband is new to me, so I'm not sure what you expect."

He asked me what type of relationships was I accustomed to, and I quickly replied, "The kind where I'm free to do what I want when I want with the person I'm involved with."

He shot back, "Like what? What would you do differently?"

"I would go to the movies, to dinner, to concerts, on trips, and what have you. And, I would make plans for tonight or Friday, or next week, or next month, and not worry that something would come up at a moment's notice, and change things." His comments were coming at me like rapid-fire, and I wanted my responses to be the same. Of course, he had no retort. He simply nodded his head and turned up the volume on the radio. It was another Freedom Friday on *The Steve Harvey Morning Show*, and they were playing another one of LaDamien's favorites. As he bobbed his head to Ice Cube's *Today Was a Good Day,* an idea popped into my head.

"Why don't we have a Freedom Friday?" I suggested.

He turned down the volume and asked me to explain. I offered that we take the day off one Friday out of every month and do whatever we liked. It could be a movie, shopping, or something fun like roller skating, or going to *Busch Gardens*."

LaDamien liked the idea. He smiled as he caressed my knee and told me that would be cool. "See, I knew you had it in you to come up with something to keep the fire burning."

Our first Freedom Friday was the following week. He and his partner Mark had a meeting scheduled in Sun City. They rode together to the meeting, which was about an hour's drive. The plan was for me to meet LaDamien afterward, and we would go horseback riding and then to a late lunch. He needed to tell Mark he wouldn't be returning to St. Petersburg with him. I didn't know what he would say, but I was looking forward to finally meeting Mark. When I arrived at the office complex where LaDamien told me they would be, the man I thought was Mark continued walking right past me, although LaDamien was about to introduce us. I pretended not to notice the slight, but it was evident that LaDamien would not let it slide. He called out to Mark very loudly. If he didn't respond, it would have been a total diss.

Mark stopped and turned around to face us. "This is my friend Mya. I wanted to introduce you to her." LaDamien said, gesturing towards me.

Mark was slow in reaching out to receive my hand, which I had extended as a show of goodwill. Unenthusiastically, he smiled and said, "Hello."

The three of us chatted for several minutes. It was unmistakable Mark wanted no part of LaDamien's infidelity. Even more apparent, he didn't want to witness or have knowledge that would one day be required of him to reveal. Nor did he want to one day be faced with a decision that would test his loyalties, not only to his partner but to his wife. Mark's apprehension screamed I don't want to have a face, a date, or an event, to confirm his knowledge of LaDamien's inability to be faithful to his marriage. By having this knowledge, he probably was forced to question his beliefs in his vows. Nonetheless, he was polite and professional as he said goodbye and again headed for his car.

"That was awkward," I stated as LaDamien threw his things into the backseat and climbed into the passenger seat.

"That's just Mark. You know he's all henpecked and holier than thou, but I remember back in the day when he wasn't so squeaky clean." LaDamien pulled me close, and we indulged in a passionate kiss. When I placed the car in reverse and looked back, Mark was still sitting there, watching us, most likely wondering if he should pull LaDamien from my car and take him home to his wife and child. As we passed by, LaDamien smiled and waved goodbye. Mark placed his car in drive and pulled out of the parking lot behind us. Again, I wondered what was said when LaDamien told him his plans included a woman that wasn't his wife.

We were both sore after the four-hour horse ride. In the beginning, we were both terrified, but as time went on, we began to loosen up. It was a typical spring day in central Florida. The temperature was in the low eighties with a light easterly wind that gave off enough breeze to combat the heat. The facilities left a lot to be desired. Even with limited space, we freshened up, using wet wipes and changing into clean clothes before making our departure. Still, the stench of the animals remained in my subconscious long after we left.

"So, what's next?" LaDamien asked as he handed the waiter his credit card. We'd had lunch at *The Crab Trap* in Bradenton, located a couple of miles from the Skyway Bridge.

There was no next. My plans ended after our lunch. So, I asked LaDamien what he had in mind. He reminded me I had not made love to him in over a week. So, the next stop on our Freedom Friday journey was my place. We arrived at my house at about four-thirty. As soon as I turned the engine off, LaDamien's phone rang. It was Kim. She wanted to know when he would get done for the day. Her friends invited her to dinner, and she needed him to pick up Ariel. He was annoyed but told her he could be there by six. Six was too late, she admonished. He needed to be there by five.

LaDamien agreed and quickly opened the car door and stepped out. He assured me that the daycare was open until six-thirty, and what he needed to do would only take a few minutes.

At six-ten, LaDamien gave me a final kiss in the parking lot at his office. He stepped out of my car and headed to his car, parked at the very end of the parking lot. My phone rang, and it was him.

"I enjoyed our day and can hardly wait for our next outing. Next time try picking something that doesn't take so much time because although I want to have fun, I also need time to do other things. His underlying message was not lost. I made sure our next Freedom Friday left time for a quick romp in the sack.

LaDamien

Freedom Fridays, that's what Mya called it. Once a month, we would take a Friday off to be free to do or be whatever we liked. Mya had such an imagination. In the past year, we had gone horseback riding, rollerblading, and ice skating. One day we traveled to *Disney's Animal Kingdom* and went on a safari. We'd watched more movies than I had seen in the last ten years, taken a pottery class, and made chocolate at a chocolate factory, and it didn't stop there. We had late-night and overnight outings that included *Orlando Magic* basketball games, *Halloween Horror Nights*, and Mardi Gras at *Universal Studio's* theme park in Orlando.

Because she knew I wouldn't be able to spend Christmas with her, we celebrated early by heading over to *Disney* one night in the middle of December. We enjoyed the holiday festivities going on in the magical kingdom. I was never one to celebrate holidays, but it was important to Mya. She loved every holiday, especially Christmas. We started the day off at Epcot, where we pretended to travel the world and learn how different cultures celebrated the holidays. As darkness began to overshadow the daylight, we headed over to *Disney's* Hollywood Studios, previously known as MGM.

We strolled down the "Streets of America" and viewed the extravagant *Osborne Family Spectacle of Lights*. It was hard to believe that these people had their homes decorated with all these lights. No wonder their neighbors were about to run them out of town. As we were leaving, fake flurries of snow began to blow through the air. It was easy to get caught up in the nostalgia of it all. I'm sure I would have allowed myself to let go even more if it weren't for Kim blowing up my cellular every fifteen minutes. Mya pretended not to notice me checking the phone and then suddenly needing to satisfy my urge to use the restroom. As we rushed to the *Magic Kingdom* for *Mickey's Very Merry Christmas Party*, I finally decided to turn the phone off.

The excuse I would give to Kim, my battery died, and I left my charger at the office.

It was twelve-thirty a.m. when we entered our hotel room at the *Embassy Suites*, on Lake Avenue, not far from *Disney*. We were both exhausted, so I told Mya to go ahead and shower while I checked my messages. She didn't complain out of gratitude for me turning the phone off earlier. No doubt she knew I would use this time to check in with Kim.

Later, we lay in bed, and I reflected on the day's events and had to admit today, I truly felt free. Forgotten were all my worries and all my responsibilities. I thanked Mya for her youthful spirit and for making me stop and smell the roses, as she puts it. Today, I didn't reply that roses smelled of cow manure. Instead, I chose to smell all the fragrances she described whenever she would stick one under my nose. Mya loved roses, so I made a mental note to buy her a fancy bouquet for Valentine's Day. We drifted off to sleep around one fifteen, saving our lovemaking for later, when we're both reenergized.

We left the room, heading downstairs for breakfast, holding hands, and giggling, making our way to the elevator. As we sat eating our breakfast in the hotel dining area, an elderly couple came by our table and asked if we were newlyweds. Mya looked down at her ringless finger. The sadness in her eyes was discernible. She replied to the couple, "not yet." The man nudged his wife to get her moving, but the woman didn't budge. She smiled and asked Mya did she want to get married, and when Mya said sometimes, the woman replied, "Well, when you make up your mind, let God know, and he'll do the rest." She patted Mya on the hand and then gave me a look I could not register. Her husband didn't make eye contact after that. He simply followed his wife as he had probably done most of his life.

After the couple left the area, Mya burst out laughing. I asked her what was so funny, and she asked me how many times had me, and Kim been stopped and asked that question. There was no need to stop and think about it. The answer was never. "That's what I figured," she replied as she cut into her pancakes and finished eating her breakfast. I asked her what was so funny again, and she stated, "Us, we're funny, LaDamien."

Mya was distant after we returned from *Disney*. She busied herself with shopping trips with her friends, dinners, and holiday parties. It was New Year's night before we saw each other again, although we talked on the phone almost daily. She insisted nothing was going on when I asked her if everything was okay. To quell my fears, she invited me over. She told me that the door would be open when I arrived and just let myself in. I arrived at her house shortly after seven, and there were no lights on. Had her car not been parked in the driveway, I would have thought she was not at home. Reaching the door, I turned the knob, and it opened. I stepped inside, and a large three-wick candle illuminated the room. In front of it was a note that I picked up and read. The note was clear and precise, remove all of your clothing, and come to the guest bedroom. Just like that, I was at full erection.

Mya must have been watching my every move. The second I removed my socks and placed them in my shoes, India. Arie's *Brown Skin* began to play.

I followed the music to her extra bedroom, and the first thing I noticed was that the entire room was bare. I had never been in the room before, so I didn't know if it ever contained any furniture.

Mya was sitting in the middle of the floor, surrounded by what looked like clay pots. In each corner of the room was a large three wicked candle. The smell of vanilla permeated the air, as India describing skin kissed by the sun. Her desire for a *Hershey's* kiss or some licorice relaxed my mind.

My God, I blinked and looked again. She was completely nude. Mya reached out to me and drew me into the warm room. She was smiling up at me, reading my reservations, knowing I don't like to be surprised like this, that I don't like it when I'm not in control.

Walking across the floor, covered with a vinyl tarp of some sort, I look down into the clay pots, but I can't see what is in them. Mya smiled slyly as she stuck her hands in two separate containers and retrieved a thick liquid substance that she smeared all over her breast. She then licked her fingers as she got up on her knees.

She grabs my hands and covers them with the smooth substance. My hands slide out of hers, and I smell. It's chocolate…warm chocolate. My erection that had subsided is back. I kneel next to Mya, who is now lying down, back arched. I pick up one of the pots and pour its contents down the length of her body. She doesn't need to do anything else.

I lift her right foot and begin licking the chocolate from her toes. I suck each toe making sure I get each drop and then do the same to her left. She's turned on. I can feel the tensing of her calf muscle as she fights the sexual arousal. It's the first time I have made love to her feet. It has been no secret I have a foot fetish. She has always obliged me by keeping them well pedicured and polished in bright, cheerful colors.

Moving from her feet to her ankles, my chocolate-covered hands grasp each ankle, and I hold her legs up as I watch the melted chocolate slowly descend her legs. I spread her legs to see if any has reached my favorite spot. Seeing that it hasn't, I reach for another pot, and with her legs still spread, I pour the mixture there. I place the pot back on the warmer that I have noticed for the first time. Mya is squirming around. I place my face where I long to be and begin lapping up the sweet substance. I never knew chocolate could taste so good. Knowing I will probably be sick tomorrow, but right now, I don't care. The mixture of chocolate and Mya's sweet nectar is feeding my hunger. The chocolate feast lasts for what seems like hours. The song has restarted several times. How many, I don't know, but every time I tune in, India.Arie croons about brown skin, lying down, and how she can't tell where her skin ends, and her lovers begin.

Mya has cum too many times for me to count. My head is covered with chocolate, and I can feel it on my ears, cheeks, and back. Crawling up to face her, we begin our slow tongue dance. We are grinding each other, the chocolate meshing into our skin. I'm so hard I feel like I'm going to explode, but I don't enter her. This eroticism has me so turned on by just touching, tasting her, being in her presence. She's reaching for me, but I push her hand away and kiss her harder. She understands, or so I thought. Her legs spread wide, and my tip is right there at her opening. She's maneuvering her body, hoping that my penis will reach that spot she's trying to scratch. I roll over onto my back, and she reaches for the last canister. Finding it, she digs out some of the creamy substance and begins to massage my rock-hard penis.

I moan out loud. This only feeds Mya's persistence. Now I'm greeting her hand strokes. Needing to grab hold of something, but there's nothing but the dried chocolate on the tarp. I decide to stop fighting it and go with it in hopes my release comes quickly. Mya is hand fucking my dick, or I'm fucking her hand, whichever it is, I'm turned on. My moans have turned into bitch yelps, and I'm riding her hand to ecstasy I have never known before. When I'm about to release a thousand babies into her hand, she slides her mouth down my chocolate-covered shaft and my brain trembles.

A half-hour later, I awaken. India.Arie is still playing in repeat mode. Mya has removed the clay pots and the warmer. The candles are gone, and a *Glades* plug-in located on one of the walls illuminates the room. She has showered, and the water dripping from her head lets me know she's shampooed her hair, as well. She laughs as she hands me a towel and rag. "That was, wow, I can't even give it words," she says as she begins to roll the tarp, forcing me up.

After I shower and dress, I join Mya back in the spare bedroom, where she has already dragged the furniture back into its place. It contains a black futon with an African print mattress, a wicker chair, and a wicker table set. I kiss her on the back of her neck and ask what she's trying to do to me. I want her to say, "Get you to leave your wife," but she doesn't. Instead, she says, "what you want me to do…freak you out of your mind."

Being sexed by Mya is something I love, but I don't like the term she has just used. I think that Mya doesn't understand the depth of my love. No matter how many times I share my feelings with her. I don't know how to get her to understand what having her in my life means to me. She looks at the clock on the wall and announces that it's after midnight, and I need to get going. I don't get it. Why isn't she fighting for me, for us, for our love? Why won't she say the words I long to hear so our being together will be normal, so people won't have to wonder so that we can be each other's dessert until the end of time?

As I make my way out the front door, India.Arie's crooning finally comes to an end. *Yes, Mya, I want to caress your beautiful mahogany skin forever and make you feel like a queen. Whatever you tell me to do, I'll do it, just to be next to you.*

LOVE...
- is patient
- is kind
- is not rude
- does not envy
- is not self-seeking
- will not lie
- does not proud
- is not quick to anger
- does not boast
- protects
- does not record wrongs
- trusts
- hopes
- perseveres
- finds no joy in evil but celebrates truth
- never fails

LaDamien

My life is in such a whirlwind right now. On most days, I don't know if I'm coming or going. Mark has advised me that he wants to dissolve the business. He says he's ready to do something new, something different. I ask him what he has in mind, and he just shrugs his shoulders. I felt it coming. Our relationship has not been the same since I introduced him to Mya. When I asked him what he thought about her, he quickly let me know that I was making a huge mistake. "You never fall in love with the affair," he had said. But my relationship with Mya was more than an affair. When I said this to Mark, he chuckled and shook his head. For some reason, he could not conceive that I could be in love with Mya and was considering leaving Kim for her.

As a result of this growing distance between us, our business is suffering drastically. Because the business is suffering, I'm having trouble dealing with my personal life. Kim has to know the truth after all this time. We are like strangers forced to live in the same space. Just knowing that Kim will be there when I arrive each evening makes me despise her even more. She's being facetious and evil by not leaving and not acknowledging what is right before her eyes. She knows I don't want to be with her any longer, but she refuses to leave. We argue deep into the night. I try to stay gone until after she has fallen asleep, but as soon as I enter the bedroom, she awakens and starts up where we left off that morning. This discord is wearing me out, and I don't know how much longer I can take it.

For a while, having Mya was all I needed to deal with the discontentment in my life, but lately, I feel Mya's love and trust slowly slipping away. She told me in the beginning that if I were serious about ending my marriage, she would stick around for six months to see if I left Kim. Six months to walk away from the last five years of my life, from my daughter, my home, my hard work in building a successful company. Mya has never been married, so she didn't understand how unrealistic she was being. So, I placed her on a pedestal to make her feel as important, if not more important, than my wife. Spending more time with her than I do with Kim, so much more someone recently asked me if Kim and I had divorced. I do everything in my power to appease her and reassure her that she's the one I love and the one I will eventually be with.

Right now, I'm sitting at my desk, looking over my bank statements. The balances have never been this low before, and I'm beginning to panic. It seems as though all of my hard work is going down the drain. Every aspect of my life spiraling out of control. In the past, I could borrow money from the business account if I had a personal expense that I could not cover. Today that isn't an option. Mark is aware of my extravagant spending trying to maintain two women. He will no longer allow me to borrow money. The folder marked Mutual Funds and Stocks is on my desk. Drawing against my investments should be a last resort in the most challenging times, but today I need to make an exception.

To demonstrate my love and commitment to Mya, I have done things totally against my character. Mya has never asked me for anything, I just see so much that she desires to have, and I want to provide those things. I have justified my actions by telling myself that everything I have done will benefit us both in the end. There are things I did just because I could. I wanted to impress her. Other things were done out of guilt, like paying off her car's balance because I felt guilty after buying Kim a *Mercedes Benz* for Christmas. Whatever incites a sparkle in Mya's eyes I want her to have. I don't care if it's a fifteen-dollar blouse from *Target* or the fifteen-hundred-dollar diamond and sapphire ring she fell in love with at *Jared's*. Her innocence moves me beyond reason. She's so gracious and appreciative of everything I do, unlike my wife.

Kim, just the thought of her brings a sickening feeling to the pit of my stomach. It's as if she has a secret code to my bank account, or she's watching my every move. Whenever I do something for Mya, it's not long before she's demanding something bigger and better. A trip, new furniture, the kitchen remodeled. She even had the nerve to ask me for a *Range Rover* months before I decided to get the Mercedes. When I handed her the keys, I could have sworn I saw a look of displeasure on her face. She later mentioned the car was not brand new but two years old. I could not believe her nerve. All the bills are paid by me, while her paycheck is hers to spend on whatever she and Ariel want, and never thinking of me. Kim could have money stashed away, earning interest in a savings account or mutual fund for all I know. She could be well on her way to being a millionaire as she drains me dry.

Mya looked concerned when I first shared my financial set-up with her. She's always worried about my well-being and says Kim is trying to send her a message that she's still my wife and isn't planning on going anywhere. I question this belief, and she explains, "Why would a man who doesn't love his wife take her to New York to see a show on Broadway for her birthday? Why would he spend thousands of dollars on a new kitchen for a home he will be leaving soon, and let's not even talk about the new car?" Then she adds, "Maybe I'm the fool, after all, maybe Kim knows you're never going to leave, maybe this is how the two of you carry on all the time."

Her accusation upsets me because I know I love Mya if I know nothing else. Why she would doubt my sincerity is beyond me. She has to understand that ending a marriage isn't that simple. Regardless of how I feel about Kim until the final decision gets made, I must do my best to live in peace and perform as a husband and father. For goodness sake, I have explained it to her over and over and over again.

My head is throbbing as I read over the documents. I think about how conniving my wife is, driving me crazy on purpose. She knows I don't love her, I don't want to be with her, yet she stays for no other reason than to torment me. Now I must figure out a way to beat her at her game while trying to hold on to the only true source of happiness in my life, Mya.

The knock on the door startles me. Seconds later our secretary, Wanda, enters my office. Wanda has been with us since the early days of Bryson Goins Enterprises. She was the third secretary to come onboard and has stayed despite the low pay and lack of benefits.

Kim has never liked, or, shall I say, trusted, Wanda. She assumes that every woman I come into contact with, I will eventually have sex with them. She has gone so far as to warn Wanda that her pursuit of me will get met with strong resistance. She claims that our relationship is unbreakable and that she would stand tough and outlast any woman who got in her way. She even had the nerve to suggest that

Wanda would get fired if she ever found out that something other than work was going on in this office.

"Fired?" What a joke. Kim has never done anything to help me succeed, not as a husband and not as a businessman. Through it all, Wanda has remained faithful to Mark and me. She has stood by the business through thick and thin. Always having our back and always putting our success first. She noticed the change in Mark before I did, suggesting to me weeks before that Mark may plan to jump ship. "But don't worry, LaDamien, we can make this business work without Mark. You can just buy him out," she said, full of confidence.

"Yes, Wanda, what is it?" I ask.

"I need to talk with you about something very delicate, and I'm not sure how you're going to take it." Wanda stood nervously before me, all six feet one inch of her tall and slender frame. She isn't the most attractive woman, but her honey-colored complexion and model-like physique give an air of confidence. It makes people stop and take notice. However, after getting to know Wanda personally, a person soon realizes she lacks self-confidence and can be downright timid at times.

I fold the financial portfolios and place them in their perspective envelopes, leaving the statement for a mutual fund out. Wanda glances down to see what it is I have been looking over. Usually, I share everything with her since she's responsible for all the business financials and some of my personal information, but not lately. "What is it?" I ask again.

Wanda diverts eye contact then decides to take a seat. She crosses her long legs and tugs at the hem of the short skirt she's wearing, making sure her goods aren't exposed. "I saw you yesterday at Baywalk. You were having lunch at Dan Marino's. You weren't alone," she adds. "Who was that you were with?"

Did she just question me? I don't believe this. "What business is it of yours who I have lunch with?" I state, more than ask. Wanda doesn't move. She's used to my bluntness, and I'm sure she knew what my reaction would be before she came in here and asked the question.

"It's just that you have been different lately. You're spending more time away from the office, and, well, the other day, I received a call from Chip over at the bank. He mentioned there was a female with you during the last two appointments you've had with him. He wanted to know if you were training someone new."

She sits up straight and looks me in the eye awaiting my response. "Well, you know it would be nice to have someone trained to do your job so you can take a vacation and not worry about the office when you need a day off. It's something Mark and I have been thinking about for some time." Wanda shows no expression, so I continue. "It wouldn't be necessary if our wives took a more active role in the business."

Having help from our spouses was one thing Mark and I agreed on. We both wanted our mates to be more involved in the operation of the business. We had talked many times about the show *"Flip That House,"* which had episodes that featured two brothers in Texas who ran a business similar to ours. Both of their wives worked for the business keeping all the money in the house. Instead, we're paying a secretary's salary and fees for accountants, Realtors, and other miscellaneous services.

"Would it be a bad thing if we brought someone in?" I finally ask. Wanda is married with three children. Her family never takes a vacation because she's always working. When the kids have appointments, her husband has the responsibility of getting them there. As I try to divert Wanda's curiosity, suddenly, I'm energized by the prospect of having Mya come work for me. Shouldn't that be the way it is anyway? A man opens a business, and his wife supports him one hundred percent.

Wanda clears her throat. "Um, I guess having a back-up would be nice, but somehow I get the feeling this isn't what it's all about."

I sit up, "What are you insinuating?"

"It's just that your body language, her body language, was not that of two people discussing a possible job opening. It was more like, well, two people with something going on. I just don't want to see you get into something since we both know how Kim can be when she thinks something is going on."

Wanda looks as though she regrets bringing up the subject. Then on second glance, it appears she expects me to spill the beans. Instead, I tell her my wife's insecurities aren't her concern, and if Mya decides to take the job, she'll be the first to know. She doesn't like my answer, and frankly, I don't care. What I do and whom I do it with isn't what she's paid to worry about. "Anything else," I ask, closing the door on this conversation. Wanda left my office, and my head began to throb uncontrollably. I decide to take the remainder of the day off.

After I arrive at the house, I take a hot shower then crawl into bed. It was one in the afternoon, and I slept until two in the morning. When I awaken, I stagger into the bathroom to unload my bladder. Sensing Kim's presence, I turn around, and there she is, ready to do battle. Not tonight. I sidestepped her and grabbed some items from the drawer. She's behind me as I walk and dress. She asks me where I'm going this time of the morning. "To the store to get something to drink," I mumble. She states we have sodas, water, and *Kool-Aid* in the refrigerator. "Well, tonight I have a taste for *PowerAde*." Kim is standing in the doorway, scowling as I grab the keys off the hook and hop into the *Mercedes*.

When I reach Thirty-fourth Street, I call Mya. She answers on the second ring, her voice groggy but still sweet. "Can I come over?"

"Can you?" she quizzes. "You know you can do anything you want to."

I chuckle, "Okay, may I?"

Mya says it's okay. She will unlock the door, and I can let myself in. It has been over a year, and I don't understand why I don't have a key. Aside from our time together, I have put almost twenty-thousand dollars into her home. She has credit cards and debit cards for my bank accounts. If this doesn't show my level of commitment, nothing will. The thought upsets me, and I turn left onto Thirty-fourth instead of right towards Mya's place.

Kim has called so many times that I finally turn the phone off. It's well after three when I pull back into my garage. Kim is still up, so I decide to sleep in the car. I'm awakened by the sound of Ariel's voice asking, "Daddy, what are you doing in the car?" Confusion plagues my mind. What *am* I doing in the car, what time is it, and what day is it? I need a moment to regroup. Ariel waits patiently for my response until her mom joins her at the opened car door.

"Come on, Ariel, we need to get going." She places her hand on Ariel's back and directs her towards the *Lexus*. Kim frowns at me but doesn't say a word.

Quickly, I exit the car and instruct Ariel to get in. Kim turns away from the *Lexus* and heads back to the Benz. She gets in and slams the door shut. I'm glad to be alone in my home. I look around the kitchen and think of the thousands of dollars we spent to remodel it. It was such a waste because since I rarely ever eat in it. Kim isn't the best of cooks, which made me that much more outraged by her request. I couldn't understand why she would ask for this, but I quickly saw her plan unfold.

Before meeting Mya, I probably could count on one hand the number of times Kim has invited my family and friends to our home. She never went out of her way to include herself in our activities or build a close bond with anyone outside her small circle of friends. This is yet another extreme between Kim and me. She can sometimes come across as aloof and snobbish. At the same time, I remember my humble beginnings and have no problem associating with any class of people.

The calendar posted next to the refrigerator has Sunday highlighted. I walk closer to read the note, 'dinner, here.' Kim has planned another family dinner. This is probably the third in as many months. She decided that it would be nice to invite the entire family over for dinner at least one Sunday out of the month without any urging from me. "You know, we can do the soul food thing," referencing the movie that centers around a tight-knit family that enjoyed having family dinner on Sundays. My siblings immediately took this as a sign that things were finally coming together for Kim and me. Little did they know this was nothing more than a farce Kim had created. So, my sisters embraced the idea and began to pass down family recipes. She learned to cook greens, macaroni and cheese, and all the southern foods that are supposed to be the way to a man's heart. I'm happy that her cooking skills have improved, but Kim has made the mistake of many Black women who can burn in the kitchen. She indulges a bit too much in her dishes, and it's showing in her already expanding hips.

Mya has been looking forward to the day that she gets to meet my mother. On so many occasions, I have wanted to take her to my mothers' apartment so the two can finally meet. The fear of my sisters catching us there keeps me from following my heart. It would look worse with Kim pretending to be the perfect wife these days. It pained me to see the disappointment in Mya's eyes when I told her of Kim's plans for a monthly family dinner. But just as quickly, she bounced back, seeing Kim's scheme for what it was…a weak attempt to hold on to what she knows she will soon lose.

Taking another look at the note, I realize that this Sunday is the fifth Sunday, not the first. Recently, my mother asked us all if we would accompany her to church. We decided on the first Sunday so we can have communion together. Kim doesn't go to church. But any opportunity to assert her place as my wife these days, she will take advantage of to get under my skin.

Since we will be attending church as a family on the first Sundays, this is the day we have the family dinner. This Sunday, I had planned on spending with Mya over in Orlando. My temples are pulsating, and I know my blood pressure is rising, so I head upstairs to shower. As I pull out my attire for the day, I see that I have a missed call on my cellular. I pick up the phone and see Mya's number. Undoubtedly, she's upset that I didn't come last night. Now, I need to apologize for not coming by, but I must also break the news that our Sunday plans are off.

As I exit the shower, I hear the phone ringing. No one calls for me on the home phone, so I ignore it. By the time I have finished my ritual of rubbing my body down in lotion and then sprinkling baby powder in those areas where I sweat the most, the caller has called back four more times. The ringing phone has gotten the best of me, and I grab the receiver off its base.

"HELLO!" I yell, annoyed, into the phone.

"Yes, uhm, is this the Bryson residence?" The caller asked, taken aback by the aggressive greeting.

I wasn't up for a telemarketer, and I knew no bill collectors were calling, so I slammed the phone down. As I fastened my belt, the phone rang again. I looked at the caller ID and saw that the call was coming from Far Rockaway, New York. "Great, just what I need. I'm sure Kim has called her aggravating ass mom talking about me again. Well, today isn't the damn day." I placed the phone back on the base and reached for my shoes. As the phone continued to ring, I put on my shoes and picked up a bottle of *Calvin Klein's Obsession*. Mya loves the scent on me, and for Father's Day, she purchased the newest collection. On the other hand, Kim treated the day like any other and didn't even wish me a happy one.

Again, the thought of Mya reminded me of the call I needed to make to her. I knew she was getting fed up with the excuses and broken promises. She deserved so much better in her life, and if she would just be patient a bit longer, I would give her everything her heart desired. I reached for my Bluetooth, and placed it on my ear, then grabbed my phone. Mya answered on the first ring.

"Hey, baby, what happened to you last night?"

No matter what I do or have done, Mya always gives me the benefit of the doubt. She understands my situation, sometimes better than I do. Even after I disappoint her, she assures me that it's a part of the situation we are in, and she knows I won't always be able to come through as planned.

"I was just so frustrated and didn't want to keep you up all night with my problems. I'm sorry I woke you up." I begin to explain that I ended up sleeping in the car when the house phone rings again. This time it's Kim. "Fuck!" I yell. "Can't I just have a minute to my damn self?" In a more tamed tone, I let Mya know it's Kim. "Let me call you back."

I grab the phone off the base, truly pissed off. Kim didn't give me a chance to answer. She's hysterical, and I can barely make out what she's saying. First, she's screaming and asking why I'm not answering the phone. Next, she asks, "Why are you hanging up on people when they call like a fucking idiot?" I wasn't about to let her talk to me this way, but her following words froze me. "My mom had a massive heart attack. She didn't make it. My mother is gone, LaDamien. She's dead."

Just like that, her mother was gone. She had just visited a few weeks ago. As usual, I made every excuse to stay away from the house, opting not to be under her scrutiny. A massive heart attack, I just couldn't believe it.

At some point, I don't know when. I left the bedroom and began wandering through the house. I entered each room I remember her being in when she was here on her visit. Eventually, I make my way to the kitchen and view the calendar, drawn to the bright red letters in the box for Sunday, "dinner here." It dawns on me that I'm Kim's only real family now. Yes, she has relatives in New York, but now that her mom is gone, how long will it be before those relationships fade.

As I step into the garage and walk towards my vehicle, I hear Kim's voice. When her mom visited last, we picked her up from the airport, stopped at *The Cheesecake Factory* for dinner before heading back to the house. Anna was happy to see her daughter and granddaughter. However, I couldn't say I felt the love coming my way.

The first couple of days went pretty well. I left the house early and headed to the gym. I kept myself occupied during the day, and by the time I returned home in the evenings, Kim, her mom, and Ariel were gone shopping or out visiting. In the brief times we were in the house at the same time, we were cordial to one another. But that all changed when I came in late one night after spending some much-needed time with Mya.

Kim was waiting in the garage and pounced on me as soon as I exited the car. "Why can't you do what the hell you're supposed to," she spewed through clenched teeth. "You know my mother is here, you knew we had plans for this evening, but you just couldn't do without that fucking bitch a few more days. Why must you humiliate me at all times?"

I climbed back into the SUV and backed out, leaving Kim behind, yelling obscenities, and making empty threats of having my bags packed when I returned. That return was not until Friday. A day and a half after I left. I spent that night in my office, where I slept on the floor. It wasn't the first time, and I was sure it wouldn't be the last. The next night, I took a chance, spending the night with Mya.

It wasn't my intention, but she asked me why, when Kim and I have fights, I never come to her. "Is there someone else," she asked. How could she question my commitment to her? I had made so many sacrifices and taken so many chances. Still, she had the nerve to question my love for her. So, I did it to show her that I would do anything to make her happy. After we made love, I was unable to fall into a deep sleep. I tossed and turned until it became apparent, I was making Mya restless and was annoying her. So, I settled down and allowed her to fall asleep. I spent the night watching her moonlit face, so beautiful and peaceful, while my mind wondered what Kim would say if I asked her if Mya could move in with us. It would make things so much easier. I finally drifted off to sleep around three a.m. but was back up by five.

Mya watched me as I showered. Something she loves to do. We make love and then lay spent in each other's arms for a few minutes. She goes and cleans herself up before returning to wipe me off with a warm rag. She joins me back in the bed, where we talk about our life together, laugh at the silly things we say and do. The whole while, she's touching me, exploring me, and learning every inch of my body. I hate for these moments to end. But as always, I have to bring them to an end. Mya must hate it as much as I do because she always climbs out of bed and follows me into the bathroom. She lets down the lid on the toilet and watches me shower. Sometimes, like that day, the peepshow isn't enough, and she slides back the glass door and joins me. Thirty minutes later, after another round of passionate lovemaking, she's sitting on the edge of her bed watching me dress in silence.

When I came in that Friday morning after taking Mya out for breakfast, Anna was waiting in the kitchen. "If you don't want my daughter, why won't you just get your black ass out of my house?" she barked.

Who did she think she was talking to that way? Kim and I had taken out a mortgage on this house, and her mother received the proceeds. So, in essence, she had sold us this house. My response was to remind her of this. But she didn't let up.

"Negro, please. This house is worth more than that measly eighty grand you borrowed. I only took that money so you could have the satisfaction of saying you bought this house for your wife. Plus, I couldn't leave here wondering if my child and grandchild would have a place to lay their heads. I'm sure if I hadn't agreed to let you take a mortgage out, you would have run out, and bought a house, and tried to figure out a way to keep Kim's name off the deed just to spite me. Yeah, you a slick ass nigga. I don't know what my daughter ever saw in you. That other asshole of hers turned out to be a loser, but you LaDamien; you are a piece of work." Anna swallowed the last of her coffee as the doorbell chimed. Her close friend Edith arrived to pick her up. The only thing that kept me from cursing her out was my respect for elders. I would never disrespectfully speak to anyone's mother.

The security guard called up to Kim's office to let her know I was here. I took the parking pass and drove through the security gate. As I pulled into a parking space marked "VISITOR," my phone rang. It was Mya. I had forgotten to call her back. "Baby, you aren't going to believe what has happened," flowed from my mouth as soon as I pressed talk.

"What?" Mya asked, with a hint of annoyance in her voice.

"It's Kim. Her mom suffered a heart attack and died. I'm here at her job to pick her up. I feel so bad, you know, things didn't go well when Anna was here a few weeks ago."

"Baby, you had no way of knowing this was going to happen. How is Kim doing? She must be a mess, as close as you say she and her mom were." Mya paused. "Babe, are you there?" Mya asked. "Go see about Kim. You can call me later."

I listened to Mya, knowing she was right. Kim needed me now, and I would be here for her. Before I got out of the car to head to Kim's office, I called my sister, Lynn. She would notify everyone and get them over to the house by the time we arrived.

Once I hung up with Lynn, I entered Kim's office. She was surrounded by her administrative assistant, Melanie, and several of her staff members. She had been crying but was now on the phone with either Debra or Karen or perhaps both. She smiled when she saw me. "Honey, you didn't have to come. I was okay to drive."

Looking around the room, from one tear-filled eye to another tear-filled eye, I suddenly realize I haven't shed a tear for Anna. Immediately, I begin to think about my mother, who has defied her minor heart attacks and was still here. I imagined the day when I would get the call that Kim had received less than an hour ago, and I pinched my tear ducts to fight back the tears that have formed. Kim ends her call and is now standing with her purse in hand.

"Debra will drop Karen off to pick up my car," Kim said as she handed the keys to Melanie. I stepped forward and pulled my wife into my arms. She let go of her professional, always in control façade and let the dam break. Melanie led the others out of the spacious office and closed the door, giving us some time alone.

"Baby, I'm so sorry," I began. "I know your mom, and I didn't get along, but I would never have wished this on her."

Kim pulled a tissue from a Kleenex box and wiped her tears away. "I know you didn't wish my mother dead. Regardless of how much you two argued, I know you didn't hate my mother."

"I'm just saying, I don't want you to think that I would be unsympathetic. You didn't have to call your friends. I knew it was my responsibility to come to get you." Kim is looking at me now like she wished I hadn't come. No matter how hard I try, it's never good enough for her. "Are you ready to go?" Without answering, Kim opens the door and leads the way out. Her colleagues look on with sorrow and pity as we walk towards the elevator. I can't help but wonder what Kim tells these people about me, about our sham of a marriage.

Kim

My mother is gone. Just like that, no warning, no good-bye, and no parting words, just a call from a distant relative letting me know that my mother has suffered a massive heart attack and succumbed. I chuckle at the terminology she used. Succumbed…to be brought to an end. My mother's life was brought to an end. At the age of sixty, it was decided that her life would be no more. Cut short and brought to a sudden end. I know it's wrong, and I can't stop the thoughts from flowing, but I immediately think of LaDamien's mother. She's twenty-one years my mother's senior. Aside from the monthly trip to church and our home, she spends her time in front of a TV. All day, she's waiting to take the next pill on a regimen of many. Then there's Wednesday night Bingo or when one of her children stop by and visit for dinner. Waiting, I guess, to succumb, to be brought to an end. It isn't fair.

On the other hand, my mother had a youthful spirit, was outgoing, and full of life. She was all I had, despite my faults, despite my lousy decision-making. She was my inspiration. She was my confidante, the only one who knew the truth about my marriage. About the depth of my husband's infidelities. She was my strategic planner, the one who suggested I "step up my game if I wanted to save my marriage." Now I'm alone, with no one.

We are on the plane heading back to Florida. Per her wishes, we buried my mother in New York. At least that is what her sister said she wanted. Although LaDamien is sure, my relatives made up the alleged conversation. He thinks they claim my mother made this testament to keep from having to come up with the money needed to fly them all down to Florida. So LaDamien and his family planned a small memorial service for her Florida friends. We flew out the next day to attend the wake and funeral in New York.

LaDamien played the perfect husband from the time we stepped off the plane until he awoke the morning after the funeral. My relatives went on and on about his attentiveness. They quickly exclaimed that he was nothing like the monster my mother had described. Of course, this was during one of his many walks down to the corner store for whatever reason. The evening after the funeral, he went on one of his disappearing acts, which I'm sure was to call his whore. While he was gone, a cousin asked me was LaDamien, my second husband. "No, he's my first."

She quickly apologized, letting me know she didn't mean any disrespect. "It's just that your mother would talk so negatively about your husband, painting him as a raving lunatic and abusive. I just can't believe this is the same guy she was talking about."

Even if my mother said those things about my husband, which I have no doubt she did, I couldn't believe this woman had the nerve to repeat them, especially during my hour of grief. The walls of my mothers' tiny apartment were closing in, causing me to feel trapped. My husband needed to be back in this small space with me, smiling and being cordial to my relatives. I needed him to understand how badly I wanted his love and support. As if she read my mind, Beryl, my unsympathetic and now nosy cousin, approached me again and commented on the number of times my husband had "run-up to the store."

"You know, they don't sell that much down there at that store. Just beer and chips, and we got plenty of that here. John, my middle son, said he saw him sitting at the park talking on his cell phone. He was laughing and carrying on like he doesn't have a care in the world. The park is in the opposite direction of the store," she added just in case I wasn't getting the gist of what she was saying.

Then she continued, "I used to be married to a man like that. He sure could put out the sweet talk and play the role of the dutiful husband when needed. But girl, that man was screwing everything that had a hole, and I mean everything if you get my drift," she chuckled.

Was she implying that my husband could be on the down-low? Quickly, I let her know that was impossible. If I knew anything about my husband, he was not prone to gay tendencies. There was no way a man could please a woman the way he pleased me, well use to please me, and be gay. Beryl was looking at me like I was crazy, as if she was reading the frantic thoughts racing through my head. It was the same look my mother would give me when I defended LaDamien. I guess it was a family trait. Unlike my mother, though, cousin Beryl wasn't patient. She picked up her glass of whatever she was drinking, gin, rum, vodka, or possibly a combination of all three, and headed out the door. No more than ten minutes later, LaDamien returned.

After the last guest left and Ariel had fallen asleep in the tiny guest room, I went to join LaDamien in the living room. He was gone. It was well after eleven, and he had left the apartment without a word. I grabbed the keys off the side table and locked the deadbolt. Not only was I tired and needed to get some much-needed rest, but I also refused to sit up and wait for him to return so another fight could ensue. Ariel was a part of all of this. Neither of us considered what our problems were doing to her.

At twelve forty-five, my husband was calling my cell phone. He was at the door and needed to get let in. As much as I wanted to leave his trifling little ass out there, I knew it would be a huge mistake. I let him in and quickly returned to the bedroom and locked the door. The stench of semen permeated the air. He only confirmed my suspension when he went into the bathroom and showered, never attempting to enter the bedroom.

We're over one thousand miles away from that bitch, and she still finds a way to satisfy my husband's sexual needs. I often wonder if she works as a phone sex operator, or maybe she's a stripper on the side. No doubt, she has worked her erotic magic on him tonight like she has many times before. I have witnessed him pleasuring himself to her words. Laying in our bed masturbating, moaning, and groaning, and speaking the words that he doesn't speak when he's inside of me. He only stops to catch his juices before they land all over the sheets. The same sheets I must return home to and sleep on at night. His Bluetooth is always illuminating near his ear, confirmation he's on the phone. After the eruption and the trembling stops, he speaks with an undeniable joy in his voice. He's at peace. Gone is the hostility he showed towards me just a half-hour earlier. Gone is the stress he has complained about. He gets up and goes to shower. I sneak back downstairs. I'm tiptoeing away from my bedroom and down the stairs in my home. I'll wait until the water stops, only to walk back up the stairs and enter the room as if I had just arrived. It wasn't a one-time thing. There have been several occasions. Always minutes after I've left the house, but returned because I left something. Or when I returned home early from an outing with my friends or one of Ariel's various practices, or when I'm just curious as to what I will catch him doing.

As I lay in my dead mother's bed crying, my husband is twenty feet away, in a deep sleep, snoring, probably dreaming about that slut. I wonder where he went to have his little phone sex capade. Was it in the park, in the alley behind the building, at a peep show, in the store's bathroom, or a gas station up the road? The thoughts make me feel dirty and disgusted. Does he have no shame, no self-respect? What if someone saw him? What if Beryl was out there watching and waiting for him to make another run to the store? What if she followed him and watched, as I have watched so many times before? "Oh, mama, what am I going to do without you? Why didn't I listen to you when you told me not to marry him? Why did I need to believe that things would work out, that he would change for me? You were right mama, LaDamien's like a silly boy. He still hasn't grown up."

Sleep finally finds me, but it wasn't a peaceful sleep. Visions of my mother filled my dreams. She was begging me to come live with her before something terrible happened. Next, I ran towards her front door, banging harder and harder, wondering why she wouldn't open the door for me. I'm awakened from my dream by LaDamien. He's pounding on the bedroom door like he has lost his mind.

"What?" I scream, my eyes filled with tears.

"Get dressed. I want to leave for the airport to see if we can catch an earlier flight."

He must be joking. We're scheduled to leave Tuesday evening, and it's only Sunday. By the time I walk into the living room, he's cleaning up the breakfast dishes. Ariel is seated on the couch, dressed. Her *Hello Kitty* suitcase is by the door. LaDamien walks past me into the bedroom, where he takes some clothes out of the suitcase and grabs his shaving bag before he heads to the bathroom. I wait for him to exit thirty minutes later.

"We aren't scheduled to leave until the day after tomorrow. It will cost a small fortune for us to change our flight to today. Plus, I have to get this apartment packed up, have the utilities turned off, and make sure all my mother's affairs are in order."

LaDamien looks perplexed. "Didn't you talk to Beryl?" he asks. "She agreed to do all of that stuff. She knows someone who is going to sublease the apartment, furniture, and all. Beryl said she'd stop by, go through your mothers' things, and donate them to various charities. You need to get whatever you want to keep and take it with you now."

"When did you talk to Beryl about this?"

To my surprise, he accuses me of sending Beryl to spy on him the previous evening. He said she approached him outside while he was talking on the phone and asked him what he was up to out there. He told her he was checking on his business and mentioned that he needed to get back home, and she made the suggestion.

Just like that, I was out-numbered and out-gunned. I made a quick run of my mother's apartment, grabbed jewelry, and her legal documents, including bank statements and tax returns. An hour later, we were exiting a taxi at JFK International Airport. It took another eight hours to get seats on a flight to Chicago, connecting back to Tampa.

We arrived home at one a.m. Ariel was cranky and whining. LaDamien is irritated by the delays and wasted time. I'm furious that I had just wasted fifteen hours that I could have used to pack my mother's things properly and extend a proper goodbye to my extended family.

I turn the water off in the shower, thinking I must be hearing things. The day's stress has my mind spinning. I could have sworn I heard a car starting. The silence embraces me as I stand there listening. Assured it was my imagination, I turn the water back on. Within seconds, I hear the garage door open, and I know he has left. After I finish my shower, I head downstairs to the garage, and sure enough, the Benz is gone. His actions anger me more than the fact that he has left. I don't understand why he has to add insult to injury by taking my car. The car he claims to have purchased for my Christmas gift but knowing full well, it was just another gift to appease me. He knew he had been spotted in Orlando at *Disney World* with Mya when he was supposed to be on a business trip with Mark in Jacksonville. I never confronted him, but he has such a guilty conscience that he showered

Ariel and me with expensive gifts. He even went so far as to put a big red bow on it as they do in the holiday commercials. He presented the car to me in front of family and friends. What was I supposed to do? Throw the keys back at him, and say give it to your whore. He played me that night like a fiddle. I had not spoken to him in a week, and the silence was killing him. Once I accepted the car, he smiled, knowing I would never mention the incident but just let it slide like I do everything else.

It is almost two in the morning, and he couldn't wait a few more hours to be with her. I want to get dressed and follow him. Go to the house that my hairstylist, Renee, took me by almost a year ago. She claimed her cousin had seen his car on numerous occasions and at various times of day and night. The same one I rode by late one night to get the address and verify it indeed belonged to Mya. Numerous times I tried to catch him with no success. Part of me prays that he isn't there when I turn the corner, which makes the reality of the situation feel less severe. I want to go right now and make a scene so all her neighbors know what a skank she is. I want to take my car while he's inside and make him wonder if it was me or if it's stolen. I know I'm not thinking rationally, but this is the depths of despair my husband is taking me to. I can't stop the tears any more than I can stop his cheating ways.

Two twenty-two, the garage door opens, and LaDamien enters the room with a bottle of *Powerade*. I convince myself that he was not gone long enough to have been with her. Perhaps he went by her house, and she wasn't home. Maybe she has someone else, and he was visiting. Right now, I don't care. I just make a mental note to add this item to the shopping list. First, it was the *Haagen-Dazs* ice cream, and then it was cheesecake from *Salem's Gyros and Subs*. Whatever he claims to be running out in the middle of the night to get, I will add it to the grocery list or pick it up on my way home from work. I will do this until he realizes how foolish it is for him to leave in the middle of the night like this.

Mya

    My heart goes out to Kim. I can't begin to comprehend the pain she must be feeling at this moment. To lose your mother so unexpectedly must make the heartache ten, no a hundred times worse. When I hang up with LaDamien, I call my mother. She doesn't answer, so I leave a message for her. I tell her that I love her and will be over after work. As I have grown older, I don't spend as much time as I use to with my family. We spend holidays together and take an occasional trip together. Still, I don't go by after work every day like I used to. I'm not sure if it's because of LaDamien or if I was already in the process of cutting the umbilical cord when he and I met. All I know is that I want to see my mother at this instant. I want to be held by her and know that she will always be here.
    Sonya, my older sister, is sitting at the table with my dad while mom puts the finishing touches on dinner. She's fourteen years my senior, so I guess I'm what you would call a "late in life" baby. My parents were in their forties when they had me. Sonja had just entered high school, and here they were with a newborn. Lucky for them, I was a quiet child who played by herself and didn't require much attention. By the time I reached high school, my parents were preparing to retire and begin traveling. Many weekends I spent at my grandmother's home. She spent the majority of her time in church preparing for the day she would see my granddaddy, the love of her life.
    My mom turns to me and says out of the blue, "I saw LaDamien the other day. He was working in the yard up the street from one of my old co-workers. She lives over in Broadwater. I haven't been over there in some years. I wouldn't have been that day, but Janice's husband passed recently, and I figured she needed the company. She had invited us over for a tea party. Well, wasn't any tea. She was just trying to sell us some of that *Noni Juice* stuff. I don't

know how folks make money if everybody is selling, and nobody is buying. Before the lady finished, she was telling us about the money we could make."

My mom went from seeing LaDamien to talking about *Noni Juice* and what was going on in all her old friends' lives. Although she forgot what she was about to say, Sonja did not. She held this look of indignation, and the second we were alone, she asked, "Now why would LaDamien be working in somebody's yard? Who does he know that stays over there?" I rolled my eyes and suggested she call LaDamien and ask him.

Sonja knows what is going on, and I'm sure she's just waiting for the right opportunity to reveal the information. I always felt she resented my parents giving birth to me and removing the only child title from her crown. After I was born, Sonja had to grow up faster, or so she thinks. She can always recount the numerous school functions and parties she missed because she had to babysit. Or the fact that she could not attend LSU as she had planned because our parents could no longer afford the cost of sending her to school out of state. She has blamed me for every failure in her life as if my being born somehow disrupted the cosmic flow in her universe. My sharp reply cuts the conversation short. Knowing that I'm not going to take the bait, she grabs her purse and tells our parents goodbye. A short time later, I follow, but not before I tell them how much I love them and appreciate the love and care they have provided to me.

I'm minutes away from home when my phone rings. LaDamien is calling to give me an update on Kim. I tell him that he should be with her right now and not cause her any more stress; he should give her his undivided attention. He must have taken my advice to heart because I don't see him again until after the funeral when he returned from New York. We spoke twice while they were there. He called after the service just to say hi and again that evening to say he will be returning the following day.

Tuesday, after LaDamien returns from New York, we take off to spend the day together. Surprisingly, he isn't trying to get me into bed but suggests we do something adventurous like ride the *Pinellas Trail*.

The trail extends thirty-plus miles from St. Petersburg to Tarpon Springs and expected to be almost fifty miles in length once completed. It began as the vision of a father who lost his son when he got hit while riding his bicycle. Coupled with the county's concern over unused railroad tracks from the *CSX* railway system, the *Pinellas Trail* came to life. It stretched from city to city throughout the area.

We decide to travel to Walsingham Park, a twenty-mile ride, have lunch, and return. After we make our plans, I reluctantly remind LaDamien that he didn't buy me a new bike as promised. We have made short bike trips to Fort Desoto Beach and downtown, but my bicycle isn't for long trips. His deep sigh resonates through the phone line, and I regret saying anything. Lately, when spending money on me, LaDamien seems reserved and almost agitated at the notion. I don't know if he thinks I'm trying to use him or if things aren't going well with the business. If I could handle the trip on my outdated *Huffy*, I would, but it would be torture. LaDamien asks me how much money I have to put towards a new bike. "A hundred at the most," I replied, and he says he will call me back.

An hour later, he arrives at my house with a rented bicycle and tells me if I like it and don't complain too much during the ride, he will buy me one in a few weeks when he has some money. "The funeral and travel expenses have drained me, and I need to cut back on my spending," he adds. The rented bike will be fine, and I will save for myself if we decide to do this more often.

It takes us nearly two hours to make the trek to Walsingham Park. We make stops along the way to rest and catch my breath, but nothing more than five minutes. Before reaching the park, we stop at a *Subway* sandwich shop and purchase lunch. We make another stop at *7-eleven* to buy water and sodas. Finally, we reach the park, and it's beautiful. LaDamien lets me know he wants to ride the park's trail before settling down, so I follow him as we take in the beauty of our peaceful surroundings. I can't think of any park in our area that can compare, but LaDamien quickly points out Fort Desoto. "But that is the beach." He chuckles before clarifying that it's still considered a park. So, I let him have that one.

We finally park the bikes and settle near the lake. Pulling out a bedsheet from my backpack and spreading it on the ground, we take a seat, unwrap our sub, and each takes a half. Although LaDamien stated he wanted Doritos and not potato chips, he has his hand in my bag. We chat as we eat our meal, and once done, we discard the trash and head back to the sheet. It's so serene I can feel myself drifting off. LaDamien pats my leg. "Don't fall asleep on me. We have to get back home, remember."

I do remember, and I'm questioning myself as to why I agreed to this. "Why don't you go back and get the car, and come get me," he laughs.

LaDamien scoots closer to me. He's sitting up, and I'm stretched out on my stomach. "Do you love me, Mya?" he asks.

"Of course." Then he asks me why I don't say it often. I tell him I thought I said it all the time, and if I say it too much, it may begin to lose its meaning. He disagrees, letting me know he wants to hear it every day. When I think about it, LaDamien tells me all the time that he loves me. So much so that, at times, I wonder if he's trying to convince himself.

"I did a lot of thinking in New York," he begins. "Death can come at any time. We're living this life right now that isn't good for me and has to be hell for you. I just don't know what I would do if I lost you before I had the chance to truly know you in the way I want to get to know you." He's running his hand down my back.

I turn on my side and look up into his eyes that have started to water. He's in a deep zone. "My life has been so different since I met you, Mya. I knew I would love you but never thought it would be so intense. I think of you all the time. When I wake up, I want you next to me, and when I come home in the evenings, I want it to be you waiting for me." He grimaces as if in pain, so I reach for him. He takes my hand into his and continues.

"I don't know how much longer I can stay with Kim knowing how I feel about you. I just wish I knew without a doubt that you felt the same way. All I need to know is that you love me as much as I love you." He places my open hand to his lips and kisses my palms. I lift and meet his lips. We kiss passionately for minutes as if we will cease to exist if we let go. I do love LaDamien, and how he can question that love is beyond me since I thought I showed him in everything I do.

We finally separate, and he looks to me for my reassurance, so I pull out my MP3 player and search for a song. He's growing impatient. The song I'm looking for comes up, and I hand him the earphones. "I listened to this song a hundred times last night. This has to be the most beautiful love song I have ever heard. If a man ever felt this way about me, I would feel so special, so loved, and I would know without a doubt that our love would be forever." I say this as he adjusts the earphones, and I press play. He listens intently as Kem crone's the words to *You Are*. When the song ends, he hands me the earphones. "Kem, huh, so you're hooked now? I never paid much attention to this track. What does it mean to you?" he asks.

"It means that I love you. That you are so much a part of me that I no longer know how to exist without you."

The intensity of his stare continues, and he responds, "If I died today, my body wouldn't be cold before you found someone else." He chuckles half-heartedly, his eyes begging for me to counter this thought.

"That's not true," I say in a defensive tone. "If you were to die, I would want to lie down and die too. Why do you question my love for you this way?" I hear the words I have just said, but I don't know where they came from. Nor have I ever said anything like this to anyone before. But then again, I have never loved anyone as much as I love LaDamien, and I hope I never will again.

He looks pleased with my admission, but still, his eyes hold a hint of unbelief. We stare into each other's eyes for what feels like minutes. LaDamien blinks first and smiles that brilliant smile I love so much. I reach for the MP3 player at the same time he reaches for the earplugs. "Put it on repeat," he says. "I want to hear this song over and over again, and Mya, you are everything in this song, and more. If something happened to you, I would die too." He kisses my forehead and pulls me closer as he lays back and props his head on his bag. We lay in each other's arms, LaDamien listening to Kem's definition of a love so intense, yet innocent, and pure, and I'm enjoying the sounds of the park and flow of the lake. We drift off into a melancholy sleep but get awakened by the presence of someone standing over us.

"Oh, I didn't mean to startle you," the White woman begins. "My name is Agnes, and my hobby is taking pictures of people in their natural state." She hands us her card along with a small form. I look at the form. It's pretty simple. It has a place for the date, location, and time, which she's completed already, and a place to write in an email address where she can send us the photos she has taken. LaDamien looks scared, maybe even terrified. He isn't buying her story, but I believe she's sincere. I jot down my email address and give it back to her. Agnes sees the concern on LaDamien's face and ensures him she isn't a private eye or some other sinister character. She just loves seeing people in love and does her best to capture the moment. "You two are a beautiful couple. I hope the pictures turn out great, and you can one day share them with your grandchildren." She checks the paper I have handed to her and places it in a small pouch. Agnes says goodbye and moves on to a mother and child further down from us. They are poking a stick in the water as if examining some creature for signs of life.

When Agnes is out of hearing distance, LaDamien asks if I believe her. I ask why not. He reminds me that he's married, and it wouldn't be beneath Kim to hire a private investigator to catch us together. "She has been so suspicious lately, always questioning my every move." Nothing I say will reassure him. I believe Agnes was doing just what she said she was. We look down at the mother and child. Just as she had done with us, she hands her a card and a small form. The mother fills in the email address and hands the paper back to Agnes. She then moves on to an elderly couple sitting on a bench.

LaDamien relaxes a bit then tells me it's time to head back. While he goes to relieve himself, I gather our things, placing them in their respective backpacks. As I reach the bikes, LaDamien returns and lures me into a fervent kiss. *"You are the air that I breathe, the half that makes me whole. I* love you, Mya. I know you probably get tired of me saying it, but it's the truth. I love you, and I don't know what to do about it."

When he's so passionate about his love for me, I'm honored but hesitant at the same time. Like any woman, I want to be loved by my man and adored, not idolized. LaDamien surprises me when he hands me a bunch of flowers that resemble Marigolds. They could have come from the Botanical Garden on-site, or he may have pulled them up from somewhere in the park. I laugh as I rub his arm and tell him that he can never tell me he loves me enough. I reach up and kiss him again. *"Marigolds in bloom,* huh? You are so amazing." I say, thinking of the lyrics from *You Are.* We eventually mount the bikes and begin our long trek back.

Agnes sent the email with the pictures attached two days later. LaDamien breathed a sigh of relief when we visited the website listed in the email. We saw all the incredible work Agnes has done and read some of her subjects' testimonials. But it wasn't until I called her and confirmed our pictures wouldn't get posted or shared with anyone else that I convinced him Kim had not sent the woman.

I told LaDamien the way he was carrying on was going to raise suspicion and have Agnes do an investigation. He finally let it go.

However, when he entered my bedroom a few days later, the tension return. He looked at the enlarged, framed photos displayed on several shelves lining my wall. It was obvious he took issue with the display.

"Baby, please relax. The only people in my bedroom beside you are people who already know we see each other." He did relax, but I knew if left to his devices, those pictures could disappear instantly. So, I made sure I kept the email from the photographer.

Wanda

Things changed dramatically after LaDamien met Mya. I thought things were crazy between him and Faye, but this Mya chick has spun things out of control.

LaDamien and Mark hired me shortly after their business venture began. When Mark decided to dissolve the partnership, there was no decision for me to make. My loyalty was with LaDamien. We would work together to recover and regroup from this setback, which was a blessing in my mind. LaDamien didn't need Mark to be successful. If we're truthful, LaDamien was a far better businessman than Mark ever could have dreamed of being. If it weren't for Mark's capital and financial savvy, LaDamien probably would have branched out on his own long ago.

Together we will survive this test and come out on top. I have always put in many hours ensuring LaDamien is where he needs to be when he needs to be there. Because his wife doesn't take an active role, I must act as secretary, accountant, and personal assistant. I will continue to do it all. LaDamien deserves so much better, and I can only wish that I had met him long before I met my husband, Horace. We are such a great team together. I step in and fill the void when he isn't one hundred percent, motivating him when he's feeling low and wants to give up. I'm the keeper of his secrets and his alibi when he needs to get away and be by himself. Sometimes I feel as though life has cheated me out of what is rightfully mine.

My husband doesn't understand my commitment. He often tells me that I'm underpaid and not appreciated. On the record, it looks like LaDamien doesn't pay me much, but there are the perks to this job, and when you factor in all the extras, I get paid quite well. My husband doesn't know about the offers LaDamien has made to pay for vacations. Or to buy the kid's school clothes because he feels so guilty about the fact he can't pay me what I'm truly worth. Plus, I can't think of any other job that will allow me the creative freedom I have here.

Hell, I pretty much set all the rules. As long as LaDamien is making money, he rarely questions anything. I could rob him blind, give myself a raise, go on shopping sprees, and he would never know, but I would never betray him that way. My admiration and respect are too strong for him even to consider such foolishness.

    Kim is supposed to be so bright and so educated, but she doesn't have a clue. Sometimes I hate her. Not because I'm jealous but because she doesn't deserve a man like LaDamien. I swear, if I had met him before I met my husband, we would be sitting on a multi-million-dollar empire by now. But it's too late for all of that. Now I just need to do what I can to get him back on track. I need to figure out how to get Mya out of the way. Taming Faye was hard, but I think Mya will give me a run for my money. I don't know what he thought when he took up with her. He's gotten involved with someone single, which is a major no-no and can cause many problems. With Mya, he may be thinking about leaving Kim. With the others, that wasn't an option because they were all married.

    It is eleven a.m., and LaDamien hasn't arrived, forcing me to reschedule a nine a.m. meeting with a potential investor. His recent behavior concerns me, and I will need to speak with him when he finally does check-in. He has missed a considerable amount of time from the office, with Kim's mother passing and this thing with Mya. I can't count the number of times I've been on my way into the office and spotted them together. They're always laughing and carrying on as though no one sees them. As though no one knows he's another woman's husband. Yet, I still make the best of the situation because I know he will not keep this business afloat without me.

    I think back to the day he said he was considering bringing that woman here to work. Laughter escapes me. Surely, he didn't think things through when he put that nonsense on the table. Good thing that notion died quickly.

    I need to run errands and go to the bank to make a deposit, but I hate to leave before speaking with LaDamien. He needs to know that the meeting got rescheduled to one p.m. If he doesn't show up, I could sit in for him. Lord knows it wouldn't be the first time. I try his number again, still no answer. It's not like him not to check in with me, especially this late in the morning. I'll finish up the open invoices and make a few phone calls. If he isn't here or hasn't called by the time I finish, I'll head to the bank and make the deposit.

LaDamien's SUV is parked out front when I return at a quarter to one. He's seated at his desk reading a message when I walk in. "I forgot I had that meeting this morning. How did it go?" he asks without looking up and without ever doubting my loyalty.

"I rescheduled for one. I hope that's okay." He looks stressed, so I may end up doing the meeting myself. Before he answers, the phone rings, and I reach for it. It's the investor. He has had a family emergency and will not be able to come down until next week. I welcome this news because we need time to regroup. LaDamien is listening and understands what has happened. After placing the receiver back on the base, I walk out to the lobby and check my schedule. We have nothing else on the books for today, so I lock the door and return to his office.

"What's up?" I ask as I step towards him. He's leaning back in his leather chair, already deep in thought.

"I want to leave my wife, I want to leave this business, and I want to leave this city," he chuckles. "What's new, huh?"

Taking a seat on the edge of the desk, I look down at him. He deserves so much better. I wish he understood how much more his life would be if he just had the right people around him. Mya is no better than Kim. He was happier at first, but now he's just as stressed as before. My attention turns to my right leg as LaDamien runs his hand slowly up and down my thigh, each time going higher and higher until he can't go any further. His eyes are closed, as usual. He's forcing them to stay that way, evident by the jittery movement of his eyeballs underneath his eyelids. I never understood that about him, and I often wonder if he's envisioning that he's with someone else when I'm here with him.

The bulge in his pants is evident as I stare into his lap. Slowly, I slide down onto my knees, pushing his chair back as far as it will go. Then I undo his belt and pull his zipper down. He lifts enough so I can slide his pants and underwear down enough to free his penis. He loves it when I take him whole, gripping the chair arms tightly as I slide his shaft deeper into my mouth. As my lips continue down his length, I allow his penis into my throat. He pushes the heels of his shoes into the carpet and moans but never calls my name. I'm thinking too much and not concentrating because my teeth catch the head of his penis. His eyes fly open for the first time. Quickly, I grab his balls and massage them as I pick up my pace. He's back in the groove. Sucking LaDamien's dick is something I love to do, probably as much as he loves having it sucked. I love it more than the times we have made love. I even allow him to ejaculate in my mouth, something my husband doesn't have the privilege of doing. He's beginning to moan a little deeper and more frequently. Just as I'm about to take him over the top, someone knocks on the door. In an instant, he's out of the chair in a state of panic. He adjusts himself, zips his pants, and fastens the belt buckle as he heads towards the door. I hear him mumble, "It's Faye." He returns to his seat and frees himself so I can finish my task.

Twenty minutes later, it's business as usual. The tension in both of us has dissipated. LaDamien is happy, which makes me happy. Faye has not been in his life since Mya surfaced, that I'm aware of, so my curiosity is peaked, and I want to ask him what made her come by. I decide to save it for another day. For now, I just want the positive energy to continue and to relish in knowing that LaDamien needed me. As usual, I was able to step right in. I know he will always need me by his side, and that is where I plan to be.

LOVE...
- is patient
- is kind
- is not rude
- does not envy
- is not self-seeking
- will not lie
- is not proud
- is not quick to anger
- does not boast
- protects
- does not record wrongs
- trusts
- hopes
- perseveres
- finds no joy in evil but celebrates truth
- never fails

Mya

My relationship with LaDamien may be over. I don't know why or what happened. One day we were fine, and then all of a sudden, we weren't. It started with a phone call from LaDamien telling me he was about to ask Kim for a divorce. It came out of the blue. I have never asked him to leave Kim. When and if he does, I want it to be his decision and his alone. Not for me or about me, but because he's ready to move forward in his life and stop living this lie. He just called one night and said he was going to do it. He sounded so sincere. Honestly, I knew telling someone you wanted a divorce and going through with it was two different things. The fact that he was even considering it meant something.

When I fell asleep that night around midnight, LaDamien hadn't called with an update. My sleep was restless, and I had a bizarre dream.

We rode down by the St. Pete Clay Company located off Fifth Avenue and Twenty-second Street. It was me, LaDamien, and Kim. The dream started when we're near the old CSX railroads located behind the red brick building that once housed a moving company, Seaboard Train Station and later Southern Transfer. The three of us were walking along the railroad tracks when I asked LaDamien why Kim was with us. He stepped away to talk with Kim in private, leaving me behind.

As I stood waiting, I heard my grandma's voice telling me that she was never going to let him go. A few seconds later, I hear my granny's voice again saying, "she will never let him go." Shaking off the warning from my dead grandmother, I turn to see if LaDamien has gotten rid of Kim. The scene has changed, and we are now by the anagama kilns at the Clay Company. I call out to LaDamien. He and the woman turn around, and to my surprise, it's no longer Kim, but Wanda, his secretary.

I'm awakened by the ringing phone at six a.m. It was LaDamien, and he sounds happy, not like someone who had asked his wife for a divorce the night before. He asked if I wanted to go to breakfast and then ride with him to Holiday to pick up some contracts. I told him I would, although the memories of my dream still haunt me.

We had breakfast at *IHOP* and made the trek up US 19 North through heavy rush hour traffic. Three hours later, we were sitting in front of my house, and he had yet to mention what took place at his home the night before. I decided that if he didn't say anything, neither would I.

That was weeks ago, and to this day, he has not said a word about that night, nor has he moved out. What has changed is his behavior. After the ride to Holiday, I didn't hear from him for about three days. When he finally returned my calls, he was very distant and aloof. His behavior annoyed me, so I ended the call. That was probably his plan because our subsequent communication was a week later when he called asking if he could come over and spend the night.

Kim was away at a conference, and Ariel stayed with Kim's friend Debra, who had offered to assist him while Kim was away. Reluctantly, I agreed to let him come over even though I was beginning to feel used by LaDamien. Gone was the excitement, and the feelings of passion, and wanton disregard. It started to feel like one of those relationships where the couple stays together because nothing better has come along. That isn't a desirable situation for me. I told this to LaDamien as we were preparing for the gym the morning after. He immediately became defensive and began talking about how ungrateful I was for all his sacrifices. How he was looking forward to this time together, but I treated him like his wife treats him. He wasn't having it. He stormed out, leaving me empty, and confused. Two days later, he called to apologize, claiming it was stress.

This web of deceit is growing out of control. My thoughts are scattered, and I'm feeling dejected. Understanding LaDamien is rebuilding his business, I know, is added pressure. Not only did Mark take his name off the building, but he took the vast majority of their contacts, as well. What cash value LaDamien had coming to him from their portfolio was all but diminished. After Mark began settling his outstanding loans and advancements, little was left. Because LaDamien didn't have the cash to repay the money, he relinquished his rights to many properties. The properties left over would need to sell for him to recoup his losses.

On most days, LaDamien only wants to talk about his business and the obstacles he must overcome. I feel so disconnected because it's not like I can step in and assume some of the responsibilities. When I suggest he needs to get Kim more involved, he becomes angry and asks why I can't do the things I'm suggesting. I want to scream *because I'm not your wife*. But I know this would be a huge mistake. Instead, I silence myself and continue to listen.

Gone are most of our outings. We have not done much of anything lately. No movies, dinners, and no Freedom Fridays. Just conversations involving his business, the lack of funds, and unhappiness in his relationship. Last week I wrote him a long letter expressing how I was feeling. Days later, I had to ask him if he had read it. His response, "I started it but didn't finish. If I'm such a horrible person, then just leave." I was dumbfounded. Nowhere in the letter did it say I thought he was a horrible person. It was as if he no longer saw me. Everything was about him, his needs, his wants, his desires. Then again, maybe it had always been solely about him. Maybe I'm too blinded by love to realize it.

LaDamien

Next Friday will mark two years since Mya and I began seeing each other. It's hard to believe it's only been two years because she has become such a constant in my life. Lately, I have been feeling like letting Mya go, but that will never be an option. I just can't see my life without her in it. Recently, I did a foolish thing that potentially could have cost me her love, and I must admit that things have changed between us since that day. It seems we have weathered the storm, although my actions continue to taunt me.

A few months ago, I decided to leave Kim. My inability to stand firm and follow my heart has been eating at my core being ever since I failed to follow through on my plans. For some reason, I couldn't bring myself to say the words.

It was all worked out in my mind and on paper. I would pay off the mortgage on the house, and the note on Kim's car, leaving her with no large debts to worry about. On top of that, I would give her a cash settlement to help her transition into her new life, no longer dependent on me to pay for everything. I'd made my decision.

After visiting my cousin Rob who had recently divorced, I poured my heart out. I even went so far as to tell him about my affair with Mya. In the end, Rob couldn't tell me if I should stay or if I should leave Kim but instead told me to follow my heart and do what would make my life better in the long run. He told me it wouldn't be easy, and I would second guess myself a million times. "Just give it a lot of thought, don't have false expectations, and most importantly, don't do it for Mya but do it because it's the right thing for all parties involved to be at peace."

A week after my talk with Rob, I made a decision. I would ask Kim for a divorce. The night I was to put my plan into action, I called Mya to let her know. "Make sure you're near the phone and be prepared for me to stay with you a few days if things get too ugly."

The reservation in her voice was undeniable, but being classic Mya, she stayed positive and encouraging. As I look back on the conversation, it may have been her reserved behavior that caused me to pause and question what I was about to do. A hundred times, I asked myself, *what if I left my wife, and Mya had no interest in marrying me?* People would think I was such a fool, and they would make me the butt of their jokes. Plus, things between Kim and I would be ruined. Then I thought about Mark. He had decided to dissolve our partnership. This brought added pressure and had me worried about the ramifications of my decision. What if things didn't work out for me, and my solo venture failed? Kim has a lucrative position that pays well. I would need to rely on her income until I worked things out. What if I needed to take out a loan for my business, her income would boost my rating? What if I became ill? Our family insurance is through her employer. The house could come into play if things didn't go as planned. There was just so much to consider that could make this a wrong decision.

By the time I arrived home and settled down, I had talked myself out of it. As if she knew something was up, Kim had dinner waiting. We ate together, which is a rarity. On nights that Kim does cook, she and Ariel usually have eaten by the time I get home. I heat up whatever is left over if I'm hungry.

After dinner, Kim got Ariel settled while I shower. When I entered the bedroom, Kim asked me if I wanted some ice cream. I told her, "yes," and she returned a few minutes later with two spoons and two individual pints of my favorite butter pecan ice cream. Her gesture immediately turned my thoughts to Mya. I wondered how disappointed she would be in me when I tell her I had a change of heart. When Kim handed me the spoon and my pint, I stared at it as if it was a foreign object. Had it been Mya, we would have shared the spoon, and the ice cream, passing the container back and forth until we were down to the last bite. I would offer it to her, and she would decline. I would then place the last of the ice cream in my mouth. Before swallowing, we would engage in a sweet, creamy kiss.

Kim took my empty carton and set it inside hers. I watch as she sets the containers on the nightstand. She turned back to me and asked if we can talk. Suddenly, my heart rate quickened, and I think Rob has called and told her what we talked about. Kim must have seen the distress on my face because she asked if everything is okay. I'm not sure but tell her that it is.

"I am going to go for my Doctorate," she began. "I think it will seal the deal on the Director of Benefits and Compensation position that should come open in the next year or so."

Janice, the former VP, had retired as planned a year earlier, but Kim wasn't offered the position. The company went with an older, more experienced candidate from another corporation. Kim never made me feel as if she thought she would get the position. Over the past few years, she seemed content taking baby steps, first becoming a supervisor and then a manager. Seeing her being proactive on her own was pleasing, and I was happy for her.

We discussed how much the program will cost, how long it will take, the responsibilities, and what it will mean financially in the long run. On paper, Kim and I make about the same. But if she becomes a director, she will exceed my total income. The shift in finances will bring about a change in her for sure. It's a proven fact that when Black women earn more than their mates, they think they are better. Worst, they eventually out-grow their husbands bringing new issues to the marriage forcing the men to leave. As I was giving her my blessings, inside, I was wondering if I should go through with my plans or stay and reap the benefits of my wife's promising future.

Kim reached over and gave me a kiss, appreciation for my endless support. She grabbed the remote from between us and turned off the television, followed by the lights. She scooted backward and pressed her rear end up against me. My manhood began to swell. I slide my hand under her gown and feel nothing but skin. She isn't wearing any underwear. I couldn't resist telling myself that she's my wife, and I'm her husband. Therefore, I'm entitled to indulge in her sweetness whenever the need arises, regardless of what I'm feeling for another woman.

Leaving Kim will require more resolve than I had at that moment. I'm thinking about finances, stability, our home, Ariel, and all the things I will forfeit if I walk out. I try to push those thoughts to the back of my mind. I'm inside of Kim, and she's warmer than usual. The slight movement of her hips draws me in deeper and deeper. The more Kim moved, the more I wanted to distance myself from thoughts of divorce and Mya. I had no idea what I was going to say to Mya when I saw her. Right now, I didn't want to worry about that. Kim rolled over to her stomach, and I followed, grabbing her hips and pulling her backward onto her knees. Moments later, I'm standing and starting to love her from behind. She's meeting my thrusts pound for pound, and I hear her calling my name, but no matter how hard I try to focus, my mind keeps racing back to Mya. What will she say, how will she feel, will this be the end for us?

I feel myself cumming, and want to yell. Instead, I smothered my moans because, at that moment, I didn't know whose name would come out. Kim was giving it to me like she used to back in the day. But my mind was consumed with Mya. I collapse next to Kim, and when I opened my eyes, she was staring at me. My heart was pounding from the exertion of our intense lovemaking, but more so because I think I called Mya's name when I reached my pinnacle moment. Kim placed her hand on my face and said, "I love you so much." I heard the words, but they didn't match the expression on her face. Relief flushed over me as Kim climbed out of bed and headed into the bathroom.

This was awful, and Kim doesn't deserve it. I should just man up and go ahead and tell her I want out, that I need to free us both from the agony this marriage is causing. Kim turned on the water, and I waited until I was sure she was in the shower before I headed to the bath down the hall with the phone in hand. I close the bathroom door and dial Mya's number. Before pressing talk, I reconsider and lay the phone down on the counter. Staring at my reflection in the mirror, I don't like the man staring back at me. "LaDamien, you have to be a man. Nothing good is going to come of this if you don't get it together." I whispered these words to myself as I stared at Mya's number, glaring up at me. Still, in that instance, I decided it was Mya that I need to remove from my life, not Kim, not my faithful wife.

All night long, I wrestled with my decision to let Mya go. But who was I fooling; my love for Mya exceeds my desire for anything and anyone else. I arose that following morning, wanting nothing more than to hear Mya's voice. As soon as Kim left the house, I called her. Instead of telling her, there had been a change in plans. I asked her to go with me to pick up some contracts. I contemplated telling her the truth over breakfast, then during the ride to Holiday. Her silence on the issue was deafening but resounding at the same time. If I had told her that I changed my mind and given her the reasons, she would have doubted my love. Surely, she would have walked out of my life forever. So I remained silent even though it was killing me inside.

After I dropped Mya off, I decided to take some time and regroup. As time passed, I became annoyed by her stubbornness, her refusal to confront me on the issue. As different as she is from Kim, the more they are alike. Why can't either of them see that their unwillingness to fight for me only drives me further away? I have shown Mya complete dedication, and now it's her turn to show me how bad she wants me.

Kim

Once again, my marriage has taken a positive turn. LaDamien has been very attentive lately and spending more time at home. When Mark dissolved the partnership, I was afraid for LaDamien. Not knowing what he would do to bounce back, he rebounded in a grand style. LaDamien Bryson Enterprises has taken on a life of its own. Wanda deserves a lot of credit. She hung in there with LaDamien, even at times when he was unable to pay her. She took on a second job and even did contract work for other small businesses, all the while doing what she could to help get his business going.

To this day, I still don't know what caused the split between LaDamien, and Mark. They didn't speak for a while, but lately, they appear to have mended their fences. Mark's wife and I have always been cordial but not friends. When Mark decided to leave, it seemed as if a wedge was between us, so I didn't know how to approach her and ask for any information she might have. In the end, I only had LaDamien's version of things. Of course, it's filled with a lot of missing information.

Cautiously optimistic is how I describe my present state. This isn't the first time he and Mya have had some sort of split, only for him to return to his cheating ways a week or so later. I just need to figure out what I need to do to take advantage of these opportunities. My suggestions have been counseling, speaking with the Pastor of our church, and attending a couple's retreat. Still, LaDamien will not agree to any of it. He tells me that he isn't having an affair, and I need to be more attentive to his needs. The main part of our problem is his denial that he's doing anything wrong. I don't know whether to laugh or cry. He looks me straight into my eyes and tells me that I imagine all the things I accuse him of doing. Nonetheless, if I'm going to stay in this marriage, I must do whatever it takes to fix what is wrong. If I have to depend on these rifts, I will, because eventually, something will have to give.

Last night, LaDamien and I put the final touches on our upcoming family vacation. It will be the first time in three years since we have taken real time off to go away as a family. When we were at *Disney World* last year, we purchased a timeshare. It's located in Orlando and owned by *Marriott*. The Grande Vista is a beautiful facility. We have access to a two-bedroom, two baths Villa, with an eat-in, fully equipped kitchen. I was sure to ask for a location overlooking one of the four pools onsite. We plan to stay for five or six days. We will take in all the amusement parks, including *Sea World, Universal Studios, and Disney*. LaDamien has already mentioned some possible business contacts in the area, so I'm not going to get upset if he backs out on an outing or two. I have promised myself that this trip will be perfect, and I will not allow anything or anyone to interfere.

When LaDamien comes in, I already have dinner on the table. He seems surprised, but I pretend not to notice. I run down the list of things that he has asked me to do and provide a full report on each. *Best Buy* is scheduled to come and install the new Plasma television and surround system. I verified that someone would be here tomorrow to fix the broken sprinkler heads. I've scheduled our annual physicals for the recertification of the life insurance policies. I spoke with all of his sisters to set a time for a family meeting to discuss their mother's lease renewal. LaDamien thanks me for taking care of these things, then heads upstairs. I follow behind him to see if there's anything else that he needs from me. He says he's okay and will be down for dinner after he showers.

Back downstairs, I get Ariel settled and place the food on the table. Fifteen minutes after the shower stops, LaDamien has not come down, so I go up to see what is keeping him. He's stretched out across the bed sleeping. The old me would have been furious. I'm learning not to take things so personally and realize that not everything is an attack on me and my ability to be a good wife.

At ten p.m. I awaken LaDamien to move to his side of the bed so that I can get in. He apologizes for falling asleep on dinner. "It's okay," I say. "I understand that you're tired."

We talk about everything from my coursework to Ariel's day in school, his new business dealings, and concerns about the direction the economy seems to be taking. It feels so good to have these intimate moments with my husband again, and I wish it could always be this way.

The following day at the office, I'm called into a meeting to discuss some changes on the horizon for our Maryland office. Changes that will require me to do some extensive traveling. This could not have come at a worse time.

I leave in two days. The Maryland office will be going through a reorganization in a few months. I'll be assisting the human resources team with displacement services. When I share the news with him, LaDamien seems almost dismayed. He's concerned that I will be gone for over a week and asks what he and Ariel will do without me. I assure him that they will do just fine.

"Where will you be staying?" he asks. "Perhaps we can fly out with you and spend the weekend." I'm happy that he wants to come and promise to look into it.

It's Sunday evening, and LaDamien and Ariel are preparing to leave for the airport. The last few days were nice. LaDamien and Ariel busied themselves on Thursday and Friday while I worked. In the evenings, they met me at the office, and we headed out to dinner as a family. LaDamien refuses to eat at chain restaurants while traveling, so I get the names of several landmark restaurants in the city. Friday, we dined at *Jerry's Famous Seafood*. LaDamien had inquired at the hotel, and everyone agreed we should give it a try, and we were glad we did.

Saturday, we took Ariel to *Kings Dominion* in Virginia. It was a long and tiring day, which is why we didn't rise until well after two today. The plane is scheduled to leave at seven, not leaving us much time to do more than pack our things and eat.

Sitting in my rental, I wave goodbye. New airport security rules enacted after 9-11 don't allow me to wait at the terminal-side with them. So I settle for hugs and kisses from my two favorite people and then watch as they disappear into the crowd. Although I'm already missing them, I'm satisfied having spent this time together. There were no phone calls, no disappearing acts, and no traces that Mya ever entered his mind.

LOVE...

- is patient
- is kind
- is not rude
- does not envy
- is not self-seeking
- will not lie
- is not proud
- is not quick to anger
- protects
- does not boast
- does not record wrongs
- trusts
- hopes
- perseveres
- finds no joy in evil but celebrates truth
- never fails

Mya

LaDamien called. His mood was upbeat, which is a rarity these days. He's in Orlando and wants to celebrate our second anniversary. He says he has a surprise for me but will only tell me what it is after I call back and confirm that I have requested the next three days off. It's Sunday, so I can't oblige until the following morning, but that doesn't stop me from begging for hints. He isn't forthcoming with information, not even when I quiz him on Orlando. I ask why he didn't take me with him if he wanted to celebrate our anniversary. He doesn't budge and only adds that he wanted to get things ready. My excitement is growing by the second, and I don't want to wait until tomorrow.

"Should I just call in or go to the office and request Tuesday through Thursday off?" I ask. He tells me to call-in, and be ready to leave as soon as I hang up the phone. "Why can't I come today and just call from Orlando in the morning?" The idea makes more sense to me, but he insists that tomorrow is when he needs me to come, and we'll leave on Wednesday evening.

The following morning I call as soon as I think Paul, my manager, is in the office. "Something has come up, and I will need to be out for several days." After assuring him and then reassuring him that everyone in my family is okay health-wise, he approves the time off.

LaDamien's voice mail picked up when I call to tell him it's a go. My heart sinks, and prayers go up because if he has set me up once again, it's going to be on and popping. His actions are growing old and tiresome, and I feel more and more like a fool the longer this continues. The clock reads ten-fifteen. If he doesn't return my call by... the phone rings, and it's him.

"Sorry about that. I got a call from a potential client and went to meet him for breakfast. So do you have a pen and paper?"

One hour and twenty minutes later, I'm maneuvering my way through the lush grounds of the *Marriott* Grand Vista Resort, looking for building twenty-three. LaDamien is on the phone directing me. His tone, impatient. Finally, I see the building and search for a parking space nearby. He tells me he's on the third floor and gives me the room number. Five minutes later, I'm standing in the living room of a plush timeshare. It's beautiful. "You've outdone yourself this time, Mr. Bryson," I say as I turn towards him and place a soft kiss on his lips. He's smiling, quite pleased with himself.

"Let me show you around," he says as he takes my hand. "Over here is the second bedroom. You can choose to use it or not. Since it's just you and me, the room is locked, so I can't show you inside. Of course, this is the kitchen. It's fully equipped. We can go pick up some groceries if you feel like making me a home-cooked meal," he says with a hint of sarcasm. "This is the living room, and the sofa lets out to a bed. Those doors lead out to the balcony, and this door leads into the master suite." We enter the master suite, and I'm in awe.

"This place is like a home away from home," I say as I step out onto the balcony with its separate entrance from the master suite and overlooking the pool area. LaDamien is right there when I turn around, asking if I want to see the Jacuzzi. I follow him back inside and past the inviting king-sized bed into the vanity area that also houses the Jacuzzi.

"Wow, I can't wait to get in." I tease. He knows I'm impressed, and he's winning brownie points. He points to the two doors ahead and advises that one leads to the bathroom, which houses a shower and the toilet. The other door leads back into the kitchen's foyer area. This place makes me want to buy my own little escape. I've seen timeshares before, but nothing like this. Then I wonder how it came to be that LaDamien has access to this one, so I decided to ask.

"I won a mini-getaway through a contest I entered. The company also offered additional nights at seventy-nine bucks. A marketing ploy used to get people to buy one, but I went along with it because I knew you would love it, and it's been a long time since we've done anything special together. So, do you like it? Are you hungry, is there anywhere you want to go or do?"

Knowing it was a freebie was disappointing. For some reason, in my mind, it would have meant more if LaDamien were paying for the condo at full price. It was silly of me to feel this way. A place like this would cost hundreds per night, and I should be thinking about how much money that left him to spend on me. But for some reason, I still felt slighted. We decide to head to *Boston Lobster* for a late lunch and then over to the Millennium Mall for some window shopping. Four hours later, we are lounging by the pool, me sipping a rumrunner, and LaDamien a Coke.

"I think we can just chill the rest of the evening, and tomorrow head over to *Sea World*. The tickets came with the package. Smiling, I agree to his plans. Despite my uneasiness, I want to enjoy this trip, but I can't ignore that Kim isn't blowing up his phone like she usually does when he's away. Something is up, but as always, I must wait for LaDamien to share, and I'm not going to ruin the mood by bringing it up.

It is midnight, and we have just finished a sexual trice in the Jacuzzi. I'm at the sink brushing my teeth when LaDamien comes up behind me. "You don't like the way I taste?" he asks as he places gentle kisses on the nape of my neck.

"Was that Kim you were talking to?" I ask as I turn to face him. He acknowledges that it was and encourages me not to let it ruin the night. I don't want to let it ruin the night, but I have to know why he just told his wife that he had put their daughter to bed and didn't want to rouse her. If Kim thinks he's with Ariel, then where is she?

"Kim is in Maryland. I told you she would be there a lot on business. Ariel is with my sister." My uneasiness returns with every word. LaDamien sees the doubt planted across my face, the face he's turning towards his. "Please don't do this, Mya. This is our time together. All of this is for you because I miss this part of us. I miss being with you this way, the freedom to walk down the street and hold hands like you love to do. Let's just be lost in this moment, in this time together." He has lifted me onto the counter and is going down on his knees. I decide to get lost in the paradise his tongue is slowly taking me to. I'm going to enjoy this trip, regardless of the circumstances. Whatever he has done, he did it for me, and that is all that should matter.

It's Wednesday evening already. The past few days have been heaven. LaDamien and I are finishing dinner at *The Cheesecake Factory*. He keeps checking his watch, so I finally ask if he has plans. He says he's concerned about the hour and me having to drive home this late at night. Since it's almost eight p.m., I let him know that I'm okay with staying the night and leaving early in the morning. He goes pale, if that is possible, with his deep mocha complexion. LaDamien takes a deep breath and pauses. His next comment is that he thinks it's probably for the best.

LaDamien awakes at five a.m. and heads into the restroom. He's gone so long that I go back to sleep. When I awaken twenty minutes later, he's out on the balcony talking on the phone. I hear him apologize for not making it back last night and say Ariel needs to go to day camp. He mentions something about a networking event that lasted longer than he expected. Whomever he's speaking to is grilling him on his whereabouts. After several tense minutes, he ends the call and leans back in the chair. I make my way back to the bed and feign sleep. Shortly after that, he steps back into the room and joins me in bed. The door is left open, allowing a cool breeze to fill the room. We lay in silence, not speaking. He's staring at the ceiling full of worry.

By nine-thirty, we are finishing breakfast at *IHOP* and preparing to head back to St. Petersburg. LaDamien tells me to go on because he remembered he left something back at the Grande Vista. I don't argue or let on that I overheard him on the phone with the concierge service. He was requesting that housekeeping have the place thoroughly cleaned by the time he leaves, which would be around ten. When we left for breakfast, I spotted two cleaning personnel near the laundry room adjacent to our villa. As we descended the stairs, I tried to look up and see if they entered the room or not. But LaDamien caught me and asked if I was looking for something. My mind tells me to follow him back to the resort and see what he does, but a part of me doesn't want to know what he's up to. We say goodbye in the parking lot. LaDamien kisses me passionately and repeats that he's happy I came and wishes we could do this more often. I agree and ask if I will see him later. He jokes, "You've seen me for three days straight. Any more, and we would be considered husband and wife."

"What would be wrong with that?"

He replies, "Nothing, except you don't want to be married to me." I shake my head, kiss him on the cheek, and enter my car. Again, I have the urge to follow him but don't want to slide down that path. I know our situation. He belongs to someone else, and if I were to catch him in a lie, what would it matter because this whole relationship is a lie? I head home.

It's eleven a.m., and traffic is at a crawl. I was making good time along I-4 until I reached Lakeland. I fear there has been a bad accident, and I'm concerned I won't make it to work by one p.m. as I had promised. Traffic inched along slowly for the next ten miles. When I approached exit twenty-five, I finally saw that the hold-up was not an accident going westbound but a wreck in the eastbound lanes. The delay on my side of the highway was due to onlookers. Traffic crept along until I was finally even with the wreckage. An older model *Isuzu* Rodeo was overturned in the median, and a yellow sheet lay on the ground close by. Someone's pinned beneath the vehicle, and that someone was dead. My natural reaction is to say a little prayer for the victim's soul and the family about to receive the awful news.

At second glance, I'm a witness to another shocker. Kim and Ariel were sitting in her *Mercedes Benz*, impatiently waiting their turn to maneuver past the emergency vehicles blocking the inside lane. I was staring so hard I must have come to a complete stop because the vehicle behind me tapped its horn. Gently, I pressed the gas and eased forward. It may have been my imagination, but I swear Kim looked straight at me with a look of total disbelief. We both lifted our cell phones at the same time. My call went to voice mail, while hers appeared to have gotten answered.

LaDamien returned my call twenty minutes later, assuring me that I was mistaken. "Even if you did see her, which I doubt it was her, I'm not too far behind you. When I passed, they had reopened all eastbound lanes, and traffic was picking up its pace." I don't know if LaDamien believes the lies he tells or if he thinks I'm crazy as hell. That was his wife and child I saw as plain as day, just as I know damn well he isn't right behind me. To prove my theory, I tell him I'm going to get off at the next exit and ask that he stops because I want another hug and a kiss. "I'll wait for you in the parking lot at *Wendy's*."

"Did you forget you need to be at work by one?" he replies. "I'll come over later, and you can have all the kisses you want." He thinks this empty suggestion and his concern for my job will quell my doubts, but he's mistaken.

It is eleven at night, and I have yet to hear from LaDamien since our earlier call. When I tried his number at around eight, the phone was off, and it remained that way until I saw his number on the call ID late Sunday evening.

Kim

Sometimes I think my husband has lost his mind. As I speed towards Orlando, far exceeding the set seventy miles per hour, my heart and mind are racing. Ariel is describing the lady who cared for her the past few days. It's the third time I've asked her to share the story. I don't want to believe her father would have a random woman in our home. But I have to be honest with myself, especially after seeing Mya heading west, back to St. Petersburg from Orlando. LaDamien laughed when I told him my suspicions and then reprimanded me for saying such things in front of Ariel. The last thing I want to hear about is how I need to be discreet and lower my tone. If my suspicions are correct, Ariel is going to hear a whole lot more.

This was to be our family vacation. I put a lot of time and planning, not to mention the money that went into this trip. We should have just rescheduled when I learned I wouldn't get back last Friday as planned. He insisted he could take Ariel over and start without me. It would be a great daddy-daughter adventure, he had insisted. Now I feel like such a damn fool. Not only has he been gallivanting around with that whore, but he handed our daughter over to a stranger to do it. The tears are streaming down my face.

"Mommy, why are you crying?" Ariel asked me.

Seeing the wet spot on my t-shirt, I reflexively wiped my face smearing my make-up. Minutes later, I pulled over at a rest stop to regroup, telling Ariel that I was just thinking about my mother and how we used to take trips like this when I was little. This was a partial truth. I was thinking of my mother and how I had no one to call and share LaDamien's latest insult. "Baby, I'm so sorry, but don't you worry, mommy is okay."

In turn, she tells me that she knows I'm crying about her daddy leaving her with the lady. When I ask why she would say that, she replied, "Because he told me to tell you I was at Aunt Lynn's house, although I wasn't, at least not the whole time he has been gone. Then I saw how mad you got when I told you daddy brought me back on Sunday and then left again. I'm sorry, mommy. I hope I haven't gotten daddy into trouble."

This thing with LaDamien was starting to affect my child, and I could not stand for that. I pulled over at the first rest stop. Ariel stayed in the car while I went inside to freshen up. While at the visitor's center, I call LaDamien to let him know that I'm turning around and returning home, and he needs to head home as well. I plan to do what I should have done long ago finally. I'm going to put my foot down and give him an ultimatum. He needs to end this affair, or I'm filing for divorce. I will not live like this another day, *not another day.*

As I listen to his voice message for the ninth time, my tears begin to fall again. Who am I fooling? He will agree to whatever terms I lay down, and in a few weeks, a month, however long it takes, he will be back at it again. It may not be with Mya, but it will be with someone. It will always be someone else.

Back in the ladies' room, I ignore the concerned stares of other travelers who have stopped to refresh, but for reasons different than mine. Looking at the other women, I wonder if they know the constant heartache that resides within me. If their men have deceitful ways like my husband? Then I wonder how many would fault me if I just got in my car and kept riding until I couldn't go any further. Far, far, far, from LaDamien, and this hell he has trapped me in. I hate my husband. As sure as I'm standing in this washroom for the third time trying to stop my tears, I hate him. I hate the day I agreed to marry him. I hate the day I conceived his child. My cell phone is ringing. Now I hate myself for not being strong enough to ignore the call. "Hello," I stammer through my mixture of rage and despair.

"Where are you?" he asks in a calm, unconcerned tone.

"We're at the rest stop right outside Orlando. I had to stop, but I'm getting back on the road now."

LaDamien doesn't care about the pain he causes. It's as if he's unable to acknowledge the pain and unhappiness in others, even when he's the source of that pain. He was making it my problem, as he always says, "he hasn't done anything wrong." He's on the other end of the phone telling me he's going to meet us at *Disney*. If needed, I should go ahead and change into comfortable clothes if I'm not dressed for the park yet. He tells me he will meet us at the ticket counter, and like that, he's gone.

I get myself together one last time. Ariel is in the car, bobbing her head to whatever sound is coming from the radio. I enter the car with a smile plastered on my face for her sake. "We are meeting your dad at *Disney World.*" This brings a huge smile to her face, which in turn warms my heart. Thirty minutes later, we are on the *Goofy* tram heading towards the theme park.

LaDamien is waiting next to the ticket window like he said he would be. He greets us like the proud husband and father he truly believes he is. I accept his kiss, playing the role of the dutiful wife who is blessed to have such a great husband who takes time out to treat his family to *Disney World.* He grabs my hand with his left and Ariel's with his right. My eyes close as I wish really hard that what I know I don't know. That my marriage is as perfect as the illusion, we present to the world. But no matter how many trips we take to this magical kingdom, we will have to return to reality. It's a reality that is full of lies and deception. A world where my husband looks me in my eyes and tells me that he loves me, and I'm all the woman he needs. All the while, the eyes staring back at me tell a different story.

After several hours at *Disney,* Ariel and LaDamien have managed to ease my guard down. We are posing before an artist drawing a caricature of us, with our *Mickey Mouse* ears and newly purchased *Disney* t-shirts. LaDamien has his arm around my shoulders, and Ariel is sitting on his lap. When the artist finished, LaDamien pays for the drawing, and we walk away hand-in-hand. He spoils us rotten for the remainder of the day. We are all exhausted from the days' activities as we patiently await the night parade. LaDamien asks me if I enjoyed myself today, and I respond that I did.

"Good, that's all I want to know," he replies.

And that was all he wanted to know for the remainder of our trip. He didn't allow me to dwell on seeing Mya while traveling to Orlando. We were not at the timeshare long enough for me to wonder what they may have done in the bed we were now sharing. We had breakfast each morning and headed out to a different theme park afterward. We visited *Animal Kingdom, Blizzard Beach,* and *Epcot.* By the time we returned each evening, we were too exhausted to do more than bathe and fall into bed.

On Saturday, we returned to the timeshare around five. We had rented videos to watch. By nine o'clock, Ariel was sound asleep. LaDamien put her to bed while I cleaned up the leftover pizza and discarded the empty boxes and soda cans. When I finished, LaDamien was in our bedroom filling the Jacuzzi. It was the first time he had turned on the pulsating jets since I arrived. He told me to get in, and I didn't hesitate. I disrobed and slid into the tub indulging in the rhythmic dance the water was playing on my thighs. LaDamien was placing delicate pecks across my back as he massaged my shoulders. He was kneeling over the side of the tub, going from my shoulders to my thighs and then between my legs. He slid his finger inside me and started a slow massage of my vaginal walls while using his free hand to tilt my head back. He lured me into a deep dance of the tongues.

LaDamien brought me to a climax using his fingers, and when he finished, he guided me out of the tub and into the shower. There he bathed me from head to toe, even shampooed my hair. He turned me around and asked me to do the same for him. I lathered the rag and slowly rubbed it across his broad chest. Washing his arms, and back but when it was time for his legs, I kneeled, taking his feet one at a time and lathering each before moving up his toned muscular limbs. When I reached his penis, I stroked its length until LaDamien began to waver, but he didn't stop me. I rinsed the soap from the rag and then used it to remove the soap from his shaft. I opened my mouth wide and took him slow but deep. LaDamien grasped the shower doors as he let out a deep moan. I sucked him long, and hard, and fast, wanting to drain every drop of cum from his body, not wanting to leave him with anything to give to anyone else. His juices should only be for me, and his lovemaking reserved only for me, and his fine body revealed only to me. Tonight, and every chance I could get, I wanted to sex him, so he never desired another woman. Damn, I wanted my husband all to myself to suck, to fuck, to love, to make love to, to cherish, to…

I don't know how long LaDamien had been begging me to stop before he finally grabbed my hair and pulled me off his soft penis. He was no longer standing erect—his body had crumbled to the back of the shower. His breathing was labored, and he could not or wouldn't release my hair. I tasted his cum now. The water was pounding on my back as I stared at LaDamien. The look on his face was a mixture of pleasure and pain. His stare centered on me as he tried to steady his breathing. After a while, he let my hair go, but as I prepared to stand, he caught my arm. "Uh uh," he mumbled between breaths.

LaDamien maneuvered his body until he was lying on his back, with knees bent. The shower was crowded with us both in there, but somehow, I straddled him. Within seconds his erect penis was inside of me. It was hard to decide what was more fulfilling, the warm jets across my back or LaDamien's warm penis riding up inside of me. He placed his arms under my legs and grasped my ankles. It allowed him to manipulate my movements so I wouldn't hurt my knees on the tiled shower floor. LaDamien was staring straight at me, daring me to look away. I was hypnotized. The harder he stared, the harder I rotated my hips, causing him to go deeper inside of me. Suddenly, he released my ankles, and reached up, and grabbed my hips, burying himself inside of me. I screamed out. LaDamien placed his hand over my mouth and pulled me down to his chest. It was an awkward position, but it felt wonderful having made love to my husband in such a reckless manner.

It was midnight when we finally settled into bed. It was the most restful night I had experienced in a long time. When I awaken the following morning, LaDamien had his arms wrapped around me. It felt so good that I didn't want to move. We stayed this way until Ariel knocked on the door two hours later.

Home, it was the last place I wanted to be. It didn't represent a place of refuge. In Orlando, the world didn't exist. It was just me, Ariel, and LaDamien. We attended the gospel brunch at The *House of Blues* in *Downtown Disney*, caught a movie, and then shopped for gifts. When we returned to our villa and prepared to leave in our separate vehicles, reality returned. The reality that when we reach St. Petersburg, Mya would be waiting. The lies would return, and I would be boarding a plane back to Maryland on Wednesday, leaving my husband to his devices. I wanted to call Adele, our VP, and tell her that I could no longer work on this assignment. Let her know my marriage was in jeopardy. I needed to be at home protecting my family and watching my husband. But I knew that would be professional suicide and could cost me my position. So I drove home in silence, praying to God for an answer to this dilemma of mine. Praying that LaDamien felt something these past few days that made him realize what is at stake. I'm a good woman, I'm a good mother, and I'm a good wife. I can provide all that he needs if he would just give me a chance.

LaDamien

I have called Mya for the tenth time since returning from Orlando. She must be beyond pissed to ignore my calls like this. Coming up with an explanation as to why I have not called since Thursday afternoon will not be easy. She seemed convinced when we last spoke. She saw Kim and Ariel en route to meet me. I was hoping I had convinced her that it was her imagination, but even I knew that was a stretch. Kim was already livid that I had left Ariel in St. Petersburg with a friend when my sister could not watch her. But when she saw Mya, all shit hit the fan. There was no way I was going to risk trying to contact Mya. My priority was calming Kim down, and I did everything in my power to succeed. In my mind, I know I should be at home with Kim and Ariel being the devoted husband, continuing to reassure her that things are okay between us. Yet, my heart needs to hear from Mya to see how much damage I've done.

It's obvious she isn't going to answer. I have driven by her house several times, and her parents, and several friends, even looked through the side window of her garage to see if the car was inside, but it wasn't. All types of thoughts are going through my head. What if she's with someone else? What if she was injured or became ill and was hospitalized. Or what if her friends have taken her out to convince her to leave me? My thoughts are frantic, and I can't settle my nerves. Seeing Mya's face and hearing her voice is the only thing that will calm me down. It's Sunday night, and I can't imagine where she could be, and the thought of her being with someone else is driving me crazy.

The phone rings, and I'm hoping it's Mya, but it's my home number on the screen. When I answer, Kim's response is simple. "Please come home." She sounds so desperate, and I can't deny her request. My worries over Mya are placed on the backburner for now as I return home. This makes Kim very happy. We settle into bed, and I wrap my arms around her, letting her know she's secure. We drift off to sleep, but later our peace is shattered by my ringing cell phone. I forgot to turn it off when I came into the house. Do I dare reach for it? The suspense gets the better of me, and several minutes later, I get up to go to the bathroom. When I return, I pick up the phone and turn it off. But first I check to see who has called. Disappointment rules my emotions when I see it was not Mya.

LOVE...

- is patient
- is kind
- is not rude
- does not envy
- is not self-seeking
- will not lie
- is not proud
- is not quick to anger
- protects
- does not boast
- does not record wrongs
- trusts
- hopes
- perseveres
- finds no joy in evil but celebrates truth
- never fails

Kim

"So what is living in St. Petersburg like?" TayJohn Neilson asked me after I informed him that his current position was getting eliminated at the Baltimore location. There's an offer on the table for him to relocate to St. Petersburg.

These past two days have been hell. Each day, I had to tell employee after employee their job was getting eliminated. Or they didn't interview successfully for one of the newly created positions. TayJohn was one of the lucky ones. He worked in production support and would get a relocation package at his current salary and tenure.

"It's definitely not Baltimore, that's for sure. St. Pete is a very slow-moving city. It's changing a bit, but not in terms of opportunities for Blacks. At times it appears to be a systematic agenda to change the demographics, both ethnically and financially. But we have some nice surrounding areas that are progressively favorable to African-Americans, and the commute isn't bad. I guess a great advantage would be a lower cost of living, and you'll be transferring, if you accept, at your current salary."

TayJohn didn't appear enthusiastic about the possibility of moving down south. He continued to finger through the documents as though he expected the offer to change. I sat silently, waiting for him to ask questions. "So I have to decide by next Monday, huh?" He stated more than asked.

"Yes. I know you were hoping to get one of the positions you applied for, but we didn't feel your strengths were in those areas, and there were stronger candidates to choose from." TayJohn continued to mull over the offer. "Why don't you take some time to think things over and then get back to me with any questions you may have."

A hesitant look clouds his eyes as he stands to leave. He's a very handsome man, well over six feet tall, with a coffee with cream complexion. A lighter-skinned version of LaDamien, I think. When he opened his mouth to speak, I couldn't help notice his perfectly aligned and bright white teeth. He either had dental implants, or his parents spent a great deal of money on orthodontia. He also has made use of teeth whitening products.

He stopped when he reached the door to my makeshift office and turned to me to speak. "Do you think you could work something out where I could maybe go to St. Petersburg on a trial basis to see if I like it? This is a huge decision, and I don't want to say yes, and forfeit my severance package only to get there and find out it isn't where I want to be."

I understood how hard this must be for TayJohn and the others who got offered a chance to relocate. My thoughts went back to when I left the company to follow LaDamien, only to have things fall apart. That was the craziest decision I ever made, aside from agreeing to marry him. Luckily, Janice, our former VP, had my back and let me return. But that wouldn't be the case for TayJohn. If he doesn't accept this offer, he'll get a severance package that is twenty-five percent less than the one offered to those who didn't get a job offer at all.

"I am not sure that will be an option. All paperwork has to get finalized so other offers can go out. If you don't want to relocate, I have someone else I need to make an offer." I smile at him. "When I interviewed you, I left with the impression that you were open to moving. Was I wrong?" TayJohn closes the door and steps back to my desk.

"When I interviewed, I said what I needed to say to stay employed. I just didn't know I would get offered a position in another state. So is there anything I can do to get a position here? Maybe you'll make an offer to someone, and they will turn it down. Maybe you could offer it to me."

I wish I could make him that promise, but I can't. "All offers are set, and alternative candidates have already been selected," I explain to him. "Your options are to move to St. Petersburg or take a severance package." My following sentence may very well get me into hot water. Out of the blue, I offer to fly him to St. Petersburg for a few days next week to introduce him to his new team, if he decides to take the position, and to show him around the area. What made me do it was a mystery, but I did, and now I had to make it happen because he graciously accepted.

Monday morning TayJohn Nielson and two other candidates facing relocation arrived at our St. Petersburg offices. When I told Adele what I had done, she was not upset and stated she thought it was an excellent idea. Relocating was a big step, and some of our candidates had families. According to his personnel file, TayJohn was single. Still, he might have a girlfriend or children, or perhaps family in Baltimore he didn't want to leave, like an ailing parent. We made these offers based on the company's needs, not the employee.

"Good morning," I say. We were all gathered in the lobby. After the greetings, I took them on a tour of the complex, making introductions to several key staff members. Next, I handed the trio off to the Director of Information Technology, who had the remainder of their visit planned. So I was surprised when Melanie called to let me know I had a visitor, and it was TayJohn.

"Mr. Neilson, what can I do for you? "I asked as soon as he entered my office. My immediate thought was he had decided not to relocate.

"I just wanted to thank you for arranging this visit. Everyone has been nice so far. Uhm, I also was wondering if perhaps we could grab a bite to eat for lunch. The others are going to a restaurant downtown that serves Russian cuisine, but that's not my cup of tea."

The gesture was flattering, but I could not accept. "It would be inappropriate for me, the Manager of Human Resources, to be fraternizing with someone who is affected by the reorganization."

He replied, "I could see how some could take that the wrong way." He stood, seemingly unsure of himself, so I asked if he needed something else. He apologized for the interruption but, before leaving, asked, "So if I agree to the relocation, and a week after getting settled in asked you to lunch, would you accept?"

Smiling, I simply replied, "If it's just to say thank you. I don't think my husband would stand for anything else." He needed to know that I was married, in case he didn't know already, and had more than gratitude in mind.

Sunday, we are scheduled to attend church with the rest of LaDamien's family and have dinner afterward at his sister Lynn's home. It's the first family dinner we've had in quite some time. The reason for the gathering is Dawn and Dexter came to town for a visit. He graduated from high school and is making college plans this coming fall, hoping to get into the University of South Florida, located in Tampa.

For some odd reason, LaDamien got up and decided to wash the vehicles. It caused us to arrive at church about fifteen minutes late, and we could not sit with the rest of the family. I was trying to get Lynn's attention when I saw a woman who looked a lot like Mya. I had to be mistaken. There's no way she could be this tacky. LaDamien seemed oblivious to my obvious distraction and the fact that I was not focusing on the service. When the choir went into an up-tempo praise song, the woman stood, clapping, and swaying, vanquishing any doubt in my mind. "How dare she?" I wanted to yell. For the remainder of the service, I'm too transfixed on her.

After the benediction, LaDamien, and I made our way to the front of the sanctuary to greet his family. Before we could reach them, Mya approached Dawn, hugged her, then turned to Dexter, and did the same. My heart sunk as LaDamien kept moving forward as though that woman was not there. Their eyes met, and then she turned to me. I believe if Ariel had not been with us, she would have remained right where she stood. But at the last possible moment, she walked away.

Dawn was the first to speak, "Hey Kim, don't you look sharp." I garnered a smile and returned the compliment. My eyes spotted Mya heading for the door, and I watched as she disappeared into the crowd. By now, LaDamien's family was moving towards the side doors. LaDamien had rested his hand on my back and was gently urging me along.

In the SUV, I asked LaDamien how long Mya had been attending church. He sighed, then responded that as far as he knew, she always attended church. He's making a direct dig at me, but I let it slide. "I mean, how long has she been attending *our* church?"

LaDamien became defensive and reminded me that it was not *our* church because I didn't attend church. Then he added that with the growth we are experiencing, many people are migrating over. "Why are you so worried about Mya?"

"I am worried because she knows your sister. I'm worried because she seemed comfortable and too damn friendly around your family." My head is throbbing, and it's hot in this vehicle, although the air conditioner is on full blast.

Pulling the vehicle into a space near Lynn's house, LaDamien suggests I ask Dawn or Mya how they know each other. Quickly, he exited the SUV, slammed the door, and headed inside leaving me, and Ariel behind. Ariel, who was beginning to act more, and more like her father, jumped out of the back seat and slammed the door mimicking his actions. Slowly, I take a deep breath, exhale, put on a big smile, and head inside.

Lynn is an excellent cook, and she went all out for this dinner. There had to be at least thirty people at her house, eating, drinking, and laughing. The women gathered inside while the men assembled on the back patio, and the kids ran wild up and down the street. The camaraderie helped me forget my concern over Dawn and Mya. St. Pete is a small town, and everybody knows somebody through somebody else. It's possible they attended school together or worked for the same company before Dawn moved to Pensacola.

After the guest had left, Lynn, Dawn, their youngest sister Pam, and I put the last of the dishes away. Dawn says she wants to thank me for opening my home to Dexter. "What do you mean?" I asked, blindsided as usual.

"LaDamien said Dexter could stay with you all until he decides what he wants to do now that he's out of school. Didn't he talk it over with you?"

"Yes," would be the appropriate response in a normal situation, but the look of disbelief on my face said otherwise. How LaDamien could decide this without my input or approval was a mystery. I'm growing so tired of not being an equal partner in our marriage. Instead of trying to sugarcoat it, I excused myself and sought out my husband. He was out back talking with Lynn's backyard neighbor.

"When were you going to tell me that Dexter was coming to live with us?" I asked, continuing before he could answer. "How could you make a decision that affects all of us and not ask for my input or blessings? You are so damn selfish and inconsiderate." My anger was apparent. If possible, smoke would have been coming out of my ears.

LaDamien and the neighbor were both looking at me as though I had lost my mind. He stepped towards me and suggested I lower my voice. "She just asked me this afternoon, and I didn't think it would be a problem. It's only temporary until he finds out if he got into USF.

If not, he's joining the military, so we are talking three months tops. If I had known our home wasn't open to my family, I would never have made the suggestion."

Stunned, bewildered, in awe, either one would do to describe my disbelief. He made the suggestion. He who is never at home? He who is running around cheating at every moment? He can't be serious. "LaDamien, this isn't us welcoming your family in our home. It's about respect, and you disrespected me by not asking how I felt." By now, Dawn had joined us outside.

"Baby boy, I thought you had discussed this with your wife. I'm not leaving my son down here if it's going to be an issue." Dawn knew whether it was an issue or not; Dexter wouldn't be returning to Pensacola with her.

If looks could kill, I would have been dead on the spot, right in Lynn's family room. The stares that greeted me when I re-entered the house were loaded and cocked. LaDamien's mom, who didn't think it was a woman's place to question her husband in front of others, was displeased with my outburst. Lynn interjected, reminding me that her husband is never at family functions. She suggested I calm down and wait until LaDamien and I were in the confines of our own home to have this discussion. "Don't put your business in the streets like that," she admonished, almost making me laugh. Did she think that I didn't know that LaDamien told them everything that happens in our house? Everything, I'm sure, but how he has cheated on me since day one. Then again, they may know that as well since everyone else in town knows.

It is almost eight, and this day has worn on me. Ariel is outside talking with her cousins. When I walk up, they grow silent. Leaving me to wonder what they were discussing, but it will have to wait. "Gather your things so we can leave." She pouts, but it's a mute issue. This visit is over.

Ten minutes later, we are in the SUV and heading home. "I'm sorry for the way I reacted back there and will call everyone tomorrow and apologize."

It's the best I have to offer to break the silence that is suffocating us. LaDamien looks straight ahead, and Ariel continues to play her PSP. My husband and daughter have me feeling like an outsider. It very well could be my imagination, or maybe I'm losing my mind, but I swear they have formed some sort of alliance against me. Several attempts to spark conversation with LaDamien garners no response. He has shut down.

    LaDamien let Ariel and me out at the house and drove off. His reaction is far more dramatic than it needs to be. Then it dawns on me that this is his way of getting me to accept the decision he has made without discussing it. He knows I can't stand to argue with him, and circumstances such as this would definitely lead to a full assault. It has been a while since we have fought verbally. I promised not to engage him after Ariel became upset one night. We were fighting, and she entered our bedroom crying hysterically, begging us to stop. That night I had slapped LaDamien and told him to get out. He left and didn't return for several days. That was months ago. What we fought about seems a mystery now. I just know it had to do with his infidelity. What was so mind-boggling about that incident is that instead of going to be with his bitch, he went and stayed with a relative.

    Hours have passed since LaDamien left, and I have had time to think things through. Having Dexter here may not be a bad thing after all. LaDamien has said many times that his nephew's main problem has been the lack of family structure and not having a male role model in his life. I convince myself that this will be a positive, not only for Dexter but for our family. Surely, LaDamien plans to play an active role, or he wouldn't have agreed to have him move in. When I hear the garage door open, I make my way downstairs to let LaDamien know that I have thought things over, and I agree with this decision. He has my blessings and total support. LaDamien is relieved by my change of heart. He informs me that Dexter is getting his things out of the Escalade.

    Dexter settled in quickly. He didn't get into USF and was thinking of enrolling at St. Petersburg College. Still, somehow that idea was lost after LaDamien offered him the opportunity to work for LaDamien Bryson Enterprises and earn some extra cash. The two were bonding well. LaDamien embraced the opportunity to guide Dexter and had commented that it was like having a son. After Ariel was born, we had discussed having more children, but that changed when it became apparent that LaDamien wouldn't be faithful. When he first took up with Mya, I considered getting pregnant again. I quickly remembered it didn't work the first time and would probably make things worse if I tried it again.

My trips to Baltimore have all but ceased. I'm so happy to be home and back into my routine. The constant travel affected my relationship with Ariel, whom I'm sure was starting to feel abandoned by me. However, it strengthened her relationship with her dad, even if that meant developing some of his negative traits.

My friends Debra and Karen have invited me to a Passion Party. When they first asked, my hesitation was evident, but after much prodding, I'm glad to be here. The party is for married women only. We have talked about everything imaginable to keep the flames burning in the bedroom. Some of these women are simply freak nasty. They are faithful followers of the new wave of urban erotica books and credit them for all the new tricks they have learned in the bedroom. By the end of the evening, I have learned new uses for various fruits, and none begin with eating them, although most end that way. I wonder if LaDamien would take fruit that had been in my vagina, retrieve it with his tongue, and then eat it. He has performed oral sex on me before, but nothing like that. But I'm willing to give it a try, as well as some other tricks tossed out during a general conversation.

Debra and Karen are teasing me, claiming that I was in with the party consultant longer than anyone else. They wanted to know what I purchased and when my order arrived if I was planning on using the items on my husband. Karen burst out laughing and added, "Or did you get a bunch of toys for yourself." They both laughed at my expense, and I had to admit the drinks from the evening had me chuckling also.

The girls dropped me off shortly after eleven. LaDamien was waiting up and curious to see what I had purchased. When I advised him that my order wouldn't be in for another week, he seemed disappointed. I quickly shifted his mood by telling him about some of the new things I had learned. He was alert and at attention immediately. Just the mention of kinky sex seemed to excite him, and I wondered if this was all it took to keep him home. If the things those women discussed were the things Faye, Mya, and the others knew would lure my husband away, then it would work for me to get him back. If LaDamien knew he could get it at home, he would undoubtedly stop running out into the streets searching for it.

His first taste was about to be served. I undressed in the bathroom, closed the lid on the toilet, and called for LaDamien. When he entered the bathroom and saw me standing there, he was taken aback. I pointed my index finger at him and gestured for him to come forward. When he was standing within inches of me, I pointed down. Instead of him dropping to his knees and tasting my delicacies as the women suggested, he took my finger and forced it inside of me. With his hand over mine, he slowly guided me in masturbating.

Convinced I knew to continue on my own, he removed his hand and started to undress. Completely nude himself, he pushed the door close and watched me intently. I could tell by the lust in his eyes that I turned him on with the show I was performing. From deep in his throat, as if he was having trouble breathing, he instructed me to get on the counter. He stepped forward and lifted my right foot onto the edge of the toilet seat. Next, he lifted my left leg, so my foot was on the edge of the sink bowl. I was so uncomfortable and no longer felt sexy. LaDamien sensed that the mood was dying and began sucking my breast as he guided my contorted body backward until I was resting against the mirror.

"Now stroke that wet pussy so I can see," he instructed as he stepped backward, watching, his breathing heavy once again. I felt like such a fool doing this for my husband. Even if it was turning him on as I had never seen before, it felt awkward. As I began to relax and focus on LaDamien, my embarrassment began to fade. I was falling into a rhythm that was taking us both over the edge. As I was about to explode, LaDamien stepped forward, and removed my fingers from my dripping hole, and filled me with his stiff shaft. He sucked the juices from my fingers. Then tongue kissed me. For a second, I tensed up, but that only made his kiss more eager, and his pumping increased. Less than a minute passed, and his whole body froze. He'd had a mind-blowing orgasm. I smiled, pleased that he was pleased.

The following morning I was up early cooking breakfast for my family. Everyone was happy and in a great mood. I looked around the table from face to face and smiled. Yes, this was my family—this was how it should always be. At least things were flowing in a tempo of my liking. Finally, LaDamien looked satisfied and happy to be here in this moment with me.

After clearing the dishes from the table and loading them into the dishwasher, I prepared for work. LaDamien and Dexter had already left. Ariel was downstairs waiting to get dropped off at school. I showered and dressed, then headed downstairs, instructing Ariel it was time to go.

No sooner than Ariel stepped out of the car, I pressed LaDamien's number into the phone. He answered on the first ring. "Hey baby, how is your day going?" It has been less than an hour since he left the house, but I'm already missing him.

"Nothing to complain about," he says. "Have you dropped Ariel off yet?" I respond that I've already dropped her off. He says, "Good, good," but nothing else.

"Do you have a busy day planned? Maybe we can grill some steaks and burgers for dinner. If you can have the grill going by the time I get home, I'll do the rest." It's the first thing that comes to mind. LaDamien laughs. "What's so funny?" He tells me he was listening to *The Steve Harvey Morning Show*, which surprises me. For as long as I can remember, he listened to Tom Joyner.

"So when did you start listening to Steve?"

"For quite some time now, you are the one who got me hooked." This makes me smile.

"Oh, didn't know I had such an effect on you," I say in a teasing manner.

LaDamien replies, "More than you know. What time are you coming home so I can have the grill ready?" I tell him no later than five-thirty. He assures me it will be piping hot when I arrive and lets me know he has to go. My need to ensure he will follow through has me calling several more times throughout the day to confirm we will be eating dinner as a family.

TayJohn has been in St. Petersburg for over a month now. We have crossed paths several times on campus. He has updated me on his relocation. Letting me know he found a condo over in Tampa and has made several new friends within the company. "You guys sure do love happy hour around here," he commented one day when we were on the elevator together. "At least twice a week, I receive an invite."

"You're prime real estate around here," I tease. "The women want a part of you." He caught me off guard when he asked if that included me. Thankfully the elevator door opened, and several people got on. TayJohn had a contagious personality, not to mention he was attractive and fine as hell. Right now, I was satisfied with what I had at home. Now that things were improving, there was nothing another man could say to make me consider looking their way. I loved LaDamien too much.

The elevator stopped on the sixth floor, and TayJohn made his way out. He turned back and remarked, "You can email me the answer if you like." He received a confused stare in response. "About the prime real estate," he said and walked away smiling.

LaDamien

Having Dexter here has been a great distraction from Mya, whom I have not spoken with, going on for four months now. To say I miss her would be an understatement. She refuses to answer my calls, and when I stop by her house, she doesn't come to the door even though her car is in the driveway. As much as I hate not being with her, I know it's for the best. Sure, I can't offer her the relationship she desires to have, and it's unfair of me to expect her to hang around indefinitely. Still, a day doesn't go by without my longing for her touch and wishing I could hear her voice. This is why I'm sitting here calling her work number and leaving a long detailed message, almost begging her to give me a call. After I finish speaking, I wait for the phone prompt that asks if I wish to discard this message and record a new one, to press whatever number designated for this action. As I listen to the instructions, Dexter jumps in the car, and I hang up. She will get the message and probably think I'm a fucking idiot. A painstaking grimace streaks my face. A sign my mind is tormented.

Kim is trying so hard, and I must admit that lately, she has turned it up more than a notch. She has been attentive both mentally and physically. The change in her makes me wonder where our marriage would be had she been this way all along. But deep down inside, I know it will never be enough. I must be honest with myself and admit that Mya is the only woman who can fully satisfy me.

"What's on the agenda?" Dexter asks, full of excitement. He has been joining me on scouting tours as I view properties and seek new leads. Dexter isn't interested in going to college. I figured this out the second day after his arrival. Because he's so undisciplined, he will never make it in the service, which is where he truly needs to be. No, Dexter is about making a quick dollar, and when I told him I would pay him to help me out, he jumped at the opportunity. That was six weeks ago. School started last month, and he has never mentioned the military or shown an interest. Although Dawn claimed that was his second option.

Kim seems to like the idea of having Dexter around. She has been incredibly supportive even when she's mulling over the fact that college and the military seem like distant thoughts to my nephew. Last night she suggested a couple of entry-level positions her employer has available. She urged Dexter to come to the office the following day to apply. But Dexter is a lot like his uncle. He doesn't want to be tied down to a desk or confined by set hours and rules that track his every movement. I thanked Kim for the suggestion and agreed to discuss it with Dexter when he came in, but I already knew he would balk at the idea.

"We have a couple of site visits to make in Tampa, and afterward, I have to meet with a contractor about some work that needs to get done on a home that has a contract pending. Why, what's up with you?" We are sitting in front of the building he just exited in the Queensmark apartment complex. Dexter has met some girl and has been spending many nights here.

Dexter looks at the apartment building then informs me that he promised his girl Sheree that he would help her and her mom move to their new place. They expect him back at four, which shouldn't be a problem. We should finish for the day by three-thirty. "Will you need any help?"

"Nah, I got it under control. Sheree has two younger brothers and a few cousins who will also help." He replies, but minutes later, he adds, "Hey, but I may need a ride home, though, cause they are moving to Bradenton.

"I guess I should start looking for a new girl cause I ain't got no transportation, and she ain't all that to stress over how I'm going to get over there to see her." Looking at my nephew, I wonder if he thinks I'm going to pick him up from Bradenton, which is almost thirty miles south of us. All for some girl, he's already thinking about dropping.

"Looks like Sheree just lost a helper," is my response as I pull on to fifty-fourth avenue and head towards the interstate.

It is almost three p.m., and Dexter has received another call from Sheree. "If you answer, it will only make it harder to say no," was my advice the first time she called. Her cousins have backed out, and she needs Dexter to come and help with the move. He listens to her fourth voice message, and then my phone rings. It can't be.

Suddenly it feels as if the air has decompressed, and my breathing has ceased. The number staring back at me in 3-D is Mya's. She's returning my call. Not wanting to hear her tell me to leave her alone and not call again, I allow the call to go into voice mail as I have instructed Dexter to do for Sheree's insistent pleas.

"You alright, Unc?" he asks me.

"Yeah, I just thought about something." My phone is buzzing, alerting me that I have a new message. Dexter can't be in the car when I listen to Mya's message. If it's harsh, my reaction will show on my face, and I will need time to digest her words. A convenience store is coming up, so I pull into the parking lot, hand Dexter a few dollars, and instruct him to run inside, grab a couple of sodas and some chips.

"*Hi LaDamien,*" the message begins. "*You are unbelievable. After all this time, you're still thinking about me. I'm sorry you're hurting and still missing me. The truth is I miss you too. After all this time, you would think that we would be over this thing we had. I don't understand why you won't be faithful to your wife since you have no intentions of ever leaving her. This whole situation is crazy, and I don't see how picking up where we left off is going to fix anything.*" She pauses, and I can hear her sigh like she's trying to make a painful decision. I'm hoping beyond all hope that she's about to agree to give me a second chance, but that hope gets dashed when she says, "*Let's just leave things as they are. Bye, Mr. Bryson.*"

When I spot Dexter, he's standing in line. Two people are ahead of him, so I decide to call Mya back. The fact that she returned my last call has given me hope that she will agree to see me if I say the right thing. She answers on the first ring,

"Hey, you called?" I ask.

"You know I called, and I know you listened to my message. Stop playing games." She doesn't sound annoyed. She sounds like a woman who knows me inside out. Mya's prepared for my return call. My nervousness comes through as I try to laugh it off.

"I want to see you," I blurt out. "Can we do something tonight, maybe go to dinner or get ice cream and walk on the beach? Whatever you want to do," she hesitates for the longest. Dexter is finally on his way back, and I need to end the call. Mya's silence lasts so long I ask if she's still there. She lets me know that she's thinking. Dexter is getting in when Mya finally lets me know her answer.

"What will be different, LaDamien? Seriously, how long am I supposed to put up with this?" She's going on and on, and her voice seems magnified, causing concern that Dexter can hear her or tell it's a female at the very least. Any other time I would have simply ended the call then pretended my battery died. But today, I can't take that risk. If I hang up, she may never speak to me again.

"Okay, pick-me-up at six. We can ride over to *The Crab Trap* in Bradenton and have dinner."

My face brightens. My world will be back on its axis soon. After ending the call with Mya, I let Dexter know he can go and help his girl move tonight. He smiles, happy he will not have to let Sheree go so soon. Then he surprises me by saying, "sometimes the pussy is so good you just can't let it go, huh, Unc?"

"What's that supposed to mean?" I ask with a defensive edge to my tone.

"Come on, man, I know you got some honey on the side. My mom's nem' be talking about you all the time. How Kim so good to you but you can't keep it at home. Shoot, my mom even told Aunt Pam that she knows one of the women you're messing with. I'm just saying, it's cool with me, and I got your back, man." Dexter rubs the stubble under his chin, unconcerned that he just accused me of being unfaithful to my wife. The topic needs to get addressed with him, but for now, I'm just grateful for the excuse to get out tonight so that I can see Mya.

It is a little after three p.m., and Dexter is exiting my Escalade and heading up to Sheree's apartment. He will have his work cut out for him hauling furniture down from her second-floor apartment. We agree that he will text me the address, and I will pick him up no later than ten-thirty p.m. This way, we will be home by eleven, eleven-thirty at the latest. My next stop is the office to check my messages and see what Wanda has been doing. Since Dexter started working with me, I have spent less time at the office and more time trying to secure new properties and sell others. With the housing market in the condition it's in right now, we barely break even on some deals.

Wanda comments that it's been so long since she's seen me that she almost forgot what I looked like. The comment draws a chuckle from me. She stands and walks around the desk to stand beside me. She has a habit of watching me read the messages, always ready to answer any questions I may have.

"Do you notice anything different about me?" Wanda asks.

The burgundy tint in her shoulder-length hair is barely noticeable. The hair color is the only difference I recognize in her appearance. "That's nice."

"Horace didn't even notice. I got it done over the weekend, and he still hasn't said a word."

Wanda and Horace have been married so long they no longer see each other. I've never noticed her calling him repeatedly throughout the day to see what he's doing as Kim does me. It probably hurt her more than she's letting on. Women don't do things to their appearance and do not care if their husbands notice. Changing their hair color was significant, so I made sure to add that the color looked good on her. Then I went so far as to retrieve two hundred dollars from my pocket and suggest she do something nice for herself. She smiled as she folded the money in half, and then in half again, and tuck the bills into her bra.

"Thanks, LaDamien. Is there anything you need for me to do before I head out?"

There isn't, so I head to my office, closing the door behind me with the messages in hand. It only took a short time to return my calls and sign the few documents from my inbox. I have no reason to hang around. It's four forty-five giving me just enough time to get home, shower, and change before Kim and Ariel arrive. My cell phone rings as I'm heading out the door. It's Kim calling again. Before she utters a word, I tell her I'm with a contractor and will call her back shortly.

Shortly, is over an hour later, but it's Kim who is calling me back. She's fuming that I didn't start the grill and not home as promised. *The grill!* How could I forget?

Kim wants to know where I'm at and what time I will be returning. She still wants to put the steaks on the grill as planned. The explanation came quickly. "Dexter went over to Bradenton to help a friend move, and I'm on my way to pick him up. We should save the steaks for tomorrow because it's getting late, and we may not be back until eight or later depending on the traffic."

Kim seems to calm down a bit but doesn't want to put off grilling the steaks. "If you will be back by eight, then I can go ahead and start the grill. Can you at least remember to stop by *Publix* and pick up some of their southern-style potato salad?"

She's testing me to see if I'm going to get Dexter. Kim is trying so hard, but I keep letting her down. The best thing for me to do is turn around and head back home to my wife and daughter. But this will not happen. It's too late to turn around. Mya is sitting next to me, arms folded across her chest, eyes staring out the window, her breathing quickening, and her fingers playing a dance on an invisible keyboard. A sure sign that my call is annoying her. This conversation with Kim needs to come to an end, or else.

We approach the toll plaza for the Skyway Bridge. Instead of traveling through the express lane for *SunPass* users, I follow the *Honda* Accord ahead of me into one of the paying lanes. The toll-taker counts out four one-dollar bills. Change for the five I have handed her. Kim is quiet, listening intently for anything that would indicate someone else is in the car. The toll-taker thanks me and bids me a good evening. Finally, Kim says goodbye.

Mya pulls her hand away before I can touch her. "This was a mistake. We should have continued our hiatus, making it permanent." She's staring out of the window. Her attention is on the sun that is setting beyond the waters of Tampa Bay.

"Don't say that. We are going to figure this out. The past four months were hell for me, and I don't ever want to go through that again. Just give me a little more time, and you won't be sorry. I promise."

LOVE...

- is patient
- is kind
- is not rude
- does not envy
- is not self-seeking
- will not lie
- is not proud
- is not quick to anger
- protects
- does not boast
- does not record wrongs
- trusts
- hopes
- perseveres
- finds no joy in evil but celebrates truth
- never fails

Mya

Letting LaDamien go had to be the hardest thing I had ever done in my life. But after his total disrespect and disregard for not only my feelings but those of his wife and child, I could no longer stomach being with him. It seemed no matter how much he did for me, how much fun we had, or how close we became, he ended up doing something to make me doubt his actions. Sometimes I think he does it subconsciously to thwart his plans to leave. Maybe it's some sort of psychosis that prevents him from taking a chance on whatever he wants for fear he may fail.

His actions had been wearing on me for some time, but the trip to Orlando was the final straw. I know what we are doing is wrong, but it doesn't mean we have to be tacky about it. LaDamien knew his family was planning to use that timeshare. Whatever happened to delay Kim and Ariel's arrival didn't give him the right to have me there knowing they were coming. It made me feel cheap and dirty, and like I had gone to their home and slept in their bed. Then to add insult, instead of coming clean when he knew it was Kim that I saw, he lied and stated he was only a short distance behind me. Little did he know, I pulled over into the emergency lane and waited thirty minutes for him to pass just to confirm he was lying. He's so smug too, knowing he got caught in his lies, he played the coward and turned his phone off. But I knew the plan already. He would return from his trip and show up at my front door with a major attitude trying to show me how I was overreacting and imagining things. You would think by now he would know I'm not his wife, and he can't manipulate me the way he does her. Knowing he would show up sooner or later, I made plans to visit a cousin in Jacksonville for the weekend. My bags were already in the car, so when seven p.m. rolled around Friday evening, I could hit the Interstate.

As I drove I-4 towards I-95, my mind told me to ride by the Grand Vista to see if they were still there. But that would have been stupid. If they were, what was I going to do, confront him? No, my problem was not with Kim, it was with her husband, and that was who my beef was with. Plus, Kim saw me as clearly as I had seen her. They were still in Orlando. I figured since he had not called. He'd probably worked his magic on her, and she had turned a blind eye to his behavior, yet again. At this point, LaDamien could have kissed my black ass. He wasn't worth the time or energy it required for me to get upset because, in the end, he wouldn't see where he had done anything wrong.

Sure, as the sun began to set on the west coast of Florida, LaDamien began blowing up my phone as soon as they stepped foot back in St. Petersburg. I turned the phone off and told my cousin Cheryl that my plans had changed, and I wouldn't be leaving until the following morning. If I planned my departure right, I would get back in town just in time for work.

A beautiful bouquet of flowers was delivered to my desk two hours into my workday. The second bouquet came three days later. As hard as it was becoming not to call LaDamien back, I knew I had to stick to my decision. This whole situation was horrible for me. There was no point in continuing to give my love to someone who didn't appreciate me or what I had to offer. When the third bouquet, a dozen long-stemmed red roses, arrived the following week, I felt my resolve slowly fading away. Instead of calling LaDamien, I called Angie.

"He's driving me crazy," I whined over wings and fries at *Hooters*. Angie was listening, being the great friend she is.

"Well, you knew this was wrong from the beginning. I was hoping you would just have a fling and get over it. Never in my wildest imagination did I think things would go this far." Angie looked pained over my situation. She never gave her seal of approval on this whole affair. She said it wasn't a good idea from the beginning. But my friend knew from the way I talked about LaDamien from the first time we met that I was going to go for it. Nothing she could do or say would have stopped me.

We stopped talking briefly when our waitress came over to ask if we needed anything. "Affairs aren't supposed to be this way. He knows he isn't going to leave Kim, so why he's acting like this is beyond me." I continued after the waitress walked away.

My head was starting to pound. Just being the other woman was never my goal, and he never made me feel that way. There was something between LaDamien and me from the start. He was the biblical forbidden fruit, and just like Eve, I ignored God's warning and greedily partook of the fruit. Now he had become Paul's proverbial thorn in my side.

Angie must have been reading my mind because no sooner did I think the thought, she spoke it. "This isn't just any affair. LaDamien does love you; at least he thinks he does. His behavior is typical of someone who is in spiritual warfare within themselves. On the one hand, he wants to be married and a good husband and father, but on the other hand, he wants to pursue what makes him happy. He probably thinks that God is going to punish him if he leaves his wife to be with another woman." Then out of the blue, she asked me if I had considered talking with my Pastor.

"And say what, 'forgive me, Father, for I have sinned' are you serious? I could never go to my Pastor and tell him I'm sleeping with a married man." Angie was tripping for sure.

"Then go to a Pastor that doesn't know you, one who doesn't know LaDamien. I'm sure you are feeling guilty about this whole thing, and if you seek counsel and pray about it, you'll be stronger and will not let him back in."

Angie was wrong about the guilt. I stopped feeling guilty when I realized what a fool Kim had to be to stay married to LaDamien. However, I was spiritually weak for allowing myself to get into this mess. Maybe it would be good if I talked to someone about this situation. I need to move forward. Thoughts of LaDamien always resided near the surface. No matter what was on the television, the radio, or in the paper, it reminded me of him, and the longing was growing more intense.

The flowers and the calls had stopped, but every now, and then I would see LaDamien drive by my house. One night, or shall I say, one early morning, I returned home from a night out with friends. My girlfriend Jaime had driven and was dropping me off. We turned on to my street as LaDamien was turning off. Jaime turned to me and spoke first, "Was that who I think it was?"

"Yeah, can you believe it? It's been six weeks."

Jaime was concerned. She pointed out it was after three in the morning, and my ex-married man was doing a drive-by. She let me know this was cause for concern. I downplayed LaDamien's behavior as he probably needed a break from Kim's annoying ass. He probably drove by out of habit. Jaime wasn't buying it, but she didn't say anything else. She waited until I was in the house and the door closed. I looked out the window a few minutes later and caught her riding by my house. It was a blessing and a curse to have friends that cared so much about my well-being.

Seeing LaDamien the night before piqued my senses, and I became more aware of my surroundings. After seeing him ride by my house that night, I started to see him more often riding up and down the main street that leads into my subdivision, near my job, or near the gym where he had not been in quite some time. My first inclination was to confront him but then figured if I ignored him, he would eventually see how ridiculous he was being and move on.

Rachel, a new co-worker, was one of those happily married women who thought everyone else should be just as happy. The second we confirmed our office friendship, she began inviting me to functions hoping that she and her husband could hook me up with "some nice guy." One of those functions was her husband's Wednesday night kickball league. Grown people should not be playing this childhood game, let alone the City sponsoring a league for it. But there I was on Wednesday nights having a blast. I sipped on Margarita's at *Ferg's Sports Bar*, where the teams and their supporters gathered afterward. Rachel pointed out which guys were single and which ones were available and safe to date. My disappointment was evident. There wasn't much to choose between. Some of these guys are playing in this league because they didn't want to grow up, while others looked like they just needed another excuse to consume more alcohol. This outing wasn't promising, and the more I ventured out with Rachel, the more I longed for LaDamien.

Aside from the fact that he was married, LaDamien was my ideal man. But according to Angie, he couldn't be my ideal man because he was married and because he's cheating on his wife. He possessed a character flaw that was not on my list of what I wanted in a mate, so I needed to stop making that assertion. Her assertion bothered me because if LaDamien were not married, he would be the man of my dreams. Instead of getting over LaDamien, it seemed the more time passed, the more I questioned my decision to leave him alone. Out of sight out of mind; or absence makes the heart grow fonder. It could be one or the other with me on any given day. Angie was right, I needed to talk to someone, and I needed to do it quickly before I lost my mind.

Pastor Timothy Epps was the Senior Pastor of First Ebenezer Baptist Church. We met at a local Urban League dinner. He was seated at the table next to me, along with his beautiful wife, Beverly. Pastor Epps looked to be in his early fifties. He noticed the absence of a ring on my left-hand ring finger. Immediately he began questioning why I wasn't married. His wife seemed embarrassed for him and kept scolding him to knock it off. Before he diverted his attention to other conversations taking place at the table, he handed me his card. He suggested I visit his church because they had some available men who would love to meet a nice young woman such as myself.

"As a matter of fact, our Singles Ministry would probably suit you well. They meet the third Friday of each month and have planned outings on fourth Fridays," he informed me. His wife, adding that they also had a bowling league that played on Tuesdays throughout the summer.

"Do you bowl?" she asked.

No, I don't bowl. After attending the Singles Ministry meeting, I knew I wouldn't participate in their monthly gatherings. The women were downright rude and made it clear they had first dibs on the few men in attendance. The ratio was something like five to one, including a couple of guys who very well could have been on the down-low. But I didn't let the experience turn me against the church. On the following Sunday morning, I decided to attend First Ebenezer's worship service.

For the last year, I had been attending Bethel Inspirational Baptist Church. It was a bit of a fluke. A friend had invited me to her church for Friends & Family Day. We never discussed the church. We just made plans for her to pick me up for Sunday Service.

St. Petersburg has so many churches that you could literally have ten or more, less than a mile from each other. Some even sat on the same city block. So it wasn't until we turned in the church's parking lot that it dawned on me that we were at the church LaDamien held his membership. The service was so fulfilling that I decided to come back the following week. Luckily, LaDamien wasn't there that Sunday, but when I told him I had attended the service and enjoyed it, he told me I should go where my soul was getting fed. If that was Bethel, then so be it, and I had been attending ever since.

LaDamien didn't attend church as much as he professed. I even questioned him a few times as to whether or not he wasn't attending because it bothered him for me to be there. He assured me that it didn't, "It just pisses me off that my wife knows how much I want us to attend church as a family, but every Sunday morning, it's a fight getting her to come. Not to mention Ariel isn't being encouraged to attend."

This bothered me because it was just another indicator that he had no intentions of ending his marriage. So on the Sundays, Kim decided to attend church, LaDamien made sure they attended the early morning service. Our paths never crossed until one Sunday when his entire family attended the eleven a.m. service. When I spotted Kim, she was staring at me so hard, and with such indignation, she could have burned a hole straight through my soul. Her glare was a constant throughout the service. When Pastor Lawrence finished the benediction, I intended to make a bee-line for the door, but someone called my name. When I turned to see who it was, LaDamien's sister Dawn was waving.

Dawn and I met one weekend when LaDamien and I drove to Destin, Florida, for a weekend getaway. Destin is due east of Pensacola, off the Gulf of Mexico, where Dawn resides. We're at the gas station filling the tank for our return trip home when a car pulled up, and the passenger yelled out to LaDamien. My window was up, so she couldn't see through the dark tinted windows that someone was in the car. LaDamien could have easily lied, but instead, he brought Dawn around to the passenger side and opened the door. She didn't flinch or seem shocked. She shook my hand and said hello. She turned her attention to LaDamien. Dawn was upset he came to town without calling to let her and Dexter know he was visiting. To make up for it, LaDamien promised to call the next time we were in the area. A month later, he did just that as we're heading to nearby Fort Walton Beach for my cousin's wedding.

It was evident that Dawn was not fond of Kim, and her drawing attention to the fact that we knew each other was proof. Since I never discussed Kim with Dawn, I didn't know where her disdain for the woman originated. I wasn't trying to forge an alliance to prove any point, especially since LaDamien and I were not speaking at the time.

We embraced each other and said a quick hello. When I turned to leave, Dawn told Dexter to give me a hug. Dexter obliged even though we were never formally introduced. Once, Dawn and Dexter had stopped by our hotel room looking for LaDamien, but he had gone off with some old college friend of his, and they quickly left, having never entered the room. That was the only time he was in my presence, but I don't believe he saw me.

The moment I saw LaDamien and Kim approaching, I released Dexter and told Dawn I'd see her later. She seemed to love the drama she was trying to create, but I wasn't going to be a participant. LaDamien and I hadn't spoken in weeks leading up to that Sunday, and I didn't want to give him any ideas. Plus, we were at church. I had enough sins to ask for forgiveness. I didn't need to add fighting Kim in the Lord's house to the list. From that Sunday on, whenever LaDamien attended the late service, Kim was by his side, staring me down and rolling her eyes. I know she was praying for my soul to enter the depths of a burning hell. She had no clue I'm finished with her husband.

Attending First Ebenezer was a much-needed distraction. The choir was fabulous, which is high on my list of priorities when it comes to church. If the choir doesn't move me, then my visit will be cut short. Another turn-off is a minister who conducts his sermon as if he were standing at a podium before a room full of college students giving a lecture. Even the best choir in the world couldn't get me to stay if a lecturer led the church. Pastor Epps wasn't a lecturer. Contrary to his articulate, highly-educated demeanor at the banquet, he was a straight-up county preacher in the pulpit. Constantly, my eyes veered up from my note-taking to reaffirm that the man jerking around in the pulpit was the same man who invited me to join his flock.

On my third visit to First Ebenezer, Pastor Epps preached about being single in today's society. On this Sunday, the Singles Ministry was in charge of the service and hosted a meet and greet afterward. Each member was encouraged to bring someone to church that was single. I scan the room when visitors are asked to stand. I want to see if anyone stood out. Again, I was left disappointed and wondering if perhaps my physical requirements were set so high that I was blocking potential mates. My wondering ended quickly. Pastor Epps answered the question when he announced his sermon title, "When You Can't See the Forest for Looking at The Trees."

"Ouch," was my mantra for the morning service because Pastor Epps was knocking on my door for sure.

"He's not tall enough, she's too fat, he doesn't make enough money, she's got kids, and the list goes on and on. If that kind of stuff is keeping you from getting to know someone, no wonder you're still alone...."

By the time the service ended, I had convinced myself Pastor Epps would be the perfect counselor. I would find peace and finally release this stronghold LaDamien had on me. The following morning at nine a.m., I was seated in his office, attempting to pour my heart out. I wanted to tell this man how I was in love with another woman's husband. How hard it was for me to move on with my life. He looked at me with no expression on his chiseled face, his long fingers interlocked and providing a resting place for his square chin. At the banquet, I didn't pay close attention to his features. Not that I didn't think he was attractive then, but because I didn't want his wife to turn out to be one of those women who thinks every woman wants her man, so I made it a point not to pay much attention to him.

I began to detail my relationship with LaDamien so he could see why it was so hard for me to move on. Pastor Epps leaned forward and waved a dismissive hand towards me. "That doesn't matter. You need to stop this foolishness and stop it now. No matter what this man has told you, he's married, and in the eyes of God, that's all that counts. He's a liar and is going to say whatever he needs to. Your actions are hurting his wife, who is innocent in all of this."

My eyes are filling with tears I refuse to let fall. This was not what I was expecting. A lecture wasn't what I needed, but that is precisely what I got. Pastor Epps was not interested in anything I had to say. He didn't want to hear that LaDamien didn't love Kim when he married her or that she wasn't a supportive wife. All he cared about was that they were husband and wife, and I had defied God by engaging in this affair. When he stepped around his desk and reached for my hand so I could stand while he prayed for me, my mind was a web of confusion. How could he minister to me if he didn't want to hear what was happening in my life? How could he counsel me if he wasn't willing to provide real solutions to my problem? Why do people think that because someone is married, that's the final say in their lives? Are there no do-overs allowed? No recognition, a huge mistake was made? He stated his position as though the marriage was a life sentence, good or bad.

His prayer sounded like the teacher in the Charlie Brown shows, wha wha wha wha wha. Pastor Epps had let me down. When I entered his office, I knew that my actions were wrong and not pleasing in God's sight. What I needed was a compassionate ear and a spiritual guide to let go of this mess. If it were as simple as leaving LaDamien alone and getting on with my life, he wouldn't still be holding residence in my daily thoughts. If it were as simple as saying poof be gone, LaDamien would have long been dust in the wind. But it wasn't that simple. The emotions I felt and the experiences we shared were real. I didn't appreciate how the good Minister was discounting those emotions or praying over me as if I had demons that needed casting out.

After my session with Pastor Epps, I knew I wouldn't return to First Ebenezer. Instead, I tried to keep myself busy both at work and at home. When the thoughts overcrowded my mind, and no one was around to calm the chatter in my head, I went to the gym and worked out. At work, I agreed to take on extra projects to consume my downtime. But when LaDamien called today and left a long, drawn-out message begging me to give him one more chance, my knees buckled, and my heart gave way.

"*Mya, it's me LaDamien,*" this was my cue to delete the message. Hearing his voice alone was enough to awaken my desire to see him. Going against my better judgment, I listened on. "*Living without you is so hard. We all make mistakes, and I know you believe what you believe, but it's not what you think. Anyway, it's been four months now, and I can't believe you are still mad. Mya, I love you so*

much, and I swear if you give me a chance, I'll fix this. I'll make this up to you. I'm not perfect, Mya. I'm just a man that loves you like crazy and needs to have you in my life. Please, Mya, we can get beyond this."
Beep

Four months had passed, and he still wanted to be with me. This was crazy. He could go out and find another woman if he just couldn't be faithful. Honestly, after our split, it seemed as though everyone suddenly had information on how big of a player LaDamien was. Somebody always knew somebody who knew him and knew for a fact that he had messed with this person or that person. But one thing they all seemed to agree on was that something was going on between him and that woman who works for him. I would just roll my eyes and keep it moving because it was a mute issue then. As I peek out the window to see if a car outside is him, I begin to think about the stories I've heard and wonder if any of them is true. It will definitely make for great conversation over dinner.

LaDamien pulled into the driveway and stepped out of his SUV. I make my way outside and greet him before he reaches the door and tries to get inside. There will be no sexing going on here tonight. We agreed on dinner, and dinner is all he's getting.

"Hhmm, I missed you," he steps back and looks me over. As soon as we met on the walkway, he pulled me into his arms and kissed me as if his life depended on it.

"Ooh, baby, that was sweet, but what about the neighbors."

"What about them? I miss you, Mya. Don't you ever do that to me again." He admonished me, taking my hand as he walked me around to the passenger door and opened it for me.

Once in the drivers' seat, he reached over and kissed me again. We explored each other's mouths like it was our first time. LaDamien's large hand cupped my chin as he allowed his tongue to overpower me. If he could have his way, he probably would have tried to sex me right there in the front seat. When we finally came up for air, I was breathless.

"So L-Boogie, you missed me, huh?" I said, sounding like a silly teenager, calling him by the silly nickname he loved.

"Yeah, I missed you, and you don't even have a clue as to how much."

"You know, babe, if you stop playing games, we wouldn't have to go through that. I don't understand why you feel the need to lie to me. By now, you should know that you can't put much past me. Baby, I know your moves, your reactions, when you're nervous, and when you're lying." I was being serious now and wanted to be clear with him that I expect nothing less than full disclosure from now on. Let me be informed so I could make my decisions. "What would you have done if Kim showed up early and caught me at the timeshare? How would you have explained my presence to her?"

"Seriously, Mya, I want to put that behind us. I know you think you know what was going on, but you don't. We've already wasted four months, so let's not waste any more time. I apologize for whatever you think I did. There was a misunderstanding. It's over now. Let's just move forward, okay?"

Man = men admit nothing. They will stick to their lie like a stamp to an envelope. No, I'm not going to argue or keep beating this dead horse. But you best believe going forward, I'm going to call you on your mess as it unfolds. I think this as LaDamien backs out of my driveway. This man is something else. How can someone be so attentive, kind, and loving, also be so devious and cunning?

"So what have you been doing with yourself while we were apart?" I ask as I massage the back of his neck.

"Besides worrying myself over what you were up to, nothing. My nephew Dexter has moved here. He's staying with us and helping out with the business. Other than that, my life has been quite uneventful."

"I bet Kim was happy to have you all to herself," Out of the corner of my eye, I watch for his reaction. But he doesn't flinch. "Did you two try to work through any of your issues?"

"Please, can we not talk about Kim? The bottom line is you're what's important to me. You're the only one whose actions make a difference in my life, so no matter what Kim tries, it's wasted effort because she isn't you."

No sooner did he finish saying all the right things, the wrong thing happened, his phone rang. No doubt, it was his wife. LaDamien is exhibiting his typical negative body language, which signifies that he's saying whatever he needs to say to get her off the phone. Looking out the window and gazing upon the calm waters of Tampa Bay, I wonder why I was anxious to get back to this. Yes, I love LaDamien and missed the fun part of our relationship, but this part I hated. This part was representative of our reality. No matter how much we missed each other, no matter how sensual his kisses, how good dinner will be, or how intimate we become afterward, it always ends this way. The reality is staring me in my face right now. I'm sitting in this SUV listening to him and his dumb-ass wife. The voice in my head is screaming, "Why, why, why, did you give in and let them back into your life?"

Kim

"*And just* like that, she's back in our lives." I'm looking across the table at TayJohn, spilling my guts about my marriage, my husband, and that bitch he can't seem to let go. His expression is blank. He's either in shock or thinks I'm the biggest idiot he has ever met. We ended up here at the *Rare Olive* in downtown St. Petersburg. It's a nondescript bar on the corner of Central Avenue and Third Street.

TayJohn caught me coming out of the ladies' room located in an obscure part of the building. It was on the same floor as his office but at the back of the building in an area used mainly for storage. Thinking I was eluding others, I took the back elevator down but ended up walking right into him.

"You all right?" he asked the second he laid eyes on me. As bad as I wanted to say yes, I couldn't. LaDamien had been in rare form lately, and it had finally come to a head the night before. He stormed out of the house the way he usually did when he didn't want to face a problem head-on. I wasn't content riding out his temper tantrum, so I called him today to pick up where we had left off.

Calling from work and not waiting until we were at home was a bad idea. The things he said to me on that call were unthinkable, and I could hardly believe they were coming from his mouth. Still, my ears were not deceiving me. It was my husband on the other end of the line. He was yelling as loud as he could that he regretted the day he ever met me, and marrying me was the biggest mistake of his life.

We were standing near an empty office, so TayJohn led me inside and closed the door. "Are you okay? What's going on?" he was almost pleading for an answer.

Taking a deep breath and releasing some of my anxiety gave me a moment to pause and consider if I wanted to go there with this man. Since he relocated from Baltimore, he had made it a weekly ritual to stop by my office and invite me to lunch or happy hour. Sometimes it was to see if I was interested in participating in an after-hours activity with our colleagues.

A couple of Saturdays ago, while LaDamien was in Pensacola with Dexter, visiting Dawn, I agreed to attend a volunteer clean-up day at Fort Desoto Beach. TayJohn participated, and the two of us ended up on the same team. His demeanor away from work was the same as when he was in the office. He was a genuinely nice person with a laid-back attitude. Two hours into our four-hour block, we were laughing and joking around like we'd known each other forever. But this was different. This was my personal life, and I could be crossing a line. As if he had read my mind, he assured me that whatever I said to him was between him and me and wouldn't leave that room. My response to him was that it was a personal matter that I could not discuss with him. I excused myself under the guise of a three o'clock meeting, but he saw straight through that lie.

"Can we grab a bite to eat after work or go get a drink? You need someone to talk to, and I'm a great listener." He smiled, and the room brightened, so I went against my number one rule in business and agreed to meet him after work.

TayJohn chose the *Rare Olive* because, according to him, it never had more than a hand full of patrons when he patronized it in the past. With it being a Monday evening, he doubted if anyone would be there. He was right. Aside from the bartender, we were the only customers. We ordered our drinks and found a table off in a corner. "So talk," he instructed, and talk I did.

"I'm having marital problems," I began. "My husband is having an affair that has been going on for more than two years now. He's had affairs before but nothing like this. As a matter of fact, and I feel so stupid admitting this, but what the hell…huh…he was cheating on me when I decided to marry him." TayJohn didn't respond, just hunched his shoulders and took a sip of his rum and coke. So I continued.

"Mya, that's her name. She's not like the rest of them. Well, I guess she's just like them since she's screwing my husband, knowing damn well he has a wife and child at home. Anyway, I say she's different because the others were either fly by night floosies or, in the case of this one tramp named Faye, they were married women cheating on their husbands." Tears started to form in the corner of my eyes. TayJohn reached over and squeezed my hand, encouraging me to go on. "I think he's sleeping with his secretary too, but I've never been able to prove it. It's just a gut feeling, you know."

He was right. He was a great listener because he didn't utter a word while I talked, not even when he signaled to the bartender to bring us a refill.

"We've been married for eight years now, and I don't believe we've gone more than three or four months where I felt like I've had my husband all to myself. His nephew came to live with us, and I thought for sure this would be a positive move, but instead, he's teaching his nephew to be as petty and deceitful as he is.

"Dexter, his nephew, lies and covers for my husband. He even has my daughter covering for him. While I was in Baltimore on business, he left my child with some woman in our home. The description my daughter gives of the woman makes me believe it's Faye. Could he be that deceitful and lowdown? He won't admit it, and when I bring it up, he flies off the handle and goes into an uncontrollable rage. I brought it up again last night, and I thought he was going to hit me."

Three hours passed, with each second filled with the insanity I call my marriage. I needed him to say something, anything, to give me a feel for what he was thinking about me. He had to be wondering how a woman with my educational and professional credentials could end up in a relationship full of ignorant ghetto drama.

"Please don't repeat anything I said to you tonight to anyone. You are the only person I have confided in any of this too. Not even my closest friends know the hell I'm living in."

"Wow, you're still there, so you must not be tired yet," he chuckled. "Do you want my honest opinion, or are you just relieved to have someone you could unload this burden on finally? I think you're the first woman I have ever heard of who didn't run and tell her girlfriends every detail of her relationship. Maybe that's why you've stayed so long."

I pondered over what he'd just said. The truth was I had no idea why I stayed with LaDamien. Maybe I just didn't want to be alone, especially with my mother gone. He and Ariel are my family, and I didn't know how to move on.

"For now, I'm just glad to have someone to unload my burden on. I'm not in the mood to get judged." Glancing at my watch, I realize it's after eight, and I promised Debra I would pick Ariel up no later than seven. I check my phone, and Debra has not called. However, I have several missed calls from LaDamien but no messages. This is my cue to get going because I know his anger has increased with every missed call.

We walked towards the door, and I stop. "You go ahead because I can't risk getting seen with you." I laugh nervously. "All I need is to get you shot over my mess."

TayJohn's body stiffens, and he looks me straight in the eyes, "Is it that type of situation? Is he threatening you, or worse, is he physically abusing you?"

Quickly, I defuse these thoughts, "My husband has never abused me, but his verbal assaults can be deadly." It was a joke, but I don't want to give him any ammunition. Another nervous laugh escapes me. TayJohn asked me to take out my cell phone and type in a number.

"Save it under Taj. That's what everyone in B-more calls me, and if he sees it and questions you, tell him it's a female, like the member of SWV." He hesitates. "Kim, if you ever need to talk, need someone to check that nigga, or whatever, just call me. Night or day, I don't care. I'm here for you, and I got your back." TayJohn placed a soft peck on my forehead and stepped back to see my response. When I didn't respond, he told me goodnight and walked out.

By the time I gathered my nerve to leave, he was nowhere in sight. So I dialed his number to let him know I made it to my car.

"Didn't I say I had your back?" I could hear the concern in his voice, "I wasn't going anywhere until I made sure you made it to your car. Don't forget, and you can call me later if you need to, or if you just want to."

LaDamien

"Kim is having an affair." This is what I said to Mya as we shared a basket of wings and fries at *Hooters*.

She dismisses my claims quickly, saying I'm paranoid and acting like someone who was doing the cheating. Then she joked and said, "Oh, you are cheating, aren't you?" She didn't know how bad I wanted to slap that smirk off her face.

There was a time when I could talk to Mya about any and everything. She would listen intently as I shared my concerns and then offering her best advice. But somewhere along the way, we've lost that connection. As I continued to share my concerns about Kim, she seemed uninterested and attempted to change the subject several times.

"Baby, what proof do you have?" she finally asked me when I wouldn't let it go.

"It's just a feeling. Kim's more upbeat, attending more after-work functions with her colleagues, and leaving Ariel with friends. Just her overall demeanor reeks of someone new being in her life."

"So you have no proof, you're just mad because she's not sitting at home moping and wondering what you're doing?" Mya had a lot of nerve speaking to me this way, especially after all the sacrifices I'd made to be with her and provide her with the things she wanted. Now that I needed something from her, she had nothing but a slick mouth and nasty attitude to offer.

"Let's go!" I was already off the stool and pulled a twenty out of my wallet. Mya sighed heavily, taking her time as she wiped her hands and then grabbed her purse, a purse I bought for her a few weeks earlier. If I could have taken it and every other gift back, I would. But despite my disappointment, she still is the love of my life.

The ride back to Mya's office was in silence. She was upset that she didn't get to finish lunch, and I was upset that she didn't take my concerns seriously. Before she exited the car, she reached over and kissed me softly on the cheek. The urge to turn and allow her to kiss my lips was strong, but it wasn't going to be that easy for her, not anymore. If today had been a test, Mya would have failed miserably.

"LaDamien, I don't think Kim is cheating on you. Just relax, and you'll see." She said this as she stood outside the car and prepared to close the door. The car started to roll off. She was pissing me off with her condescending attitude. She slammed the door and stepped back as I sped away.

That was three weeks ago, and today I'm back where I was six months ago, missing her like crazy. She tried to call a few times, but I refused to answer the phone. The last thing I needed was to lose Kim and then have Mya thinking she could talk to and treat me any kind of way she chose. My focus needed to be on my wife and saving my family. Even Dexter had turned his back on me. We had a big argument one day when he didn't show up for work. He had been spending more and more time in Bradenton. When I chastised him about being irresponsible, he dared to throw my relationship with Mya in my face.

"You are the last person who needs to be talking about responsibility. Where is your damn responsibility to your wife?" he yelled through the phone. After all I had done for him. He had switched out just like that.

After that blow-up, he worked for me a few more weeks, and then he announced to Kim and me that he was moving out. He had found another job and gotten an apartment. Now he and Sheree were living together. It seemed no matter what I tried to do, who I tried to help, they always moved on without a second thought for what I had done for them. Mya was the last person I thought would treat me the way she has, knowing I would do anything for her, but she was no different. Still, I longed to have her, to be with her, to hear her voice at this moment.

"Hello," Mya sounds groggy. It's seven in the morning, and she's still asleep.

"What are you doing?" That was a stupid question but the only one that came to mind. She lets out a deep breath leading me to think she doesn't want to be bothered with me. Or maybe she isn't alone. This thought angers me, and I regret dialing her number. "I'm sorry, I shouldn't have called," I say before I hang up.

Minutes later, my phone rings, and when I look at the caller ID, Mya's name flashes across the screen. At least no man is there with her, a relief to my agitated thoughts.

"When is this madness going to stop?" she asks me.

Mya has no clue how bad I want to be able to answer that question. The madness will not stop until she's mine, and we're together in every sense of the word. But Mya hasn't proven herself to me or shown me why I should leave my wife for her. She has no idea the emotional turmoil she has caused. Mya has refused to step to the plate and show me that she's worthy of the sacrifices she wants me to make.

"You were on my mind this morning, so I thought I'd call and say hi, but I could tell that it was a mistake by the way you reacted." I don't know why these words flow from me when what I want to say is, *I Love you so much, Mya, and want to see you. Can I come over?* Again, she speaks my thoughts.

"Want to come over and get in bed with me? I'm off today."

Thirty minutes later, I'm deep inside of Mya, loving her with every ounce of my being. She's very moist, letting me know that she misses me as much as I miss her. Her body is squirming beneath me, prompting me to press my hands into hers, preventing her from going too far. My sex is intense and powerful. She's had two orgasms to my one but reaching a third. She's almost to her climax. I retreat, pulling her up from the bed and carrying her over to the dresser. There, I place her atop and spread her legs wide. I just stand looking between her legs for the longest before getting on my knees and sliding my tongue inside. Mya uses both hands to push herself up from the dresser, but I lower her back down and hold her in place. She screams with pleasure as I bring her to full climax.

"Mya, what are you doing to me? What are you doing to me?" I ask over and over again. We're back on the bed, and I sex her from behind. Her warmth engulfs me pulling me deeper and deeper until I can't go any further. Even then, I want to find a way to go even further inside her, if it's at all possible. She's trying her best to keep up with my thrusts as she grips my right hand, which I'm using to massage her clit. The harder my thrusts, the further her knees spread, and the deeper I feel myself inside of her. Suddenly she tightens her vaginal muscles, and all hell breaks loose. I'm quivering, trying to grip anything in reach. Mya falls forward, and I follow, the sudden movement sending another orgasmic surge. "Ohhh, shit, don't move, don't move. I love you, Mya. You just don't know." I moan.

We remained bound to each other as we drifted off into a deep sleep. Tranquility engulfed us for almost an hour but was interrupted by an announcement from my phone letting me know I have a new message. I reached for my phone, which was on the nightstand. It was a text from one of my friends.

"Since when did you start using text?" Mya asked as she tried unsuccessfully to wiggle from beneath me. My mouth covered hers preventing her from speaking further. Minutes later, we are back in a groove. It dawns on me that if I could make love to Mya like this every day, all day, I would be the happiest man in the world.

Mya and I have gotten our groove back. We aren't at each other's throats like we were before. Finally, I think she gets it. She understands how badly I need her to keep me steady and not present the same problems and attitude I get from my wife. She has stopped with the sarcastic jabs and become more attentive to my needs. We are even doing more things together as we did in the past, like going to the gym, bike riding, and weekend getaways.

On the other hand, Kim is making it too easy for me to be with Mya, which increases my suspicions that she's having an affair. We are like two strangers living under the same roof. Kim has always maintained a weekly hair and nail appointment and spent more time at the mall shopping than the law should allow. I still could sense something different about her. The main thing being we hadn't made love in months. Grant it, me and Mya had been more intimate lately, exhausting the majority of my energy. But if my wife needed me, I would have been able to perform. The problem was she hadn't, and this had me on guard.

Mya and I had made plans to go over to Orlando for a basketball game between the Magic and Suns. The day before the game, I walked in on Kim talking to someone on the phone. She reassured the caller that I wouldn't be home, and they had nothing to worry about. "He's going to Orlando tomorrow and won't be back until late."

Immediately, I called Mya to let her know we couldn't go to the game, but she quickly defused that idea. We didn't change our plans. I just ruined the trip for us both. Instead of Kim calling every twenty minutes to see what I was doing, I was the one claiming to have to use the bathroom or wanting something to eat or drink so that I could call her. When I wasn't calling, I was sending her text messages. It didn't take a rocket scientist to see what was going on, and Mya had no problem letting me know how obvious I was being.

"If calling doesn't bring you home or stop you from doing what you're doing, what makes you think it's going to stop Kim if she's with someone else?" It was a reasonable question but one to which I had no answer.

Mya let me know she disapproved of me ruining her evening with my petty jealousy. She told me it made no sense for me to be cheating on my wife and getting angry because the tables have turned. But the biggest revelation came days later when we were about to make love, and she retrieved a condom from the nightstand drawer.

"What is this?" I asked when she handed the packet to me. Mya chided that I knew what it was and then told me that if I believed Kim was having an affair, we would be using condoms from now on.

"You are the only person I'm sleeping with and have slept with for the past six years. If you believe your wife is cheating, then I can't take a chance that she's using precautions with this guy."

There it was, the realization that my wife could be having sex with another man. Kim and I had been sex partners for years before getting married, and I knew she had been with other men. But somehow, her now being my wife and possibly sleeping with another man angered me. I refused to use the condom Mya handed me, and she refused to make love to me. Not just that day but many that followed. Mya and I weren't having sex, and neither was Kim and me. Every time the urge hit me, the thoughts of her with some other guy unnerved me, and my shaft went limp.

The pressure was building, and I was about to implode. Everyone seemed to be moving about their business, but I felt stuck in a bad dream. The need to do something, anything, to get out of this rut was consuming my every thought. It wasn't just the lack of sex in my life, but the control I felt I was losing in both my relationships. Mya, who claims to have been celibate over three years before getting together, had no problems denying me. Kim didn't either. It wasn't like we ever had an active sex life. Our intimate moments ranged from one extreme to another. She was either feeling as though she was doing me a favor or thinking she was keeping me out of another woman's bed.

To get my mind off my problems, I decided to focus more on my business by joining several civic organizations and exploring new networking opportunities. One of the associate pastors approached me and suggested I join the men's ministry and become a more active member. This led me to bible study on Wednesday nights and joining a mentoring program for young boys. Both Kim and Mya thought this change was good for me and encouraged me to follow through. I laugh when I compare the similarities between these two very different women. The main one being, they both enjoy the benefits of having me as their man, but neither wants to go the extra mile to ensure my happiness. This has to be a cruel joke. God can't hate me this much. All I ask for is someone to love me completely, and in return, I get two women with very little to offer.

"Hey stranger," the voice behind me was not one I needed or wanted to hear. It belonged to Faye Austin. I was exiting *Walgreen's* drug store after picking up some shaving cream and deodorant. Faye had been in and out of my life for at least ten years. We met during a period when she had become bored with her husband. At the time, they had already been married seven or eight years, maybe longer. Talk about freaks in bed. Faye was a straight-up freak, and that's the only thing we had in common. Aside from the sex, we stayed in touch through the years for other reasons. She and her husband owned a travel agency. Her connections often came in use, rendering huge discounts on airline tickets and hotel rooms. For that reason alone, I keep her number in my Rolodex.

"What's up?" I say as I turn and greet her. She's coming towards me, so I know this will not be a passing exchange. I also know the potential for where this can lead.

Faye is wearing a pair of white Bermuda shorts and a black tank top. Her hips fill out the shorts nicely. She has put on a few pounds over the years, but she still looks good. Her hair is braided and pulled up into a ponytail that hangs midway down her back. We are now standing at my car door. "You're looking good as ever, Mr. Bryson."

Faye is flirting with me. There was a time when I would have followed her lead, and we'd be getting buck wild somewhere, most likely the backseat of my car. But since Mya came into my life, Faye no longer had that effect on me. Only Mya can calm that beast, so I needed to get in my vehicle and leave before she talks me into something I will later regret.

She senses my hesitation and asks what's wrong. Quickly, I come up with the excuse that Kim and I have plans, and I need to get home to shave and shower. Faye asks if Kim is home, and I tell her yes. If she thought otherwise, she'd be trying to follow me there. We stand around kicking pebbles for a few more seconds then I let Faye know I need to get going.

"Alright, big daddy, I'll let you go but see if you can get out later. I'll wait for your call." Faye saunters off towards the store leaving me something to consider. To stave off her advances, I call Mya. Her phone rings four times and transfers to voice mail.

"Damn! Why can't she ever be available when I need her?" Faye is looking better now that Mya has disappointed me yet again. One thing I can say about Kim, no matter where she's at or what she's doing, she answers the phone on the first ring when I call. But Mya never hears the phone ring, and she purposely ignores my text messages because, according to her, "texting is so impersonal, and immature."

When Faye exits the store, I'm still sitting in the parking lot. She's heading my way when the phone rings. It's Mya. "Thank God." I wave to Faye and back out of the parking space. "Hey, I'm on my way over. Be ready when I get there."

Mya and I ride out to St. Pete Beach and get ice cream from *Dairy Queen*. We then ride along Gulf Boulevard into Treasure Island

and over to Madeira Beach. "When are you going to start treating me right?" is my question to her.

"When you make me the only woman in your life," Mya doesn't hold back. She's thumbing through my planner, being nosey. Since I have no secrets, I don't stop her. She stops on July 4th and slams the book closed. "Maybe, when you stop planning annual trips to the Essence Festival with your wife." She's pouting now.

"I made those plans before we got back together. If I'd known we were going to make-up, we could have attended together this year." Mya thinks I'm bluffing, but I'm not. I don't know how I would have pulled it off, but I would have if she asked me to.

"Tell you what, plan a trip for us, and I'll make it happen." Mya's eyes brighten, and she picks up the planner and begins thumbing through it again. She stops in March then turns to me.

"*Jazz in The Gardens* is at the end of March. I want to go." I think I've been set up.

"What is *Jazz in The Gardens*?"

"It's a music festival held down in Miami Gardens for the past few years. They have an awesome line-up this year, and your boy Kem will be performing."

"I have never heard of this festival before. How do you know about it?" Mya tells me she heard about the event while surfing the net looking for concerts. When she tells me that Stanley Clarke is also in the line-up, I've made up my mind. We are going.

"Seriously, LaDamien? Don't have me making plans, and you're just talking. I want to do this, and if you're not serious, say so, and I'll get Angie or someone else to go with me. You can just foot the bill like you did last year for Essence." She's calling my bluff, and I plan on standing and delivering. So I tell Mya to make plans and let me know the cost so I can give her the money. When we had our break-up over the *Disney* incident, I canceled Mya's bank and credit cards. To this day, she has not asked to have them back. She has to be the most fickle woman I have ever known.

"That was the last time I foot the bill for you and your friend. From now on, if we don't go together, we don't go at all."

"Oh, does that include this year's Essence Festival? Are you going to tell Kim she can't go?" Mya is playing, but little does she know. All she has to do is say the word and mean it, and Kim would be history. Why she can't see this is what unnerves me the most.

It is almost nine when I drop Mya off at her house. She doesn't invite me in but kisses me goodnight in the car. My anger resurfaces, but I don't mention how she's treating me. I wait for her to enter the house and then head home. Two blocks from my house, I receive a text message. It's from Faye. "Meet me at Coquina Park. U know the spot." Fifteen minutes later, I'm pounding Faye in the backseat of my Escalade.

Faye

LaDamien, and I have had an on-again, off-again relationship for almost ten years. I shouldn't refer to it as a relationship because it's purely about sexual gratification. I love to have sex, and I love the way he gives it to me. LaDamien came into my life during a time when my husband and I were considering divorce. There was no fire in our marriage. My husband had been ill for about a year, causing our sex life to diminish. He knew I was disappointed and unfulfilled, so he tried to make up for it by spoiling me with gifts and unlimited freedom to come and go as I please.

I met LaDamien one Sunday afternoon while pumping gas. He pulled up behind me, and as he exited his vehicle, an old Camaro, he noticed that I was checking him out.

"Hi," he said, followed by a brilliant smile. From that moment on, I'm hooked. We ended up pulling our vehicles off to the side and talking for almost an hour. He was single, recently back in the area, and looking to put his college degree to use. After the gas station, we went to *Shirley's Soul Food* to grab a bite to eat. Our next stop was an inexpensive motel where we screwed for nearly three hours. That night I returned home refreshed and renewed. When I came in, my husband looked at me, wanting to question my whereabouts but fearful of the answer. That is how it has remained ever since. I'm the dutiful wife who takes care of the home, and he accepts the fact that I have needs he can no longer fulfill. Turning the other way, and biting his tongue as I leave to be with my lover, and not uttering a word when I return.

When word got out that LaDamien had married, Luke, my husband, acted as though he were the lucky groom. I'm sure he had convinced himself that this turn of events would send me back to him. Little did he know, LaDamien's marriage was nothing but a farce. He was down on his luck and married Kim more as an opportunity to regain his footing than it was about true love. I wanted so badly to tell Luke that LaDamien and Kim's marriage wasn't a good six hours old before he called me and asked if we could hook up, which we did. That bit of information would have chilled him to his bones, but I didn't say anything because I knew he would figure out that nothing had changed soon enough.

But things did change between LaDamien and me. He claimed he was tired of fooling around and was ready to be a better husband to Kim. If that was the case, I could have accepted it, but I knew LaDamien all too well. There's no denying that we're cut from the same cloth and have the same desires. Even if he wanted to be the faithful husband he spoke of, he couldn't. Kim would never be able to keep up with him and his insatiable sexual appetite. Aside from that, he was appalled by her weight gain. Until the day he tried to end things, he complained about her laziness around the house, her obsessive attention to their daughter, and her bad spending habits.

My first thought was Wanda had butted her nose in where it didn't belong. She was like a mother hen protecting her eggs. Always fearful someone is going to come in and bust her hustle. Kim had to be the biggest fool I knew. How a woman could allow another woman to come in and take the reign in steering her husband's dreams was unthinkable. When LaDamien shared Kim's lack of interest in his business, I thought he was just talking. Or it was another way to get my sympathy, so I would step in and lend my secretarial skills for free. But it didn't take long for me to realize he was telling the truth. Before I knew it, he was going on and on about some chick named Wanda they had hired and how grateful they were to have her there. Now that his business partnership had failed, and he was doing his thing, Wanda was right where she wanted to be.

At first, I thought nothing of it. I figured Wanda was just some chick in need of a job and tried to make the best of what could turn out to be an ideal situation. Then the signs started to surface. She was always calling while we were together. No matter the day of the week or time. She even had the nerve to show up one day we were at lunch claiming to need his signature on some contracts to meet a deadline. When I came out and asked LaDamien if he was fucking this woman, his insistent denial gave me all the confirmation I needed. He was guilty as sin. At that point, all I had to do was catch them in the act.

Catching them wouldn't be hard. LaDamien isn't the romantic type. He will fuck wherever and whenever the urge arises. I knew without a doubt that if he was doing Wanda, it was happening right in his office. For the next two months, I tried my best to come up with a plausible reason why I would need to come by for a visit, especially since this was a no-no. LaDamien never forbids me from coming to his office, but it was an unspoken rule. We got together whenever we could and took it from there.

My opportunity finally came late one night when he and I were out riding. Wanda called and began questioning him about some documents. To get her off the phone, he agreed to go by the office and retrieve the documents so he could review them and have an answer for a client the following morning. We went to the office, and as usual, one thing led to another. Before long, I was lying on his desk. Skirt pulled up to my waist, legs spread wide while LaDamien teased my clit with the head of his dick. We fucked on his desk, on the floor, and in the bathroom. We were cleaning up when we heard the key in the door. LaDamien ran to his office and closed the door as he put his shorts and underwear back on. We thought it was Mark. Shortly after, I heard a female voice questioning him about his disheveled appearance.

"What were you doing?" she asked.

"Why?" he replied. The two went back and forth until LaDamien finally asked, "Why are you up here, Wanda? I said I would come up here and find the papers."

Bingo! Wanda's response gave me the evidence I needed. She was silent for a few seconds as though she had to plan her response. Her next words were all I needed. "I thought since you were coming up here, and I was still out, I would stop by so we could," she paused briefly, "you know it's been a while since we've done anything, and I was just hoping tonight we could."

LaDamien must have been startled or stunned because he didn't respond for the longest time. I didn't know if I should stay put or bust in on them. This woman needed to know that I had that part of his life taken care of, and she just needed to worry about answering the phones and typing memos. My curiosity got the best of me, and I threw all caution to the wind, not caring that I was a married woman with so much to lose. I charged into his office just in time to see Wanda caressing the bulge between his legs as he leaned back on his desk. The desk he had just screwed me on, I might add. It was evident by the expression on his face that he was impressed with himself. LaDamien had me hiding in the bathroom while he was about to get busy with his secretary right under my nose. I coughed. They both looked in my direction. Wanda embarrassed, LaDamien smirking.

Wanda didn't hesitate in making her departure. She simply glared my way and excused herself. LaDamien didn't even try to apologize or justify his actions. I asked him why he lied when I asked if he was sleeping with her, and he told me because it wasn't significant enough to him or frequent enough to acknowledge. "You heard what she said. It's been a while," he exclaimed as if it mattered.

LaDamien sat down in his black leather chair and pulled me into his lap. "Since you know now, I have a proposition."

"Oh yeah?" I quizzed.

"I've been thinking about it for a while. I want us to have a threesome, you, me, and Wanda." As he talked, he slid his finger in and out of my pussy, making me wet all over again. Then he turned my face to his and lured me into a hurried kiss. In seconds I was bent over his desk as he thrust his big Mandingo dick up into me as far as it could go. Six weeks later, we had our first and only Ménage á Trois.

I pretended like I didn't want to do it, but the truth is, a threesome is something I always wanted to try. LaDamien knew I would go for it because I would get moist between the legs whenever he brought it up. Convincing me wasn't the problem. It was convincing Wanda.

After months of trying, we finally devised a plan. Since Wanda would disagree, we would just have to set it up and trick her into it. The plan was for me to rent a room, and LaDamien would bring Wanda there, not knowing I would be hiding in the closet. Once he got her in a compromising position, I would join them.

I rented a room at The *Marriott* on Roosevelt Boulevard in Clearwater. The hotel location is far enough from the main road that our cars wouldn't get spotted. The hotel itself was one of many grouped nearby and designed to serve business travelers flying in and out of St. Pete/Clearwater Airport, less than a mile away.

The room is perfect, and I like the setup. When you entered, there was the bathroom, next was the closet, and then the sleeping area. Once LaDamien had Wanda inside the room, the closet wouldn't be in her view. I hated that I wouldn't be able to watch the two of them before my joining in.

Shortly after I entered the room, I undressed and hung my clothes in the closet. My cell phone rang twice, and then the caller hung up. It was LaDamien letting me know that they were on their way up. Grabbing my purse and room keycard, I headed into the closet. A minute later, the door opened. I listened in amusement as Wanda tried to turn the event into a romantic moment. Still, LaDamien was rushed and ready for business as usual. How delusional this woman must be. She believes LaDamien has some sort of romantic interest in her. LaDamien played the part. He told her what she wanted to hear. He kissed her and prodded her to undress. Wanda tried to drag it out. She asked him why the rush. Then she wanted to watch TV for a while. Next, she wanted to talk, anything to prolong their time together. LaDamien held his impatience in check. He undressed and climbed into the bed. Then suggested she do a striptease for him. She giggled but agreed.

I pictured LaDamien lying spread eagle in the middle of the bed, stroking his dick. The thought was turning me on, prompting me to start fingering myself, getting excited about what was to come. The room was quiet, and then I heard an all too familiar sound. She was sucking his dick. Damn, I wanted to watch. With my face pressed to the slates in the closet door, I could view them in the mirror that faced the bed. Yep, I was right; Wanda was giving him a blow job. It must have been good to him because LaDamien's toes curled tight, and he had his hands above his head gripping the headboard. LaDamien let out a deep moan as he began to fuck Wanda in her mouth. I had to admit. The girl had skills. She was handling his thrusts like a pro. Now I knew why he thought I could take him down my throat if I just "relax, and give it a try," as he would always say.

A good ten minutes went by before I finally exited the closet and climbed on the bed, startling both of them. I guess Wanda was working her magic so good that LaDamien forgot I was there. Wanda jumped out of bed and searched for her clothes.

LaDamien sat up and grabbed her wrist, begging her not to leave. "Please don't go, I want this so bad," always thinking of himself.

Wanda was clear she didn't want any part of this. She wasn't trying to have sex with a woman. She wasn't that way. LaDamien told her it didn't mean anything like that. The threesome was something he wanted to share with the two of us. He didn't want there to be any secrets. He wanted us to have an open relationship.

He was starting to get on my nerves. I wasn't trying to do any more with this woman than share this sexual moment with her. Wanda was not happy and wanted out. She continued to pull away from him in an attempt to grab her things and leave. He finally asked me to go into the bathroom and give them some time. Begrudgingly, I obliged.

The conversation was muffled and lasted a good half hour. LaDamien finally came to the bathroom door and summoned me out.

"Come on. We're just going to lie down together for a while."

A while for me and LaDamien lasted a good thirty seconds. We had him sandwiched between us. I had one leg draped over him as I fingered the tight curls of his chest hairs. He took my hand and placed it on one of Wanda's small breasts. She flinched but didn't remove it. LaDamien took this as his cue.

"Can she suck your nipples?" he asked Wanda. Without a response, I lifted myself over him and began to tease her nipple with the tip of my tongue. LaDamien began rubbing my ass. Soon he had me straddling over Wanda with my butt in the air. He entered me from behind and pounded for several minutes as he instructed me to "suck those titties, ooh suck them like I love to suck on yours." Just as I was about to cum, he withdrew. He slapped me on the behind, indicating it was now Wanda's turn. I noticed her looking over at the nightstand.

"Where are the condoms?" she asked him.

"We don't need them. You're both safe," he replied.

I began to think about all the times he and I had sex without protection, and now I knew he had been doing the same with Wanda, and I know with his wife. I didn't use protection with my husband, and I'm sure Wanda didn't use it with hers. This whole thing seemed so out of control at that moment.

"What's wrong?" I heard LaDamien ask, not knowing if he was talking to me or Wanda, the disappointment clearly showing on his face. Wanda and I looked at each other and then at him. She was the first to speak.

"I'm leaving. This was a mistake. You two do whatever you do, but I won't be a part of it." This time LaDamien didn't try to stop her. We waited in silence for the door to close before he finally spoke.

"You're leaving too?" LaDamien asked in a low tone. Of course, I wasn't going anywhere. I picked up where we left off and gave him enough to make up for Wanda's absence.

Since that night, Wanda and I had sort of an understanding. We respected each other's space and stayed out of each other's way.

Then came the change in LaDamien. Little did I know, there was a new chick on the block.

LOVE...

- is patient
- is kind
- is not rude
- does not envy
- is not self-seeking
- will not lie
- is not proud
- is not quick to anger
- protects
- does not boast
- does not record wrongs
- trusts
- hopes
- perseveres
- finds no joy in evil but celebrates truth
- never fails

Kim

"**Ah, come** on, Big Red, it'll be for my eyes only." We are relaxing on his oversized leather sofa. I'm wearing nothing but my silk navy blue full-slip. It's mid-afternoon on a Tuesday. TayJohn is on a scheduled day off. His schedule has changed to twelve-hour workdays with a rotating three days on and three days off. But I have taken the day off to spend with him. Once again, he's begging me to allow him to take pictures of me…something I can't allow to happen. The thought that my body turns a man on is exciting and a massive boost to my self-esteem. But I must be smart and realize how quickly the simple gesture can backfire if things turn ugly between us.

It was never my intention for things to get this far. I love my husband and want my marriage to work. LaDamien has put me through so much, and the past few months have been the worst. Once again, I have suggested counseling, but all I get from LaDamien is I know what I need to do to keep him home. I don't know because if I did, I would be at my office right now and not in the arms of another man.

Sometimes I tell myself that this is all LaDamien's fault. That he drove me to this, he forced me into the arms of another man, that he made it easy for me to take the leap.

TayJohn, or Taj as he prefers, had been flirting with me since the day he arrived in St. Petersburg, but I knew my role as a wife. I was committed to my marriage despite my husbands' infidelities but the harder I tried, the more things LaDamien did to push me away.

LaDamien started spending so much time away from home, and our arguments were increasing. He would be gone until late into the night, come home, get ready for bed, and once I was asleep, leave again.

His trips were increasing. They use to be once every three months or so, but now they seemed every other week. Sometimes he wouldn't even give advance notice. He would wait until he knew that I was at work, out with Ariel or my friends. He'd then call and say he's on his way to Miami, Jacksonville, Orlando, or wherever. When I questioned him, he insisted the trips were business-related, or he was frustrated and needed some "alone" time. Nothing could have been further from the truth. LaDamien stayed stressed about finances. When he and Mark were in business together, I knew more about the company finances. Now, I get shut out of his business dealings.

Aside from never being at home and the frequent trips, some other outlandish things were happening. One day I called LaDamien's cell phone, and a woman answered. Thinking the lines had crossed somehow, I apologized and hung up. Seconds later, my phone rang, and the same woman informed me I had the correct number. "LaDamien is busy right now," she chuckled. "What do you want anyway?"

My reaction was to slam the phone down. As soon as LaDamien came in that evening, I was all over him. He had the dumbest confused look on his face but denied I had called his phone, and a woman answered. Even after I tried to show him the call history on our home phone, he responded, "Kim, you call me every five minutes, so exactly what are you trying to prove?" He was right. It was my word against his, but I know what I know, and some tramp, probably Mya, had crossed the line.

Shortly afterward, LaDamien made some excuse about going to the store. This appeased me a little because I knew he was leaving the house to address the issue with whomever he thought had disrespected me that way. Never had any of his women been so bold as to communicate with me.

No sooner had that episode died down, another one popped up. LaDamien was away on one of his last-minute trips. He had offered to drive one of his elderly uncles to a funeral in Mississippi. They had left early Friday morning and were due back late Sunday evening.

Saturday morning, Ariel and I went to get our hair done, and afterward, we headed over to Westshore mall in Tampa. We had been at the mall for a good thirty minutes when I saw a woman I thought was Mya. I'm sure LaDamien was in Mississippi with his relatives.

However, it wouldn't be beneath him to have taken her along, so seeing her would be a welcomed relief.

My attention was diverted by Ariel asking to go into *Lady Foot Locker* to see if they carried *Pastry* sneakers by Angela and Vanessa Simmons.

After leaving the sneaker store, we were walking past *White House Black Market* when I spotted the woman again. She was paying for a purchase. I scanned the store looking at the attractive black and white ensembles that I would love to own but couldn't because they didn't come in plus sizes. For the first time, a tinge of jealousy consumed me. I never considered Mya my equal on any level. Not in looks, intelligence, nor professionally. She was nothing more than an obstacle to my marriage. But seeing her in this store purchasing what I couldn't made me look at her differently now. Ariel grabbed my hand, urging me along.

"Mama, please come on, let's go to *Macy's*."

An hour later, we were leaving *Macy's*. I had purchased a new suit for work, matching shoes, a new *Marc Jacobs* handbag for myself, and several outfits for Ariel. Shopping always made me feel better, and after seeing Mya, I needed a huge boost to my esteem. But that boost didn't last for long.

We entered *Ann Taylor's Loft*, and exiting the store was Mya. She looked me straight in the eyes, smiled, and said, "Hi." Never missing a step or waiting for a response, she strolled out the door. My reaction wasn't anger. It was more annoyance. I walked through the store, looking over my shoulder to see if she was lurking outside. I realized I was trying desperately to figure out if that was the same voice that answered LaDamien's phone the week before.

I eventually decided on a pair of white Capri's and a top to wear with them. The salesgirl was a young White woman with a bubbly personality. She totaled my purchase and folded my items as I made out my check. When I handed it to her, she looked at the check and remarked, "Wow, what a coincidence." I asked, "what," and she handed me the final blow to my gut. "The lady I waited on before you is also married to a guy named LaDamien Bryson."

"Wh—what do you mean?" I stammered. Ariel was no longer milling about but awaiting her response too. The clerk punched some keys on her register, and still smiling, confirmed, "She paid with a credit card that belonged to a LaDamien Bryson. Look at that. The same bank issued the card as your check."

She had to be a complete airhead because it never registered on her face, and probably not in her feeble mind that it was the same person. Or my husband and I could have been the victims of credit card theft. At that very moment, my thoughts bounced back and forth. I debated calling this girl's manager to complain about their lack of protocol regarding possible identity and credit card theft. I also wanted her to call mall security and have Mya stopped and returned to the store to explain how and why she had my husband's credit card.

In the end, I simply said, "What a small world." I took my purchase and led Ariel out of the store and the mall and back to the sanctity of our home. My house seemed to be the only place we were safe from the grips of that wretched heifer.

LaDamien finally answered my call, claiming he had little or no reception where they were. "Why is Mya at the mall shopping with your credit card?" I asked, cutting to the chase.

"Mya doesn't have my..."

"Yes, she does, she was at the mall today, and she was using one of your credit cards. When you get home, I want all the credit cards to set up online accounts to monitor the activity. I want access to all the bank accounts, the business account, and your personal account, everything LaDamien." Tears were streaming down my face, and I was shaking uncontrollably.

LaDamien was silent as my rant continued. When he decided to speak, he told me I could have access to whatever I wanted. He even told me if I wanted to, I could call Wanda and have her bring the paperwork to me. Then reality set in. Of course, I could have access to everything because they probably had secret accounts that no one but them knew about but them. I decided to tell him we would also be pulling credit reports first thing Monday morning to outsmart him. I also wanted access to his cell phone to pull the call logs and a text message history. His tune changed quickly, and we were no longer in perfect harmony.

Weeks passed, and LaDamien never produced the credit report. Whenever I broached the subject about the credit report and the phone access, an argument ensued, and I eventually gave up. However, to appease me, he did change his cell phone number.

He thought he was so smart, and I was so dumb. One morning he went to wash my car. While he was gone Lynn called, and asked if

I could go pick up a prescription for their mother. Of course, I said yes. I grabbed the keys to the coupe, which we rarely drove anymore. As I was sitting in the drive-thru lane, music started playing, and a buzzing sound came from the glove compartment. I opened the door, and to my surprise, it was a cell phone. I pulled the phone out, and the number flashing on the display screen was LaDamien's cell number. I pressed talk and didn't say anything—LaDamien hung up.

I went through the phone logs, and there were no text messages, no numbers, no nothing, so I retrieved the phone number and wrote it down. Later that evening, I would call the number to see who answered. Imagine how perplexed I was when LaDamien answered the phone. He was out back working in the yard. I looked out the window, and sure enough, he had the phone to his ear.

Why was I shocked? I don't know. In the past, we have had arguments about his phone and women calling him. He has the number changed, and bam, they end up with the new number. I guess he thought he'd outsmart me by getting a second phone. It all made sense now. He had washed the coupe before he took the Benz to have it detailed. He must have left the phone in the car then. He just worked too damn hard at deceiving me.

The night that I removed my blinders and acknowledged the passes TayJohn was throwing my way, LaDamien and I were supposed to meet his family at Veronica's home. By two pm we'll be there. The family was meeting to discuss making a trip to North Carolina to attend a family reunion. LaDamien left the house at nine a.m., claiming he was going to work out and would be back no later than ten-thirty.

We spoke at ten forty-five, eleven-thirty, and noon. Each time LaDamien assured me he would be home in time for us to get to the meeting. At two-fifteen, he told me to go ahead, and he would meet me there. By six p.m., I was on my way home, fuming mad that LaDamien never showed up. The looks his family members displayed varied from sympathy to disdain to apathy for my situation.

When Ariel and I reached the house, it was clear that LaDamien had not been home. My last conversation with him was at four. Instead of claiming he was on his way as he had on previous calls, this time, he claimed to have received a call from Wanda about a lead on a foreclosed property. He had to jump on it as quickly as possible.

Ariel entered the house, went straight to her bedroom to get on her computer, and play games. I planned to call LaDamien and see where the hell he was, but my cell phone rang, and the name "Taj" appeared. No sooner than I said hello, I was spilling my guts about my husbands' latest show of disrespect.

TayJohn stopped me before I could finish the story. "Where is your daughter?" he asked me.

After sharing that she was in her room deep into a game, he instructed me to go into my bathroom and run a warm bubble bath. Not much later, I was in the tub listening as he told me all the things he would do if he were my man. The funny thing was, the majority of the things he mentioned were things that LaDamien did already. Hearing it come from another man made it all seem brand new. Perhaps it was the passion in the way they said it, or maybe it was the anticipation of having it done by someone who was doing them because he wanted to please me.

TayJohn was a thoughtful lover who wanted to please me. He told me I was beautiful, and I believed he was sincere. Unlike LaDamien, who would say those same things to me then pursue the ugly bitches that he gallivanted around town with for everyone to see. My husband says I'm beautiful, my weight doesn't bother him, and my education doesn't make him feel inferior. Yet, he chooses women that were the complete opposite of everything I represented. Everything that made me who I am.

On more than one occasion, I asked TayJohn about his past relationships. So much so until one day, he handed me an old and worn CVS one-hour photo envelope. Inside were pictures of several different women. All were full-figured, light-complexioned or Hispanic, shoulder-length hair or longer, and about my height. "I like what I like, now can we get past this? If I weren't turned on by what I see, I wouldn't waste your time or mine," he said.

Seeing the pictures was a double-edged sword. Yes, I was happy to confirm that I was TayJohn's type, but it also caused concern that he still had these pictures. Now I wanted to know the story behind each and if she was entirely out of his life. More importantly, why was he holding on to the pictures. He did everything in his power to dispel my curiosity. As we have this conversation about him taking my picture, the memory of that day resurfaces.

"So did you tell Vonda, Tammy, and Renita that their pictures were for your eyes only?" TayJohn placed the camera on the coffee table and turned to me.

"I only showed you those pictures to prove a point. Plus, they were everyday pictures taken at parties or in public places. What I want from you is something I can look at to get my mind off of you lying next to your husband when I want you to be here with me. I'm not asking you to take your clothes off, just some sexy poses in your lingerie." To add to his plea, he rubs his hand up and down my thighs while staring into my eyes. "Pretty please, with sugar on top." We both laugh before indulging in a kiss.

Once I made the first step, it became easier to continue seeing him, not because the loving was so great, but because LaDamien picked up on it quickly. Like Denzel said in the movie Training Day, *"It ain't fun when the rabbits got the gun."* Now he was the one calling to check on my whereabouts. It was him worrying that someone else was getting what was his. And him doubting *my* every word. For once, my husband was catering to my needs and making me feel wanted. It felt good, even if it was out of jealousy. I found myself wondering what the hussy was thinking every time he picked up the phone to call home. Or what she thought when he received and replied to my text messages all evening long. It must have been driving her crazy because lately, I have begun receiving hang-ups, at home, on my cell phone, and at work. I spoke to LaDamien about it, and he insists he isn't fooling around on me and then insinuates it must be "that nigga you screwing."

TayJohn senses that my mind is drifting away. He gets up off the couch and reaches for my hand. Once I'm standing, he slides my slip up and over my head. He leads me into the bedroom and over to the bed. "Can I make love to you all afternoon?" He asks me this with such sincerity as if he wouldn't object if I said no.

"When we're together, it hurts me to know you are still thinking about your husband. I want your undivided attention, lady, and if that means sexing you the entire time you're here, then that's what I'm going to do."

Now I feel bad. No way do I want him to think this is only about sex for me. If so, then that makes me just as wrong as my husband. But still, the fear of falling in love with him frightens me.

"I'm sorry," is all I say before he guides me backward and fills me with his warmth and his slow grind...never rushed, never hurried, never aggressive, just pure sexual healing for my soul.

Mya

It is the fourth Friday of the month and the time for my monthly book club meeting. I prepare to leave when my phone rings. I look at the caller ID and see that it's LaDamien. He knows I'm supposed to be at Angie's in fifteen minutes, so I'm pissed that he has called on the home phone. I answer against my better judgment. It's not that I don't want to speak with him, but he tends to call when he knows I have plans. He starts in with his woe is me, routine. It goes downhill from there. I never give in to his tantrums or cancel my plans. After all this time, he should realize that I can't give up who I'm to appease his insecurities.

"Hi baby," I say as I answer the phone.

"I thought you were going to hang out with your friends tonight?"

"I am. I was on my way out the door when you called." I don't know why we have to play this game, but I go along.

"Well, I don't want to hold you up. I just wanted to see you before I head inside. I'm around the corner. Can I stop by?" My delayed response is enough to spark his furor.

"I understand," he starts. "I know you have your own life to live and don't have time to worry about me and what I'm going through." He pauses then continues when I don't respond. "You don't know how much I love you, Mya, do you? All the things I do for you, and the hell I'm catching at home because of you means nothing, does it?"

Plopping down on the bed, I wonder why I answered the phone, why didn't I just call him on my cell as I drove to Angie's. "Baby, please don't start. You knew I was going to this meeting tonight. Can we get together afterward? Leave your phone on, and I'll call you as soon as I leave Angie's." He isn't going to go for this. It's either his way or no way.

I check my watch, and it's five minutes to seven. My meeting starts at seven. Ten minutes have passed, and LaDamien is nowhere in sight, so much for being just around the corner.

"You know Mya. I always find time for you. I'm always there for you when you need me. Now that I need a little bit of your time, you put your friends ahead of me. Go ahead to your little meeting, and don't worry about me." He ends the call.

I knew it was coming and have grown accustomed to it. I can't understand if LaDamien is so miserable in his marriage and life, why won't he make a change. I slide my feet into my shoes and grab my purse. As I back out of the driveway, I pull out my cell phone and dial his number—the third number since we met. I don't know if Kim goes through his phone and finds numbers or what, but every now, and then he pops up with a new number. This last time, it came with a second phone. I could not believe he was trying to relegate me to some undercover hoe phone that he was trying to hide from his wife. A week after I confronted him about it, he turned the phone off and gave me the new number to his regular phone.

He doesn't answer, as I suspected he wouldn't. He will time my travel, and when I'm minutes away from my destination, he will return my call. We will banter back and forth, and to appease him, I will agree to meet him somewhere.

"You called me," LaDamien says when I answer.

"I didn't know if you hung up or if the call dropped." Not wanting to encourage him, I stop and leave the door open to continue the conversation. If he genuinely wants to see me before I go into this meeting, he will need to spell it out.

"Call me when you leave. I'll still be out, so don't be all night." LaDamien hangs up as I pull into a spot near the home next door to Angie's.

"Sorry I'm late, girls," I say as I enter the house. Angie is in the kitchen while our friends Brigit, Aubrey, Roxanne, and Jaime gathered in the living room, downing frozen Margarita's and Strawberry Daiquiris.

Aubrey is the first to speak. She's married to her high school sweetheart, whose name is Keith. Both Aubrey and Keith are school teachers. They have one child, a son who will be graduating from high school this year. "What's been up with you, Missy? Have you finally come to your senses and realize that no good nigga ain't no good for you?"

"See, this is why our education system is failing our kids." Roxanne chimes in, "If the teacher is talking like the kids, then who is teaching the kids?" We laugh.

Roxanne and Jaime are the other two single women in our little group. Roxanne is ten years my senior, while Jaime is a few years younger than I am. I know the women discuss my relationship with LaDamien when I'm not around, each having their own opinions. Of them all, Brigit is the most vocal. She's married and blames women *like me* for her marital problems. The truth is her husband was a creep when she married him. No matter what he does, she stands by him. When he became strung out on drugs, she mortgaged their home to get him into a drug treatment center. When he got arrested for buying crack cocaine a month after leaving rehab, she borrowed money from anyone who would give to get him out. This has been their story for almost twenty years. I don't think Brigit resents my relationship with a married man as much as she resents the fact that a married man does for me what LaDamien does. I think she compares her husband to LaDamien, and can't understand why she's in that situation.

"Well, Mya? What's new with LaDamien?" Aubrey asks, wanting to know the answer.

After LaDamien and I broke up over the Orlando incident, I made the mistake of sharing the details of my relationship with her. If I thought for one second, I would forgive him; I would have never opened my mouth. But I was so hurt and distraught.

Typically I would have called Angie. I didn't want to get consoled this time, so I called Aubrey, knowing she would understand and bring humor to the situation. Plus, she was one of a few friends LaDamien didn't know well enough to show up at her home, even if he knew where she lived. Aubrey was a great support system, but twelve hours later, she had shared my business with everyone else. Claiming she didn't see the harm since we were all girls, and eventually, everyone would know LaDamien, and I had parted ways. "So I just saved you the trouble," she mused.

Since then, I have refused to get in-depth and personal about my relationship. I still shared details with Angie, but I just shared the fun stuff with the rest of the ladies, like our upcoming plans to attend *Jazz in The Gardens*.

Jaime chimed in next, "How can his wife not know what is going on? Man, is she that damn crazy?"

"I don't think she's crazy at all," this is Roxanne talking, "I mean, think about it, she lives in a nice house, drives a nice car, her bills get paid, and hell, most men cheat, so why should she give all that up. I bet Kim has a man on the side and isn't thinking about LaDamien's crazy ass."

"I know that's right," Brigit began. "She's probably thanking you for getting that creep out of her hair," she laughed more than necessary.

Angie came from the kitchen and rescued me. "First of all, I think it's sad that two people are married and living separate lives. I also hate that Mya got mixed up in this mess. We need to be trying to uplift her and motivate her to get out of this situation, not sit here and make jokes about it like it's nothing. Second, we talk about LaDamien but what it must be like for Kim and that poor daughter of theirs. No one in that house can be at peace. I just think it's a sad situation all around."

"You know, Angie is right," Aubrey is now speaking. "But still, I don't know one hundred percent that Keith isn't cheating on me, but I do know if he were to cheat, it would be all about getting his freak on. You know, doing some nasty mess I won't do. I know he wouldn't be taking money from our home, giving it away like it's nothing. Does this woman have any clue how much money is leaving her house? And look at all the time you and he spend together. How can a man be gone that much, and she not know or not care? I swear if Keith said he was going to the gym, and I thought something was up, I'd be getting up going to. And every time he said he was going away for the weekend, that car wouldn't leave without me in it."

It was now Jaime's time to put in her other two cents. "The thing that gets me is how your husband can own his business, and you aren't involved. I told you, Mya, I have heard several people say that he's screwing that secretary of his. Maybe you need to quit your job to go work for him. I would get that heifer out of there."

My head was starting to hurt, and when Brigit got started, I knew it was time for me to go.

"So what if he's fucking the secretary, he's not Mya's husband, so it's not her problem. What she needs to do is remember where she came from, ask God for forgiveness, and leave that woman's husband alone."

Angie begged me to stay, promising we would eat dinner and get on with the book discussion, but I'd had enough. My friends were right. I was in something wrong, and no matter how much I loved LaDamien, and no matter how much he did for me or how good he treated me, he was still someone else's husband. It didn't look like that was going to change any time soon.

As I was telling the girls goodbye, my co-worker Eric showed up. Just when I didn't think it could get any worse, it did. Eric gossiped twice as much as the average woman. He knew everything about everybody and didn't hesitate to repeat any and everything he heard. "Hey girl, I thought that was your car. What're you, ladies, up to in here?"

Before responding, I take a deep breath. "It's our monthly book club meeting, but I was about to leave. My head is killing me."

Brigit takes it upon herself to correct me. "Headache, my ass, you just mad because we are calling you out on your mess," Angie tells her to hush. She invites Eric in, meaning I have to stay as well since he's my friend.

Eric knows me well enough to sense something is amiss, and I need to leave. So he explains why he has stopped by. "Thanks for the offer, but I just saw Mya's car outside and wanted to invite her to a cook-out I'm having tomorrow. The more, the merrier, so if you divas aren't busy, please stop by." Eric rattled off his address and followed me out to my car.

"What was that all about?"

"Nothing, just my girls looking out for my well-being, you know how that can be. I can't make any promises, but I'll do my best to make it tomorrow." Eric hugged me, and we went our separate ways.

Before I can pull my phone out, LaDamien is already calling. "Hey Baby, I'm leaving the meeting early. So what do you want to get into?" Surprise, surprise, he says my panties.

I'm sitting in church feeling like such a hypocrite. At times I feel like the entire congregation knows my sin. Whenever adultery gets mentioned, they are all pointing a shameful finger at me. Reverend Lawrence extended the invitation as he does every week, but today I feel that the moment is prolonged. I hang my head in prayer, and I'm fighting back the tears as I ask God for forgiveness, guidance, understanding, and to have mercy on my sinful soul.

Reverend Lawrence says that the Holy Spirit won't allow him to close the invitation because someone else needs to come to get loosed from a stronghold. I battle with my spiritual desire to do what is right and my earthly desire to hold on to what makes me feel good. When I have convinced myself that it's me, God is calling to get up and start anew, the congregation begins to clap, and someone touches my back. I open my eyes, and the young girl seated next to me is getting up, preparing to go forward. This is my opportunity. I can just get up and follow her, but I'm glued to the pew, paralyzed if you will. Minutes later, the opportunity is gone. Twelve people have accepted the call and are on their way to redemption.

Attending Eric's cook-out wasn't in my plans before church, but now I felt like I needed the distraction. Cars lined both sides of the narrow street, which surprises me because I didn't know Eric knew that many people. He greeted me at the door, asking if any of my friends were coming.

"I haven't talked to any of them, so I don't know." He looks disappointed but brushed it off as he began introducing me to his guest. I recognized a few faces from work but everyone else I was meeting for the first time. Eric handed me a wine cooler and instructed me to make myself at home.

"Hi, I'm Nikki, Eric's fiancée," I was shocked. Eric always talked about his fiancée. However, it was a long-running joke amongst us that Nikki was a figment of his imagination since no one had met her. Regardless here she is, flesh and blood.

Nikki laughs when I share with her that I thought Eric made her up, and it was great to meet her finally. After chatting for almost fifteen minutes, Nikki excused herself to welcome the new arrivals.

Ever since I entered, I noticed one of the guests kept watching me. My curiosity got the best of me, and I decided to learn who she is.

"Eric, come here for a second. Who is that sitting outside in the lime green top?" I ask.

An hour had passed since my arrival, and this woman had not taken her eyes off of me. Eric said he didn't know her personally.

She'd arrived with one of Nikki's friends. I tried waiting to catch Nikki when she came by, but she was busy being the perfect hostess. Finally, I strolled out to the patio, sat next to the woman, and started a conversation by asking if we knew each other.

"Well, you don't know me, I don't think, but I know who you are. My name is Faye."

Sometimes you can ask God for something, and it can take a lifetime to come to fruition. Then there are times you can ask him for something, and it gets done in a blink of an eye. That's how I felt about my meeting Faye at Eric's gathering. Just hours earlier, I had asked God to open my eyes and help me see beyond the love I had for LaDamien, and show me if we could ever have a future together. Just like that, God laid it out for me.

Two hours, two whole hours, this woman talked to me about a man I thought I knew and loved but didn't have a clue who he was. Faye shared with me how she met LaDamien, their affair, his countless other affairs, and so much more. I often wanted to cover my ears and run away, but I had gotten caught like a deer in headlights. A train wreck I couldn't will myself to turn away from, not even when Eric stopped by to see if everything was okay.

It took Brigit and Jaime arriving to free me from Faye's captive audience. We had left the cook-out and stood out front, close to the street. Jaime knew right off the bat that something was amiss and refused to walk away when I insisted things were okay. Brigit was busy asking questions, "Now who is this? How did you meet? You look familiar…"

Faye knew the show-and-tell was over. She asked Jaime and Brigit for something to write with, then jotted her number down and handed it to me. "Call me if you need to."

"She said what?" Brigit asked as I replayed as much of the conversation as I could between their questions and gestures of disbelief. We were at my house, having left the cook-out immediately after I told them who Faye was.

My mind is spinning, and the days' activities have me mentally drained. I continue to talk as if I need to hear myself repeat the incredulous stories to believe them. "Faye said for over ten years they were involved and that he's screwing his secretary. Remember the whole Orlando fiasco? Well, according to her, she stayed at LaDamien's house with Ariel one of those nights. I feel sick. I heard LaDamien on the phone, and I took his word that it was his sister when all along he was talking to some chick he's getting freak nasty with." My emotions were all over the place. Anger, sadness, embarrassment, it was all there.

"And you say she's married? What kind of bullshit is that?" Jaime was asking some stupid questions, but I answered each one. "Do you believe her? I mean, I'm sure some of it's true, but what married woman in her right mind would go around talking freely about an affair and in such detail. She doesn't know you or who you know. What if you found out who her husband is, and went back, and told him? I would take what she said with a grain of salt, but don't let it stop you from confronting LaDamien."

Confronting LaDamien regarding Faye and the myriad of information she provided to me was something I knew I had to do. I just didn't know how. I'm lying in bed, the shock of the days' events still weighing me down. Brigit and Jaime didn't leave until ten. After they left, I called Angie to let her know what happened. She was just as astounded as I was. When you consider LaDamien is lying to his wife to have a relationship with me, it shouldn't be so far-fetched that he would do all the things Faye said. Yet, I still couldn't get a firm grip on her words and make them stick.

I'm thinking about how nicely the pieces fit into the puzzle. All the unanswered phone calls when I knew he wasn't home. The times he went away, claiming he needed to be alone. The angry outbursts followed by disappearing acts. The times Kim was away, or they'd had a fight, and he never came to me. What hurts the most is having this woman share stories about things they'd done together. The stories mirrored many of our activities together. And the stories about Wanda, his secretary. I want to vomit at the thought of the three of them together having some sick orgy. Although Jaime said I shouldn't believe much of what Faye said, I still tried to sort through what was probably the fact and what was probably fiction. In the end, it didn't matter because regardless of how intense their relationship was, LaDamien was a liar, and I deserved so much better.

Everything he's ever said to convince me he's truly in love with me runs through my mind. He loves me more than anything. He'd dreamed of being with me since the first time he saw me. Now that he finally had me, he wasn't going to let me go. None of it made much sense.

It's twelve-thirty, and dawning on me that LaDamien hasn't called. I wonder if he knows I have met Faye and know all of his dirty little secrets. Or is Faye waiting in the cut for me to confront him and do the dirty work for her? What if it was all a set-up to get me out of the picture? "Ugh, this is just too much. I need to get it together. I didn't ask for all of this," I said into the darkness, but of course, I asked for it. There's no way you can do wrong and not pay the price. This was just my dirt settling back at my front door.

LaDamien called early Monday morning, claiming he was unable to get away yesterday. It was first Sunday, and they'd had a family dinner at one of his sisters' homes. He had become ill, and after returning home, slept for the remainder of the day. Nothing in his voice gave way to having spoken to Faye. How would I even know? According to Faye, LaDamien was the master deceiver and had pulled the wool over my eyes for two and a half years. If I were to believe Faye, it was she that LaDamien couldn't live without, not me. It was she that knew his inner-most thoughts and was the keeper of his secrets.

As I listen to LaDamien, I debate mentioning yesterday's incident. What will waiting accomplish, I don't know. I can't help but wonder if this is what Kim goes through, knowing her husband is cheating on her. If she weighs her options and decides it's easier to stay, or if she stays out of spite to keep the other woman or women from having what is rightfully hers. What is it with LaDamien? Why can't he be satisfied with what he's given? How does he keep up with the lies required to live this lifestyle? I have a hundred questions, and even if I ask them all, there's no guarantee I will get the answers I so desperately need.

LaDamien breaks my train of thought by asking if everything is okay. "Just tired from the cook-out yesterday," I say.

Referencing the cook-out doesn't seem to raise any concerns. He just tells me to get dressed so we can go to the gym. After agreeing, we end the call. I will meet him in thirty minutes instead of him coming to pick me up.

The more I see LaDamien, the less I want to see him. We have to talk about Faye soon. Our trip to Miami is the following weekend. Still, LaDamien has made no indication that he's aware that I know what he's been up to all this time. However, he has commented several times that I have been distant. It's Thursday afternoon, and we have plans to meet for lunch. My mind is made up. We will have our talk today.

We decide on *Cha Cha Coconuts*, a Caribbean-themed restaurant chain located downtown at The Pier. The attraction has been dying a slow death for at least fifteen years, if not more, hanging on by the City's financial life support. I hope that the place will be near empty, in case things get out of control. LaDamien doesn't like being forced into a corner and will get defensive to avoid facing issues.

"Baby, you have not been yourself all week. What's wrong?" LaDamien has opened the door so many times this week, but I have refused to enter. Today, I take a deep breath and allow the chips to fall where they may.

"Tell me about Faye." There, I had said it, it was on the table, and LaDamien didn't miss a beat.

"What do you want to know about her?" He was ready, probably had rehearsed his response all week long, but I wouldn't relent. It was full speed ahead.

Taking a sip of my iced tea, I replied, "Everything. How did you meet, how long have you known her, but most importantly, when was the last time you fucked Faye?"

LaDamien looked up from his Grouper sandwich and eyed me suspiciously. "Where is this coming from? You think you know the answers, so let's just cut to the chase. How did you hear about Faye?"

Cut to the chase. Is that what he just said to me? No concern, no shock, and awe that I'm on to his game. A sarcastic chuckle escapes me. "I heard about Faye through Faye. She was at the cook-out Sunday and extremely chatty. She had so much to tell me that it took over two hours."

Finally, I get a show of emotion from LaDamien. He wasn't expecting to hear that I had spoken to Faye directly. No, he thought someone had dropped a dime on him. Now that I had his attention, I shared every detail Faye had shared with me, from how she had played the wife in his home while Kim was away to the ménage á trois she shared with him and Wanda.

"That was all before you and I started seeing each other. When we started seeing each other, I cut Faye loose. I've been honest with you. Remember, I told you I'd had an affair before. It was with Faye. If she told you we still see each other, she's lying."

The last two years of my life replayed in my mind, and not one reference to an affair did I recall. I can't believe he just sat there and claimed to have told me that he'd had an affair before me. Nothing is resonating, and I know deep down inside we have never had this conversation. There's no need to argue about it because LaDamien will swear to the end that I just don't remember.

"So I guess you told me you were sleeping with your secretary also. You are unbelievable, LaDamien. How can you sit here, and look me in my eyes, and dismiss this bullshit like it's nothing? It's bad enough I have to deal with the guilt of this affair, but now I've learned that you've been cheating on me too, or are you cheating on Faye, or is it only cheating on your wife because we don't count?

"I don't get it. I don't get you. I just don't get any of this. If you've been seeing this woman for over ten years, why in the hell did you need to involve me in your mess? Your wife isn't good enough. Your secretary isn't good enough. Your mistress isn't good enough, tell me, what will it take to satisfy you?

"You know what, don't answer because I won't believe you anyway. Everything about you is a damn lie." There's nothing left for me to do but grab my purse, and walk out, which is what I do. The elevator takes several minutes to arrive. When I reach the main floor, I see LaDamien crossing over the circular drive to the sidewalk. He must have taken the scenic glass-enclosed elevator located on the front of the building. He's walking swiftly as he dials a number on his cell phone, Faye's, no doubt.

Faye

LaDamien didn't give me a chance to say hello. As soon as I pressed talk, he began ranting and raving like a lunatic. "How could you do that to me, Faye? Why would you do that? You know how I feel about Mya. She's not Wanda, who you can play stupid ass games with for fun. You are fucking with my life, and for what? You're not going to leave Luke, so why fuck-up my life?"

I wish I had an answer for him, but I couldn't even rationalize my behavior to myself. The minute Mya walked in, I began plotting how I was going to approach her. Not to tell her about LaDamien but to see what type of person she was. When she approached me, something snapped in my mind, and I wanted to break her down, pull her off the pedestal LaDamien had placed her on. But she wasn't going to let on that she was romantically involved with him. She just stood there with a smug-ass look on her face, listening to me like I was keeping her from something more important. The longer we stood there, the more I wanted to break her spirit, to kill whatever she felt for LaDamien, but nothing worked. Mya just kept shaking her head and asking me what I was expecting from LaDamien, why I was placing *my* marriage in jeopardy.

Not once did she let on that she and LaDamien were anything more than friends. Then her friends showed up, and she suddenly wanted to get an attitude. Mya didn't know that I didn't give a damn about her friends. Hell, I'm sure she went back and told them everything anyway. I think what pushed me over the edge was when she asked me in that smug-ass tone, "Now how old are you?" I wanted to say, "bitch, how old are you? We're both old enough to know it's wrong to fuck somebody else's husband." She was a snooty bitch, if nothing else. But when I told her I'd been in LaDamien's house and slept in his bed, the light finally dimmed in her eyes. I had one up on her, that thing she had never done with him.

LaDamien was going on and on, every other word a curse word. I had never heard him talk like this before. "Don't ever fucking call me again, bitch do you hear me? Don't fucking call me again. If you do, I'll destroy you. I'll tell that faggot ass husband of yours everything. You hear me, Faye, do you hear me? I hate you bitch. I hate your fucking ass." He ended the call and must have turned his phone off because my calls went straight to voicemail when I tried to call him back.

Should I give him some time to cool off and then apologize? It's scary not knowing where he is, what he's doing, and what he's thinking. I have driven by his house numerous times, but there is still no car in the driveway. Since he bought Kim the Mercedes, he parks the Escalade in the driveway. It's gone, making it obvious he isn't going to answer or return my calls.

It is one in the morning when I ride by for the last time. Luke is calling and asking where I'm at and when I will be home. He senses that something is amiss. Perhaps LaDamien is right. I need to leave him alone and focus on the man who loves me, despite his inability to please me in bed.

Luke is a wonderful husband, and we have been married too long for me to risk losing him behind this childish mess. LaDamien is never going to leave Kim, that's for sure. So what if he had some stupid ass girl thinking she has a future with him. LaDamien isn't half the man he thinks he is. If it weren't for that big dick dangling between his legs, he wouldn't be in my life at all.

LaDamien

Something has to give, and soon. Everything is a mess, and I feel like my life is spiraling down into a black hole. It's one o'clock in the morning, and I'm pulling into the parking lot of a *Comfort Suites* hotel in Jacksonville. When I get to my room, I turn the air down to fifty, undress, and lay naked in the middle of the king-sized bed. Tears are streaming down the sides of my face, and I feel helpless, hopeless, and so alone. Things are so screwed up in my life that I want to do everyone a favor and just disappear. Kim, Mya, my family, everyone would be so much better off without me and my neediness.

Kim is cheating on me, and she knows that I know it. For some reason, she thinks it's going to bring us closer and somehow save our marriage. That's funny to me. Nothing she has tried has made me want to stay in this God-forsaken union, so why in the world would she think screwing another man would. *Hmph, he can't be that good because he hasn't made her forget about me.*

Some nights when I think about her having been with that nigga, and then bringing her ass home and crawling into bed next to me, I want to pull my forty-five from under the bed and blow her brains out. Oh man, how did this turn into *my life*!

Reaching for the box of tissues on the desk, I see Faye's name flashing across my phone screen. I pick the phone up and throw it across the room. "Damn! God, what did I ever do to deserve so much unhappiness?"

If I could ball up into the fetal position and return to my mothers' womb right now, I would. I'm such a failure. The things I want the most in life continue to elude me, and I don't know why. Is this all life is meant to be for me? Don't I deserve happiness and love at some point? I've spent a lifetime loving Mya and dreaming of the day we would finally be together, and it has been nothing but a nightmare. Our first year together was the best, but since then, it has been downhill. If she ever loved me, she no longer does. She doesn't believe in me any longer and only stays because she doesn't want to be alone herself, but if the right man came along at the right time, I know she would give him a chance. All she had to say was, *leave Kim and be with me.* That's all, and she refuses to will herself to do it.

Lately, all I have wanted to do is be alone. No Kim, no Mya, and no business to run. The sexual trysts I have been having with Faye have just been another part of this never-ending nightmare. Another sign that my life is out of control. Mya no longer desires me that way. She makes me feel that making love is a favor she extends and not a desire she wants to fulfill. If I could, I would just throw in the towel and walk away from it all…the bills, the responsibilities, the worry, the desire to just be loved.

One day recently, while at breakfast, a news story came on the television in the eatery where Mya and I were seated. A man had killed his estranged wife and her lesbian lover, their two young children, and then turned the gun on himself. Mya commented in her usual dry humor, "When people get to that point, I don't understand why they never think to start with themselves."

I chuckled at the comment, but deep down inside, I wanted to cry. I wanted to scream, *because after all we've suffered, it wouldn't be fair for the others to go on and be happy without us.* At that moment, I wanted to share with Mya all the dark feelings I had been having lately. If she loved me, she would understand. The Mya I met at *Jackson's* over two years ago would have taken me into her arms and loved the hurt away. But the woman sitting on the barstool next to me at the *Central Avenue Coffee Shop* that day was not the same woman I thought I would love through all eternity.

Now I have to deal with Faye's betrayal instead. What did she think when she confronted Mya at that party? I will probably never know because I will never speak to Faye again. Of all the people in the world, I never would have thought she would be the one to turn on me this way. When I asked her why she did it, all she could say was, "I don't know." First, she answered my phone and got smart with Kim. Now she's gone and destroyed my relationship with Mya. What else was she capable of doing? What if I stooped to her level and told her husband what a nasty freak his wife was and how she loved to suck my dick and lick my asshole. I bet she wouldn't think that was too funny.

Rubbing my hand over my tired face, I try to think about my future, but all I see is Kim there and the hell I'm already living in. I don't know why I feel connected to her or what I think will happen if I break the bonds of this so-called marriage. The feelings of abandonment always resurface, and I convince myself that, good or bad, thick or thin, Kim isn't going anywhere. I could pack my bags tomorrow and leave, and she would sit right there. If I decided a week, a month, a year later to return, she would let me. My wife keeps me shackled to her this way. Subconsciously, she's feeding off my insecurities. Kim knows my fears and my weaknesses. She knows that if she stands steadfast, she will outlast any woman I become involved with. When things are going well between us, she believes that I'm finally seeing things her way and have decided to concede.

Mya was to be my savior. But she didn't know how to be. I wish I could have taught her, but it's a gift, a trait she had to come into on her own. Before Faye betrayed my trust, Mya claimed to love me, and she probably did, but she was impatient and selfish. She, too, was insecure but in a different way. She didn't want to risk laying her guard down completely and giving me one hundred percent of herself. She said it would be stupid of her to do so since I can't give her one hundred percent of me. When I countered that I already did, she would reply in that nitpicky way of hers, *"LaDamien, how can you give me one hundred percent of you. You're married and leave me to go home and pretend you're happy to be there? When you are with me, and Kim is calling and sending text messages every five seconds, and you respond, you surely aren't giving me one hundred percent then."*

I laugh. It doesn't matter now, thanks to Faye. But Mya is part to blame as well. If she had been handling her business, I never would have slipped back into Faye's grip. Faye turned everything around. Yes, she stayed with Ariel while I was in Orlando with Mya, but she did it as a favor, not because anything was still going on between us. She turned things around, repeating stuff I had told her about Mya and me. Faye lied, making up stories claiming she and I had shared the same things. Talking about Mya to Faye, I now realize, was a mistake, but had I known then what I know now, I would have kept my mouth shut.

Looking over at the clock, I realize it's almost three a.m., and I need to shower. Hopefully, it will calm my nerves, and I will sleep the rest of the night peacefully and most of the day. When I awaken, I'll return home and fain happiness, or contentment at the very least.

The water is hot and feels good on my skin. A nice hot shower is usually all I need to lift my mood. The water is calming, and the heat is soothing. I stay in the shower for almost forty-five minutes. The great thing about hotels is the water rarely runs cold. I lather my body with the hotel soap, a task within itself. As my hand guides the soapy rag down to my limp shaft, I begin to think of Mya. I wonder what she's thinking. She has not tried to call me, and I have not tried calling her. Still, I wonder if she's still angry, relieved to have me out of her life, worried, or if she even cares anymore. I continue to stroke myself, but my penis refuses to cooperate. I'm too stressed and too uptight.

My thoughts from earlier in the night begin to resurface, and I can feel my brain churning, tightening, and resisting the negativity that's trying to consume me. The tears I'm fighting back are burning my eyes as I resist the urge to give way to my true feelings. If I do, they will take me far beyond my sexual addiction to Faye, my overwhelming need for Mya, and my conflicted marriage to Kim.

Giving in to the fear that resides deep inside me is something I've never done. Buried beneath layers of failed relationships, disappointments, anger, and resentment of everything that has happened in my life are places in time I refuse to revisit. Using the rag to wipe away the tears and the memories dancing at the surface, I turn the temperature level as far left as possible. The hot water will help me claw my way back to the present and back to my dreams for a better life.

After stepping out of the shower, I dry off and locate my phone to ensure it's not damaged. Placing it on the nightstand, I pull back the bedding and climb in. Lying there waiting for sleep to overtake me, I try to put everything into perspective. Leaving Faye alone isn't that hard. All I need is for Mya to forgive me, be more attentive to my needs, and be more consistent in our lovemaking. She needs to understand that she can't go weeks or months without making love to me. When I get back home, I will call Faye and let her know that it's time for me to move on for good, so there's no doubt in her mind that we will ever have anything together. She needs to focus her attention on her husband and try to get him to understand her sexual needs like I need to have Mya understand mine.

The talk I will have with Mya when I get back will center on my need for her to show why I should leave my wife to be with her. It's one thing for her to say she wants us to be together and that she loves me, but something different for her to demonstrate what I will have if I make that decision on her behalf.

Divorcing Kim is more than me leaving one woman to be with another. We have a history that exceeds our years of marriage. Despite our lack of compatibility in marriage, she's my friend and the mother of my child. Kim will always be a part of my life. That aside, I must consider the ramifications of walking away from my daughter. Plus the effects of not being there during her formative years. I will be leaving my home and the comfort of knowing Kim is there for me no matter what. Starting over with Mya will be no walk at the park, but she will need to make my transition as painless as possible.

The sun is peeping through the break in the curtains, and the clock located behind my vibrating cell phone reads eleven thirty-three. It has been six hours since I fell into a tranquil sleep. The number flashing before me belongs to Wanda. "What does she want?" I ask out loud. "Hello."

"Hey, are you busy?"

"No, what's up?"

Wanda rarely calls me on the weekends unless something has come up involving one of my properties. But the tone of her voice doesn't lend to that notion.

"You sound sleepy. Did I wake you?" She's wasting time, so I decide to get her to the point of this call.

"Is something wrong?"

"You were on my mind, and I thought I would give you a call. *American Gangster* is on, and I know how much you love it, so I wanted to make sure you knew it was on."

Where this is coming from all of a sudden is perplexing. Wanda is hot and cold. When I think she's gotten over her feelings for me, I get a call out of the blue. So I tell her thanks, that I will check it out. Next, I lie and say that Kim is home and I need to go. She appears to buy it. The truth is, I don't care if she did or not.

Wanda, Faye, both women, are obstacles in my way. I don't know why, but minutes later, I dial Wanda's number and share Faye's deception with her. "Why do you think she did it?" I ask.

Wanda is silent for the longest, and then replies, "So are you now admitting that you're having an affair with Mya?" Without a second thought, I hang up on her.

Mya

"*Mya, don't* say anything, just let me talk." It's LaDamien on the phone. We have not spoken since I confronted him about Faye on Thursday. It's Tuesday, and I'm preparing for work.

"Make it quick. I have to get going."

"Faye and I met a very long time ago before I was even married. I was sleeping with her up until about two months after we started seeing each other, and then I broke it off with her. Although we weren't sleeping together, we still talked to each other. She's the one that works the deals for me on my travel. She and her husband own a travel agency, and I needed that connection. She has only been to my house once, and that was when you and I were in Orlando. Ariel and I were in Orlando together, but it wasn't the same without Kim being there. I'm not good with my daughter when we are alone. I took Ariel back Sunday night. She was going to stay with Pam until Wednesday night, I would pick her up, and then when Kim came in, we would head back to Orlando. Pam was on vacation, but there was an emergency, and she had to go in, and no one else was available to pick Ariel up from school, so I asked Faye. It got too late for you to leave, so I asked Faye to stay and drop Ariel off at school the following morning.

"Mya, I love you, and things weren't supposed to turn out like this. After we broke up over the Orlando incident, and you refused to see me, I did sleep with Faye a couple of times, but after we made up, that was it. I swear I have not been with her since."

"And what about Wanda? What fantastic story do you have to tell about that?"

"Nothing is going on with Wanda and me, never has and never will be. I have no idea why Faye made that lie up. I have never been involved with Wanda. Never!"

The silence stretches the conversation out. After LaDamien's speech, I have nothing to say. Honestly, I don't care at this point. I know what needs to get done. I can force myself to do it. I'll just hang up on him and this whole mess. But before I can, he asks about Miami. "So what are we doing this weekend? Is Miami still on?"

"Is that all LaDamien? I need to go." I've grabbed my purse and heading out the door. The trip to Miami is the last thing on my mind, and why did he have to bring it up? "I don't know about Miami. Why don't you ask Faye?"

My comment has incensed him. I can hear it in his breathing. He's clenching his teeth as he fights the urge to say something cruel. "Call me later, and let me know what we're doing. Just know I still want us to go. It doesn't have to be intimate, but I think we need to talk, and it will give us a neutral setting away from everything and everybody. Okay?"

LaDamien

As we make our way across Alligator Alley towards Ft. Lauderdale and into Miami Gardens, Mya's solemn mood is causing me to regret forcing the issue. She never said she wasn't going to come. Instead, she made me beg and grovel for her to accompany me. I was ready to throw in the towel and just give her the tickets and transfer the room into her name when she said she would go. Now, her gloomy demeanor has me reconsidering.

We arrive at the hotel, check-in, and get settled in the room. Honestly, I'm at a loss as to what I should be saying or doing. We're here together, and I hope we can enjoy the weekend. While Mya is in the bathroom changing into what she will wear to the festival, I take the opportunity to call Kim and let her know I have arrived. She believes I'm at the festival with my long-time friend Joseph, celebrating his fortieth birthday. Joseph's wife is a Lieutenant currently serving in Iraq. He's here in Miami attending the festival, and his room is across the street from our hotel. If things go south with Mya and me, he's prepared to let me crash there.

"Just wanted to let you know I'm here," I say.

Kim says she's at the store grocery shopping. She and Ariel are making pizza for dinner, and then she tells me she ran into one of our old teachers at the gas station. Mya steps out of the bathroom and sees me on the phone. She lets out a deep sigh and rolls her eyes. I immediately tell Kim I have to go.

"Sorry, I was just letting her know I made it. Are you hungry? Do you want to go somewhere and eat or take our chances at the stadium?" Mya is indifferent. She isn't going to make this easy. So I let her know I prefer to eat first. Minutes later, she follows me out the door, out the hotel, and into the car, still not saying much.

We have lunch at Esther's, a soul food joint not far from Dolphin Stadium. We exchange petty conversation but not enough to allow me to put my guard down. It wasn't until we were at the festival that Mya began to relax. She was enjoying the music and letting her resistance subside. George Benson had her moving her head, George Duke brought a smile to her face, and by the time Stanley Clark took the stage, her hand was caressing my shoulders. I looked over at her, and she smiled up at me, letting me know we were going to be all right, and we were. Even when Kim began her ritual of calling every half hour, Mya didn't fret. She was in a zone enjoying the musical artist gracing the stage.

It was getting late, and the last act, the O'Jay's, had yet to come on stage. The weather was excellent, and I was happy to be back in Mya's good graces. We hadn't moved from our seats since our arrival, more so because I didn't want to risk being seen by someone who knew Kim. Our seats were three rows from the stage, and there had to be ten thousand people behind us. During the intermission, I asked Mya if she was hungry or needed anything. She said she needed to go potty and could use something to drink and eat. Reaching into my pocket, I retrieved a fifty-dollar bill and told her to get whatever she wanted.

Once Mya was out of my sight, I stood to stretch and take a look around to see if I recognized anyone. To my horror, Faye and her best friend Sharon were sitting two sections back. I quickly turned back around and took my seat. Five minutes later, Faye was making her way down my row.

"Hey, who are you here with?" she asked, looking around. "Where are you staying?"

"I thought I told you to stay away from me? We have nothing to talk about." My voice is weak, and my heart is pounding as I look in the direction Mya walked when she left.

Faye followed my gaze. Her curiosity peeked further. "Tell me, or I'll just sit here until they return."

"Leave me alone, Faye. What difference does it make? I'm not here with you. I don't care to see you, so stop worrying about what I'm doing and who I'm doing it with, okay. Get away from me before I call security and have them move you." This situation has the potential to get ugly. If Faye sees Mya, there's no telling what she might do. It may be best if I change my tone and try to be nice to her. Whether I tell her it's Mya or not, she's going to watch me the rest of the night and figure it out on her, and then what?

Faye allowed me to squirm in my seat several more minutes before she decided to let me off the hook. "Okay, LaDamien, have it your way. I'm not going to let you ruin my weekend. Go ahead, and do what you do." She stomped off, never looking back.

Thirty minutes passed, and Mya had not returned. Fear began to take hold of me. What if she saw Faye and had left? I had the keys to the car, but that wouldn't stop Mya. She'd hail a taxi, catch the bus, or, depending on how mad she was, walk back to the hotel. Faye could have seen Mya and stopped her, feeling her head with more lies.

As my mind conjured up scenarios to explain the length of her absence, Tom Joyner introduced the mighty O'Jay's. The crowd rose to their feet in a round of applause. I needed to find Mya. Excusing myself as I slipped down the row, I bumped into Mya, sliding through in my direction.

"Man, was those lines long." She had a plastic Solo cup in one hand and a foam takeout container in the other. I pointed into the direction she had come from, instructing her to head back. When we made it to the end of the aisle, I told Mya I was ready to leave.

"Do you want to see them?" I asked, referring to The O'Jay's. "We can make our way out and catch them on the Jumbo-Tron near the exit."

"I'm fine. Let's go." Mya didn't know how relieved I was that she said that. The O'Jay's wowed the audience and kept them on their feet. I used the opportunity to maneuver out of the area and away from Faye without being seen.

Mya ate her food, a mixture of fried rice and an array of grilled seafood and vegetables. Her drink was Chardonnay and not Sprite as I had thought and hoped. Although I was thirsty, knowing Mya was getting her drink on gave me hope that I might get lucky tonight. During the fifteen-minute ride back to the hotel, we talked about the various acts and which ones we enjoyed the most. I pulled into the hotel parking lot, which was near capacity, and found a space in a row facing the street. After exiting the car, my worst nightmare appeared; Faye and Sharon exited a vehicle at the *Marriott*, located across the street. The same hotel where Joe was staying. "Damn," I said out loud.

"What's wrong," Mya asked, getting out of the car. Normally she would have waited for me to walk around and open the door for her, but I guess I was taking too long.

"Nothing," My phone rang, and hesitantly, I looked to see who was calling. Relieved, it was Kim. I held the phone up to Mya and exclaimed, "It's Kim again. Go ahead on up while I take this." Mya didn't argue. She took the key card from me and walked away.

The room was dark when I arrived. Mya had showered and was in bed. In the bathroom, I wiped the remaining steam from the mirror, pulled out a coconut-scented incense from my travel bag, placed the lit stick on the edge of the counter, turned on the shower, and took a seat on the toilet. The message on my cell phone read, *"Come back down, and play, I'll make it worth it."*
"Don't fuck with me, Faye. It's over."
"It won't ever be over between us, never."
"This time, it's Mya who I desire."
"Kim is your wife, and that is the only one I respect."
The conversation could have gone on all night long if Mya hadn't knocked on the door. "What are you doing? I thought you were talking to Kim downstairs."
"I'll be out in a second." Putting the phone down, I undressed and stepped into the shower. Stung by the cold water, I reached forward and turned the handle to alter the temperature. My shower was quick, and as I rushed to dry off, I received another text from Faye. "I'm downstairs in the lobby…come down, u won't regret it."
Oh shit, I thought to myself. This can't be happening. Should I call the lobby and make sure they don't let her up? Should I risk calling and talking some sense into her?
"LaDamien, it's one in the morning. What are you doing?"
It was settled. The phone was powered off. Quickly, I brushed the ashes up, and dumped them in the toilet, pressed the handle to flush, and opened the door showing Mya all my glory. "I didn't think you were going to give me any, so I was handling my business." I teased.
Mya looked down at my limp shaft. "You must think I'm stupid or something. The only time you are that limp is when you're stressed about something. There's no way you just jacked off." She turned and returned to the bed, nestling under the covers. The room is cold, just how I like it. Mya doesn't like the room this cold, so I know she did it just for me. Fooling around with Faye, I may have missed my opportunity to make love to Mya.
"Hey, come here," I say to Mya as I pull her body close to mine. "Let me warm you up." She doesn't pull away but allows me to spoon her.

"Take off this nightshirt so that I can feel your skin on mine." Mya allows me to lift the shirt over her head. Touching her body helps me get over my nervousness and forget Faye may be lurking downstairs.

"Umm, that's what I'm talking about." Mya hums when my stiff rod brushes her thigh as I make my way down to my treasure.

She turns slightly and spreads her legs so I don't waste any time beginning my late-night feast. I love going down on Mya more than I love being inside her. I've just begun, and she's already squirming, forcing me to grip her ass and hold her in place. My tongue is working feverishly as I work her clit, and suck her juices. Mya's body is tense, and she's trying to raise her hips. I crave fingering her, but if I let go, she'll get away. My goal is always to bring her to climax, but she tries to resist, although I always win the battle.

"LB, stop," she begins to moan and then whine. Her resistance is building. I place my left arm over her right thigh and rise onto my elbow. She relaxes enough for me to start massaging her vulva as I flick my tongue on her clit. The more she swells with excitement, the more excited I become. Mya is drenched, letting me know not only is she enjoying it, but she was looking forward to making love to me. I hate I had her waiting and worried Faye was going to do something stupid.

As I suck her clit, I slide my index finger inside and begin massaging her vaginal walls. Mya loves this, and is starting to rotate her pelvis in conjunction with my fingering. When I add my middle finger, Mya moves from a slow grind to more intense gyrations, driving my libido over the edge. I stretch out onto my stomach, using the bed to massage my enlarged penis, as I meet Mya's thrusts with my tongue and fingers. She loves every second, evident in her moans and movement. I'm about to cum, and need Mya to come along for the journey. When I try to insert a third finger, her vaginal muscles tighten, and I hear her murmur, "uh, uh, too much, baby." Her pleas only intensify my desire to make her cum. She's so wet and so sweet I yearn to suck every drop of her juices out of her. Although she's enjoying our foreplay, she's still trying to wrestle from my grip. I pretend to release my hold long enough for her to relax a little. The second she lets her guard down, I grip her inner-thighs and spread her legs as wide as they can go, then pierce her vagina with my tongue as deep as I can, moving it in a circular motion. All hell breaks loose. Mya grips my head as her body begins to convulse. She's trying to push me away, but my need to cum is stronger. I'm licking her with long stiff swipes while my finger penetrates her anal opening. Mya arches up, and her fluids stream down onto my hand. As always, I only require one swift motion, and I'm inside Mya, but the slightest movement of her hip causes my dam to break. She lifts and pulls my right nipple into her mouth to punish me and began to suck. I'm now the one trembling, but unlike Mya, I can't control my desire, and the entire third floor probably heard my release. It only took me a minute to recover before I had Mya on top of me, riding me to ecstasy once again.

    I don't know what had gotten a hold of Mya, but she was hanging with me and enjoying our lovemaking. Not once did she tell me to slow down or stop because she was tired or getting sore. We were starting our third round. She was on her knees, and I had just entered her from behind when the hotel phone rang. It startled us both, causing my rod to slip.

    "Don't you dare answer it," Mya said with authority. Remembering my cell phone was turned off, I reached over her to grab the receiver. Mya grabbed my hand.

    "If you answer that phone, and it's that bitch across the street, you better be prepared to take your ass over there."

    "But it might be Kim," I said, knowing it probably wasn't.

    "Or it might be a wrong number. For once, LaDamien put me and my feelings first. Just once, realize that you aren't slick, and the only person you're fooling is yourself." The phone rang for the fourth and final time, and since the mood was gone, I fell to the bed and pulled Mya with me. A few minutes later, she had me by the hand, leading me into the bathroom. She slides back the shower curtain and turned on the water. "Come bathe me. I love it when you do that."

    Thirty minutes later, we were relaxed and spooning again. Mya had my left arm draped over her waist while she held my hand close to her heart. I didn't know if she was trying to hold on to me as a show of affection or if she was trying to restrain me from leaving the bed or answering the phone if it rang again.

Mya

Friends shouldn't let friends drive drunk, nor should they encourage their friends to stay in crazy adulterous affairs. LaDamien kept asking me about the trip to Miami, and I was determined not to give in. But Jaime kept calling to check on me and to inquire about the Faye situation. When I told her I was over LaDamien, and this whole mess, she laughed.

"Girl, stop tripping. You love that big black hunk of a man too much just to walk away. If his wife hasn't caused you to leave him alone, why would you let some skank ass married hooker run you off?"

"So what am I supposed to do? I can't be out here fighting over somebody else's husband."

Why was I even talking to Jaime? She and I didn't talk in a year, as much as we'd talked since Eric's party. We usually saw each other at the book club meetings, and on rare occasions, we all got together and went to dinner and the club. Now, since the Faye thing, she had become my new best friend.

"No, you can't, but that doesn't mean you just let that heifer run you off. LaDamien may be a jerk, but he does care about you. If nothing else, go to Miami, have a good time, go shopping, and spend as much of his money as you can. He's desperate now, so you can get whatever you wish out of him. In other words, make him pay for the hurt he's caused you."

Like a fool, I listened to her and agreed to come to the jazz festival with LaDamien. When I first saw Faye, I didn't think much of it. LaDamien had said she owned a travel agency, so it wouldn't be odd for her to be here. There was a girl I knew a while back named Sheila that owned an agency and made most of her money booking trips to various festivals. Plus, I needed to make the best of this weekend, and letting LaDamien know she was here would only be a distraction.

My radar didn't fully engage until we returned to the hotel. LaDamien said Kim was on the phone and for me to go to the room while he talked to her. As I waited for the elevator, I remembered I had taken off my earrings and placed them in the cupholder. Making my way back outside to retrieve them, I saw LaDamien walking across the street. Thinking he had seen his friend Joseph, I preceded through the door, but it wasn't Joseph he was meeting. It was Faye. My first inclination was to follow him, but what was the point. LaDamien didn't care how his actions affected me, so I turned and headed back inside. In the room, I showered and readied for bed. Before I got in, I walked over to the window and looked out. LaDamien had only made it to the low-cut shrubs that lined the *Marriott* property. His body language let me know he was not happy having Faye and her friend across the street.

"This is so messed up," I thought to myself. "LaDamien is married and leaves Kim home, Faye is married and leaves her husband home. Maybe LaDamien and Faye should be together driving each other crazy. I watched them for a few minutes, satisfied he wasn't going any further than the curb. In the room, I slid under the covers and counted the seconds until I heard the door open. Instead of coming around and checking on me, he entered the bathroom and closed the door. Secret code for, I'm about to get on the phone, and I can't let Mya know who's on the other end.

He was annoying me, so I got up and knocked on the door. He pretended to be using the bathroom, had the incense burning, and everything. A short time later, I had to knock again. What was it with him and that woman? She wasn't even attractive and looked older than we were. LaDamien didn't have a type. Or maybe what they said was true. All coochie looks the same.

I finally got him out of the bathroom and into the bed. I planned to make love to him and get his mind off of Faye, but the more I considered it, the madder I became with myself. I was not in competition with this woman. LaDamien needed to grow up, and it wasn't my job to help. It wasn't my place to try and lure him from anybody. He climbed into the bed and pulled me in his arms. As much as I tried to resist him, it felt so good, so right, that I gave in to my feelings and made love to him because I desired him and not because I was trying to prove a point.

"You need to do something about Faye." I said as we dressed later Sunday morning, "Not for my sake but because she's dangerous and poses a threat to your marriage." LaDamien cut his eye at me when I said the last part. "Now I don't feel like I can let you out of my sight, and I don't like to feel that way."

He didn't get it. I seriously was beginning to believe he just didn't comprehend the severity of the situation. Perhaps he had lived his whole life with women fawning over him and fighting for the right to be his main squeeze. But I wasn't one of those women and didn't feel up to the challenge.

Of course, he didn't see it my way and insinuated that my insecurities were the problem and nothing he had done. If I wanted to prolong the drama, I could have brought up seeing him talking to Faye. But I didn't bother. In the end, I would only frustrate myself. We planned to go shopping and have an early dinner at a restaurant named The Mahogany Grille. Afterward, we'd head over to the stadium where Chrisette Michelle and Kem were among the artist performing.

LaDamien and I grab a bite to eat at the hotel before heading out. Faye's car is not in the parking space they had pulled into last night. This gives me a slight sense of relief. Hopefully, she has found other means of entertainment to fill her time. We're headed to Dolphin Mall. I always enjoy the opportunity to walk freely with LaDamien, holding his hand and stealing kisses. It's times like these that I feel like we're meant to be together. Our interactions are fluid and feel so natural. It does help that LaDamien is so accommodating.

He's giving me the keys to the candy store and prodding me to try outfits he selected and modeled them for him. We don't leave a store without a purchase. Some are for him but primarily for me, including an all-white sundress he has decided he wants me to wear to the concerts later. I return from the fitting room. LaDamien is at the counter holding an array of silver bangles, silver hoop earrings, and a long necklace consisting of silver hoops linked together by thin serpentine chains.

"Do you need some shoes to go with it?" he asks. I do a quick mental inventory of the five pairs of shoes I brought with me and let him know I have a pair of wedge-heeled white sandals that will go perfectly. "You know the ones that wrap around my ankles." He recalls the shoes and agrees. It's after one p.m., so we make our way to the exit and head back to our hotel in Miramar, where we dress and head to dinner.

LaDamien tries with all his might to get me back in bed when we get to our room, but I force myself to resist his advances. As it is, we will probably miss a portion of Chrisette Michelle's performance. Kem isn't scheduled to perform until seven, and he's the main act I want to see. The Mahogany Grille has an hour wait. It's three when we arrive. They're still serving the after-church crowd and just starting to work the many festival-goers. It looks like they received the same glowing recommendation as LaDamien, and I did.

With fifteen minutes remaining on our estimated one-hour wait, I believe we have both let our guard down. It's the only explanation for why neither of us saw Faye until she was standing right in front of us.

"Don't you two look cute," she begins. "How long have you been waiting?"

LaDamien grabs my hand and heads towards the car. "Why are we leaving?" I ask. But he hastens his pace. "You can't let her ruin our time together. Why can't you just ignore her?"

"Because you can't just ignore Faye, she will keep coming at you until you say or do something that you may later regret, so I prefer just to walk away."

"But, what about dinner? They were about to call us." We are to the car, and LaDamien is opening the door for me. I look back, and Faye is following us.

"What do you want?" I ask without hesitation but annoyed.

"I was just going to say you don't have to leave on my account. I was just being friendly." The smirk on her face says otherwise. This woman knows how to push LaDamien's buttons, and she's working them now. He's livid and insisting I be quiet and get in the car.

"Leave us alone, Faye, leave *me* alone." He says through clenched teeth. Faye just smiles and continues to taunt him. She makes her way to the driver's side door blocking him from entering.

"Move out of my way," he demands, but Faye doesn't move.

I am afraid this is about to get ugly. This woman has some serious issues, and I have no idea what she hopes to accomplish by exhibiting such childish behavior. She and LaDamien are exchanging words, and I don't know if I should get out or not. The parking lot isn't that big, and people are starting to take notice. LaDamien uses his remote key to lower the window and toss the keys inside. He tells me to move over to the driver seat and take the car. Before I can ask where

I'm supposed to go, he walks away with Faye following, still taunting him. Looking in the rearview mirror, I slowly back the car out of the tight space. LaDamien is walking at a quick pace towards the street.

Faye's friend is approaching from the restaurant's direction. As I turn the car towards the exit and the direction LaDamien is walking, a man approaches him. I stop to see what is going on. The man appears to know LaDamien, which may be a bad thing depending on who he is. He talks to LaDamien while Faye's friend lures her away. The expression on LaDamien's face when he enters the car's passenger side is a mixture of embarrassment and sheer anger. There's nothing I can say at this moment that is going to make him feel better, so I head back to the hotel to give us a chance to regroup.

"I'm sorry," he mumbles, barely audible as we pull into a parking space.

"How did you ever get involved with someone like that?" I ask.

LaDamien gets out of the car and stretches. I walk around to him, and before handing him the keys, I wrap my arms around him and reach up, planting a soft kiss on his lips. "If you ignore her long enough, she'll go away, but you can't let her upset you like this."

"I have to leave. I don't want to risk running into her at the concert, she knows where we are seated, and I don't need to get into another confrontation. On top of that, Joseph was the guy I was talking to in the parking lot, and that was the last thing I needed."

He knows this isn't what I want to hear. Why should we alter our plans because of Faye? That's just what she was looking to do, and I let him know this. Still, thirty minutes later, we are checked out of the hotel and heading home. It was a long ride because neither of us said a word. LaDamien was troubled and worried, and I was fuming that he allowed that woman to ruin our trip after all.

LOVE...

- is patient
- is kind
- is not rude
- does not envy
- is not self-seeking
- will not lie
- is not proud
- is not quick to anger
- does not boast
- protects
- does not record wrongs
- trusts
- hopes
- perseveres
- finds no joy in evil but celebrates truth
- never fails

Kim

TayJohn will be away for six weeks. Our company has sent him to Denver for software training. He will be the lead support for a new system we're implementing. While LaDamien was in Miami with Joseph I did some much-needed soul searching. I decided to use this break to work on my marriage. It was never my intention to let things go this far. Falling for Taj was so easy. He knew all the right things to say and do. Our time together is increasing, and I'm starting to tell lies to spend more time with him. A few weeks ago, I went so far as to pretend I was at a three-day conference right here in Tampa, but the company had made it a requirement that I stay at the host hotel. Meanwhile, TayJohn and I were cooped up in his apartment the entire time.

Now that I have LaDamien's attention, I take advantage of the opportunity to introduce something new. When he returned from Miami, he seemed troubled. I asked him why he had returned early, and he claimed to have not been feeling well. He moped around for the next few days. On Wednesday, I suggested we grab a bite to eat and go to the. Something we have not done in ages.

During dinner, I ask if we can start having couple's time. Each weekend we would send Ariel to stay the night with a friend or relative. LaDamien and I would do something together on Friday night and Saturday morning. We would pick Ariel up Saturday evening, and as a family, we would attend church together on Sunday morning. LaDamien is all for it, and I'm thankful. Hopefully, by the time TayJohn returns from Denver, he will be out of my system. I have already committed to not calling him while he's gone. Also, I won't take any of his calls, reiterating *to myself* that this affair was a colossal mistake.

The first weekend LaDamien and I ended up going to Piccadilly's for breakfast and to the mall just to window shop. It wasn't much, but it felt so good to be spending quality time with my husband again. The following Monday, LaDamien told me to go online and purchase tickets for the Clearwater Jazz Festival the following month. Kem will be one of the headliners and is one of his favorite performers. He was a little dismayed over missing his show in Miami.

My joy only lasted a moment because, after about three weekends of couple's time, LaDamien began to drift away again. No matter how hard I tried to keep a positive attitude and fight for my marriage, my efforts were pointless if my husband wasn't cooperative.

My friend Debra and her husband aren't doing well either. She learned he's lost his job for the second time in as many years and has not shared the news with her. The last time he had been unemployed for six months before she finally put the pieces together and decided to show up at his place of employment. She spared herself major embarrassment when she ran into an acquaintance in the parking lot and asked if Todd was in his office. According to Debra, the woman's face transfixed into a perplexing frown as she shared the bad news. Todd was part of a sexual harassment case and got terminated months earlier.

Debra looked mortified as she shared with Karen and me how Todd had displayed no signs that things were amiss. He had gotten up every morning, dressed, kissed her and the kids goodbye, and headed off to work. His behavior left more questions unanswered than answered. Like where he had gone every morning, how he spent his days, and why there were no signs that an income was missing from their household, a very significant income.

When she confronted Todd, Debra explained he appeared happy to have the burden of his deception removed from his shoulders. He shared that he was too embarrassed to let her know what was going on. He thought the allegations against him would blow over. Not once did he believe his position with the company was in jeopardy. Although a hearing was scheduled, an HR Consultant had assured him it wasn't anything serious. According to him, management presented sworn statements by at least three other women. They were all friends of his accuser, stating he had made unwelcome advancements against them also. Todd said his termination was devastating, and he didn't know how he could face her with the news.

The first few weeks of his unemployment, he spent searching for a new job. He had several promising leads, but all fell through as word reached the potential employer that he'd gotten fired for sexual harassment. The more rejections he received, the more depressed he became, and the harder it was to tell her the truth. Days turned into weeks, and weeks turned into months. The more time went by, the easier it was to keep the lie going. He figured it was just a matter of time before something came through but that something never emerged. In the meantime, he used money from his 401k to keep the charade going. He had laid all this out to Debra, and she had shared it with Karen and me.

I admired Debra's bravery and wished I could be as forthcoming with my husbands' deception, not to mention my affair. As I listened to her story, I realized that the gossip that had been abuzz was about Todd. I'd heard bits and pieces at the beauty salon, nail shop, and while attending professional mixers. Thinking back, those doing the talking knew Debra and me were friends and probably tried to bait me for more information.

Todd *was* fired for sexual harassment, according to those rumors. Still, he was having an affair with his accuser. The deed that did him in was that the woman had pictures, voice messages, emails, and additional proof of their affair. She had turned on Todd when she learned he was messing with another woman within the company. There was no way I could share this information with Debra. She was already down over the whole mess as it was. I didn't need to be the bearer of more bad news. I guess, deep inside, I knew that my friends were aware of my husband's deception. I didn't want my skeletons exposed while trying to shed light on Todd's.

Debra was handling the situation the same as I was. She was standing by her man through thick and thin, for better, and right now for worst. Her only options were to stand by her man or to let him go.

For fourteen years, Todd had been the ideal mate. They had been best friends since college. Debra weighed the pros and cons and decided her marriage was worth saving. She and Todd did some soul searching, went to counseling, and renewed their commitment to each other. Debra called in some favors within the community, and two months later, Todd was working. His income wasn't nearly what it had been previously, but it was better than nothing. Now here it is a year later, and like déjà vu, it had happened again, but this time with more ramifications.

We are at *The Cheesecake Factory* at International Plaza in Tampa. Karen and I offered to take Debra out to dinner when she called with the news. I desperately want to be as open and honest with my friends about my marriage but can't. Debra is now sharing that Todd's accuser this time around is pregnant. No denying that he was involved with this woman. His overall attitude is negative. He doesn't seem interested in finding a job or stepping to the plate and trying to right this wrong. Unlike with his first firing, there are no funds from a 401K to draw on. They are in financial trouble. Debra needs him to pull himself together and get a job because she will not be paying the child support, he will be ordered to pay soon.

Karen asks Debra if perhaps it's time to reconsider her marriage. Debra doesn't want to consider this as an option. She loves Todd too much to give up on him. Debra thinks he's depressed because he's failing his family. She takes her vows seriously and will stand by her man no matter what. Karen looks dismayed. She's a no-nonsense woman. Years earlier, after learning of his infidelity, Karen gave her husband an ultimatum. Patrick took the hint and hasn't strayed since, that we know.

"He's a grown man," Karen began. "This isn't the first time he has done this. The first time I understood you standing by him, but I don't get your devotion now. He's taking your kindness for weakness, and what about the kids? What type of example are you guys setting for them? It's okay for daddy to be a trifling bum out in the streets having unprotected sex, making babies with other women, and placing their mom's health and life in jeopardy. Come on, Debra, you're smarter and better than this!"

I see the hurt in Debra's eyes. She knows she's better than this. Hell, we are both better than our marriages. However, I can sympathize with Debra because she and Todd have invested many years into their marriage.

Debra excuses herself to go to the ladies' room, and I take the opportunity to criticize Karen for her brassiness. "You could be a little less blunt and a lot more compassionate," I tease. Karen smiles and lets me know I'm right, but it's ridiculous what Todd is doing to his family.

"Come on, Kim, Debra is a beautiful, intelligent sister with a bright future. She has too much going for her to allow her life to get derailed over Todd's stupidity. She doesn't have to stand for this bullshit. Todd knows exactly what he's doing. They are too old for this childish behavior. She needs to take a stand and be firm. She needs to put his ass out and not let him back in until he gets his act together."

I know Karen is right, but she doesn't get it. Her marital problems occurred two years into the marriage. They were still young, and starting over was a feasible option. Plus, she and Patrick didn't have kids unless you count their two dogs. There's so much to consider when you have invested so much into making your marriage work. You have the kids, the perception of family, and friends, financial matters, and not to mention the emotional aspect.

Debra is returning from her trip to the ladies' room, and she's talking on her cell phone. For the first time, I think of LaDamien and the fact that I have not spoken to him since earlier in the day. I check my phone for missed calls, and there aren't any. I need to excuse myself so that I can give him a call.

"So, Kim, how are things with you and Mr. Bryson?" Karen asks after she sees me checking my phone. Debra has taken her seat and chimes in to save me.

"I know LaDamien has his issues, but I don't think he would ever put you through what Todd has put us through. I never thought I would say this, but LaDamien turned out to be okay. He's a great provider. I wish Todd did half the things for me that LaDamien does for you. If he did, we wouldn't be in the mess that we are in now. We are two months behind on the mortgage and coming close to falling at least a month behind on other payments. If Todd doesn't find a job soon, I will try to get a second job. I'm considering bankruptcy."

Silence has descended over our table. Now I need to call LaDamien, not only to check on his whereabouts but to see what, if anything, we can do to help Debra and Todd. He won't be happy about the request. He's commented on several instances when I have shared stories that he thinks Todd is a poor excuse for a man. He, of all people, believes Debra can do bad by herself.

"Ladies, speaking of LaDamien, I need to go check-in. I'll be back in a minute." They both smile when I stand.

As I'm walking away, I hear Karen say, "Debra, you and Kim are a mess." I immediately feel naked and wonder how much they know about my marital troubles. Do they know the depths of my husband's infidelities and are just waiting for me to come clean?

"Hey, what's going on?" I ask LaDamien when he answers the phone. He's in a jovial mood, asking me how the war council is going. I fill him in on the latest and share the news of Debra and Todd's financial situation. If I'm not mistaken, he sounds happy about my friend's misfortune, or maybe he isn't paying me any attention. Preoccupied by his hussy, who I'm sure is nearby.

"Where are you?" I ask. He says he's on I-4 heading back from Lakeland. He had to check on a property to see if it's ready for a scheduled open house. I note that he told me this same thing just three days ago when he came in past midnight. There's a long break in our conversation, so I listen to hear whatever I can to prove or disprove my suspicions. But all I hear is Luther Vandross crooning loudly through the phone. LaDamien asks me if I need anything else. When I say no, he ends the call. My mood has changed when I return to the table, and Karen picks up on it immediately.

"So what's lover boy up to?" she asks. Is she hinting at something, or am I paranoid? I shrug it off and repeat the lie fed to me. They both nod with skeptical looks. Who am I fooling? They know. They have to know like everyone else who has called with questions—asking me why LaDamien was at this place or that place. It's almost always the description of Mya. The same people gossiping about Todd in front of me are surely gossiping about LaDamien to Debra and Karen, hoping to receive confirmation of our tattered lives.

Later that evening, when I drop Debra off at her house, Todd sits in his favorite chair playing a video game with their eldest son. He barely speaks when I say hello. Debra looks frustrated. My reason for coming in is to retrieve some discs Debra has from when she was in her doctorate program. Once she hands them to me, I make a hasty exit.

During my drive home, I think about Debra and wonder what she must be going through. How embarrassing it must be for her to share her story. I feel like such a hypocrite. Sitting there listening to her pour her heart out, too scared to let on that I'm in the same boat. Somehow, I have convinced myself that my situation is better than hers. LaDamien is too proud of what he has accomplished to lose it. He's too consumed with appearances and what others think to allow any hint of financial troubles to surface, like him cashing out one of his mutual funds. He claimed it was to invest in a business venture with an old college friend. I know his business is struggling because of his out-of-control spending habits. Another reason to confront him before he squanders our future away, but I don't know how.

Unlike Debra, I have found a distraction, a source of comfort, to keep me from going crazy. TayJohn will be back next week, and instead of telling him that it's over, I'll be picking him up from the airport and going to his place to get the loving my body has been missing since he left.

LaDamien

Mya and I are on International Drive in Orlando when Kim calls. She's telling me about her friend Debra and Debra's husband, Todd. When Kim finishes, she holds the phone, not speaking. I look at Mya and roll my eyes upward. She chuckles. We know this is Kim's way of trying to figure out if I'm alone. You would think that after all this time, she would know that it's not going to work, but time after time, she does it.

Like Debra and Karen are to Kim, Mya is my best friend. No matter what we go through or how bad things get between us, and we have had our share of bad times, like the trip to Miami that ended in disaster, she's the person I trust with my deepest thoughts. We haven't fully recovered from that weekend, and things have been tense, but she's still here, and that's enough for me. Aside from the drama, she's the person I call first with the news, good or bad. She's who I roll my ideas off of most of the time. Lately, she's the person whose opinion I seek when I need advice, personal or professional. That is one of the things I always loved about her. We can debate an issue for hours, and in the end, agree to disagree. When I'm upset, she has a way of moving us from the topic back to the place where only our love for each other matters. So when I end the call with Kim, I turn to her and share the latest on Debra and Todd. She shakes her head and displays a look of disbelief.

"Well, they say birds of a feather flock together. No wonder Kim is so passive towards your infidelity. She's hanging with people who think as she does." I ask her what she means by this, and she doesn't hesitate to expound on her comment.

"Seriously, LaDamien, Kim and her girls are all educated women with professional careers. Appearances with these are more important. They're worried about what people think. So they choose to live a lie rather than risk anybody knowing they have the same issues as everybody else. Just look at Kim. She's calling you talking about Debra like her situation is any better."

Mya will probably never marry, I think to myself. She sees everything in black and white. She would never cut a brother any slack, and I wonder why she even bothers with me. Mya thinks she knows so much about relationships when she doesn't know half of what it takes to be married. On top of that, she doesn't understand commitment and staying together no matter what. If she and I were to get married, she would leave at the first sign of trouble. Still, I try to get her to understand where her thinking is off-center. "How do you know they aren't just standing by their men because they love them and want the relationship to work?"

"Standing by your man is being there to support his dreams and encouraging him to keep going when he feels like giving up—not giving him a pass to give up. If Debra were to get real with herself, she'd see that Todd probably doesn't want to be with her anymore, but he's too much of a coward to say so. He's probably acting this way in hopes that she'll get tired and leave him. But she can't do that because that would mean letting people know that her marriage wasn't all that she claimed it was." Mya pauses for a second and then continues. "What about counseling? Maybe Todd is depressed. You know Black men would rather die than admit they have some sort of mental illness.

"Then look at your wife. She walks around like her world ain't crumbling before her eyes. You and I both know the truth about that. So you tell me, how can Kim stand by and let you cheat on her if she loved you? There's no way my husband could be running around town with another woman, and I just sit quietly and take it. You aren't even my husband, and I want to beat you down over this Faye mess. If you don't find a permanent solution to that situation, I'm going to be history." Mya looks agitated. The last thing I desired or needed was for her to think about Faye.

"Mya, Kim doesn't even know about you," I blurt out for some unknown reason. Kim has thrown Mya in my face during many arguments, and Mya knows it because I have told her. "And if she does, it doesn't mean that she doesn't love me. There's a lot to consider when you are talking about ending a marriage."

Mya laughs. "Why are you getting defensive?" she asks. "The truth is the truth. Why do people exert so much energy into putting up a façade for people who don't mean anything to them? Who are you and Kim, or Debra and Todd, fooling by pretending all is well when it isn't? Regardless of what you think you're showing others, the fact is, at the end of the day, your marriage is broken, you aren't trying to fix it, and you're not happy. As for me, happiness supersedes appearance any day. I would rather be alone and happy than married and miserable."

I want to say to Mya, and *that's why you are alone*, but she can be so mean at times that she would probably jump out of the car and walk back to St. Pete. Instead, I pull her close and kiss her forehead. She smiles, a sign that she realizes she has gone out in left field somewhere. We have arrived at my favorite men's clothing store. Mya decides to walk over to *Ross Dress for Less* while I shop for a new suit. Thirty minutes later, she's meandering outside the store, so I motion for her to come inside.

Malik, the store manager, is showing me a brown suit. Mya smirks and starts looking through the suits hanging on a nearby rack. She refuses to come near me until Malik has left to assist another customer. On many occasions, we have come to the store, and I think there's an unspoken language between Malik and Mya. She doesn't value his opinion. It's obvious she's put off by his sales tactics. Now that he's gone, she makes her way over to me. I ask her about the brown suit, and she says it's nice, but she prefers the one with the peach and navy pin-strips. I signal for Malik, but he pretends not to see me. Mya chuckles, satisfied that he's respecting the invisible boundaries she has set.

Mya points out a few more suits that she likes and hands them to me. Malik makes his way back to me, and Mya cops a feel on my behind, her flirtatious way of letting me know she's ready to go. As I discuss my impending purchase, Mya is making sexual gestures towards me. She's tracing her lips with her tongue, smiling seductively and blowing kisses. When that doesn't get me to the register as quickly as she wants, she approaches and becomes very clingy. Now she's leaning on me, massaging my shoulders, and whispering that she loves me. I tell Malik I will take a navy suit and white shirt that he's holding. He then offers to throw in a tie and cuff links for an extra twenty dollars. Mya sighs, and I decline the offer. We leave the store, and I ask her if there's anything in the Ross store that she liked. She says no. When we get in the car, I tell Mya that she's rude, and she laughs. "It isn't funny, and you need to knock it off."

"It's not my intention to be rude. Malik disregards what you are asking him for and starts pulling out suits that look like a pimp would wear."

"That's being a good salesman," I say. "He doesn't have the suit that I ask for in my size, so he shows me similar suits that I can fit. If he just told customers he didn't have the suit they asked for in their size and left it at that, he wouldn't be in business very long." Mya is quiet, so I continue, "You're messing up my hustle, baby. Malik looks out for me, so I need you to be nicer when we come over here. Okay?"

She smiles, and says "Okay."

"Are you hungry?" I ask, and she says she's not. For some reason, I'm not surprised. Sometimes I think she's indifferent just for the sake of being indifferent.

We have been together since ten this morning, and it's now after six. We grabbed a bite to eat at Wendy's around noon, and I'm starving. Since Mya says she isn't hungry, I rule out going to a restaurant, and we stop at a *Subway* sandwich shop.

Mya places our order while I go to the restroom. When I return, she's sitting at a table by the window with a foot-long club, a large soda, a bag of plain chips, and three Macadamia Nut cookies. I unwrap the sandwich and give Mya half. Although she claimed not to be hungry, she takes the sandwich and bites into it.

As hungry as I was when we came in, I'm satisfied thirty minutes later as we walk back to my car carefree. Holding hands, acting as though two hours from now she will not be at her home alone, and I will not be answering Kim's unending questions about how I spent my day.

We are about ten miles past Lakeland, and Mya is singing along with Mary J. Blige's *Be Without You*. When she gets to the line where Mary says, *'come on, put your hands up,'* Mya starts waving her hands in the air like she's at a live concert. I ask her why she's faking, and she replies by singing, *"Anybody who's ever loved ya know just what I feel, too hard to fake it, nothing can replace it."* Her horrible singing makes me laugh.

Reflecting on the song's lyrics and thinking back to our earlier conversation about marriage, I wonder how Mya can sing this song with such conviction. Yet, she has such strong opinions about what she would and wouldn't tolerate from her man. "So what do you think Mary is talking about in this song?"

Mya explains. "She's talking about two people who are in it together through thick and thin, good or bad. No matter what they are going through, it isn't bigger than the two of them together. Sorta like me, and you, ride or die." She reaches for my hand.

"So how is that different from Debra standing by Todd?"

She pulls her hand away and lets out a deep sigh. "Why are you bringing that up again?"

"Because I need to know how you define love and how deep your love is for me. You say Debra is wrong for standing by Todd, Kim is wrong for standing by me, but you're sitting here singing about a love that can sustain anything. I just want to know what the difference is."

"The difference is I love you because of who you are and how you make me feel. Not because of what you can do for me or because we fit some mold society has decided makes us a perfect fit. My love won't change based on what you have materially. If you lost everything you have, my love for you wouldn't change. But on the other hand, I'm not going to let you disrespect me just because I love you. Grant it, I don't know Debra or Todd, so I can't say what their deal is, but as for you and Kim, based on what *you* say, I wouldn't be in that situation."

"What situation Mya? Exactly what do you think is Kim and my situation?"

Her posture has stiffened, and her response is just as hard. "Why are we having this conversation, LaDamien? I feel like you're purposely trying to pick a fight with me. You claim you don't love Kim, that you made a mistake marrying her. You're afraid to leave because you don't want to leave your daughter, which is a joke when you consider the little time you spend with her. Then there are the finances you keep talking about you don't want to lose to Kim in a divorce. Still, if you talked to an attorney, you'd know Florida is like a community property state. Since Kim is gainfully employed, you wouldn't have to pay her alimony. Do we want to get into the Faye situation or the fact that you keep asserting that Kim is having an affair? If you love your wife and don't want to leave her, just be honest, and say that so we can stop playing games. It's just too much madness otherwise."

I'm taken aback when she brings Ariel into the conversation. This is the first time she has done this, and I let her know that Ariel is off-limits. If nothing else, I love my child. Mya says she doesn't want to talk about this anymore and for me to change the subject. I can tell she's tired and wants to be left alone, so I put in a mixed CD, and Rick James, *Deeper Still,* replaces the silence. We are well into Tampa, and Mya still isn't talking, so I decided to bring up a subject I know will lift her spirits.

"I thought we could go to Savannah for your birthday?"

Mya's body language changes, and she turned towards me. I see the smile I love so much, and she lets me know she's interested. Placing my hand on her thigh, I ask if she wants to go for the weekend or during the week.

Savannah is one of the places Mya has mentioned she would love to visit. She's intrigued by old Southern towns and wants to tour the Victorian-style homes and have dinner at the famed *The Lady and Sons* restaurant. Like Miami Gardens, I'm going to have to plan to pull this off, so Kim doesn't up and decide she wants to come along.

My hand is now under Mya's skirt, and I'm running my finger under the elastic in the leg opening of her panties, searching for my mound of gold. "Take them off," I instruct, and she obliges.

I place her hand in my lap, and she takes it from there. She gently massages the growing muscle under the denim fabric of my shorts. Minutes later, she's unzipping them and placing her hand inside my underwear. It feels so good, causing me to lean forward a bit, one hand on the steering wheel and the other fingering Mya. She's relaxing back in the seat, enjoying the pleasure I'm bringing to her. As my rhythm quickens, so do her strokes on my erect penis. We pass the Roosevelt exit to Clearwater when I remove my finger from her wet vagina and free myself. If Mya doesn't protest, she can get me off before I reach her house, and then I won't have to go inside. I intended to get a room in Orlando to chill for the afternoon, but we became sidetracked.

Placing my hand behind Mya's neck, I guide her head towards my pulsating member. She slides her lips down my shaft, and the car veers into the next lane. Quickly, I place both hands on the wheel. She's unrelenting. Each bump in the road increases the sensations gripping me deep into my groin. I can't control the rotation in my hips, and it's becoming impossible to keep the car steady. A quick glance at the speedometer indicates I'm below the speed limit. When we reach the next exit, I tell Mya I'm getting off the highway. She slows her motion but doesn't stop completely. I pull into the parking lot of a nearby business. In seconds, I've placed the car in park and reached over to flip the lever on the passenger seat. It reclines backward. Mya is looking at me in horror as I maneuver from my side of the car to hers.

"What are you doing?" she finally musters, but it's too late. I'm inside of her. Mya is stiff as a board, making it much more awkward to maneuver in the small space.

"No one can see us." I'm assured of this since we are in the corner of the lot where no one parks and blocked from the street by bushes. Her embarrassment is turning me on. For some reason, my mind goes to Faye. This is the type of tryst that excites her.

I stroke faster but not hard as I peer out the tinted windows and then back to Mya. She's telling me to hurry up, but the exhilaration of this act is keeping me aroused, and my orgasm remains on edge.

Mya seems to take note of this somehow and begins to move her hips under me. She lifts my shirt and begins teasing my nipples with her tongue. This drives me over the edge, and my juices burst through. Mya has covered my mouth, blocking my loud groans and restricting my breathing, prolonging my orgasm. She moves her hand as I begin to whimper, kissing me before pushing me away.

"Get off of me, boy, you are crazy," she says.

"I can't believe we just had sex in this damn parking lot." Mya covers her face. She giggles which comes out as a mixture of embarrassment and a bit of excitement.

I make my way back to the drivers' seat, which is a little more complicated than when I crossed over. Mya opens the glove compartment and hands me some wipes. While she does this, I turn the defroster on full blast. Once the windows defrost, I switch to the A/C. When we are both cleaned up, I place the car in drive and head back to the interstate. Mya is all the woman I will ever need. She's a mixture of everything a man could ever desire. She represents stability and adventure. Mya can love me gently and be a freak when I need her to be. She knows when to put me in my place and when to let me have my way. She's everything that I wish my wife would be.

As we sit in the car outside her house, Mya tells me that she will go inside and write this experience in her diary. This may not be a good idea, but at the moment, I'm still reeling from the incredible sex we just had, and whatever Mya decides to do is fine with me. We kiss for what feels like an eternity. I yearn to follow her inside, but I know if I get out of the car and go inside, Kim will never see me again. Knowing this, I force myself to leave and prepare for the act I must put on at home, pretending I'm happy to be there.

LOVE...

- is patient
- is kind
- is not rude
- does not envy
- will not lie
- is not self-seeking
- is not proud
- is not quick to anger
- protects
- does not boast
- does not record wrongs
- trusts
- hopes
- perseveres
- finds no joy in evil but celebrates truth
- never fails

Kim

TayJohn feels so good inside of me. His large hands are exploring my backside as I ride him into ecstasy.

"Kim, you feel so good," he says over and over and over again. The harder we grind, the deeper I want him to be inside of me.

He paced his lovemaking to a point where it drives me mad. He tells me not to rush but to savor every second, but by the time we can be together, my body is fiending like a crack addict.

I try telling myself that we have a lifetime ahead of us, that I can relax and enjoy the moment. But deep down inside, I know this isn't entirely true. Each second we're together is a moment I'm stealing from my marriage, my daughter, and my husband. I try to shake off the feelings of guilt plaguing my mind, leaving me wondering if these types of thoughts ever enter LaDamien's mind when he's with other women.

"Earth to Kim," TayJohn says. "Where're you at, baby?"

"Trust me, I'm right here," I say as I place kisses on his hairy chest. "And here, and here," sliding down the length of his body. "And here," taking his shaft deep into my mouth. TayJohn is shivering, which moves me to please him more, and more.

Hours later, as I'm preparing to head home, TayJohn asks me to sit down for a talk.

"So is this all we have, stolen moments, afternoon sex, and then lounging in front of the television?" He asks me this as he runs his fingers through my micro-braids, one of the many changes he has inspired in me. "I don't want you to think this is only about sex for me."

To be perfectly honest, it never occurred to me that he wanted more. The notion that I could offer him more is frightening. Infidelity is so easy. Here I'm with a man who isn't my husband, having walked out of the house this morning under the pretense of going to a study group and then shopping with my friends. There wasn't a hint of guilt in my voice as I told LaDamien the lie. He may or may not have believed me. To him, it may have simply been one less lie he had to tell to be with Mya. Could I be turning into my cheating husband? Does this put me on the same level as him?

"What are you suggesting we do?" I finally ask, shaking the guilt that is seeping from my subconscious.

Instead of answering, TayJohn takes me by the hand. Once I'm standing, he slips on a pair of leather slides, leads me out the door, and to his *Toyota* Camry parked in front of his building. Minutes later, we are at Starbucks enjoying Caramel Macchiato shakes and blueberry muffins. We laughed and talked like we were a real couple with every right to be seen in public holding hands and partaking in lover's kisses. I didn't want the afternoon to end, but I knew it had to, if for no other reason than I was a mother, and Ariel needed me.

On the ride back to his apartment TayJohn asked me if I enjoyed myself. "Wouldn't you like to be able to do that all the time without fear of being caught by a man who treats you like shit? Don't you think I want to be able to go out in public with you and show you what I'm all about?"

He's right. This whole mess is unfair to him. He should be able to do whatever he wants with his woman, but instead, he can't truly express himself, and neither can I.

"Kim, you're torn, I know. Just promise me you'll think about what sharing you with him is doing to me, especially knowing what an asshole your husband is."

Smiling, I make the promise but internally, I know I wouldn't leave LaDamien for another man.

Back at his place, TayJohn tried his best to get me back inside. When it became evident I wasn't taking the bait, he placed his hands on my cheeks and slid his tongue in my mouth. We enjoyed a passion-filled kiss and then a strong embrace before I departed. In my vehicle, as I drove out of the parking lot, I watched him out of my rearview mirror and wondered if I've gone too far-knowing very well that I have.

LaDamien isn't at home when Ariel and I arrive. No surprise there. We watch a movie and order pizza for dinner. Once Ariel retreats to her bedroom, I head to mine. Taj has sent me a text message. *Send me a pic*, it reads. I giggle. Not much later, I'm stepping out of the shower. Glancing over at my cell phone, I see I have another message. *Please, fancy no, sexy yes.*

Dropping the towel, I aim the camera at my hairy mound and snap the picture. Viewing the image, it shows a glimpse of my thighs but mainly my pubic area.

As I'm about to send the picture, a text from LaDamien comes in. *What r u doing?* It reads. I reply, *getting settled.* Before I can press send, a text comes in from Taj. *Don't make me beg.*

I clear TayJohn's message and send my response to LaDamien. The picture I was preparing to send to TayJohn is gone. I check my outbox, but there's no pending message. I don't recall sending the picture. Next, I open my sent folder, and it's not there either. Checking my picture mail, I see one sent message. It's to LaDamien, dated with today's date and timestamp of three minutes ago. My heart stops. The next ten minutes, I stand waiting and watching for my cell phone to ring, or worst, for my husband to come storming through the door. How could I be so stupid?

The suspense is killing me. I muster up my strength and dial LaDamien's number. He answers on the second ring; nothing in his tone suggests he was expecting my call.

"Hey, did you get the picture I sent?" He says no, and asks what picture. I laugh nervously and prod a little further. "You didn't like it? I feel so silly. Please delete it."

LaDamien swears he didn't receive the picture, so after ending the call, I contact TayJohn. As soon as he answers, he asks about the picture. He's upset I haven't sent one. Knowing that LaDamien received the picture and is acting as though he didn't have me confused and concerned. I explain what happened to TayJohn, but instead of sharing my concern, he says he thinks the picture didn't transmit, but my gut feeling is that it did.

The days following the picture mishap, LaDamien seemed to watch my every move. He was on my heels as I maneuvered through the house. Instead of calling me on my cell phone or sending text messages, he started calling my desk phone and having me paged when I didn't answer. Each day I came in from work, he was there.

One evening, he had the nerve to go through my phone and question why my call and text history was blank. On the one hand, I was relieved this little distraction only lasted a week. But on the other, it made me realize that I was becoming the distraction, and someone else, Mya, undoubtedly held his attention now.

"I want a divorce."

TayJohn asks me if I'm serious or just talking after my revelation. I don't know, but something has to give.

"We are too old to be carrying on like this, and I don't see things getting better. LaDamien has to be tired after all these years of living this way. Hell, you and I have only been together a couple of months, and I'm overwhelmed."

TayJohn smiles seductively. "So we're officially together?" He teases as he tickles me. "I'm honored." His brown eyes stare into mine as if he's trying to see if I'm serious about divorcing my husband.

"Divorce is a huge step. You need to think this through and make sure it's what you should do. From what you say about your husband, he will not be too happy about your decision. Guy's like him want to end things."

I consider what he's saying. LaDamien would be upset only because it would damage his pride, but he would get over it. Besides, he would then be free to love Mya.

TayJohn tells me he doesn't plan to spend our time together talking about my husband and a divorce that will never take place. His lackadaisical approach to the topic troubles me. I would think he would be happy and push me in that direction so we can be together. Then I think about the amount of time LaDamien has been cheating with Mya. My life's caught up in a vicious tornado of betrayal and deceit that will ultimately consume me and spit me back out.

Melanie entered my office carrying a beautiful bouquet of roses. She placed them on the console, located near the door, and then handed me a large white packet. "Oh, somebody's been good, it's not your birthday or Valentine's Day, and you're getting expensive roses." She stands there waiting for me to open the envelope, but I don't dare. Chances are the flowers are from Taj, and I can't risk her seeing the card. Melanie gets the hint when I lay the envelope down, step around my desk, and walk over to the roses. I inhale the sweet fragrance and smile.

"They are beautiful, aren't they?" I say this as I finger the rose petals, which are cool yet soft. Melanie agrees, then backs out of the door, closing it as she heads back to her desk.

I return to my desk and take my seat as I reach for the envelope. The anticipation is killing me as I rip the envelope open and remove the card. To my dismay, it isn't a card but a large piece of white card stock paper folded in half with something tucked inside. Suddenly, several pictures slip out and land on my desk. Horrified, I stare at a picture of Taj and me sitting at a table outside *Starbucks*. Another of him and me embracing outside his apartment. The third one is of us lounging by the pool at his complex. A note is on the inside of the paper. *Guess you aren't the innocent victim after all.*

"Melanie, do you know who delivered the flowers? There isn't a florist card attached."

Melanie informed me that she would call downstairs to the receptionist to see who signed the guest registry. She asks me why and inquires as to whether there's a problem or not. *There's a problem, or I wouldn't be asking,* but I don't let her know that there is. I simply ask that she get the information for me.

My next move is to call TayJohn and let him know about the flowers and the pictures.

"Do you think it was Mya?" he asks without hesitation.

The truth is, I have no clue. Of course, she's the obvious choice, but who knows what my husband is out there doing or who's doing it with him. I think back to the phone call several months ago where someone answered his phone. That was a one-time incident.

TayJohn is talking, trying to help me figure out the mystery.

"You said one of the pictures was of us at *Starbucks*, well we've only been there once, and that was a couple of weekends ago. Do you remember where your husband was that day?"

"Baby, do you not listen to me? I never know for sure where LaDamien is or who is with him. On that day, all I know is when I arrived home, he wasn't there and had been gone all day. There is five pictures total, and in each one, we're wearing something different, which means somebody is following me. Do you think it's LaDamien? You know he has been acting strange since I sent that picture message?"

"Some of the pictures were taken before that day," he reminds me.

Slouching back in my chair and absorbing the absurdity of the whole mess, I'm startled when Melanie enters my office. I quickly grab a folder, place it over the pictures, then press end on my call. "What's up?" I ask, looking guilty as hell, I'm sure.

"Jessica, the receptionist downstairs, says whoever delivered the flowers didn't sign the florist's name. Is everything okay, Kim?" Melanie is concerned, but I have to assure her that nothing is wrong.

"I'm good. The flowers look expensive, and I just wanted to know where they came from."

After Melanie left my office, I looked at the pictures again. This time I noticed the date stamps in the lower-left corner of each. It was clear the sender wanted me to know that they could show that my affair was going on for a while. Back on the phone with TayJohn, I share my frustration. This is a very childish game that a grown person is playing. I just have to figure out how to let my husband know he needs to get his bitches in check without mentioning the pictures.

Mya

My heart fluttered at just the thought of him. I had never known such happiness and desired to shout it to the world, just like that White man in the *De Beers* diamond commercial, *Declaration*. He's standing on the steps of Piazza San Marco Square in Venice, Italy, professing his love for his woman. "I love this woman. I love this woman. I love this woman!"

I was so giddy with joy that I must have had a lapse in common sense. What other logical explanations would explain my sitting here telling my Grandmother about this man? About this forbidden fruit I had taken a succulent bite from with little regret. My Grandma Janie, the woman who began taking me to church when I was a wee bit toddler of two or three. The woman who claimed if she hadn't introduced me to God, my soul would have been lost. My Grandma Janie, the woman who loved, married, then buried her soulmate. A man she claims to have loved every second of every hour, of every day, of every week, of every month, of every year, sixty-three years to be exact, that she was blessed to have known him. My Grandma Janie, the woman who had taught me to be a self-respecting, Christian woman who loved the Lord and feared his wrath. So why was I shocked, hurt, even saddened, when she looked me straight in my eyes, showing all the wisdom of her eighty-nine years, and said, "Baby, God ain't gonna bless you with another woman's husband. Not today, tomorrow, not ever."

I sat straight up in my bed, gasping for air and searching my surroundings. Sometimes my dreams seem so real. Oh, how I wish I were sitting in my granny's kitchen eating her sweet potato pie and drinking iced cold sweet tea. Tea made in a glass jar by the power of the sun in a large glass jar placed on a tree stump. The stump is the remnants of an oak tree we once spent our days climbing and trying to build a treehouse in. This was before the violent winds of a tropical storm downed the old oak. Grandma Janie would always use Sweet'n Low instead of sugar, even before they began selling the substitute sweetener by the box. She said sugar would settle to the bottom once the tea was chilled, so breaking open all those individual packets was worth it. "Sometimes you just have to do a little extra to make something you love just right," she would say.

    I grab my pillow and hug it tight, smothering my sobs. It's been ten years since she passed peacefully in her sleep, and I still miss her as much right now as I did the day we received the call from my cousin letting us know she was gone. I look at the digital clock, and the large green numbers scream back at me. It's three a.m. Always three a.m. Too late to go back to what could have been and too early to decide which direction to go next. Three a.m., the bewitching hour that paralyzes the soul. I'm reminded of a novel, *Something Wicked This Way Comes*, by Ray Bradbury. We read it in middle school English class, and every time I'm awakened by a dream at three a.m., the fading memories of this book spook me. I stare out into the darkness. There's no moon and no stars to greet me. It's just me, and my dreams and the stern admonition of my dead Granny, "baby, God ain't gonna bless you with another woman's husband. Not today, tomorrow, not ever."

    "Mya, can you come to my office for a second?" Paul, my manager, asked when I answered the phone. I welcomed the distraction since my thoughts were not on work but my dream from last night. Seated in his office, he announced that our location was merging with our Orlando office. Management has decided that this location would close.

    "Some people will be offered a relocation package. Other people will be offered severance on the condition that they stay until we close down completely. I called you in because you are one of the people who will get offered a position in Orlando." Paul gave me a moment to absorb this bombshell. It had been years since I was in the job market. I'd become quite comfortable in my current position.

    "So, do you think you would be open to moving?" he finally asked.

"Wow, I never thought about it. I mean, I guess it's an option since I'm single and have no children. Other than starting over in a new place, there isn't anything that would stop me. Plus, it's only an hour and a half away."

I tried to be positive, but inside I was panicking. Moving was not on my radar. My main concern was leaving LaDamien. What would this mean for us? Why I was thinking of our relationship in terms of it being a hindrance was beyond reason. If anything, this move would be the perfect opportunity to get my life back on track.

"Mya, you are only one of three Business Analysts who'll get offered a relocation package. A formal announcement won't happen for several weeks.

"In other words, this is a private conversation, a heads up because I'm your favorite employee," I joked with Paul but knew that was precisely what he was saying. "Will you be moving?" I asked.

"No, they already have managerial people in place. Plus, my family is pretty rooted in the area." Knowing Paul would no longer be my manager changed things a bit. He was a great guy to work for and was pretty flexible. If I relocated, I could be walking into a different environment that may not be favorable. This decision was going to require some serious consideration.

Angie agreed to meet me for lunch. We're dining on Shrimp Creole and crab cakes at *Chappy's Louisiana Kitchen*. I decided to share my recurring dreams of my Grandma telling me to leave LaDamien alone. Then I went into the details about my job situation.

"Girl, you know you're in a mess when you start stirring the souls of the dead. If my Grandma were coming to me in dreams, I'd be taking heed. This job relocation is simply a confirmation that it's time for you to get on with your life and leave LaDamien alone. Face it, girl, if he were going to leave his wife, he would have done it by now."

Angie was so right. This was my opportunity to start fresh and leave all this mess behind. Faye hadn't been a problem since we returned from Miami, but LaDamien was no closer to leaving Kim than he was the night we met.

"Orlando is nice, and it's growing. In a way, I'm excited about the possibilities, but it's also hard letting go of what's familiar. Well, the drive isn't bad, so I could always come home on the weekends and hang out. Maybe I could get LaDamien to keep up the mortgage on my house." Angie didn't like that idea and didn't hold back on letting me know. She believed this was God extending me an opportunity to get my act together. To continue working LaDamien into the equation was only going to stir His wrath.

"God is a forgiving God, and he gives us more chances than we deserve. But don't mock Him Mya, or He will show you that although we have free will, He's still very much in charge."

The mood had changed, and Angie was about to go into preaching mode. I looked towards the restaurant's front and was surprised to see Mrs. Epps, Pastor Epp's wife, coming towards us.

"Hi, how have you been doing," Mrs. Epps asked as she reached our table. "I haven't seen you in quite some time. Were we not what you were looking for to continue your spiritual journey?"

Mrs. Epps was dressed casually in khaki capris and a nice red print top. A far stretch from the sophisticated formal gown she was wearing the night of the banquet. Or the stylish suits and matching hats she wore a couple of visits I made to First Ebenezer.

Before replying, I scanned the room to see who she was here to meet since she had entered alone. Picking up on my curiosity, she informed me that she was placing an order at *NGI*, the reprographics shop a few doors down. She saw us come into the restaurant.

"You just touched me the first time we met, and I wanted to make sure your spiritual needs get met." Mrs. Epps pulled out a business card for the church and handed it to me. "I don't mean to intrude on your time with your friend," I took the opportunity to introduce her to Angie. "So, please give me a call so we can talk," she finished.

Taking the card from her, I realized that her husband had probably told her about our session. That's what she wants to talk to me about, I'm sure. Our eyes met in a moment of recognition, and I let her know that I would love to meet with her.

"You know, there's something I would like to speak with you about also. My company may be transferring me to Orlando, and I don't know what I should do." Mrs. Epps understood, and before she left, we made plans to meet for breakfast the following morning.

Six o'clock the following morning, LaDamien was calling my phone. It had been a long time since he'd called first thing in the morning. Our early morning work-outs and breakfast outings were a thing of the past, as were many of the other things we use to share. Although we still spent a considerable amount of time together, it was obvious things had changed. Maybe complacency is what kills most relationships. Couples begin to take each other for granted, or maybe the hunt is what makes relationships exciting. Once he conquers the prey, the hunter loses interest. On any other day, I would have welcomed the call and the invitation to meet at the gym and then head over to *IHOP* for breakfast, but today I'm meeting Mrs. Epps. We're meeting at *Munch's*, a small diner near the southeast neighborhood of Coquina Key.

"What do you mean you have plans?" LaDamien barked. He wasn't giving one hundred percent but still expected me to be readily available to him.

I had not shared with him the news about my job yet. If I told him I was meeting with a Pastor's wife, he would immediately jump to conclusions. He'd insinuate I no longer wanted to talk to him about my problems. My first thought was to lie and say I was meeting one of my friends, but I had no reason to lie. He wasn't my husband, and I didn't owe him an explanation regarding my whereabouts.

"I'm meeting with Beverly Epps. She's the wife of Pastor Timothy Epps…"

"Okay, Mya, bye." LaDamien ended the call. There was a time when I would have cared and called back. The more he does things like this, the less likely I'm to fight for this relationship.

"Mya, tell me about your job possibly relocating," Beverly Epps asked after the waitress placed our orange juice on the table. "Do you know when you would be required to move?"

I let her know that my company was closing its local office altogether. Supposedly, I was one of a few people who will get offered a chance to relocate. She asked me if I thought this was an opportunity I was taking seriously and whether or not I could take my career on a new path. I was candid with her. The truth was I didn't have a clue what I would do when they make the official announcement. Currently, I was basing everything on a heads-up given by my manager. He said the announcement was months away. Therefore, anything could happen between now and then.

"My parents and my sister are here in St. Petersburg, as well as all of my friends. The saving grace is that Orlando is less than a hundred miles away, and since I'm not a social butterfly, it may prove to be an easy transition."

Beverly Epps nodded her head in agreement with my assessment. We stopped chatting long enough to say grace over our meals, then flowed back into our conversation. "What about your love life?" she asked out of the blue.

Clearing my throat and wiping my mouth, I let her know I wasn't in a real relationship at the moment. "That won't be a problem. I'm single." She didn't miss a beat in transferring into the real reason for this little meeting.

"You're single? So who is the brother I see you around town with all the time? You two use to work out at the gym together? Is he no longer in the picture?"

Was she serious, or was she baiting me? The conversation I had in her husband's office might have remained in his office. If she has seen LaDamien and me out together, chances are she knows very well that he's married.

"That's my friend, LaDamien Bryson," I answer.

"Friend? That's interesting because, from the looks of things, you two are more than friends. I'm not going to play around with you, Mya. I know LaDamien is married. Although I don't indulge in gossip, I have heard the rumors surrounding you two. Plus, you sought counsel with my husband last year, and you stopped coming to our church right after that meeting.

"You appear to be a smart woman. I know it's hard for women, especially Black women, to find a suitable mate. But getting involved with another woman's husband isn't the answer. Now I may be overstepping my boundaries here, but I want you to know that if you need someone to talk to, I'm here for you. I won't judge you, just listen, and provide advice when asked.

"See, I've been on both ends of the fence. I've been the other woman who cheated and the wife who got cheated on."

Boy, did she say a mouth full? I could not imagine this righteous woman being someone's mistress. She was implying that her husband, the pastor, had cheated on her. I know it was wrong, but I was more interested in hearing her story than I was in sharing mine.

"Wow, I never would have thought that about you."

She chuckled, "Like you probably don't think people know what's going on with you, and LaDamien? We can dress up, put on make-up, and walk around smiling and thinking our sins are covered. To some, they may be, but God knows all, and he sees all. As corny as it sounds, the only person we are fooling is ourselves."

Ouch! She was right on target. "Three years ago, if someone had told me I would get caught up in this vicious web of lies, I would have laughed. I don't think too many women wake up in the morning and decide they will get involved with a married man. At least I didn't. It just all happened so fast, and I couldn't, no, I didn't want to stop it. LaDamien was everything I ever wished for in a man, except for the gold band he used to wear on his left ring finger."

"Used to?" she asked with a confused look on her face.

It's now my turn to chuckle. "It's one of the little things that stand out in my mind. He never wore his ring around me, but I knew he had one. Some days it would be in the cupholder. Other days, it would appear on the dresser or nightstand as if he had been wearing it, and I hadn't noticed.

"One day, I was in a funk, and I noticed he was wearing the ring, and I went off. To appease me, he took the ring and placed it... Well, that's not something I care to repeat." Her eyes widened and revealed her curiosity, but there was no way I was going to finish that thought.

"Anyway, I don't know what happened, but the ring disappeared. He stopped wearing it. The slight discoloration on his ring finger was gone. The ring wasn't in the cup holder, and it just turned into one of the many subliminal things that made me think he was sincere about his love for me." As I tell her this, I start to see the pattern and how this whole affair was so easy for me to get into and stay. LaDamien had been a master manipulator.

"The wedding ring symbolizes the unbreakable link between a husband and wife. I can see how his disregard or a blatant disrespect of his wedding ring could lead you to believe he did not commit to his vows. But think of it this way Mya, he does these things to convince you that he doesn't love his wife or no longer cares to be married. I'm sure you've heard people say he's never going to leave, no matter what he says or does. This may or may not be the case, but just think about it, he has shown you who he is, and that places you at an advantage."

The waitress came over to check on us, and Mrs. Epps dismissed her quickly so she could continue. "As I was saying, his wife may not have had the benefit of knowing what her husband was capable of, so she stays because she feels the need to honor her vows. But he let you know without a doubt that marriage vows don't mean anything to him. When things aren't going the way he wants or becomes boring, he's going to cheat, and he's going to do it with absolutely no regard for you. Is that what you're looking for in a mate? Is that all you think you deserve?"

I felt as though she was no longer ministering to me and my situation. She seemed to have gone to a place in time that had caused her many hurts—a low point in her life that she didn't want another woman ever to experience.

We stood in the parking lot next to her Mercedes S-series and embraced. Beverly Epps was only a few years older than me, which made me feel like she was the big sister I always dreamed of having. Sonja would never have pulled me aside for a talk like the one we just had. The only time I ever heard from my sister was when she called to repeat something she'd heard about LaDamien and me or relay a message from my mother.

My soul felt good having had this heart-to-heart talk. I left Munch's with much to think about in terms of my relationship. Mrs. Epps assured me that she didn't expect me to end things with LaDamien just because we'd had this talk.

"Regardless of how wrong this is, the heart is real, and what it feels is real, love is an emotion that can consume our entire being. Your love for him is real, so it's going to be hard to walk away from that. I'm going to pray over the job situation because it may take distance to break this stronghold. Honey with prayer, and time, you can move from this place in your life. But first, you have to acknowledge that nothing good is going to come from this. God has something better in store for you if you just trust him."

I watched as she drove away and wondered if God could turn my life around and let it work in my favor. No, I didn't think I could stand being a preacher's wife, but despite all she'd been through, Beverly Epps had a great life and a husband she adored and who adored her.

"Where are you coming from?" I asked LaDamien when he rang my doorbell after midnight. He had called asking if he could come over. When he entered wearing the same white linen shirt and cargo-Capri's he wore the second day of the festival down in Miami, my radar went into full activation.

"Mya, don't start. I was out with friends and just wanted to see you before I headed home." LaDamien was all over me with hurried kisses and heavy groping. He was not turning me on, and he knew it.

As he tried to back me into my bedroom, my mind was running a mile a second. Thinking hard, trying to remember if anything was going on tonight that would explain his being out and dressed in attire he usually wouldn't wear. It hit me like a brick when he said, "Mya, you are everything to me."

"KEM! You went to see Kem, didn't you?" In one hard push, he fell over. "I can't believe you."

"You're wrong, Mya. I didn't take Kim to that show. Mark and his wife were supposed to go, and..."

"Stop lying. Damn. You promised to take me to that show to make up for us missing him in Miami. When I told you Saturday's concerts sold out, you knew you already had tickets, and you and your wife were going. What the hell LaDamien, where is she? You dropped her off at home and then came here? What kind of nonsense is that?" I don't know what this man told his wife, but there's no way my husband and I would go out, and afterward, he drops me off and leave.

"I'm sorry I didn't tell you. Kim bought the tickets as a surprise. She knew how disappointed I was that I missed him in Miami. I knew if I told you, you'd get pissed."

"Why are you here, LaDamien?" The question is laced with my frustration with him and his antics. I refuse to allow him to drag me down this slippery slope with him.

"Because the whole time Kem was performing, I was thinking of you, and how I wished it was you standing beside me instead of her. I told her some friends were hanging out and had called several times for me to join them, so I needed to go by really quick and say hi."

"And she fell for it? Just said drop me off, and go on, and have a good time? Is this the kind of crap you're going to pull when we're together...if we ever get together?"

The longer he's here, the more I think about my meeting with Mrs. Epps. LaDamien and I have seen our best days together. It's only downhill from here. I need to end this. He thinks this is flattering me, that I'm somehow special because he came up with a stupid lie to tell his wife to get out of the house this time of night. She got to go to a concert he promised to take me to, and as a consolation prize, I get fucked. I don't think so, and I ask LaDamien to leave. He begged to stay, offering to go down on me and claiming he just had to taste me. In his mind, this was supposed to turn me on. Instead, I felt repulsed and needed him out of my home with the quickness.

LaDamien

"*Fuck!*" I yell as I slam my palm into the stirring wheel. Mya has just put me out of her house. She treated me like I was some average joker off the street or an old boyfriend who happened to stop by unannounced.

I planned to take her to see Kem, but after we returned from Miami, she was so negative and acted as though she didn't want to be bothered. On the other hand, Kim was being very accommodating and desired to work on our marriage. She had come up with the idea of couples' time. It was the first time in a long time she had shown an interest in our marriage, so asking her to get the tickets seemed like the right thing to do at the time.

Mya keeps insisting that Kim isn't cheating on me. Sometimes I think she's so adamant because she doesn't want me to leave Kim. Any other woman would have been agreeing with my assessment and building a case against my wife. Even tonight, why would she try to send me home instead of keeping me out all night and hoping that a fight would ensue when I returned home in the wee hours of the morning? The longer I sit here, the madder I become. Mya needs to tell me something, and she needs to tell me now.

"Open the door, so we can talk," I command when I see Mya peeking through the blinds. She opens the door with attitude. "If you don't want to be with me any longer, then just say so because I don't need this shit. I'm tired of bending over backward and kissing your ass to make you happy when I'm the only one making any sacrifices in this relationship." My heart is beating fast as I fight the anger raging inside of me. She's standing here looking as though I'm annoying her. Well, all she has to do is say the word, and I'll be history. There are too many women looking for a good man for me to keep begging for attention and her love.

Mya folded her arms across her chest and leaned on the open door. "Are you serious? You come to my house in the middle of the night after you've taken your wife to a concert you promised to take me to, and you have the gall to confront ME! She points to her chest. "Why don't you do everybody a favor and grow up? I can't believe you thought you were going to come over here and climb into bed like nothing was up, knowing where you had been. Now you're standing here giving ultimatums. You can't be serious."

"Are we going to stand out here and wake the whole neighborhood, or are you going to let me in?"

Mya is so sexy, and when she's angry, it turns me on even more. She knows I wouldn't be here if I weren't craving her, which is probably why she came to the door in her tee and no cover-up. If she lets me in, I know I'll be between her legs in minutes, but she hasn't budged so far. "Can I come inside so we can talk, please?" Still, she doesn't move, so I start towards her.

"You're not coming in, LaDamien. You can just go home to your wife, call Faye, or go screw, Wanda. I don't care, but you're not coming in here. Now, if you don't mind," she backed up to close the door, but I pushed my way inside.

"I don't want to go home to my wife, and I damn sure don't want Faye or Wanda."

Mya is trying to be tough, but she doesn't know I will take it tonight. She tries to elbow me, but I wrap my arms around her in a bear hug and cover her mouth with my hand. As I back her up, I use my foot to close the door. Once the door is closed, I turn her around and press her body against it. She's still resisting, but not as much.

"I love you, Mya. Why can't you see that? Why do we have to go through this drama?" My body is pressed against hers, not allowing for much movement.

"LaDamien! Get off me," she murmurs as she tries to push me off. My hands are roaming her sides as I attempt to lift her t-shirt. "So you're just going to do whatever even though I'm telling you to stop. Last I knew, they called this rape."

To stop her senseless ranting, I put my tongue in her mouth and kiss her deeply. If she considered this rape, she could easily bite my tongue, knee my groan, or resist a little harder. My penis is so engorged it feels as if it's going to rupture. I bear down on Mya so she can feel my desire, my overwhelming need for her.

"Please don't make me leave," I moan. "I promise to do better, I promise. You're right. I was wrong about taking Kim to the concert when I knew I had promised to take you. I'll never do it again. Just forgive me."

Mya probably thinks I'm saying whatever it will take to get her to let me stay, but I mean every word. Her resistance is subsiding, and I undo my pants. In no time, I have freed myself, grabbed her thighs and pick her up. She cooperates and wraps her legs around me so that I can penetrate her warm, moist opening. "Ooh, ah, ah, uh, uh, my god, Mya…"

The clock on Mya's nightstand is showing two-thirteen. After our brief sexual encounter at her front door, she relented and allowed me to come in and make sweet love to her. Mya urged me to get going once we showered, but I wasn't ready to leave. I wanted to stay and hold her.

My phone has been flashing for an hour now. Kim has called at least twenty times. If Mya is still awake, she's doing an excellent job pretending she's asleep. All hell will break loose when I return home, so I'm in no hurry to get there. I don't know what it is about this woman that makes me break all the rules. Just hours ago, she put me out of her house. Had that been anyone else, I wouldn't have looked back. Instead, with Mya, I begged my way back in. It seems the more she rejects me, the greater my desire for her, leaving me wondering how much longer we can go on this way. Since we can't live without each other, we should be able to get it together and do the right thing, which is to be together for real. The light on my phone is lighting up again. The phone is on the nightstand closest to Mya. This time she stirs and turns to face me.

"You need to get going, so your wife can get some sleep."

"I know, but I'm not ready to leave." Pulling Mya closer to me, I reach over her and grab the phone. Going through the missed calls, I see the first seventeen are from our home phone, and the last four are from her cell phone. My heartbeat starts to race as I roll away from Mya and look for my clothing.

"What's wrong?" Mya asks as she sits up and turns the light on as if it will clarify things for her.

"Kim is up to something. She's calling from her cell phone. I'm sure it's a scare tactic, but I need to get going just the same."

Mya makes her way into the living room and peeks out of the window. "I don't see her car, but you do need to get going. The last thing I need is you and your wife to bring your drama to my doorstep." She smiles as she says this, her way of letting me know that she's kidding. Subconsciously, I wonder what she would do if Kim knocked on her door. Would she send me out clothes and shoes in hand and lock the door? Or would she cuss Kim out and run her away from here. Somehow, I don't see Mya putting up much of a fight for me. She certainly didn't do so when confronted by Faye, and that pissed me off.

At the door, I place my hand in the small of Mya's back, pull her close, and kiss her goodnight. "Thanks for letting me stay."

"I didn't have much of a choice, now did I?"

"Regrets?'

"No."

"Then that's all that matters. I love you." Mya tells me she loves me too, and I head to my car.

As I'm backing out of the driveway, headlights come on down the street. I stop and wait, but the car doesn't move. My first thought is to go in that direction, but I place the car in drive and speed off the opposite way. About a mile away from Mya's house, I get stopped by a red light. A car pulls up next to me, and when I look to my right, Kim is gesturing for me to roll down my window. The light turns green, and I proceed towards home.

We arrive at the same time. The garage door opens, and Kim allows me to pull in first to maneuver the coupe inside in front of the Escalade. I stand by the kitchen door and wait for her to exit her car.

"Did you leave Ariel here alone?" I ask in an annoyed tone.

"Ariel is asleep, like you, and I should be. Why would you leave this house and to be with that ho? I should have packed your shit and took it over there since that's where you want to be." Kim brushed past me, headed inside, and pulled the door shut in my face.

Two weeks have passed, and Kim continues to give me the cold shoulder. It takes a call from Ariel's school to get us to talk to one another. They've scheduled a conference to discuss our daughters' behavior. According to her teachers, Ariel has been blatantly disrespectful, refusing to do her work and talking back. Kim has no qualms about placing the blame on me.

"You think you can just run the streets not paying any attention to us, and she doesn't feel there's some sort of disconnect between her parents."

Who was she to talk when every time I turn around, Ariel is with Debra?

"I think we both could do a little better. There's no need to point fingers. We just need to get her back on track." Kim sucks her teeth loud enough for me to get the point. She isn't going to bear any of the blame. Everything is my fault, as usual.

"Family counseling" is what Mrs. Fitzpatrick, the principal at Ariel's school, suggested. Ariel is concerned that Kim and I are getting a divorce. She confided in one of her teachers that I'm rarely home, and when I am, all her mom and I do is argue.

Kim has set this up perfectly. I'm not sure what she's feeding my daughter, but when we get home, I'm going to let her know that I don't appreciate her antics.

I watch as she gleefully accepts the information on the counselor Mrs. Fitzpatrick recommended. "Whatever is going on, Dr. Sampson can assist you with it. He's the best in this area."

"So is this what you had up your sleeve all along? To send Ariel in there telling our business so you can get us into counseling."

We were barely out of the school office when I lit into Kim. She ignored me and continued at a hurried pace to her car. She claimed to have an important meeting that she could not cancel, leaving me to take Ariel home. Her teacher had walked her back to class to gather her things, so I followed Kim to her car.

"I'm not going to counseling, so don't even bother scheduling an appointment."

"Fine, LaDamien, I'll just let them know it will be Ariel and me since my husband, her father, could give less than a damn about our family. Now get out of my way." Kim slammed the car door and pulled off, missing my foot by inches. I let out a deep sigh, thinking, my wife has lost her mind.

When Ariel makes it back to the office, I'm leaving a message for Mya, asking her to call me at once so I can fill her in on Kim's latest antics.

"Ready to go, baby girl?" My daughter smiles and says yes. We go down to Baywalk and grab a bite to eat at Johnny Rockets, a popular themed hamburger place. Ariel eyes the Muvico sign and asks if we can see a movie. This isn't how I planned my day, but I have to beat Kim at her game, so I agree. Two hours later, as we walk to the parking garage located across the street, Kim is calling. I send her calls to voice mail and let Ariel know we are going to the mall, where I will buy her whatever her heart desires.

Kim

"*Kim, please* stop crying, and tell me what happened." Debra is doing her best to console me, but the tears keep flowing. I yearn so badly to tell her what happened today. To do so, I would have to explain why Ariel thinks LaDamien and I are heading for divorce. That would lead to my having to admit his infidelity and, ultimately, my transgressions. Why confiding in my best friend is so hard for me to do? She tells Karen and me everything, always looking for our words of encouragement and sisterly advice. Karen, just the thought of her getting the wind to any of this would be a huge debacle. She would kill me herself if she knew the hell I had been going through with LaDamien.

"Let me get myself together, and I will call you back. Don't worry. Everyone is okay. No one has died or anything." Debra didn't want to hang up the phone, but I assured her I would call back. Evidently, she didn't believe me because she and Karen were ringing my doorbell twenty minutes later.

Whew, I had let it all out, and I must admit it felt good to no longer have those secrets buried inside me. Both Debra and Karen were looking at me like I had grown a second head or something. Debra was sympathetic to my situation and kept mumbling that she was so sorry I was going through all of this. Karen waited patiently for me to get it all out before she let it rip.

"You're having an affair in response to your husband having an affair, and now your daughter is acting out because she sees the two of you acting the fool. Did I leave anything out?"

When she put it that way, it minimized the depth of my despair and trivialized the mess my marriage and life had become. "It's not that simple, Karen."

"Oh yes, it is. When you first found out he was cheating, you should have given LaDamien an ultimatum. No woman should be disrespecting you this way., and what was the picture bullshit all about. Who does stuff like that anyway? Seriously, did she hire a damn private eye? Did she call *Cheaters* pretending to be the wife? LaDamien, he sees nothing wrong with any of this?" Karen was too through with me. It was apparent in her tone and her dismissive body language. Then she asked to see a picture of TayJohn.

"Well, we might as well see LaDamien's competition and how he looks. Tell us about him because I don't need to hear anything else about Mr. Bryson's trifling ass."

Just like that, the mood had changed from tense to light. My fear that these two women would judge me or see me differently because my husband was having an affair was unfounded. However, Debra commented that she didn't understand why I felt I couldn't come to her and talk about it sooner. A question I didn't have a rational answer to at the moment.

The pictures I had received at the office remained at the office, locked in my desk drawer. Karen was serious about seeing a picture, so I called TayJohn, and asked him to send me one quickly.

"Goodness gracious. Girl, he's hot." Karen exclaimed.

Debra chimed in, "Yes, he's. So you found him in B-more and brought him back with you?" They both laughed. We joked around for several minutes, and then the conversation turned serious again.

"So what are you going to do, Kim?" Karen asked.

"Honestly, I don't know. I just know it can't continue like this. At this point, a divorce is a serious option."

"Let me ask you something?" This time it was Debra. "If this TayJohn guy were out of the picture, would divorce be an option? How does he feel about you? I mean, how do you know he isn't just enjoying the moment while it lasts but has no intentions of it going any further?"

"All I can go on is what he says and how he makes me feel. I know women are biting at his heels every day, and he doesn't give them a second thought, which was going on long before we got together. TayJohn aside, LaDamien placed the divorce card on the table with his crazy behavior. I have tried everything I could think of at this point. For him to say he won't go to counseling even with Ariel involved says a lot about him and his feelings about this marriage."

"I just feel so bad," Debra began. "I've been hearing the rumors but decided to wait until you said something. I had no clue it had gotten this bad."

"Oh Lord, are you serious?" Karen said in an exacerbated tone. "It's been going on for years, and you never said anything. Is there anything you've been hearing about my husband because I have to know? there's no reason why Kim has been dealing with this all this time."

"Come on, ladies, let's not fight about it. I'll figure it out sooner or later."

"Seriously, Kim, you don't need to figure anything out. Your husband has shown you exactly what he's, and that's a low-down dirty dog. I'm sorry if I step on your toes, but you need a dose of reality. Have you considered the ramifications of his actions or your actions? Is he using protection when he's out screwing around? Are you using protection? The fastest-growing number of HIV/AIDS cases is African-American women between the ages of 25 and 44 or something like that. The media convinces us to believe that it's poor ghetto women sleeping with every Dante, Kwame, and John that throws them a few dollars that's causing this epidemic. But nothing could be further from the truth. The numbers include women like the three of us, educated professionals, married to educated professional men. The same men who are out fucking for the sake of fucking, and not using condoms, and let's not even get into the ones fucking other men."

Karen could be so brash at times, and right now, I didn't want to acknowledge the reality of the words she was speaking. LaDamien and I never used condoms before we were married, and not since...not even when we were just sleeping around. I also have to be honest with myself, TayJohn, and I have slipped up a couple of times and not used them.

I look over at Debra, and she's dead silent. After Todd's fling turned up pregnant, she had to face the reality of his infidelity. He had sex with another woman unprotected. I went with her to get the HIV test and was the one who read the results when they came in. I ignored that situation as if I was somehow immune to it.

"What's your plan, Kim?" Karen talked to me in a harsh tone, and I realized I had zoned out for a moment.

"I'm sorry, this is just too much for me to consider right now," I said in a timid voice.

"Right now? Right now?" she repeated. "You've had almost three years to devise a plan. What is keeping you in this marriage? Kim, look at you. You're an attractive woman who still has what it takes to pull a fine brother. You have a position with a Fortune 500 company that pays you well. You can afford this house on your own. Your car's paid for, so what is making you stay with LaDamien?" Karen wasn't holding any punches.

"He's still my husband, and I have to exhaust all options. I think now that everything has hit the fan, he will see how crazy our lives have become. If faced with divorce, I believe LaDamien will get his act together and stop taking me for granted."

Debra finally chimed in. "Well, that's what worked for me. When Todd realized I'd had enough and was seriously considering leaving, he did a total turn around. Things have been great for us lately, and Kim, don't give up on the counseling. Todd refused to go, so I started going on my own. I stopped whining and begging him to change. Instead, I started focusing on my future and my kid's future. It was then I accepted the possibility that it may not include him. He started to take notice and eventually agreed to join me. So as bad as it seems now, there's hope. Too many people are quick to up and divorce, but that should only be an option after you've exhausted your very last option."

Karen let out a deep, loud sigh. She didn't care to hear Debra's words of encouragement. She never liked LaDamien. If my husband were anyone else, she would have been preaching the same sermon as Debra. Because it was LaDamien, she had no room to compromise. I took in both of their advice and concerns, but I couldn't commit to anything. I looked at my watch. The one, my husband, purchased me recently, for no other reason than he was thinking about me, or so he said. It was after nine.

"It's getting late, and I'm sure LaDamien is circling the block waiting for you two to leave. We can get together for lunch or dinner after I have had time to think things over. I love you two, and I'm so glad to have you as friends."

Before I could finish, Debra was on her feet as if she was waiting for an excuse to leave. Karen, on the other hand, probably would have sat right here and waited LaDamien out. I just prayed he wasn't in the driveway sitting in the parked car, waiting for them to leave as he has done in the past.

Twenty or so minutes passed, and no LaDamien and Ariel. He was so petty, keeping her out this late on a school night just to spite me. My cell phone rang, and I pressed talk immediately.

"So, did your girlfriends like what they saw?" It was TayJohn.

"How did you know it was for my girlfriends?" I asked.

He chuckled, "because you've never asked for a picture of me. Plus, if you wanted to see me, you could have come over."

Sharing my days' adventures with TayJohn felt right. My husband's disrespectful behavior angered him, but like Karen, he thought I needed to be making an exit plan.

"Divorce is rough, I know because I've been through it. Believe me, when the dust settles and all is said and done, you'll realize that peace of mind is something you never want to let go of once you have it. Even though I was the cause of my divorce, I still didn't want to end my marriage. We were both miserable, and the negativity permeated around us. When friends and family no longer wanted to come around, we started hating on them too. It's just a bad place to be, and even now, when I think back on that time, I can't believe I thought that was normal."

TayJohn had told me he was divorced. He and his high school sweetheart married young and were together for about three years when things turned nasty. They didn't have a clue what it took to be married, and the relationship soured quickly. He eventually started stepping outside the marriage with other women. She would follow him and make scenes, forcing him to return to a place where he no longer found joy. This lasted for over six years, and then one day, he came home, and she was gone. She had packed up everything and left. In hindsight, he realized that she had been planning her exit for a while. His wife had stopped her direct deposit and put enough money in their joint account to cover her half of the bills. She started having yard sales every weekend to get rid of stuff she called "useless clutter." He said she must have had a moving truck waiting around the corner for him to leave for work because it had to take a good seven to eight hours to pack up their place. After she left, he looked for her everywhere. No one knew where she was. Her job stated she had given two weeks' notice. Her family just wanted him to go away and leave her alone, "she'll contact you in due time," they had told him.

Due time was a year later when she served him with divorce papers. He begged for forgiveness, declared himself a changed man.

Their time apart taught him how to appreciate her more. He said he found God as if God was lost. He was ready to be a husband. According to TayJohn, she told him all that was great, and hopefully, his next wife will reap the benefits, but she had moved on. At that point, all he could do was accept it, and soon he realized it was the best thing that ever happened to both of them.

"All I'm trying to say is, baby, you've already wasted a lot of time on this marriage. It's time for you to decide that this isn't how you're going to live. If your hubby desires to be with you, he needs to step to the plate. If not, then you need to get you and your daughter out of the line of fire. I mean, damn, if you learned tomorrow that you only had one month to live, would you spend it worrying about him or begging him to be your husband? Or would you choose to be free and happy to live out your final days in love, surrounded by people who love you and care about you?"

"As crazy as it sounds, I do believe he loves me. He just needs to see that this isn't how it's supposed to be." I say.

"So you would live those thirty days as you've lived the past eight or nine years, begging someone to love you who has no concept of what love is. That's sad, Kim."

"What do you mean eight or nine years?"

"Kim, come on, this mess didn't start with the Mya chick. It's been going on since you and he got together. The only difference is he's feeling something for this woman that he didn't feel for the others. Now you're scratching and clawing to regain control when you never had any control.

"And to be honest with you, baby, I thought you were much more intelligent than this. Like my ex and I started to drain on other people, you're starting to drain on me. I care about you, Kim, but I can't just be this shoulder you keep crying on. I have needs too, and although I pursued you, I was thinking clearly about what it means to be *with* you.

"I guess, I thought at our age you'd recognize that you can't change your husband. You can only change yourself. If you don't demand better, he's not going to give you better, and you're going to end up bitter and eventually alone because men loathe weak women.

"Look, I have to go. Holla!"

Holla, what the hell was that? How dare he? I try calling TayJohn back for the remaining forty-five minutes LaDamien and Ariel are gone. When they enter the bedroom, I'm in the bathroom washing my face. My eyes are red and puffy. Ariel bursts into the bathroom carrying several bags full of goodies she wants me to see.

"Mommy, what's wrong? Why are you crying?" Before I can answer, LaDamien is behind her, staring at me like I'm some freak of nature. He's waiting for my explanation as if I couldn't be crying over him.

"Nothing, baby, mommy is just emotional right now. I've been calling you two all evening, and I was just getting worried that something bad happened. Come here, and let me see what all you have in those bags." As Ariel showed me countless new outfits, LaDamien seized the moment to make his exit. Good riddance.

Wanda

***"Did you** know The Berkshire Company may be closing?"* I asked LaDamien when he entered the office. His mood had been so foul the past few days, and I guess this is the reason why. He's probably contemplating how he will bring Mya aboard when she loses her job, but I will not tolerate it. He can yell, kick, scream, and threaten to fire me, but she will not come and work for the company I have slaved to build.

"Are you okay?" LaDamien asks me as he stares at me with a concerned look on his face. At this moment, I feel my heart racing and the sweat beads have formed on my forehead.

"Yes, it's that time of the month," I suggest. "Isn't that the company your friend Mya works for?"

"Why are you worried about Mya?" He's becoming agitated. This lets me know he's already considering the possibilities.

"Just small talk, no need for the attitude. Those poor people, I can't begin to think about how tough it will be to find something in this market. Hopefully, they received fair severance packages."

He isn't taking the bait. Instead of joining the conversation, LaDamien heads off to his office and closes the door. I need to find out what his plans for Mya are so I can defuse them immediately. If he brings her in here, it won't be long before he's trying to push me out of the door.

"Wanda, I need you to fax these contracts before one p.m. Also, tomorrow morning I was scheduled to attend a breakfast with the Chamber of Commerce, but I need you to attend in my place."

Before I could respond, LaDamien was heading for the door, leaving me to wonder what he was doing tomorrow morning that would prevent him from going to the breakfast.

The following morning I headed straight to the Commerce breakfast held at *Café Alma's*. Attendance was good, and I have an opportunity to network. I wish LaDamien had purchased a vendor table to showcase the business like a couple of our competitors. These are the type of things we have got to get on top of if we plan to grow.

"Hey Wanda, I see LaDamien ducked out on us again." LaVette Gray, one of the members of the chamber, exclaimed as she reached for my hand. "He has to be the busiest man in town."

LaVette joked, but deep inside, I know she, like most women, yearned to get her hooks in LaDamien. She sends her invitations directly to his home, avoiding me altogether. LaDamien must have contacted her directly to RSVP. This event wasn't even on his calendar, leaving me to wonder just how much contact they have with each other. Shame she had to squeeze all of that butt and those forty-four D's into that too little dress for nothing. LaVette is still talking when something catches my eye. Quickly, I excuse myself and focus on a sign-up sheet lying on the *WorkNet* table near where we're standing.

WorkNet is a government-run agency created to match employers with qualified individuals seeking employment. The representative seated at the table explains to a man next to me that the register is for people interested in being on their distribution list. What caught my eye was the name Mya Blake and all of her contact information. As they converse, I pull out a pen and piece of paper and try to jot down the information. I get an email address and fax number before the woman diverts her attention to me.

"Can I help you with something?" she asks. I tell her I have all I need and walk away after picking up a pamphlet.

After I leave the breakfast, I head back to the office to figure out how useful this information can become. No sooner than I pull out the piece of paper, LaDamien walks through the door.

"Mr. Kenwood says he didn't receive the fax I told you to send yesterday." He isn't in the best of moods.

"The fax kept ringing busy, so I was going to try again today."

"You'll need to take them to him. He and his realtor are at the property. I need to make some phone calls so I'll stay here, and cover the office. Do you have the Mincey contracts ready because they need to go out this morning? I think they are going to accept the asking price."

For someone who is about to earn close to fifty grand, LaDamien is awfully detached. I grab the papers from my desk and hand them to him.

"Here is the Mincey contract. Everything looks to be in order, but you can go over them. When I return, I'll send them off."

LaDamien takes the papers and heads into his office, leaving me wondering what I can do to improve his mood. *Maybe I should stop somewhere on my way back and pick up one of his favorite meals. We can have a little lunch session here in the office.* I think to myself.

"Wanda, where is the latest property listing? And I also need the fax number for Rupert Johnson. How much longer are you going to be?" LaDamien asks when I answer my cell phone.

This man acts like I'm fifty people in one. He sends me on an errand that is twenty miles away and expects me to get there and back in five minutes.

"The listing should be in a green folder in my outbox, and the phone number for Rupert is on my desk. He called the other day with a new number, and I haven't created a new insert for the Rolodex. I should be back in about fifteen minutes if you need me to send it."

"No, I can do it. I have to head out for a lunch appointment and want it taken care of before I leave. Chances are I won't be back in the office today. Bye."

Oh well, so much for my surprise.

Mya

*"**Hi Mya,** this is Beverly Epps."*

I was surprised when I answered the call. I had not spoken to Mrs. Epps since we had breakfast over a month ago. Placing the last of the dishes into the dishwasher, I replied, "Fine, and how are you?"

"I'm doing good. Do you have a few minutes? I have some good news for you."

She had my full attention because good news was something I needed. Hell, anything good would have been a welcomed distraction. It seemed no matter how hard I tried to focus my attention on other things, LaDamien consumed my every thought.

I could no longer keep up with his mood swings. One day he was upbeat and wanted to spend every second with me. Other days he was angry at the world, or should I say his wife, whom he seemed to have no desire to leave, yet expected me just to sit around and deal with it.

Truth be told, I have been anxiously awaiting the offer to relocate to Orlando. Angie has told me time and time again that running away isn't the answer and that I need to confront this demon head-on so I can break the stronghold it has on me. Well, I keep telling her the stronghold will be much easier to break a hundred miles away.

"Mya, I hope you don't mind. I didn't mention this at breakfast, but one of my sorority sisters works for your company's Orlando location, and I decided to give her a call."

Oh Lord, yes, I did mind. What if she revealed the information Paul had shared with me, and the company had reconsidered? Ten different scenarios played in my mind, but I decided to hear her out since she said she had good news.

"The information your manager provided was accurate. Alicia Faison is my friends' name, and I told her that I knew of someone who may be moving to the area and seeking employment. About a half-hour later I had all the details on the company's plans to close your office and relocate some key employees. From that point, I took the opportunity to let her know I knew you and hoped you wouldn't be adversely affected by this decision. We chatted a little while longer, and then this morning, she called to let me know that she did some checking. I was one of the people that would get offered a relocation package. They're making the announcements next week. So what do you think? Have you given it much thought? I've been praying about this, Mya, and God's desire is for you to make this move."

"Wow! That *is* exciting news. Paul was under the impression that it would be several months. Did she say how long I would have before the move?"

Hearing her say God wanted me to make this move reaffirmed what I had already decided I needed to do. After the night, LaDamien showed up at my home at midnight after taking his wife to my concert, sealed the deal. I was so angry at myself for allowing him to weasel his way into my bed. It let me know I had no self-control when it came to LaDamien. Now that our affair was causing his daughter to act out in school, I know it has to end between us now, more than ever.

"Your office will close in thirty days, so once they make the offer, you'll be expected to accept or decline probably within forty-eight hours. You'll then have time to find a place in Orlando and get your affairs here in order. So are you going to say yes?" she asked, a little bit too excited.

"Yeah, I'm going to accept. I've been praying about it also. Since our last talk, things have gotten crazier between LaDamien and me, and I know now I have to end this affair, now."

My call with Mrs. Epps had to end abruptly due to the phone alerting me that someone was trying to send me a fax. I promised to call her back in ten minutes.

Someone had made a terrible mistake, and it was either LaDamien or Wanda. The fax I received was from LaDamien Bryson Enterprises. It was a listing of his properties. My first thought was to let him know they had faxed it to the wrong number. Then I wondered how they knew my fax number since I had just had the line added when I learned the company I work for might be closing. I needed to get my ducks in a row just in case. My confusion quickly changed to shock as the pages continued to print out. The property listing ended, and a personal letter began.

...you just don't know how hard it is for me to sit by and see you in such misery. Don't you know by now I would leave my husband in a heartbeat to be with you? I have invested so much time and energy into helping you become the businessman you are because I believe in you and love you. You and I make a dynamic team, and those other women, including you know who can never appreciate you for the man you are. Baby, I understand your wants and needs. I'm committed to your success. I would never place my needs before yours...

For five pages, it went on—no names, no signature but the characters evident. Wanda had written this letter to LaDamien, and the things she exposed caused my knees to buckle. They've been having an affair since she started working for him. This woman knew intimate details of his marriage, and other affairs, just like Faye. She wanted to leave her husband and kids to be with LaDamien.

I read the letter several times, trying to figure out when it was written. She talked about him giving her his credit cards to buy Christmas gifts for his wife, child, and family. There was mention of a Valentine's Day spent at the *Renaissance Vinoy Resort and Golf Club*. They had the couple's spa treatment and lunch at *Marchand's Bar & Grill* before retreating upstairs for some much-anticipated lovemaking.

Her letter then turned solemn as she talked about him slipping from her grip and how she wished she knew what it would take to get him to see how unconditional her love is.

It was overwhelming. Who faxed this to me? How could LaDamien deny to me over and over again his involvement with this woman?

Who, if anyone, should I show the letter to? I call LaDamien, but he doesn't answer, so I leave a message. Three hours later, and he still hasn't returned my calls. The last one I went so far as to mention the letter. Ugh, this is just too much for me to deal with right now. Tired of waiting, I take the letter and fold it up and then place it in a drawer until I can rationally deal with its contents, if at all. God, I get it. As hard as I try not to, I do get it. LaDamien is a creep with a capital C. How this landed in my hands isn't important. The fact that it did is what matters.

Our monthly book club meeting is at Aubrey's home. She and Keith live in a mini-subdivision called *Ahali Place*. The development is comprised of homes starting at the half-million-dollar mark and moves higher. All homeowners are African-American, including a professional boxer and a local politician. The multi-level home is beautiful, but I don't understand how they can afford it on their teacher salaries. Since she's never asked me to make a payment or contribute to one, I don't worry about it either.

We are out back on their oversized lanai that houses a swimming pool, separate Jacuzzi, full bar, and outdoor kitchen. I have chosen this gathering to announce that I'll be moving to Orlando at the end of the month. I also want to see if they can go apartment hunting with me next weekend.

"WHAT?" Brigit says in a loud tone. "What about your house? Are you going to sell it?"

Of all the questions she could have asked, she's worried about my house. But she lets me know why. She hopes to rent it. This woman has to be joking if she thinks I'm going to let her crack-head husband move into my house.

"Since they are paying my mortgage for six months, I'm going to take my time figuring out what to do with it. Plus, I would hate to have someone move in, and then two months later, I decide Orlando isn't for me, and I need to move back."

Angie and Aubrey breathed a sigh of relief as I wiggled my way out of that one. Still, neither one of them would've allowed Brigit to move into their homes with that husband of hers.

"Well, let me know what you decide because I'm going to need a place in a few months?"

"Why?" We all asked in unison.

"We got served with foreclosure papers last week. James stopped the direct payments on our mortgage and has been withdrawing the money. He comes home for lunch every day to steal the correspondence that has been coming in the mail. Remember when we got our number changed a few months ago? Humph, that's what he was covering up. I can't believe after all these years, and all I've done for him, he deceived me this way." Brigit was tearing up. It was Roxanne who pulled her into a consoling embrace.

"Oh no, Brigit, I am. I mean, we all are sorry to hear this. Those drugs are a mess and have people doing all sorts of crazy things."

Brigit wiped her eyes as she pulled away from Roxanne. "It's not drugs this time. If it were, I wouldn't be leaving him because that's an illness. He has another woman, and they have a baby together. He's been stealing from me to set up house with some ho." She looks at me as she says the last part, willing the venom in her words to poison me, her friend.

"What do you mean set-up house? He left you?" Aubrey asked the question I, and probably the others were all thinking.

"Not yet, but that was his plan. He thought he'd be gone by the time I learned the house was in foreclosure. His dumb ass was sitting around, reading all those articles about how long it's taking the courts to foreclose on houses. He didn't ever think that the bank has to file the papers first, and that's what caused the backlog." We all chuckle, not because Brigit is hurting but because men are so dumb at times.

Despite her jabs, I'm concerned about Brigit. If she's serious about leaving James, I would consider allowing her to stay in my house. She's consistent, if nothing else, and poured her heart into their home. I hate to think that she's about to lose it.

"Have you tried negotiating with the mortgage company or going to one of the seminars Congresswoman Castor has been putting on around the state?" I ask.

"If I wanted to keep the house, Mya, there's a lot I could do to save it. But my house isn't the same without my husband. He took the last of his things the other night, and he has not answered any of my calls since. I went to his job yesterday, and his manager told me that if I returned without James's permission, they would have to file a no-trespass warrant against me. They just don't want any trouble." The tears were unstoppable now. How embarrassing that must have been for her. We all did our part in consoling and reassuring Brigit that things would work out.

Suddenly Jaime came to life, "Okay, hold up a second. You have stood by James for twenty-something years while he was on drugs, bouncing from job to job, and not supporting you, now all of a sudden. Are you ready to throw in the towel over some trick? I don't get it. Twenty years is a long time." Jamie raised some excellent points, but I would have left James a long time ago if it were me.

"Jaime, you know there comes a time in your life when you realize you've given all you have to give. As I said, drug addiction is an illness, and all the stuff with the job and stealing from me, resulted from the addiction. James has been drug-free for five years.

"James having an affair and making a baby with someone else was a clear conscious decision. Do you know how low and inadequate that makes me feel? He's gotten from someone else the one thing I refused to give him because of his addiction. He wasted my child-bearing years, and now he's gone and started a family with some twenty-something-year-old who will never do for him what I did."

This was terrible. I had no clue Brigit didn't have kids because James was an addict. I don't know what I thought about the fact that they didn't have kids.

Angie finally spoke up. "No disrespect Mya, cause we all have our cross to bear, but this is just another prime example of how infidelity destroys lives. Brigit, you are a strong woman, and you have done everything according to God's plan. Don't think for one second you being home when those papers got served was a coincidence. He needed you to see what was going on and knows that you have been faithful to James in all things. Now James has to deal with what he has done to you and your marriage. Hold your head up. You don't have anything to be ashamed of."

After hearing Brigit's ordeal, it was hard to rejoice in my decision to move. It was also difficult to get through the evening, knowing that we all were thankful Brigit's marriage was over. She deserved so much better than James would ever be.

I know they were all looking at me sideways when I stated I didn't understand why women stay with men who bring nothing to the table. Or why people think they have to stay married to someone who is causing them more harm than good. When Aubrey's clock chimed, representing the nine o'clock hour had arrived, I steered the conversation back to my relocation.

"Mya, we're sorry," Roxanne began, "I am definitely up to helping you find a place. What about you ladies?"

Everyone but Brigit was down for the ride. However, I knew by the time we left Friday afternoon, Brigit would be in Angie and Bernie's Ford Excursion. She would complain that Angie was too tiny to be driving such a monster of a vehicle the entire ride. Questioning why men go out and buy big SUVs, and after a month or so, start leaving the house early so they can take the wife's sedan.

Telling LaDamien about my decision was the hardest, which is why I waited to tell him last. My parents were okay with my news. Their only concern was to get an apartment big enough to have a place to stay when they came to visit. I assured them that I would. Sonja, on the other hand, was her usual pessimistic self. For some reason, she insisted my move was just another example of my selfishness. My sister claimed I was only doing this to keep from helping with my parents as they grew older. I might add the same parents, come and go as they please, and travel more than she and I combined.

Now it was LaDamien's turn, and his reaction could be mild or totally outrageous. It just depended on his mood. To say I'm not looking forward to this is an understatement. I have never had to end a relationship with someone I genuinely love. Then again, I have never been in love with someone who was turning my life upside down.

The highs and lows I have experienced while with him have been crazy. I wonder if this is what it's like being a drug addict. You know you are doing yourself harm when you're sober, but when the euphoria of the drug have you entranced, only that moment matters.

As I sit across from LaDamien, I think back to the night we met, our first date, and our first time making love. It seems as though a lifetime has passed. This isn't the man I fell in love with, and I keep telling myself that Maya Angelou said it best, *"when a person shows you who they are, believe them the first time."*

The problem is, I don't know if LaDamien is the kind, compassionate, caring man who professes to love me, and only me. The one who is afraid to let his guard down and love completely and be loved in return. Or if he's the lying, cheating, selfish, narcissistic dog, I'm trying to escape. It's so frustrating. I wanted him to be angry and to scream and yell. Instead, he's looking at me like the kid picked last for the kickball team during recess.

"Why are you doing this, Mya, when you know how much I love you and want us to be together? Is there someone else? Is that why you have been so distant lately, you've decided to move on without me?"

"No, LaDamien, there's no one else in my life. I don't even know how you could think that. It's like I told you, I have this opportunity, and I want to take it. It's time for me to make a change."

"By a change, you mean to get away from me?"

Everything is about him. It's as if he has not heard a word that has come out of my mouth since we sat down.

It's Tuesday afternoon, and we are having lunch at *Chattaway's*. I intended to have this conversation Sunday afternoon. That way, I would have the remainder of the day to deal with the aftermath, but as usual, something came up, and he wasn't able to get away. That only confirmed once again that I was making the right decision. It seemed the more time passed, the harder it was becoming to spend quality time with him. A lunch now and then or a ride to this or that place was no longer cutting it for me.

I don't get excited when I hear his voice. Now I wish for the last-second phone call saying he can't make it or praying that he'll fall asleep and not call at all. These things used to annoy me to no end. My emotions swing like a pendulum. One minute I need to walk away, and the next, I want to stay. One day, I need him to drop everything and come with me. The next, I wish he'd get over me so I can move on with my life. Knowing what I came here to do supersede my doubt. This has to end.

"LaDamien, why does everything have to be about you? Why can't I make a decision about my future that is totally about my future? What are you offering me aside from a few stolen moments and sex?" The last part struck a nerve. I could see the pulsating in his temples. The truth was that I wasn't getting anything out of this anymore, not mentally, emotionally, physically, or financially, so what was the point.

"It hasn't been about me in quite some time, Mya. You don't think I see and feel the change in you. You're distant, always claiming you're going somewhere with your friends when you know damn well you have met somebody else."

"LaDamien…"

"Don't fucking LaDamien me. Do you think I believe that your company is relocating you to another city when they could hire someone off the street? What makes you so special that you get an offer to move, but everybody else is losing their job? You must think I'm stupid."

Yes, I do think you're stupid, I think to myself, but don't dare utter the words. Stupid for thinking that there's someone else. That I, a single woman, would have to sneak behind your back and find someone else. That I couldn't just say to you that it's over, and I'm moving on like I'm trying to do now. So I take a deep breath and try to explain.

"It's not that I'm special. It's the position I hold, and it's not just me. The company offered other people the same package. It just depends on what you do."

"And what do you do, Mya? I'm sure whatever it is, you can find another job here doing the same thing."

I'm not sure, but I think he's insulting me. LaDamien has never asked me what it is I do for a living. But hearing him talk this way places a few things into perspective. He had no regard for my job. He's always asking me to take off, call in, or leave work early as if I could just find another job if they fired me. Or the doubt that laced his voice whenever I said I had a meeting to go to or was on a teleconference. Since this is the prelude to our end, I thought I'd ask.

"What do you think I do, LaDamien, since you think I can just go anywhere and do it?"

"Why don't you tell me since you know I don't know because you've never told me?"

"I never told you because you never asked. I develop processes for my business unit, as well as research the market for new..." He sighed and rolled his eyes. Incredulous!

"How much does it pay, that's what matters? If you can find something here that pays what, thirty to thirty-five thousand, then you could stay."

I snicker, "That's a good starting salary, but why would I get a job starting at half of what I make." His eyes grow big.

"Thirty or thirty-five?" he asked.

"What difference does it make? You're not promising me anything that would make me reconsider. I've given you my all for three damn years, and all I've gotten in return are lies and empty promises. We don't even do a fraction of the things we use to. For all I know, you're probably still screwing Faye and...and, what about this LaDamien?" I reached into my purse and pulled out Wanda's letter.

"I left you a message days ago about a letter faxed to me, and you have yet to ask about it. Why in the hell did you or your secretary fax this bullshit to my home?"

He took the letter and glanced at it briefly. Did he recognize it, was he confused by it? His face contained no expression whatsoever.

"What is this, Mya?" He asked too calmly.

"It's a letter faxed to my house along with a property listing for your business. There was a cover sheet addressed to someone I assume is an associate of yours. LaDamien if you read the letter, it's quite clear Wanda wrote it, and she's talking about her relationship with you. Now Faye has already stated you were screwing both her and Wanda. This letter just confirms what I already know, so my question is who sent it to me, and how did they get my fax number."

"Since I didn't know you had a fax number, it couldn't have been me, and I doubt if Wanda wrote this because it's all a lie, none of this happened. If anything, Faye is up to her tricks." LaDamien folded the papers and handed them back to me, but I quickly let him know that those copies were for him. I had the original fax. He looked at me perplexed and asked, "Why do you need to keep a copy?"

"Just in case, I need a reminder of what a cheating liar you are."

He inhaled then let out a deep sigh before completely dismissing the issue. "So your mind is made up, you're leaving, *leaving me*, you didn't even think enough of me, and our relationship to discuss this with me when you first learned about it. I could have taken care of you until you found another job. You could have come and worked for me, but this is what you wanted all along."

Although we were trying to keep our voices down, Debbie, one of the owners, came by twice to see if everything was okay. The second time LaDamien requested the check. After we made our way to the car, he asked me again if I was leaving to be with someone else. My inner voice was screaming, *hell yeah*, but I wouldn't lie. So I repeated my earlier answer, and like before, it went in one ear and out the other. Like my previous comments about not being satisfied, the letter, and him still being involved with Faye.

By Sunday afternoon, I had decided on a beautiful two-bedroom, two-bath townhouse in a flourishing planned community ten miles from downtown Orlando. It was like a city within a city. Aside from work, I would never have to leave home if I didn't want to. The town center had a *Publix* grocery store, boutiques, and numerous restaurants. But what caught my eye was the waterfront with its bike and walking trails. The rent was steep, but I was sure I would be able to pull it off. If not, I would just have to find something less expensive. For now, I've signed my lease, and I'm moving in a couple of weeks.

"Mya, I'm so jealous of you," Brigit said. As I thought, she decided to come along at the last minute. "You just live your life as you damn well, please. When my divorce is final, I'm going to take on your approach, just say the hell with everything and everybody, and live my life doing what makes me happy. To be honest, I never thought you would move and leave LaDamien behind, but you are smarter than I gave you credit for being."

"Girl, I was just tired of that foolishness, and it wasn't like he was going to leave his wife, so what's the point of hanging on."

"Do you think LaDamien is going to let you walk away without a fight?" Roxanne asked as we pulled into my driveway. I didn't see it as LaDamien letting me do anything. He wasn't my husband, and I was not beholding unto him.

"Let? LaDamien doesn't own me, and I don't answer to him. Trust me, after a few weeks, he'll be preying on someone else. Hell, he's probably already back with Faye if he ever left her alone at all." My declaration was falling on deaf ears. None of my friends appeared to take me seriously.

"Bernie said he could help if you need it," Angie said. Aubrey added Keith would be available also to assist with my move, both ignoring my comments regarding LaDamien.

"That will be great. Well, let me get everything planned out, and I will let everyone know what I need. Thanks so much for making the trip with me. It was a great weekend, and Brigit, you can come to stay the weekend anytime."

LaDamien

The thought of Mya moving away scares me. She's just going to walk out of my life like it's no big deal, leaving me alone like we never meant anything to each other. How could Mya claim to have loved me all this time then make such a huge decision without consulting me? She didn't even ask for my help finding a place in Orlando. I realize I was being an ass at lunch the other day and called to apologize. When I offered to go with her to find a place, she informed me that she and her friends already had plans to go apartment hunting. She's been gone all weekend and hasn't answered any of my calls. It's late Sunday evening, and the lights are finally on at her house. I've been parked outside for almost a half-hour. She still isn't answering the phone, and I'm contemplating walking up to the door and ringing the bell. The fear inside of me won't allow me to do it; I don't want confirmation that she's planning to move on without me, literally. My phone rings and shakes me out of my trance.

"Are you going to sit outside my house all night?" Mya asks in a harsh tone.

"Why wouldn't you answer the phone so I can ask if it's okay to come in?" I retort.

"It's over, LaDamien, so please don't make it harder than it has to be. We aren't going to see each other anymore, I'm leaving, and I can't take any additional baggage with me. Please respect my decision, and don't come by here or call me again."

Her tone was so final. She had made up her mind and wasn't concerned with how it was affecting me. The moment was too much for me to absorb at once. There was no hug, no kiss, no making love to her one last time.

It wasn't right or fair after all I had done for her. What was I supposed to do with all the love I had for her? Before I realized what I was doing, I had exited the car and was now banging on Mya's door.

"Open the damn door, Mya. You owe me more than this." Who did she think she was dealing with at this moment? "Open the door, Mya!"

Mya yanked the door open in a furor that far exceeded mine. "Leave LaDamien. I have nothing else to say to you. It's over between us, what don't you understand. You are full of excuses, and what you can't find an excuse for you just pretend isn't so."

"So you don't love me anymore, you're just tossing me to the curb like I'm nothing? We have a history together. I love you, Mya. Why are you treating me like this?"

I could feel tears forming in my eyes, but the problem was I didn't feel them running down my face. Mya's furor turned to disgust. Instead of pleading my case, I was now begging her to allow me to be in her life. She didn't love me and never had. It was all a game to her. She just used me to get what she could out of me. Now I was angry. At that moment, I wanted to reach out, and grab her skinny neck, and choke the shit out of her.

"What is wrong with you, LaDamien? Please just leave and go home to your wife. Or to Faye, or better yet to your secretary who has devoted her life to you. Use this opportunity to get your life back on track because that's what I'm going to do. Stop looking at me like that," she yelled.

Mya is a cold-hearted bitch. She has to see the pain I'm in, but she doesn't care. She's plunging the knife deeper and deeper into my soul. When I step forward, she slams the door hard. She learned from our last interaction and made sure I didn't get in. I look around and see that one of her neighbors is standing in the yard.

"Yo man, what's up? Didn't she ask you to leave?" Totally humiliated and defeated I turn, and head back to my car, not saying a word as I passed him. "Man, come on, play the game, don't let the game play you."

What the hell was he talking about? This was no game, this was my life, and I was losing the only thing that mattered to me.

"Man, back the fuck up so I can get out of here," I said when he came over to my car, still trying to talk.

"I know where your head is at, man, and I'm just trying to say stop and think about it. It's too many women out here to flip over one. Man, you got a wife and a kid to think about..."

"You don't know me." Who is this dude? I've never seen him before. Could he be Mya's new man, the one she's leaving me over?

"No, I don't, not personally, but my wife knows who you are. But that doesn't matter right now. I'm just saying, this one got away, but you still have your wife. Chalk it up to the game, and move on just like she is doing. Shake it off, man, it's gonna be alright." He grabbed my hand and shook it.

What he was saying was right, but he didn't understand my heart was breaking. Mya went about this all wrong, making it harder than it should have been. She was lying about a letter she claimed to have received. It would have been a huge coincidence for me to transpose the fax number, and it turns out to be hers, and if I accidentally faxed the property listing to her, that's all it was.

When I left Mya, I went straight to the office and checked the paperwork. There was no letter behind the documents that remained on Wanda's desk inside a file folder. Nevertheless, we could have fixed things, I could have moved with her, there are so many options, but she chose this one, and it doesn't make sense. She has to have someone else in her life that's making her act this way.

Mya's birthday is coming up, and I'd planned to take her to Savannah. She's moving in a few days. I'm not privy to where she's moving, no address, no phone number, nothing. The closer it gets to her departure, the more I begin to panic. My thought is to call and remind her of the trip. Or maybe I can send her some roses with the details of the trip enclosed. It could be a going-away gift, a peace offering of sorts.

When I turn the corner, Mya is outside with two guys, loading boxes into a *U-Haul* truck. Several vehicles line the street, belonging to her girlfriends. Slowly I make my way up the street. The easiest thing to do would be to turn in a neighbor's driveway and go on my way. I haven't seen Mya since the day we had our argument, and this may be my last opportunity.

"Hi Mya, can I talk to you for a second?" I'm standing next to my SUV, which I have parked in front of her friend Angie's *Ford Excursion*. "I just came to say goodbye."

The two guys are now standing guard, awaiting Mya's command. My anger is building. A few months ago, things were fine, and I have no clue how it came to this. Mya walks towards me at a hurried pace.

"You shouldn't be here, LaDamien." She says as she approaches.

"Can we go for a ride? I just want to say goodbye and let you know how much I'm going to miss you."

"No need for a ride. You just said it. I'm going to miss you also, but it's for the best."

I don't know what possessed me, but I blurted out, "Savannah." Mya looked confused. "I was supposed to take you to Savannah in a couple of weeks for your birthday. It's all planned. Remember I suggested it a while back? It was going to be a surprise."

Mya wasn't moved. "We can't do that now. Take Kim and Ariel, you can have a good time with your family, like Orlando last year. Remember how you forgot about me and enjoyed your time with them. Do that with this trip, do it as a new beginning. I have to go now, take care LaDamien."

There was nothing else for me to say or to do. So I got back in my SUV, and I drove away. At first, I was going to wait and then follow them to Orlando, but four hours later, all the vehicles were gone except Mya's and the moving truck. She had not left yet. I still had a chance to convince her to let me know where she was going.

I got out and rang the bell. No answer. The lights were on, and I knew she was inside. I rang the bell again, and again, and again, but Mya refused to answer. The longer I stood there, the more I wished I could see her. Suddenly my phone rang, and I prayed it was Mya. To my dismay, it was Faye. I had not heard from her in months, so why was she calling now. Letting the call go to voicemail, I rang the bell again and again.

My phone announced I had a new message. I looked at the screen, thinking it was a 'please call' message from Faye. I was wrong. Mya sent me a message asking that I please leave her alone or she would call the police. This infuriated me, and I picked up a decorative brick from her flower bed and slugged it at her living room window. The brick hit with great force and bounced back into the yard.

Hurricane strength windows that would take a projectile traveling at seventy-five miles per hour to break, at least that's what the salesman said when I ordered them. Guess he was right, I think, as I begin to laugh at the absurdity of this whole situation. Mya is leaving me, and she doesn't want me anymore. I take a seat in the cushiony chair on her porch, trying to breathe, trying to see my way through this mess. Trying not to kick in that damn door and…and…and I don't know what.

She's rejected me, and she doesn't even care about me anymore, and to prove it, she's called the police. There's nothing left for me to say or do, so I get up and leave as the sirens near. My phone is ringing. It's Faye again. I get into my Escalade and drive off. When the phone rings again, I answer. If nothing else, Faye will help me calm down and be the distraction I need to put this behind me.

Faye

For months I have been trying to figure out a way to get back into LaDamien's life. One thing I can't stand is to feel like I lost at something. When my friend Celeste told me that the company Nikki's fiancé worked for was closing, I sent her on a hunt for information regarding Mya. Learning that she was moving to Orlando had me jumping for joy. It was just a matter of time before LaDamien would be calling and asking me to come back to him.

On occasion, I would drive by Mya's house just to see if he was there. It didn't matter if his car was there or not because I knew deep inside his heart was. Seeing the moving van in her drive let me know my wait was over. It's almost one a.m., and we're going for round three. The first hour after LaDamien arrived at my hotel room, he talked about how his relationship with Mya ended. He thanked me for calling when I did because she had called the police on him. Had he not left when he did, things would have gotten ugly, and he didn't think it would have ended well.

Deep down inside, I resent the hold she had over him. In all the years since we met, LaDamien has never given me any indication he felt that way about me. Yes, there were times when we had our spats. I would tell him to get lost, and he would fain a broken heart. That was because he knew it turned me on, and we would have great sex as part of our make-up.

Great sex is what he needed right now, and that's what I would provide. When the time was right, I would let down my guard and ask for what I crave, and that's for me and him to be together, but for now, I need to help him forget that stupid bitch, Mya.

"Ohh, baby, I love it when you do that," I stammer as LaDamien drives his big dick deep inside of me. "Uhm, don't stop, please don't stop," and he didn't stop until four in the morning.

We fucked all over the room and into the bathroom. Outside we went at it again in the backseat of his Escalade before he drove off. If LaDamien had asked to go back upstairs, I would have happily obliged. Unfortunately, his wife was calling, beckoning him home. He told me the last time he stayed out late like this, she showed up at Mya's house, although she didn't get out of the car. The way Mya was acting, he said, he didn't know what she would do if Kim knocked on her door.

"Faye, where have you been? I have been calling you all night long. This has got to stop." Luke was waiting for me when I came in. Sitting in the living room like my mother used to do when I was a teenager. LaDamien had me high on his loving, and I wasn't about to let my husband bring me down with his nagging ass.

"If you didn't complain about everything I do, you wouldn't have to call all night. You'd just roll over, and I would be there. Now I'm tired and don't need this tonight. I'm going to bed, and please don't wake me when you leave for church."

Luke had given his life to Christ several years ago, and with that commitment, he spent a lot of his free time helping out at the church. He was over one of the youth groups, led a bible study class, and taught Sunday school. Lately, he spent a lot of time praying for and over me, begging me to join him at church and to give our marriage a second chance. All of that was fine and dandy, but unless he learned to sex me like I yearned to be sexed, I wasn't interested in investing too much more into this marriage.

"Faye, we can't go on like this. You can't keep running the streets. I won't tolerate it much longer. For heaven's sake, I'm your husband, I'm a man, and I can't let you continue to walk over my manhood like you've been doing." Luke was near tears.

I burst out laughing at his trite attempt to man up. He sounded so pathetic, almost pleading for me to allow him to wear the pants in his house.

"Fine, Luke, whatever you say. I'm going to bed."

LOVE...

- is patient
- is kind
- is not rude
- does not envy
- is not self-seeking
- will not lie
- is not proud
- is not quick to anger
- protects
- does not boast
- does not record wrongs
- trusts
- hopes
- perseveres
- finds no joy in evil but celebrates truth
- never fails

Mya

My move to Orlando started rough, but here it's four months later, and I love it. LaDamien was acting a little crazy the day before I left, and I was afraid he would do something crazy. He tried to throw a brick through my window, and my total being became constricted in fear. He had lost his mind for real, but thank God the window didn't break. I was scared he would do something else to gain access to my home, but he must have heard the sirens in the distance and took off. It turned out to be fire rescue and paramedics, not the police. I feared that my nosey neighbor who confronted LaDamien a week earlier had seen him throw the brick and called the police.

Sleep didn't come easy my last night in the house. At four am I was up pacing and wondering if I'd handled the situation the best way. When I last spoke with Mrs. Epps, she told me the most effective solution was to cut ties quickly, not leaving room for negotiation.

"The longer you drag it out, the harder it will be to end it," she said to me during lunch.

Although she had given me great advice, she didn't provide step-by-step instructions on carrying it out. Ending the relationship was going to hurt no matter what. I felt my actions were crass, and LaDamien didn't deserve to be treated that way despite all the bad things he had done. Several times I picked up the phone to call him and apologize. Each time, I pressed 'end' instead of 'talk' on my cordless phone.

Bernie, Angie's husband, arrived first. He and Keith were going to drive the moving van for me. The girls wouldn't be able to come over today, so the plan was for me to unpack as much as I could on my, and the following weekend everyone would come over and help set up my new place.

"How are you doing, Mya?" Bernie asked when I opened the door.

"Very tired. I didn't get much sleep last night," I told him as we stood in an awkward moment.

Bernie had never been to my home without Angie. Was I supposed to invite him in, step outside, and ask why he was here an hour early? Or should I ask if Angie would mind if he came in? Before LaDamien, these thoughts never would have entered my mind. Now I'm suspicious of any married man's actions. Plus, I didn't need anyone to take his being here alone and draw the wrong conclusion. Bernie broke into my thoughts when he asked why I couldn't sleep.

"Regrets, nervous, excited, what kept you up?"

"Fear," I joked, although I was serious. "LaDamien came by yesterday, and it got ugly. No matter how hard I try, I can't figure out how I allowed that to become my life."

Bernie took a seat in the same patio chair LaDamien had sat in when he failed to break the window. A few seconds later, I joined him in the matching chair.

"We all do things in life that we look back on and wonder why we did it. The important thing is whether or not you learned from it. I've known a lot of men who have had affairs, present company excluded," he clarified in all seriousness. "But I've never seen anything like what Angie described was going on with you and this guy."

"So you know the whole story?" I asked as I folded and unfolded my arms.

"Pretty much," Bernie replied.

"Care for some orange juice or water? I have some stuff in a cooler by the door." A minute later, I returned with our juice and took a seat back in my chair. "Do you think I'm a ho, slut, tramp, or whatever for having an affair? Does Angie?"

Bernie choked on his orange juice. I didn't mean to be so blunt, but I had to know what people were saying and thinking about me.

"Wow, Mya, I wasn't expecting that. Honestly, most men wouldn't consider you any of those things. It's not like you're going around sleeping with this man and that man. Now most women, especially married women, would think that."

"What about Angie? What does she think?" Would he answer the question truthfully?

"Have you asked her? You two are pretty close and can talk about anything." He took a sip of his juice, avoiding answering the question.

"She says she understands, she prays for, and with me, giving advice, but that's what friends do. It doesn't necessarily speak to their true feelings."

"True, true, she doesn't think you're any of those things. If so, she'd be here with me." He laughed.

"So she sent you over here an hour early?"

"Busted, she wanted to make sure he hadn't weaseled his way back in and made you unpack the truck." Bernie had jokes this morning, but I decided to play along.

Bernie and I sat on the porch talking and enjoying the lovely Spring morning until Keith arrived. He allowed me to drill him on how a man thinks. He even suggested we stop at a bookstore along the way and pick up a copy of Steve Harvey's *Act Like A Lady Think Like a Man*. But I wasn't interested in Steve's book; I listen to him enough on the radio to know his way of thinking wasn't the most up-to-date.

During our conversation, I asked Bernie if he thought LaDamien loved me or was it some sick game he was playing. He didn't want to give me hope or a reason to change my mind, but he did try to be honest.

"Obsession is what comes to mind when I think about your situation. Men sometimes crave what they can't have, but it doesn't stop them from pursuing it. Most men know not to cross that line, but some don't have that control. A man like LaDamien has probably had his way all his life, so when a woman says no, he hears yes, but he's going to have to work for it."

"But I said yes, he said he loved me, did things for me, and shared a lot of things with me. It wasn't like what people say affairs are all about, you know, a selfish man looking for extra-marital sex."

Bernie stretched out his right leg and began squeezing his thigh muscle like he had a cramp. He placed his empty cup on the ground and leaned forward. "What does it cost someone to profess their love to another person? About three seconds of their time? I love you, I love you, I love you, and if you say it enough, eventually, you may begin to believe it yourself. At some point, it just becomes natural, but it doesn't make it true.

"Then you say he provided for you, at what cost Mya, he has money, he owns his business, and could probably make-up what he gave you in a snap. He didn't pay off your mortgage, and you aren't rocking diamonds on every finger. Do you have a bank account with thousands of dollars earning interest?" Bernie wasn't holding back.

"Mya, in essence, it *was* your typical affair. He didn't leave his wife to be with you. Most men don't, but some men do, and he wasn't one of those men, and that's what you need to take from this. No matter what he said or did, it wasn't enough to make him leave his wife and start a life with you. That's what it boils down to."

Keith pulled up, and Bernie looked relieved. He stood, satisfied that he had fulfilled his obligation to his wife, which I'm sure was to drive home that last point.

Keith walked up to the porch, handed me a card and a gift bag, and said it was from Aubrey. He and Bernie shook hands and walked inside to get the last of my boxes. After they loaded the last of my items, they got into the truck and backed out of the driveway. I took a final walk-thru of my place, making sure I wasn't leaving anything important behind. Turning off the lights and walking outside, I inhaled, exhaled, locked the door, and headed to my car.

My parents were awaiting my arrival so we could say "so long," never goodbye, as my mom put it, because we would see each other again real soon. When I arrived, she had a full spread breakfast waiting. Sonja had even stopped by to say farewell and offer to follow me over and help unpack. I told everyone they're welcome to drive over next weekend when the official unpacking would occur. After hugs and kisses, Sonja followed me outside.

"I'm sorry you have to move away to end things with LaDamien. I had no idea what you were going through. You could have talked to me, Mya?"

I had no clue where Sonja was coming from with her empathy towards my situation. How did Sonja know what I was going through with LaDamien? Where was she getting her information?

"I'm leaving because I don't feel like being unemployed. It has nothing to do with LaDamien or what you think is going on with him." At that moment, my phone began to ring, and when I looked at the caller ID LaDamien's name was emblazoned across the screen.

"Sonja, I'll see you next weekend, okay?" We embraced, and I promised to call her when I arrived.

I watched Sonja head back inside my parent's house as I listened to my phone ring again and again until finally, I turned it off. The card and gift Keith handed me caught my attention. Inside was an inspirational card from the *Maya Angelou* collection and the new CD *Epiphany* by Chrisette Michelle. Aubrey had written a note inside encouraging me to keep my head up and use this opportunity as a chance to find the man God truly intended for me.

"We've all done stupid stuff in the name of love. Believe it or not, more women have had affairs than they are willing to admit. Think about it, if most men cheat, who are they cheating with...LOL.

I bought this CD for you because you said track four was going to be your anthem. Stay true to yourself Mya, I love you and can't wait to see you next week. Aubrey."

I had a great set of friends and wouldn't trade them for anything in the world. When I looked up, my mom was at the door, asking if everything was okay. Smiling, I nodded in the affirmative and waved as I placed the car in drive and drove off. I placed the CD into the player and pressed forward until I reached *Blame It on Me*. This song was definitely what I needed to hear.

Yes, LaDamien, *I love you, but I gotta lose you, freedom's where I want to be...yes, I probably will always love you, but I'm moving. I gotta do this for me...*

The first night in my new place, I cried myself to sleep. Reality and the enormity of my decision finally hit me like a ton of bricks. I was in a new city, a new place, and all alone. My phone had been off most of the day. It seemed as if every time I turned it back on, LaDamien was calling.

As I lay in bed that night, I decided to confront my mixed emotions. What was the worst that could happen if I moved on without him? I'll be alone, not necessarily lonely because I control that, but alone until I meet someone new, single and available. If nothing else, I would have peace, and peace of mind is something you can't put a price tag on.

Days turned into weeks, and weeks turned into months just like that. Our Orlando location was much more technologically advanced, and the building more modern. The atmosphere was different as well. Whereas the St. Pete location was very relaxed and casual, this office is more business professional. My entire wardrobe needed to be revamped, not that I was complaining.

Getting settled in my new place, updating my look, and just settling into the flow of life left little time for me to fret over what was or could have been. Or wonder when life begins to happen. You're going with the flow. You barely notice the changes occurring around you. Like the guy who stopped me at the grocery store and asked when I would stop pretending, he wasn't flirting with me. It was sheer coincidence that we were at *Publix* every Wednesday evening at seven, doing our weekly shopping.

"I would love to take you to dinner?" he asked, and the following week, after consulting with my friends back in St. Petersburg, I accepted.

Kim

Ding dong, the witch is gone! My prayers are answered, at last. Mya is out of our lives. It only took a company shutting down and a thousand people losing their jobs, I think sarcastically.

I am so sorry for those people, some of whom I ended up hiring. Mya is gone, and I'm ecstatic. Rumor in the business world had it that a local company was closing its doors. When I opened the newspaper and saw the announcement, my first reaction was that LaDamien would have more time to spend with her. She would be unemployed, and he would try to support her, something I was prepared to fight him on tooth and nail.

It was my former beautician who delivered the good news. I severed our business relationship soon after she advised me that my husband was having an affair, and I needed to check him. Each time I would visit her shop, she made a point of letting me know she'd seen his car at Mya's house.

Her cousin who lived on Mya's street had called to tell her that Mya was moving to Orlando, and in turn, she called to fill me in. "She was one of a few employees offered the opportunity to relocate to their company headquarters." She had said in our brief conversation.

Secretly, I wished Mya lost her job, home, and eventually everything else; karma for sleeping with my husband even if he was partly to blame. As a woman, she owed it to me not to cross that line, not to betray another woman as she had. But Mya would get hers eventually. One day she'll fall in love and start a family, and some trifling trick would come along and destroy what she was trying to build.

Not only did I hate Mya for what she did to me, a woman, a wife, and a mother, but I hated her for what her actions drove me to do. She forced me to step outside my marriage, break my vows, and bring me down to the same level as her and my husband.

My affair with TayJohn was a huge mistake that I will have to live with for the rest of my life. The feelings I developed for him are real, our interactions, real. I never thought I would love another man as much as I love LaDamien, and even though my love for TayJohn is different, it's still real.

He walked away from our affair for several weeks, and it was then that I knew I had fallen in love with him. Those weeks, seeing him at the office and being ignored was too much to bear. LaDamien was tripping big time, Debra and Karen pushed me to leave him, and TayJohn refused to talk to me. Things changed after I received a picture text of LaDamien entering the side door of what looked like a hotel. It was attached to a message asking if I knew where my husband was that night. My first thought was to reach out to TayJohn. He was there for me, which led to us making amends.

"This has to end," I said to TayJohn when he allowed me to enter his apartment that evening. "He's at a hotel right now with only God knows who."

TayJohn just stood at the door looking at me, allowing me to get it all out, and when I finished, he simply asked if that was everything. When I nodded in the affirmative, he stepped to me, and took me in his arms, and made sweet love to me in the middle of the living room floor. His desire met mine with every thrust, and he filled me up completely. In the recesses of my mind, I justified the elation of being with TayJohn again by reminding myself that LaDamien was off with someone else. That he didn't love me the way he claimed or the way TayJohn professed his love for me.

My husbands' kisses didn't set my soul afire. His touch didn't ignite my flesh, and his tongue dancing across my clit no longer drew orgasms that caused massive soul-shaking explosions. Not like the one I experienced that night with TayJohn. No, as much as I loved my husband, I knew I was no longer in love with him. But what was I going to do about it?

TayJohn and I have only been intimate twice since that night. Not long after Mya moved away, LaDamien agreed to family counseling. He came in one evening and asked when the next appointment would be, and as promised, he attended. We've had family counseling that included Ariel. It has helped tremendously in getting her back on track. Our couple's counseling unleashed some deep-rooted issues in my marriage.

It was hard sitting there hearing LaDamien admit he wasn't in love with me when he asked me to marry him. He proposed because he no longer wanted to live alone and knew I would be a good wife. Someone who would run the house and one day become a great mother to his children. But when he admitted his proposal's abruptness came out of desperation, I felt the need to retaliate.

"I had lost my job and was a week away from being evicted. My life was on a downward spiral, and I needed something solid to grab hold to, and that something was Kim." He said this to Dr. Sampson like it was an everyday occurrence. Like men just up and got married every day because they couldn't pay their bills. How could I have been so stupid? Why didn't I recognize that he didn't love or want me but just needed a safe place to lay his head?

"Well, I guess we both said I do for reasons other than true love. See Dr. Sampson, LaDamien came back into my life after I had experienced a rough break-up with someone I *was* in love with," he flinched. "At the time he said, and did all the right things, and I just figured what the hell, it can't be any worse. Boy, was I wrong."

Dr. Sampson saw straight through my lie and insisted that I be honest with my feelings. He already knew my story, knew I was madly in love with LaDamien and would do anything for him back then. Remembering the things I had revealed to him in earlier private sessions frightened me. I knew when we addressed LaDamien's infidelity, I might get asked if I have ever stepped outside our marriage. The good Dr. Sampson would see straight through me and know I had been cheating on my husband.

Many nights I have weighed the decision to come clean with everything. Not only because it's the right thing to do but also because whoever sent the pictures and text messages may still be playing games. Evident by the hang-ups I continue to receive.

"What do you think would happen if I told LaDamien about our affair?" TayJohn and I are at *Savannah's Cafe*, a southern-themed restaurant located on Central Avenue, just east of Thirteenth Street.

Not too long ago, I wouldn't dare allow myself to be seen in public with another man. Considering my husband never seemed to have a problem gallivanting around town with his women, so why should I. Besides, no matter how cautious I thought I was being, someone could still find out about TayJohn and me.

TayJohn looks past me, not making eye contact. I turn to look behind me, but there's no one sitting at those tables. "Are you okay?"

"Yes, just wondering why you would tell your husband about us if you have no intentions of leaving him." TayJohn picks up a fried green tomato and dips it in the Remoulade sauce he has requested over the house sauce of roasted red pepper puree with goat cheese and pecans. "I don't care to be a pawn in your game, the one you can fall back on if things blow up in your face. I'm not some toy, okay." His eyes are intense, although his full attention still isn't on me.

"He's in Gainesville," I say, hoping it will quell his fears that LaDamien is going to walk up on us.

"Who's in Gainesville?" he asks, looking at me confused.

Chuckling, I ask TayJohn again if he's okay. "My husband, silly. He went to Gainesville for the weekend. He's going to check out some properties and then catch the Gators tomorrow in their home opener.

"Why didn't you accompany him? If you wish to work things out, you should be going with him and showing an interest in the things he enjoys doing."

Did I need my lover telling me how to work my way into my husbands' good graces? Shouldn't he be basking in our time together? "Because I'd rather be here with you," I respond.

TayJohn seems annoyed by my response instead of turned on. Something is up with him. "If Debra can watch Ariel, would you like for me to spend the night with you?" He slides his large hand from underneath mine and picks up his glass of lemonade.

"What I desire, Kim, is for you to stop playing me like a chump." He glances over at me. I assume he catches my glimpse of dismay because he apologizes and agrees to come over.

"Maybe I'm just tired and need a good massage," he hesitates, and then continues, "and some good company," he taps the back of my hand and smiles, "and some good loving." Now I'm smiling.

The more my desire for TayJohn grows, it seems the more my husbands' desire for me grows. LaDamien has become more intimate lately, and I'm just not in the mood, for him, that is. He tries his best to have his way with me. At first, I gave in, but the more time goes by, the less I can tolerate him on top of me.

We have begun to argue again, and he's accusing me of having someone else. I laugh at the notion and insist that I wouldn't still be here with him if there were someone else. Unlike before, when Mya was here, he doesn't run out of the house. Instead, he stays, and gloats, and knocks things around.

My time with TayJohn is becoming limited because LaDamien's suspicions are growing, and he's watching my every move. It's Saturday night, and we have plans to go over to Orlando to the *House of Blues* to see Jazmine Sullivan in concert.

LaDamien planned this trip alone and surprised me with the tickets at dinner last weekend. TayJohn's best friend from Baltimore was in town to celebrate his fortieth birthday, leaving him little time for me. Rather than sit around pining for him, I put on a happy face and let my husband know I'm looking forward to our evening together.

LaDamien

She left, it's been months since Mya moved, and I still can't believe she did it. I don't know what made her do it, or who got to her, or what got into her, but she left and never looked back. Things will seem like they are mellowing out, and then I'll pass by the Blake's home or Mya's house, and her car will be there. She has been home several times, and not once has she tried to contact me. When I call her, she never answers. She just sends my calls into voice mail. My pride refuses to allow me to leave a message professing my love for her, so I opt to hang up instead.

One Sunday, I saw her car at the church. Instead of going inside and agonizing over not being able to touch her or speak to her, I opted to park around the corner and wait for her to exit. Kim had long since stopped attending church with me. She claimed it was hypocritical of me to attend church on Sunday morning and then run around town screwing everything with a hole Sunday afternoon through Saturday night. She said it as if her salvation was connected to mine somehow. But that day, I was grateful she hadn't come.

Two hours later, Mya exited the church and separated from a group of parishioners parked in the same lot as her. She headed out and turned left. I assumed she was on her way to her parent's home. I maintained a safe distance so she wouldn't spot me. As I was thinking of turning off and heading over to visit my mother, Mya continued straight, whereas she would have turned if she was going by her folks. I couldn't risk losing her, so I continued to follow. She drove until she reached the on-ramp to I-275, heading north. Without hesitation, I followed suit. We were almost to Thonotosassa before realizing how crazy it was for me to follow her back to Orlando. I had to question myself, my motives, and my anticipated outcome. In the end, I decided Mya would call the police the second she saw me, and things could quickly escalate, and where would that leave me. No, it was best not to face the unknown. Mya had made her decision, and I needed to find a way to live with it.

After a month or so, I decided it was time for me to move on with my life. Soon, I was back to attending church regularly. After one moving sermon on the man's role in the family, I decided to ask Kim about the counseling sessions. As hard as it was for me to admit, the sessions have done a lot of good.

Dr. Sampson has helped me see what a gem I have in Kim, but it may be too little too late. My wife is no longer in love with me, nor does she desire me sexually. She insists there's no one else, but in my heart, I believe there is.

Kim doesn't know it, but I have had a few private sessions with Dr. Sampson, as well. He has made me realize the damage I have caused and says that my thinking Kim is having an affair is simply a result of all the dirt I have done. When I shared with him my love for Mya, the doctor wasn't the least bit surprised. Although he didn't say it, I believe Kim has probably told him the whole sordid story.

Dr. Sampson didn't hold back any punches. He looked me in the eye, man-to-man, and asked, "Are you going to leave Kim and go after this other woman?" He hesitated and waited for me to answer. The wait was met with silence, so he continued, "If not, you need to put her behind you and focus one hundred percent on your marriage. Can you do that, LaDamien?" He asked the question as if he were talking to a child, and at that moment, I felt like I was ten again.

"I don't have a choice, do I?"

"We always have choices, LaDamien. It's just a matter of acting on them. Right now, you have the choice to honor your marriage, or you can be honest with Kim and let her go so that you can pursue Mya. Just know no guarantees are awaiting you. Or you can continue living in this web of deception you have created. But for once, consider not yourself but everyone else you involve when you live out these lies. Consider Kim, Ariel, and Mya, and then consider the other women you're involved with and their husbands. Your actions adversely affect many people. You seem oblivious to this, which is systematic of other things that may be going on with you. Things we can discuss when you're ready." He peered over the rim of his reading glasses as if to alert me that now was as good a time as any.

As much as I enjoyed our one-on-one sessions, I stopped requesting to meet with him alone. I thought I had made my choice. I was going to save my marriage. Kim and Ariel are my main priority.

My resolve was firm. At least it was until I took Kim to Orlando to see Jazmine Sullivan in concert. As I scanned the room, my heart froze. Mya was there with another man.

Mya

"**Mya Myambi,** umm, I don't know about that," I teased Rashad as I prepared for the concert. We had been dating now, going on three months.

Rashad Myambi was a tall, muscular but slender brother with neat shoulder-length dreads. Both of his parents were American, but his father was of Ugandan descent. Rashad was definitely what the doctor ordered. Ever since he approached me in *Publix* claiming to have been arriving each week at seven p.m. just to get a glimpse of me, he had gone out of his way to assist me in mending my scarred heart. Angie, Aubrey, my folks, and even Sonja agreed that he was a Godsend. Having a man that I could call mine and not have to worry about who's watching or being caught by his wife and all that other nonsense seemed a lifetime ago.

Rashad owned a computer repair business by day and attended college by night. He was studying to become a pharmacist, which was his lifelong passion. According to Rashad, he became sidetracked his first run at college after getting caught up in the social life. After leaving school with a degree in business administration, he enrolled in night school to learn computers. Although Myambi Computer and Network Solutions was a booming business, he was committed to fulfilling his destiny.

A part of me thought he should stick with what was already working. Still, another part of me was happy he was trying to pursue something that would pull him away from entrepreneurship. I was not too fond of the idea of him being in people's homes where he could easily commit devious acts, and no one would be the wiser. LaDamien is to blame for my thinking this way. Before getting involved with him, I never would have equated a man running a successful business to limitless opportunities to cheat. I'm mindful that Rashad isn't

LaDamien. Not all men conduct themselves in such a haphazard manner, but still, I find myself wondering.

"So, Miss Mya, are you saying that if we were to marry, you wouldn't carry my name?"

"That is precisely what I'm saying. Then again, you haven't asked, so I don't know exactly what I would do." Rashad comes up behind me and kisses me on my neck.

"I love this up-do you have going on here. Your neck is so sexy, and I could plant kisses there all night. Are you sure you want to battle I-4 to get to the HOB? We could just have dinner and listen to her CD while sharing a bottle of wine." My deep sigh answers his question. We are going to the concert.

Young Jazmine Sullivan surprised the music world with her mature raspy vocals and grown-up lyrics. Many people didn't know of Jazmine until she appeared on *The Steve Harvey Morning Show*. Still, she had an extensive resume' preceding the release of her debut CD *Fearless*.

"What a turn-out," Rashad commented as we took our seats.

The House of Blues' concert hall was at total capacity as we awaited Jazmine to take the stage. I hadn't been in Orlando that long to look for anyone specific in the crowd but what caught my attention was the number of familiar faces from St. Petersburg.

Fifteen minutes before showtime, I excused myself to go to the ladies' room. Thankful that the line was short, I used the potty, freshened up my make-up, fixed my hair, and quickly made my exit. As I was making my way back, two faces I never cared to see again were staring at me. This had to be a delusion; LaDamien and Kim were not here. But they were, and neither seemed able to take their eyes off of me.

Taking a deep breath and shaking off the negative energy, I bypassed them and made my way back to Rashad. I was just in time for the show's opening. My mood had changed, and I was not enjoying myself. As if I had no control over my movement, my head kept turning in their direction. Each time I looked, a hostile glare from Kim greeted me, matched with sadness mixed with longing in the eyes of LaDamien.

I began to feel the vibration of my cell phone as my bag rested against my leg. I pulled the phone out and saw I had two text messages. The first read *"Hi,"* and the second, *"I miss you."* I willed myself not to turn around, but my resolve was weak. Now only Kim's stare greeted me. LaDamien was gone. Probably in the restroom, I figured. The phone vibrated again, *"Do you miss me?"* By now, Rashad was distracted from the show and was watching me.

"What's up? Is everything okay?" he asked, looking at the phone more so than at me.

I closed the phone after turning it off and placed it back in my purse. Sliding closer to Rashad, I forced myself to focus my attention on Jazmine Sullivan. However, my mind was twenty feet away.

Jazmine was halfway through a commanding rendition of *In Love with Another Man* when I realized I was fighting back the tears. What in the world was wrong with me? Rashad and I were happy, he was everything I hoped for, but here I was, focused on LaDamien, and wondering why he couldn't leave his wife if I were who he desired. The crowd was going crazy as she put gut-wrenching emotion into every lyric of this powerful song. By now, I was trembling from her every word, which was chilling me down to the bone; then Jazmine began to speak directly to the screaming women in the audience.

"Ladies, how many of you have been in love before? Uh uh, y'all don't hear what I'm asking. How many of you have ever been in love before, I mean, in love with a man, and no matter how hard you try, you can't shake that feeling. You could have a good man who treats you like the world, but he just doesn't make you feel like that other man." Women were testifying, and if Rashad didn't have his arm around me pulling me closer, I would have been one of them.

"Damn, she singing that song," he exclaimed. "Could you imagine her in a church? She'd have people signing up to go to heaven." I try to chuckle at his humor, but my soul is entranced.

Jazmine has resumed singing and is now on her knees crawling as she belts out, *"but I love that man…I'm so sorry, sorry, baby."*

This song needs to end before I lose my mind. For some reason, I wonder if Kim realizes the torment I'm in over her husband, and what is LaDamien thinking? Is he reading my body language or wondering what I'm thinking? Finally, Jazmine has ended my torture and moved into a more upbeat tune. The crowd has moved on with her, and I decide to do the same. My body is swaying to the beat, and my momentary lapse into insanity is a thing of the past.

It's two a.m. when I look over at the clock. My cell phone is ringing somewhere in the room, but I'm more focused on who would be calling me this time of night. Rashad left around twelve-thirty, and I'm sure he's home and asleep by now. The phone stops and starts again. Remembering I laid the phone on my dresser after checking my messages, I roll out of bed and shuffle over to it. "Hello."

"Can I come to see you?" It can't be, but to verify, I look at the display and confirm it is...LaDamien!

"Why are you calling me?" I ask as I make my way back to the bed. "Where is Kim? Where are you?"

"Mya, seeing you tonight, let me know I will never get over you no matter how hard I try. We've got to work this out." LaDamien sounded so pitiful that my desire to hang up and turn the phone off disappeared.

"Where is your wife, LaDamien?"

"She's at the hotel. I told her I didn't want to drive back to St. Pete tonight, so we got a room."

"You didn't want to drive back to St. Pete, but you're out after two in the morning? Where does she think you are?" This was crazy, just like our whole relationship. Nothing good was going to come of this. Why couldn't I accept it and move on with my life?

LaDamien has a hint of impatience in his voice. "She's probably sleeping by now. I told her I was hungry, but she said she wasn't hungry, nor was she getting up to ride with me to find something. Where do you live Mya, I have to come over and just hold you for a few hours, and then I'll leave? I know that joker isn't there, or you wouldn't have answered the phone."

"I answered the phone because I was worried something was wrong, had I looked at the display first, I wouldn't have."

"Where do you live?"

"Please go back to your hotel and your wife. We don't need to rekindle our relationship LaDamien. We don't have a future, so what's the point?" I know he wasn't taking no for an answer, and the only thing for me to do was hang up the phone. Part of me wanted to, but the stronger part couldn't. At that moment, I wished I had taken my new friend Glenette up on her offer to attend church last Sunday. My soul was weak.

"Mya, what's the address? I'm just riding around. Please, I just need to hold you for a couple of hours."

"Won't Kim wake-up, and worry about you?

"I don't care."

"This is wrong."

"No, it's not."

"You can't come over."

"Please, Mya, what's the address?"

"No!"

"Mya, don't do me like this. I love you. You just don't know what this is doing to me. If I can't have you, what's the point?"

"Don't talk like that."

"What's the address?" he demanded.

LOVE...

- is patient
- is kind
- is not rude
- does not envy
- is not self-seeking
- will not lie
- does not proud
- is not quick to anger
- protects
- does not boast
- does not record wrongs
- trusts
- hopes
- perseveres
- finds no joy in evil but celebrates truth
- never fails

Kim

"Baby, what's wrong?" Taj asked the instant he heard my sobs.

"That bitch was at the concert."

"Huh?"

Through my sniffles, I said, "Mya, she was at the concert, and he couldn't take his eyes off of her. Now he's gone, and I know he's with her. It never ended; he's been coming over here fucking her the whole time." I didn't know this for a fact, but the hatred in my husband's eyes as he leered at Mya's date let me know he still wants her.

"It's after three in the morning. Where are you? This isn't making any sense. How did he leave? Did you fight?" He was rolling the questions off so fast I couldn't keep up, so I took a deep breath and tried to explain, but the more I talk, the faster the tears flowed.

"He…he…he said he was too tired to…to drive back home, so we got a room," It was hard to control my breathing, but I continued, wiping the tears and mucus from my face. "After I got settled in the bed, he claimed he was hungry and was going to go get something to eat," I repeatedly sniff to catch the fluid seeping from my nostrils. "I chose not to get up, and that was two hours ago. He even turned his phone off."

Being the rational person he is, TayJohn asked if something might have happened, like a car accident. It was a possibility, but I knew LaDamien, and I knew what my gut feeling was telling me, he was with her. No drive-by or repeated phone calls or sitting outside her house until he came home. He'd return when he was good and ready, and there was nothing I could do. I didn't even have transportation back home, so I had to wait for him to return and listen to whatever lie he will have conjured up to explain his absence.

"Do you need me to come to get you?" The offer was tempting, but what if LaDamien returned before he arrived. As if he was reading my mind, he replied, "If he arrives before I do, go in the bathroom and send me a text. As a matter of fact, type the text now, and save it as a draft. When we hang up, bring it back up, and if he comes back, press send. What hotel are you at?"

"*The Best Western* on International Drive, but you can't do this, it's too risky, and I'm sure he will try to make it back before he thinks I will awaken." Having Taj coming to rescue me sounded so good, but I couldn't place his safety at risk because as wrong as LaDamien was right now, he would flip out, and things could turn ugly.

"What are you going to say when he returns if you find out nothing happened to him, and he was with her? How much more disrespect are you going to take?" He was making sense.

"Please don't get mad at me and hang up as you did before. Not seeing you was the worst feeling in the world." I say.

"More so than your husband leaving you in a hotel…and a cheap one at that…to go and be with his mistress?" That was a cheap shot, but he was right. If I forgave this transgression, then shame on me.

"I'm going to leave him? Can Ariel and I come live with you?" I ask.

"Come live with me? It's your house. He would need to leave." He didn't answer the way I wanted, although I was joking. I remember Karen telling me if I leave LaDamien, do it for Ariel and me. Not because I think TayJohn will be a suitable replacement.

"What if he becomes violent and refuses to leave? Then what? I'll have to leave at least until the police can get him out."

"He'll be pissed, but I don't think it will come to that." TayJohn counters.

"I love you." I don't know why I said it, but I did. I guess it was true, but if he didn't say it back, then what.

There was a brief hesitation, but he finally said, "I love you too, Kim, but this can't continue. Are you sure you don't want me to come? I'm up and dressed? Just say the word.

"Can I spend the day with you so you can help me sort this mess out?" His yes was like music to my ears.

My husband had crossed the invisible line of no return. I will see TayJohn tomorrow and allow him to boost my confidence, and then I will return home and tell LaDamien I want a divorce.

TayJohn stops my contemplation when he states, "Kim, I'm on my way. I'll be there in forty-five minutes. What room are you in?"

LaDamien

Seeing Mya with another man changes things, and seeing her happy with another man changes them drastically. The moment Kim and I entered the room, I knew she was there. I could feel her presence long before seeing them, holding hands, smiling, and laughing like we used to do. If Kim weren't with me, I would have confronted them.

He looks nothing like me, and I wonder what she sees in him. My thoughts soon turn to whether or not they are intimate with one another. Anger engulfs me, and I feel as though I'm suffocating. Kim sees her at the same time I do, and her body language changes. She knows what I'm thinking and what I'm feeling. Whatever this evening was supposed to hold for us, it's now gone. We sit staring at Mya, both angry but for different reasons. It becomes unbearable when Mya crosses our path and head for the ladies' room. As I prepare to follow, Kim grabs my arm, "Wait. I'll go with you. I need to freshen up." Her comment surprises me. She saw Mya and knew I would try and steal a few minutes alone with her.

"I wasn't going anywhere. Did you want a drink or something?"

Kim smiles, "Oh, I thought you were headed to the restroom."

"No, I wasn't," is my response.

Kim keeps her eyes on me until Mya heads our way. Mya's demeanor changes, and I realize she has spotted us for the first time. Now we are looking at her, and she's looking at us. This evening is going downhill fast.

"You know what, I think I do need to use the restroom," but this time, Kim doesn't offer to tag along. As soon as I'm out of her sight, I pull out my phone and send Mya a text. I wait for her to reply, and when she doesn't, I send another. Peeking around the corner, I see her looking at the phone. Her date says something to her, and she presses what I think is the end button and drops the phone into her bag.

Quickly, I dial her number, and the call goes straight to voicemail confirming what I suspected.

Back at the table with Kim, I do my best to divert my attention to the show happening on stage. Things were going well until Jazmine Sullivan began singing her hit *In Love with Another Man*.

My heart begins to yearn for Mya all over again. Kim has a smirk on her face, probably wondering if Mya is in love with the man she's with and has left me alone in the cold. But my thoughts lead me to believe that Mya thinks that as much as she wants to love this guy, her heart will always be with me. Yes, she secretly desires me, and that chump or any other man will never take my place. Jazmine is on the floor singing with all her might, and the expression on Mya's face lets me know I'm consuming all of her thoughts right now. This makes me feel so much better. Now I just have to figure out a way to get back into her life.

The concert is over, and I don't feel as if I can leave Orlando. If Kim weren't with me, I would follow Mya and her date. I wouldn't leave without learning where she resides. Do they live together, I wonder. Is he staying the night? I have to know.

Heading to our car, I advise Kim that I don't feel like driving home. "I'm going to get a room. It's too late for us to drive back tonight." Kim looks at the clock that is showing ten fifty-seven on the display.

"If you're tired, I can drive. Debra has plans tomorrow morning, so we need to be home to get Ariel pretty early," she retorted.

Thinking quickly, I say, "We'll call Lynn to get her," and I bypass the on-ramp to I-4 that would take us west and back to St. Pete. Twenty minutes later, we are checking into a hotel. Once Kim showers and gets situated in bed, I announce that I'm hungry and about to grab a bite to eat. Mya would complain and eventually drag herself out of bed, but Kim won't. She's going to catch major attitude then turn away from me as I grab my keys. "Do you need anything?" I asked, reaching for the doorknob.

"I'm not hungry. Just don't be gone long." That was easier than I thought it would be.

For nearly an hour, I drive through Orlando, wondering where Mya could live. If I call her number, will she answer, and if she does answer, what will I say to convince her to let me come over? The thought that her date could be lying next to her when I call is driving me insane. Each time I prepare to press send, my nerves get the better of me. Immediately, I begin to wonder if she's with him. Are they making love? Is he holding her in his arms the way I use to, unable to turn her loose for fear she won't be there when he awakens? Then the thought hits me, what if they went back to his place? These what-ifs are excruciating. I need to know. I have to know, so I muster up my nerve and press the button to call Mya's cell phone. She answers, and all my doubts evaporate temporarily. Mya informs me that she didn't look at the caller ID before answering, and had she known it was me, she wouldn't have, so I get straight to the point and tell her why I've called.

Mya and I banter back and forth on whether or not I can come over. She refuses to give me her address and eventually suggests meeting me at a twenty-four-hour eatery. She says it will take her almost forty-five minutes to get there. I'm not sure if she lives that far away or if she's trying to divert me away from where she truly lives. Whatever the reason, I'm just happy she has agreed to meet me.

Glancing at my watch and noting that it's almost three-thirty, I begin to wonder if she set me up. Calls to Mya's phone go unanswered, and my hope begins to dwindle. As I start my car and prepare to leave some fifteen minutes later, a car pulls into the parking lot, and I recognize it as Mya's.

She exits the car and heads inside. I exit my car and follow her. We take a seat in a booth, and I reach for Mya's hand. The need to touch her is too much, and feeling her palms' softness in mine is orgasmic. Mya has a devious smile on her face. It's the same smile she displays whenever she desired me but didn't want to admit it—always choosing to make it seem as if I was the one with a robust sexual appetite. I wonder if she will allow me to make love to her tonight, maybe right here in the restaurant's bathroom. It wouldn't be the first time we've done it or the second.

"Your wife is going to kill you when you get back to the hotel; you are so insensitive to her feelings." Mya kills me with her concern for Kim. If she cared about Kim's feelings, she wouldn't be sitting here with me.

The waitress comes over to take our order. Mya gets her usual omelet, and I, the works, pancakes, eggs, and country ham. "Your appetite is the same," she joked.

"I miss you." It was what I longed to say all night. Mya was sitting here as beautiful as ever, with no worry and no signs of stress. It's as if we never separated.

"What are you doing, LaDamien? Why can't you let it go?" I can't believe she's asking me this. I have left my wife in the middle of the night to hunt her down. Shouldn't it be obvious what I'm doing, that I can't let it go?

"I've said it a thousand times, and I will say it a thousand more, I love you, and I want us to be together." Mya begins to giggle.

"Please stop it. If you loved me and wanted us to be together, we wouldn't be meeting in the middle of the night. We would be together, no Kim, no late-night creeps, no more games." She was right to a certain extent.

My love for her was real, but my fear of the unknown was bigger than us both. But this separation was an eye-opener. It was time for me to take a chance and go after what I desired. Her confidence in me has dwindled, and it's going to take a lot to get her to give me another chance.

Mya releases a deep sigh before continuing. "Say what you have to say, LaDamien, so that I can get back home. I have plans tomorrow." She's trying to play tough, but deep inside, I know she's longing for me. I just have to bring that emotion to the surface.

"Baby, I know I have screwed this whole thing up royally, but if you give me a chance, I'll make it up to you ten-fold."

"You can't make up for disappointment, LaDamien. You can't reclaim the tears, the spent emotions, the hurt feelings. I have said this to you before. You have taken me through the wringer, wasted so much time, and I know it's not completely your fault, but I trusted you, and I believed in you, and all I got in return were lies and games."

She was right, again. We had been through a lot due to my failure to man up and be who I told her I was, but one thing she can never doubt is my love for her. "I'm sorry, Mya, for all that has gone wrong." It was the least I could do. A simple, heartfelt apology drew a slight smile from her soft lips that let me know I was making headway.

"I'm ready to do it, say the word, and I'll ask Kim for a divorce as soon as I get back to the hotel." Mya shakes her head.

"It hasn't changed, LaDamien. You can't divorce Kim for me. You have to do it for yourself. I will never tell you to do that, and I won't promise you anything will happen between us if you do.

Divorce your wife because you don't love her, you aren't willing to be her husband, because you have no intentions of doing better. Whatever the reason, don't do it for Faye or me or anyone else."

Mya hadn't changed a bit. Everything she wanted and needed was at her fingertips, but she refused to claim it. Instead, she wanted the burden to be all mine. That way, if things didn't work out between us, she could have a clear conscience.

"Okay, I'll do it for me because I have to be free to love you. Can you at least promise me that you will end things with that guy you were with at the concert and focus your attention on me?"

"I can't make a promise like that. What if I end things with Rashad, and you never leave Kim? What if this is just another lie, or you back down as you did two years ago. I'm not stupid, LaDamien."

"No one said you were stupid. Look, baby, I'm going, to be honest, here. I love you more than life itself, and I would give anything for us to be back together. I love you, Mya, and this separation is killing me. Now that I'm here with you, I know I can't ever let you go again. But on the other hand..." Mya cut me off.

"There can't be an other hand, LaDamien. No more butts or what-ifs, or I'm afraid. You have got to make up your mind what it is you want and make it happen."

I smile deviously at her and rub the back of her hand, which is resting on the table. "Can I make love to you tonight?" She half laughs, half sighs, and then turns to look out the window. I use the opportunity to lift her hand and gently kiss it. "Please?"

"What about your wife?"

"What about her?"

"It's after four a.m. It would be daylight before you returned."

"Maybe I don't want to return. Take me home, and I'll call and let her know I won't be back. Like Richie told his wife in *Harlem Nights*, *"...I ain't never coming home no more."* Mya thought I was joking, but I wasn't.

"Go back to the hotel, and tell her you want a divorce. Go back to St. Pete, and start making arrangements to do that, and when you have your divorce decree, call me, and ask me out on a date." Mya grabbed her purse and slid out of the booth. "Don't even try to follow me, just show me you are for real."

Mya hurried out of the restaurant and hopped in her car, leaving me to wait for the waitress and pay the tab. My moment had passed. Chances are, I would never see her again. I could kick myself.

After leaving the diner, I didn't care to return to my hotel room. My frustration would only mount seeing Kim and wishing it were Mya. "Damn!" I yell out as I drive onto I-4 and head east. Before I know it, I'm at I-95 at the exit for Daytona Beach. It's after five a.m. "Great! Kim is going to kill me."

My phone, I begin to think, has been turned off since I left. Kim is probably losing her mind with worry. She may have called the police, thinking something has happened to me.

The display shows no messages. Once I'm turned around and heading west on I-4, I call Kim's number, but she doesn't answer. This happens for the remainder of my drive. Remembering that I called the hotel from my phone, I grab the money saver guide to hotels. After locating the *Best Western*, where we're staying, I locate the number on my phone.

"Room 304," I ask the operator. She transfers the call, but no one answers. My heart is racing. Twenty minutes later, I'm rushing up the stairs. When I open the door, the room is empty. Kim is gone. There's no trace of her anywhere. There's no pocketbook, shoes, note, nothing. Then I think she must have taken a cab home or called one of her friends to come to get her. Maybe she knows someone here in Orlando who could have come and gotten her. My mind is drawing a blank. I call her number again, and this time I leave a message.

"Kim, I'm worried sick about you. Please call, and let me know you are okay. I won't leave Orlando until I know you are okay."

At nine a.m., I decided to call my home number, and when Ariel answers the phone, I'm both relieved and angered. "Where is your mother?" I ask a little harsher than I needed to.

"She's outside talking to Aunt Debbie. Where are you, daddy?" Ignoring her question, I instructed my daughter to get her mother on the phone. A minute later, the call was disconnected. When I call back, my calls go straight to our voice mail greeting the remainder of my ride back home.

Turning onto our street, I noticed Debra's car first, and then Karen's *Infinity*. I could only imagine what they're saying about me. My first clue was to keep going, but I decided against it and met my jury head-on. Karen was placing some items in my Escalade when the garage door opened.

"What the hell are you doing?" I yelled.

"What Kim should have done a long time ago, packing your shit." Karen stuffed the clothing into the backseat and headed back into the house. "Kim!" she yelled, "LaDamien is here."

Kim met me at the door. "You have disrespected me for the last time," she said through clenched teeth as she poked me in the chest. "Get your ass out of here, now."

"Out, what do you mean? This is my home." Her arrogance had me confused. "Get your friends out of here so we can talk."

"No, you get out of here. It's over, LaDamien. I'm not doing this anymore. Take what we've packed, and just leave. You can come back on Monday when I leave for work to get the rest of your stuff. I'm filing for divorce."

"You, you can't be serious. How did you get back here? You got some other nigga you think you're going to move into my house?" Kim looked dumbfounded. Did she think I was just going to leave without a fight? "Where am I supposed to go, Kim?" I asked.

"To hell, I don't care. Go back to Orlando with that bitch." Karen and Debra were now standing by her side. If they weren't here, no way would Kim be speaking to me this way?

"You didn't answer my question. How did you get back?"

"What difference does it make? If we had come home last night, none of this would be happening. Do you really think I don't know where you were or who you were with, LaDamien? How could you treat me like this? Now get out!"

Kim threw a box of shoes in my direction and rushed back into the house. Karen closed the door as she entered last and locked it. This was not happening to me; Kim didn't just put me out of my home.

I rushed to the door and inserted my key, but it wouldn't turn. Confused, I tried another key and then another. None of the keys on my ring worked. Kim had changed the lock. I rushed to the front door only to discover the locks are also changed, and when I headed to the back to try the patio doors, I get stopped in my tracks. She's also changed the lock on the gate for the privacy fence. Her friends had put her up to this. How in the hell had she gotten a locksmith here this quick to change all the locks? Then it hit me, whoever picked her up in Orlando probably stopped by *Home Depot* or *Lowes* and picked them up. Now I know for a fact she's fucking someone else. This infuriates me to the point where I feel like I need to hurt somebody, but then I think about Mya. It's time for her to show and prove. I make my way back to my Escalade and back out of the garage. Instead of reaching out to a friend or family member, I find a hotel and reserve a room for three days.

"It's official, Kim, and I are getting a divorce." Mya doesn't sound fazed by my revelation. I thought she would be ecstatic knowing we will finally be together, but the enthusiasm went undetected.

"So what brought this on? What happened when you returned to the hotel?" Do I tell the truth or act as if I've done this because I can't live without her? As if she read my mind, Mya chimed in, "The truth LB." She hadn't called me LB in a long time, and it caught me off guard. I loved it when she referred to me by this pet name.

"She was gone when I returned. Her other man came and picked her up, and then they rushed back here and changed the locks."

"She did what? Who is the guy? Was he there when you arrived?" Mya was asking the questions faster than I could answer.

"No, he wasn't, but Debra and Karen were, all smug and happy to witness the end of my marriage, but I'm not going to let this break me. It was inevitable, and now you and I can be together. There are some things I need to work out, but I think I can manage them. How would you feel about me moving to Orlando?"

"When? What about your business and Ariel? Kim is just angry. I'm sure Karen or Debra came and got her from Orlando. You two are just tripping, you'll kiss and make-up, and it will be business as usual in a few days." If I didn't know any better, I would think Mya was having second thoughts about us being together.

"If this hadn't happened, I would have asked her for a divorce. I meant what I said, Mya. I want us to be together. I've even thought about moving the company to Orlando. Would you help me?"

Getting Mya to take me seriously about the demise of my marriage took almost two days. I still had not gone to the house to get the remainder of my things. However, I did keep a vigil to see who was coming and going. No man showed his face, but Kim and Ariel didn't get in until around ten both nights. My mind was all over the place, trying to figure out where they were. I rode by her job, the homes of her friends, the office of Dr. Sampson, but she was nowhere to be found.

Mya finally called on Wednesday morning and asked if everything was okay. She asked if Kim and I had talked and if I was still staying at the hotel. I tried my best to convince her and myself that my marriage was over. My resolve was failing, and I was starting to miss my family and my home.

"I'll be checking out of the hotel today. I can't afford to stay any longer. If Kim doesn't let me back in the house, I'll have to tell my family what has happened and move in with one of them." As soon as I mentioned moving in with my sister, something occurred to me. Mya's house was still empty. She was supposed to let a friend move in, but no one had. Since she hadn't offered, I decided not to ask. Again her inaction had me second-guessing her commitment to me.

After ending my call with Mya, I dressed, checked out of the hotel, and headed to the office. Wanda arrived simultaneously and wasted no time asking why I had "all those" clothes in the car. I had no reason to lie. If things were over between Kim and me, and I decided to move to Orlando, she would have no choice but to find another job.

"She put you out? How tacky of her. You must be devastated. Do you need me to check into some of the properties and pick one out for you? I can take care of the furnishing as well if I choose one not staged. LaDamien, I'm so sorry that you're going through this. You know Kim never understood you or your vision. She didn't support your dreams. The split is for the best. You're hurting now, but as time goes on, you'll see that you are better off without her."

By now, Wanda has made her way to me and has slid her arms around my waist. She's taking too much pleasure in my despair, and she has no clue what she's talking about either. I step back and out of her embrace.

"One of the properties, the thought never entered my mind. Can you check the Lakeland and Orlando area? I'm going by the house tonight to try and work things out with Kim, but just in case..."

Wanda's entire demeanor changed, and her body became tense. "Lakeland or Orlando?" she hissed. "Why?"

"Why?" Do I tell her now that the business will be moving if things don't work out with Kim, or should I wait? "Because I'm tired of St. Petersburg," I say instead

"So you're going to drive back and forth. That doesn't make sense."

I wasn't going to debate this with Wanda. If she didn't want to find me a place, I would do it without her, and I let her know just that.

Later that afternoon, I decided to go by Ariel's school to check on her. Our drama had to be very traumatic for her. There's no telling what Kim had told her. Nor what she's discussed in front of her while Debra and Karen were around. Debra's champagne-colored Audi A6 pulled into the parking lot as I waited at the red light a half-block away. I drove slowly past the school and turned on a side street to park and watch. Ten minutes later, she exited with Ariel secure in the front seat, smiling as if she had forgotten about me already.

Fuming was not the word to describe the anger that rose inside of me. If Debra was picking Ariel up from school, then where was Kim. Did Ariel go with her every day while Kim was out doing whatever she was doing with this joker she was fooling around with? Reaching for my phone, I dismissed Wanda's incoming call and called Kim's office. She didn't answer, and her voice mail stated she was out of the office and press zero to speak with Melanie.

"Uhm, hi Melanie, when is Kim due back in the office."

"Hi LaDamien, how's it going?" She asked in her normal upbeat tone. Good, she didn't know Kim and me were having problems.

"Good, just trying to reach my wife." No need for chit-chat. Just answer my question.

"She just left and probably isn't even in her car yet. Why don't you try her cell phone? Bye, LaDamien."

The thing I liked most about Melanie is she was a no-nonsense type of person. She wasn't looking for conversation or trying to be in her boss's business like my secretary.

I pressed end and headed for Kim's office. As luck would have it, she turned on to the interstate as I was exiting on the other side. Quickly, I changed from the turning lane and headed across the street to take the same on-ramp. We drove into Tampa and then towards Lutz. If Kim knew I was behind her, she didn't let on. Probably thinking she's so damn smart that I couldn't figure out what was going on. Forty-five minutes later, she turned into a gated complex, and the guard opened the security gate allowing her access. She made a right turn, and I followed along on the outside, side street. Not long after, she pulled into a parking space and exited her car, the car I had purchased for her. "Damn!"

A car came up behind me, forcing me to move along. The low shrubberies lining the six-foot fence were a big enough distraction from the street activity. I turned into a parking lot and maneuvered around, so I was facing the building she was now approaching. She knocked on the door, and a man of my height and stature, but several shades lighter, greeted her. He surveyed the area for a few seconds and then stepped back so Kim could enter. Before closing the door, he took a second glance. Now that was odd, I thought to myself.

My anger was at an all-time high. How long had this been going on? Who was this guy, how did they meet, is he the one who picked her up and changed the locks on my house? The questions were running through my mind faster than my heart was beating.

"Sir, if you don't know who you're visiting, and you don't have a phone number, I can't let you in." This Barney Fife-looking wannabe cop for hire didn't know how bad I wanted to jump out of my vehicle and blow his brains out. "Sir, are you okay, I don't want any trouble, so it may be best if you just leave."

Things were happening so fast I didn't remember driving the block from the parking lot to the complex gate.

"Leave, leave, that's it? My wife is in one of these units, and I need to talk to her, and you're telling me to leave. Motherfu...." I saw the red button he was about to press, and I knew it was a direct line to 911. I was so furious I thought I was about to suffer a stroke. My eyes filled with tears, and I wanted to kill this man who was only doing his job. Instead, I slam my hand into the steering wheel.

"Sir, I'm sorry, but I can't let you in. Your phone is ringing. Maybe it's your wife. Please back-up. I can't let you in." Barney Fife stepped to the back of my SUV and jotted down my tag number before instructing the cars behind me to move over to the resident's lane. Mya was calling, thank God. She would have to help me through this.

"Baby, I'm so sorry. Are you okay?" No, I'm not okay. Why would she ask me such a stupid ass question?

"If it wasn't over before, it's definitely over now. The slut..."

"Don't LaDamien, you haven't been a saint in all of this. Where are you now? Where are you going to go? Do you have a place to stay tonight?" Mya rambled on as I headed back to St. Petersburg, and calmed me when I turned around and headed back towards Lutz. It was nearing eight p.m. when she suggested I stay at her house tonight and then come over to Orlando tomorrow. "We'll talk about what's going on with you, what you should do, and how you're going to get through it. Okay?"

"Okay," I mustered.

"Brigit has the extra set of keys. I'll call and have her place them in the mailbox. LaDamien, if you love me half as much as you say you do, please don't do anything stupid."

Don't do anything stupid. Mya was chiding. Nothing made sense to me right now. My marriage was coming to an end and not on my terms. Wasn't I the one who was unhappy and miserable, having made the worst mistake of my life? Still, Kim was my wife, and she had allowed an outsider to steer her away from me, to break our bond.

"LaDamien," Mya called out. "I'll see you through this. Please, if you feel like you're going to try, and confront Kim, call me. Baby, I love you, trust me, things are going to work out."

Wanda

Kim kicked LaDamien out. How did I not see it coming? What could have possibly happened to bring about this chain of events? I laugh to myself. This is precisely what I've prayed for, and now that it's happened, it seems so surreal. LaDamien leaving Kim was something I never betted on. Deep inside, I knew she would have a breaking point, and something pushed her to that point. Regardless of what it is, my work is cut out for me. Getting LaDamien to understand this is for the best will be difficult but doable. Once he has accepted it as their fate, I will have to get him to see we're meant to be together once and for all. "Wow, my dreams are within reach, and I'm totally unprepared."

LaDamien startled me when he entered the office the following morning. "How are you doing today? Where did you stay last night?"

"Wanda, please stop with all the questions. Let's just keep it business as usual and leave my personal life out of it." He looked as if he hadn't slept all night long and probably hadn't eaten either.

"Okay, how about I go next door and pick up some breakfast, and then we can go over the list of properties I came up with."

"That won't be necessary," he began. "Mya is letting me stay at her house while she's in Orlando."

So he was still in contact with her. His world is falling apart, and he contacted Mya instead of coming to me, the one who has proven their self loyal to him. "How long will she be in Orlando?" I ask, although I already know Mya moved to Orlando months ago.

"She lives there now and is considering selling her home here, and I was going to help her with the sale if she decided to go that route. She said I could stay there as long as I need to, now. Can we please discuss work?" I'm wise enough to know not to push him. He will open up in due time. Knowing he has not returned home is enough to satisfy me and buy some time until I can devise a plan.

A week has passed since LaDamien and I last discussed his marital situation. It has also been that long since I have seen him. On Friday, he left for Orlando and didn't return until yesterday. We have handled our business transactions over the phone, through text messaging, and email. He has been with Mya all this time, I'm sure, allowing her to comfort him in his time of need. This was supposed to be our chance. I was to be the one who got him through this ordeal. He'll be in the office today, and I plan to tell him exactly how I feel and what I think we should do about it.

LOVE...

- is patient
- is kind
- is not rude
- does not envy
- is not self-seeking
- will not lie
- does not boast
- is not quick to anger
- is not proud
- protects
- does not record wrongs
- trusts
- hopes
- perseveres
- finds no joy in evil but celebrates truth
- never fails

Mya

No sooner than I ended my call with Brigit did Jamie, Aubrey, and Roxanne begin blowing up my phone. I had already spoken to Angie and knew she wouldn't reveal the details of our conversation. The disappointment was apparent in her voice when I confided in her that I was letting LaDamien move into my place. Also, the two of us would probably give it another try if he indeed divorced Kim.

"Mya, are you sure this is what you need to be doing? What about Rashad, have you broken things off with him?" Angie asked right out the gate.

Rashad knew all about my relationship with LaDamien. It was one of the first things we discussed after we started dating. He asked about my last three relationships and shared his with me. He said he could tell so much about a person based on their past relationships. According to his analysis, he could tell that once I fell in love with someone, it was hard for me to let that love go even if I found out they weren't all they pretended to be in the beginning. "This is the source of so much heartache for you," he said.

The day after the Jazmine Sullivan concert I called, and let him know that I had seen LaDamien at the show. I was honest about how I felt seeing him again. Since I was being honest, I even confessed to our early morning rendezvous. Although he appreciated my honesty, he was hurt and disappointed in how easily I looked back. "You know what happened to Lot's wife when God told her not to look back, and she disobeyed his commandment?"

"She turned into a pillar of salt," I replied without hesitation, not understanding its relevance to the conversation.

"Well, sometimes we have more control over our destiny than we think. You're a grown woman Mya, free to make your own decisions. I knew what I was up against after you told me about this man, but I wanted to believe I could be all the man you would ever need. I can't fight for you. I can't beg you not to love him or go back to him. But I can ask that you think about this long and hard because a leopard rarely changes his spots." Rashad kissed me on my forehead and left my townhome without a backward glance. He didn't say we were over if we could still be friends, if he would call me, or anything. He just walked out the door and closed it behind him. His actions stung but not as much as his words. He said he couldn't fight for me or beg me to love him. LaDamien, in his way, had done both. And that mess about Lot's wife, what was that all about, I wondered?

    Now that all my girls knew what was up, I knew where they all stood on the matter. Angie and Aubrey were both very disappointed and wanted nothing to do with the situation. Angie's hurt came from her love for me and her desire to have the same love and happiness she had in Bernie. Aubrey was "just through with the whole mess," as she put it, her anger coming through in her words. Without a doubt, our relationship is damaged. But I know if things worked out with LaDamien, she will be happy for us. If it doesn't, she would proudly say, "I told you so," until the day she died, but I would still be her girl.

    Jamie called to say that she knew it was just a matter of time before LaDamien weaseled his way back into my life. "As crazy as this shit is, you and LaDamien are meant to be together. I never understood why people stay in unhappy marriages making each other miserable. He loves you, and she loves this other guy if she let LaDamien go, so don't worry what people say, do you, and be happy." This would have meant more if it came from Angie…not that Jamie didn't mean it…but she was happily single and had no intentions of settling down with anyone.

    Roxanne was her usual neutral self, and then Brigit, when I asked her to give LaDamien the keys, she cursed me out. My friend called me all kinds of names, and none of them Mya. She then called back and apologized, saying she was still upset over her personal problems.

    LaDamien called after they met and said the two talked for a while at the house. "Your friends care for you, Mya, and you are so lucky to have people like them in your corner. Brigit didn't hold anything back, so neither did I. We parted ways with a clear understanding. All any of them want is for you to be happy, and that's what I promised her, to make you happy."

    In the end, I know all my girls will have my back. Good or bad or indifferent, we will be there for one another. I needed so badly to call Mrs. Epps and let her know about the latest turn of events in my life, but I talked myself out of it. Seriously, what would I say, "Thanks for ministering to me, helping me to move forward in my life, but I've tossed caution to the wind and backslid to where you found me?" In the end, I decided it was best not to contact her. Once LaDamien's divorce is final and we are officially together, I will contact her.

I can hardly believe the turn of events that got us here. Never in my wildest dreams did I think Kim would garner the nerve to ask for a divorce, let alone have an affair. If someone had asked me how LaDamien would respond to something like that, I would have said, "Not too well." As much as I love him, he has always struck me as the type who would go ballistic if he learned his wife was cheating, even if he was doing the same. The day he told me he was outside the complex where Kim was with the other guy, I began to panic. Fear overtook me, and I said whatever came to mind that would calm him down. I offered my home, love, encouragement, and even a second chance at our love. It was the latter that caught his attention.

We spent hours on the phone that evening, both of us afraid to end the call for fear of what could happen if he confronted Kim. What is weird is that as afraid as I was for Kim at that moment, I never felt that my relationship with LaDamien could take that same turn. He checked into a hotel that night, and after a 3-way call with Brigit, he decided to take me up on my offer to stay at my house until he figured things out. By Thursday afternoon, I had agreed to let him visit me at my townhome in Orlando. It was awkward at first because he was visibly upset over all that had transpired in the past week. But slowly, the negative energy subsided, and as the evening unfolded, we found our way back to each other.

LaDamien was surprised when I cooked him a good old-fashioned southern meal of smothered chicken, lima beans, rice, and cornbread. We finished the meal off with his favorite, Haagen-Dazs butter pecan ice cream.

"What're you trying to do, make me fall in love with you?" he teased as he came up behind me and placed kisses on the nape of my neck. "Is this what I'll get all the time?"

"Nope! This isn't healthy eating, but on special occasions, I'll lay it down for you." He seemed to like this, made his way to the barstool nearest me where he sat, and watched me until I placed the food on the table.

"This is nice, Mya," he said, referencing my new home. "The whole area is nice. You did well for yourself. Tomorrow, while you're at work, I think I'll take a drive and see if there are any subdivisions nearby where I can buy a place."

LaDamien was saying all the right things, as usual. He was also moving fast, too fast if you asked me. My next move was to slow him down. "I'm taking tomorrow off so we can talk; talk about your situation. This is all fresh, and you don't know how it's going to play out. You're talking about buying houses, and you haven't even filed or gotten served divorce papers." He appeared to understand what I was saying. In Florida, a married person could not buy a house without their spouse signing off on it. Kim would have to agree to the purchase and then do a Quit Claim Deed back to him after the closing. LaDamien had to know this since he dealt in real estate.

"I'm just anxious to move forward in my life. This marriage has been weighing me down, and I feel like I have wasted so much of my time. So much of your time, valuable time, we could have been building our future together."

Later that night, as we lay in bed, I envision the possibilities of our future. Things are transpiring quickly, and it scares me. I've been telling LaDamien to slow down, and now I'm getting caught up in the whirlwind. Jamie says I need to pounce on the opportunity. To take control and make this be what I want it to be. My heart is saying go for it, of course, but my mind is telling me to pump the brakes, wait for him to get a divorce, and then take things slow.

"What are you thinking about?" LaDamien asked.

It would have been easy to lie and say nothing, but I chose to tell him the truth. He needed to know what I wanted and what I expected of him, as well as my fears and reservations surrounding our future. "The truth, baby? I'm scared that Kim is going to call and say she reconsidered, and you'll take the easy route and go back still expecting me to be here for you."

"Can I share something with you?" he asked. "I'm just as scared as you are. It's easy to hang on to what's familiar and what's safe. For as long as I can remember, Kim has been both."

LaDamien sat up and rested his back on the headboard. "Come here," he beckoned and pulled me to him, resting his arm around my shoulder. As I rest my head on his chest, he began telling me a story he says he has never shared with anyone else.

"You know my dad left when I was young. Growing up in a house full of females without him was hard. My mom had to work a lot to pay the bills, so I was left with my sisters a lot." He stroked my hair as he talked as if it was therapeutic. I didn't move, just laid there and let him talk.

"As we grew older, my sisters made friends and then had boyfriends. Their lives also included after-school jobs and extracurricular activities. I soon found myself spending more and more time alone. I missed my dad a lot. He would try to come by and spend time with me for a while, but his visits slowly became lesser and lesser until he stopped altogether. With my mom at work and my sisters out doing their thing, I was left to my devices. To entertain me, I started hanging out with some older boys, playing ball at local parks, sneaking into the movies, fooling around with girls." I could tell he glanced down at me to see how I felt about the last part, but I laid still and continued to listen.

"There was this one girl when I was about eleven. She was fifteen. She would always find me. One day she asked me if I wanted to go to her house and watch TV. We went to her house, and shortly after we got there, she asked if I wanted to see a movie. Little did I know I was about to see my first porno flick. "You want to do that to me?" she asked me. I didn't want to at all, but I just sat there. She took off her clothes, and then got on top of me, and started to grind."

At that moment, I knew this story was about to go somewhere deep. Reaching for LaDamien's hand, I pulled it close to my heart and caressed it gently, letting him know he could continue, and I wouldn't judge him once he finished.

"Man, I was scared half to death. My sisters had brought boys home while my mom was at work, and I had seen them having sex, so I kind of knew what to do. I just didn't want to do it at eleven, but she made me, so, at eleven, I lost my virginity, and every day after that, she came looking for me. For a while, I just came home from school and wouldn't go back outside. After I ignored her for a while, she told everybody I was hiding from her. My sister Pam started hearing the rumors, and she told my other sisters. When my mom found out, she thought I was out being mannish and beat me. I was so mad at all of them. When the girl came looking for me again, I went with her out of spite. We would have sex at her house three or four times a week, and not just kid sex but grown-up sex like in her mom's porno movies."

"That's wild, LaDamien. Most people think boys are always looking for sex and never think about a girl making a boy do something he doesn't want to do. Thanks for..."

"I'm not done," he said. "This went on for months, and I eventually started looking forward to it. The guys in my neighborhood knew what was going on, and they thought I was the man. But then one day, I went to her house. Her older brother and some of his friends were there. I would have left, but he told me to come on in, so I did. She was upstairs having sex with some guys, and he made me go up there and join them. He told me I was the shit, a little runt, but I was banging his sister.

I didn't want to punk out, so I took off my clothes and got in the bed with her and two other guys. They had to be in their twenties because her brother was around that age. I was nervous as hell wondering why these grown-ass men wanted to watch a boy having sex with the teenage girl they had just fucked. They had been drinking and smoking weed because I could smell it in the air and on them. She was looking at me kind of strange. When I got on top of her, one of the guys started rubbing his hand on my butt."

"LaDamien, don't," I pleaded. What he was about to confess became more evident.

He sniffed, and I turned to face him. The tears were streaming down his face. "Please let me finish, Mya. You are the only person I have ever shared this with."

The truth of the matter, I didn't want to be the person he shared this with, even if he trusted me with the secret. I didn't want to be a part of this side of love. In this unabashed part, two people are entirely naked, mentally and spiritually. This side of love is where there are no secrets. You have to accept the good, the bad, and the ugly. It didn't get any uglier than what he was sharing with me now, his way of proving his unequivocal love for me.

"For the next few years, I battled with feeling what ranged from shame to thoughts that I may be gay. I never wanted to be alone, so I learned how to play ball, and I excelled at it just to have people around. Girls wanted me more and more when I was in high school, and I took full advantage of them to prove I was all man. After a while, I found myself unable to become emotionally attached to anyone. As much as I love my mother and my sisters, a part of me blames them for what happened. In return, I began using them the same as I did the dumb girls throwing themselves at me. This continued through college and into my adult life. I was probably in my mid-twenties when I finally stopped and realized how much pain I was causing others. Now that I have you, Mya, I see I haven't changed. I've been inflicting the same pain on you and Kim as I did everyone else when I was younger."

"I'm sorry those things happened to you." What else was I supposed to say? What else did he need for me to say?

"Yeah, so what now? Are you going to abandon me like everyone else? Are you going to decide it's just too much to deal with, that I'm too damaged both physically and emotionally? Besides being sorry, Mya, what are you going to do?" His anger was a defense mechanism, so I decided to tread lightly.

"Why me, LaDamien? What is it about me that makes you want to be different?" I asked, biding time to think.

"…Because as corny as it sounded when I first said it to you, and as corny as it sounds now, I have loved you since the first time I saw you. If anyone loves me despite everything I've been through, it will be you."

"Why not, Kim? You chose to marry her. Why?" This is the one question I always needed an answer to for some reason.

"Convenience, companionship, desperation, choose one or choose them all. All would be correct. She was there when I needed someone to hold me up. Kim is a nice person, she doesn't require much to be happy, and I had never been happy, so we seemed a perfect match."

"Desperation, explain that," I prompted.

"Have you ever been on that ride at the fair where you stand up against the wall in that circular room, and then it goes dark, and the room feels as though it starts to spin? Lights are flashing, and the music is blaring, and you feel as if you need to grab hold of something or you'll get tossed around the room. That's how I felt when I asked Kim to marry me, my world was spinning out of control, and I needed so desperately to grab hold of something. But like everything else in my life, I eventually ruined it."

"Uhmm, that has to be a frightening feeling."

"It was, then I walked into that ballroom, and it all subsided except the fear of abandonment. But right now, I don't even fear that because I just told you the worst thing that ever happened to me, and you're still here and still holding my hand."

I turn to face him and wipe the tears from his face, but they have dried on my skin. "I love you, LaDamien, and I'm glad you decided to release that demon, and you trust me this much. The next step is to deal with the anger and the other residuals of what happened to you. That may require counseling." This was more than I bargained for, but we were at this place and time for a reason, and if I truly loved him, I couldn't turn back. Oh, I needed to talk to someone, but there was no one I could share this information with before. No one, no way, no how. He had handed this thing off to me, and I took it, so now I had to help him fix it.

Kim

"**My marriage** was over, and it had ended on my terms over three months ago. The divorce papers are filed, and the marital assets are divided. LaDamien gave me the house in exchange for my signing over my rights to a home he would buy in Orlando. He had what he wanted. Mya took him in without hesitation. So much for "men only cheat because of sex," which is a misguided myth that married women use to ignore their deficiencies in their marriage. Looking back, I can't think of anything I could have done to save my marriage. Plain and simple, LaDamien was not a willing participant. Without his desire and initiative to make things work, we were doomed from the start.

Mya probably thinks she has it all figured out, that he will somehow be to her what he was unable to be to me. She's in for a rude awakening. LaDamien is unable to be faithful to anyone. I don't know what it is, but something keeps him from achieving the necessary level of commitment required to have a successful relationship. I thought something must have happened before we met, or maybe it was just the attention he received from so many women that drives his desire.

My relationship with TayJohn has not ignited as I thought it would. After he rescued me from that humiliating ordeal in Orlando, things heated up between us and then quickly slowed after I filed for divorce. According to him, he didn't want to interfere or be seen as an instigator. Only last week did I have the opportunity to introduce him to Debra and Karen. I planned to host a dinner party at my home, but he stated he wouldn't be comfortable in my house until after the divorce became final. "Until then, it's still LaDamien's home, and I just don't need any mess if he decides to show up."

Show-up, LaDamien hadn't done that but three times. The first was when he returned from Orlando after leaving me in the hotel room. The second time was a few days later. He came by the house cursing and fussing about having followed me to an apartment in Tampa and seeing me enter a man's place. He described TayJohn to a tee. Where he was hiding was a mystery to me, and knowing he had followed me some forty miles without my knowledge was unsettling.

That night I was terrified and thought for sure he would kill me. Had Ariel not entered the room crying, he probably would have. He was so angry, and evidence of his pain was visible through his bloodshot eyes. To think he could cry over having seen me with someone else but couldn't cry over the end of our marriage was a slap in the face. Not once did he apologize for his numerous affairs or beg me for a second chance. He just lit into me about having an affair, cheating on him, and abandoning our marriage for another man. No matter what, he just didn't get it.

The third visit came a month later after he was formally served with divorce papers. This time he came by begging and pleading with me not to move forward. He promised he would change and that he would resume counseling. Anything I asked he would do if I just dropped the divorce. To be honest, I was tempted several times, but my saving grace came in his inability to admit he had done anything wrong. I could have easily demanded that he apologize. It wouldn't carry the same weight as if he had done it on his own. That was what I desired the most. For my husband, the man I married and vowed to love until death, we do part, to say that he was sorry for the pain he had caused. Apologize for loving another woman more than he loved our daughter or me. To apologize for not being who he promised me he would be, a husband, a lover, and a friend. LaDamien left my house that night looking more defeated than when he entered. Three days later, he called and said he would grant me a divorce if I didn't stake a claim to his business. If I would sign on the house, he wanted to buy and then do a quitclaim deed relinquishing my property rights.

TayJohn had nothing to worry about, but he insisted he did. He claimed he was afraid that LaDamien would change his mind at the last minute, which would devastate him. Little did he know, I was afraid he had changed his mind, which was devastating me. Instead of the dinner party I was planning for us, we all ended up downtown at *Café Alma*. It wasn't the ambiance I envisioned, although the restaurant and its food were superb. In the end, Debra, and Karen, along with their husbands, had the opportunity to meet TayJohn, and give their stamp of approval.

Now here I sit, wondering if we even have a future together. Three months ago, we were spending every free minute together. Now

I may see him once or twice a week, and his explanation is the same, "You need to be sure about what you're doing. I can't put me all into this only to have you renege at the last moment."

Our court date is set, so I guess TayJohn will need to show and prove in two weeks.

The knock-on my office door shook me from my reflections. "Come in." I summoned my guest. To my surprise, it was TayJohn. Although it was well known that LaDamien and I had separated, we still kept our relationship under wraps.

"How are you doing, beautiful?" he asked as he closed the door behind him and locked it. The gesture caught me by surprise.

"To what do I owe the honor?" I say as I stand and walk around the desk to greet him.

TayJohn takes my hand and pulls me to him. He then slides his hands around my waist, and as he kisses me, he glides them over my derrière. "Uhmm, I missed not seeing you this weekend, and it was driving me crazy sitting at my desk knowing that you weren't that far away."

"Well, you are the one that has placed yourself in exile. I have offered you not only the key to my home but the key to my heart as well." He tenses up. It could be my imagination, but I don't think so. I could invite him over, but my heart can't take the rejection, so I allow him to lead the way in this impromptu visit.

"Melanie at lunch?" he asked.

"She's out today," I respond, curious as to where this is headed. He reads my mind and lures me into another sensual kiss. His hands explore my body, and when he reaches my breast, he tries to unbutton my silk blouse.

"What are you doing, baby?" I ask breathlessly. His touch feels good, but he can't go any further, so I step out of his embrace and return to my desk. The barrier is more for me than him because this man brings out a weakness in me, and there's no telling what he can talk me into at this point.

TayJohn seemed put off by the rejection, but it's time for us to get serious and be honest with one another. I need to know where he stands in all of this drama. If he wants to be with me or if this is all just a game?

"Sit down, baby," I say, cutting through the tension that is now clouding the room. He sits in the chair opposite me and rubs his chin.

"What's up to Kim? I thought you'd be happy to spend some time with me. Please don't tell me LaDamien has weaseled his way back into your good graces." He can't be serious, but I know he's.

"This isn't about LaDamien. We are moving forward with the divorce. My reservations are surrounding us. I would have thought that my filing for divorce would have brought us together, but instead, it seems to have pulled us apart. What's up with that, Mr. Neilson?"

He appeared to be at a loss for words. Was he not feeling what I was feeling? Did he consider his sneaking up to my office spending quality time together? There's that look again. He's avoiding eye contact with me. "Is something going on with you that I need to know about, like maybe you've met someone else?"

"No, I haven't met anyone new," he begins. "I just don't care to get my hopes up about us only to have them squashed because your husband would rather live in misery than see you happy with someone else. That's all baby, I've just had my heart broken one time too many, and I can't go that route again."

This brings a level of relief to me. Now I just need to figure out a way to calm his fears. "We sign the papers next Friday. How would you like to go away afterward, to celebrate? I heard about this boat that travels down to Key West. We can leave Saturday morning, stay the night, and then return Sunday. I think it would be fun, and relaxing, and sort of a coming out for us."

He does it again, that look of uncertainty. "Next weekend, I have plans. Let's do something this weekend, you know. I can plant a seed to remind you of what's to come after your divorce." He smiles.

"Sure," I say unenthusiastically. "So what do you have planned for next weekend?" I ask.

"Baltimore. I'm going home for a few days., I leave next Wednesday, returning Sunday night."

His trips to Baltimore are becoming more frequent, and I'm afraid he may be considering moving back. If I ask, he will probably deny it, so I don't. But I will have Melanie see what she can learn about him from some of his co-workers. I simply need to figure out how to get the information without letting on that we are already involved.

"Can I see you before the weekend?"

"You're seeing me now," he jokes.

"I'll take that as a no," I reply before walking over to the door and opening it—his signal to leave.

TayJohn stands and faces me. "What's up, Kim? Why are you so tense, baby?"

Why does he have to ask? I'm about to end my marriage, and the truth is told, I thought we had a future together, now I'm not so sure.

"You're starting to make me feel unloved and unwanted, like LaDamien use to do. You should know better than anyone else how vulnerable I'm right now, but you seem to have your own thing going on, so maybe I shouldn't include you in my new life."

"That's a bit extreme, Kim, don't you think? I've been here for you, and for you to insinuate that I haven't is disappointing. But I will say this. I don't think you should place all of your focus on me. You've been through a horrible marriage and endured a lot of emotional abuse. It may be best for you to take some time for yourself and re-evaluate what you desire and what you need in a mate." He met me at the door, and kissed my cheek, then walked past me without looking back.

Back at my desk, I took a deep breath, tried to absorb, and then dissected his final words. What was he trying to say? Does he want out because that's what it sounded like to me? My next move is to call Debra and Karen to get their thoughts on this change in TayJohn.

"Maybe he's right, Kim," Karen begins, "Maybe you should give yourself some time before jumping into a serious relationship."

"Karen, we wouldn't be jumping into a serious relationship. Hell, I thought we were already in one." Debra wasn't able to join us for lunch, but Karen dropped what she was doing to meet me. An hour later, we were seated at *Chili's* sharing chicken fajitas.

Karen wiped her mouth with her napkin and took a sip of her soda. "Kim, you're doing exactly what you said you weren't. You're divorcing LaDamien hoping you, and Taj is going to be together. It can't work that way."

She was right, but the thought of being alone, starting over again, and even being rejected again was frightening. "I don't want to go through this alone," I admit.

"Sweetie, you won't be alone. You have Ariel, who will need you more than ever, and you have Debra and me. Don't set yourself up to be hurt all over again, Kim, please don't do that." Karen had pushed the skillet aside and was reaching over the table. I took her hands as she continued. "Kim, you are a beautiful and smart woman.

You need to learn your self-worth and recognize that having a man doesn't complete you. You have to complete you."

I laugh a little at her last comment. "But I'm the marrying kind. I do need a man to have the complete package. Karen, family means a lot to me. The last thing I want to be is a desperate woman like Mya settling for someone else husband because I don't have what it takes to get me. It's important to me to come home in the evening and have a complete family. I don't want to be a single mother, lowering my standards just to say I have a man."

"Listen to yourself. You're falling into that same trap that so many women get caught up in all the time. If you think about it, you've always been a single mother." Karen stopped, although it was evident she had a whole lot more to say. Rather than continue her lecture, she fixed another fajita. To let her know I was okay, I asked if she and Debra were planning a party to celebrate my divorce.

"It's the in thing to do, nothing fancy, but I don't wish to be alone next Friday night. Taj and I are going to do the boat ride to Key West on Saturday, and I'm so excited, but the weekend after, he will be in Baltimore." Karen let me know her, and Debra would definitely be available to help me celebrate the end of my union with LaDamien.

"Taj, oh, he's definitely taken," Melanie replied when I asked if she knew if TayJohn was seeing anyone. It's Thursday morning, the morning after he and I spent an intimate evening together. I asked the question under the guise that I had a friend who was interested in meeting him after the two met at a recent Urban League fundraiser. I was taken aback when she called him by his abbreviated name, something I thought was reserved for personal friends.

Trying my best to conceal my angst, I ask her if it's someone within our organization. To my horror, she tells me that she believes he has a fiancé back in Baltimore who is supposed to be moving to Florida real soon. Suddenly it all made sense. The disappearing acts, the frequent trips home, the weekends he didn't call, and our conversations were rushed when I called.

He called me yesterday afternoon to invite me to dinner. Afterward, we returned to his place, and he made tantalizing love to me. He loved me the way he did when we first met. It felt so good being in his arms and being caressed tenderly. His kisses were so sensual, and when he entered me, my soul melted. I held on to him as he worked his magic, not wanting ever to let go. Because I had recently hired a nanny for Ariel, I was able to stay the night. Waking up in TayJohn's arms meant so much and felt so good. Standing here listening to Melanie tells me that he doesn't have a girlfriend, but a fiancé makes me feel like I'm the biggest fool ever to step foot on earth.

What do I do, what do I say? Should I tell Debra or Karen? So many questions are swarming in my mind, and I feel sick. The best thing for me to do is end the conversation and come up with an excuse to leave for the day.

The mailman is leaving as I pull into the driveway. He motions for me, letting me know he has a package that requires a signature. Putting on a happy face, I greet him and sign for the large, thick envelope that has an Orlando Title Company listed in the return address. Opening the package, I remove copies of the closing documents for the home LaDamien plans to buy. The closing is set for next Thursday, the day before our divorce. I wonder why, since the original date was pushed out several weeks, he didn't wait until after the divorce was final. That way, he wouldn't need my signature. Placing the documents back in the envelope, it occurs to me that he can't afford the home without me. My cell phone rings, stalling my anger temporarily. It's LaDamien.

LaDamien

In a little over a week, my marriage to Kim will be over, and I will be free to be with Mya. It all seems so surreal right now. If anyone had told me that things would have ended between Kim and me, I would have thought they were crazy. Learning that Kim was having an affair nearly killed me. I'm reminded of all the times I thought she was with another man and allowed others to tell me otherwise. People would say I imagined things, or my infidelity made me think the worst about my wife. Now I know it wasn't. I was right all along.

If Mya had not opened up her heart and home, there's no telling what I would have done. In return, to show my gratitude for her love, I shared a part of my life that I never shared with anyone else, not even Kim. Now the most significant challenge standing before me is getting Mya to agree to marry me. She wants to wait, to see what it's like dating one another, and getting to know each other as two single people. There's nothing else I need to explore to convince me that she's the one. Like I tell her every day, I knew she was the one the first time we met.

Regardless of my history with Kim, I'm, as they say, "the marrying kind." Being married, providing for my family, and having the security of someone at home waiting for me, longing for me, and most of all, needing me is all I have ever desired. Despite this, being married to Kim has taught me that those things are hard to achieve if you are married to the wrong person. A part of me mourns the loss of my marriage because I know Kim loved me and wanted all those things with me. None of this was her fault. It boiled down to my loving Mya more than I ever could have loved her or any other woman. Hopefully, the guy she was screwing around with will be able to give her the happiness she deserves but a part of me doubts it. The day I followed Kim to his place, I saw a lot of myself in him. In just that brief moment, as he opened the door and looked around, I knew Kim was not the only woman in his life. I just pray that she's the most important because she deserves that much.

Kim refused to discuss him with me. It took Ariel telling me his name even though she had not met him, which pleased me to know Kim was not exposing my child to another man. She said his name was Taj, "that's what I hear mom and Aunt Debra call him."

I didn't want to grill my daughter about her mothers' actions, but it was the only way I could learn anything. Not only did Kim shut me out, but she also cut off my family, claiming they were just as guilty as I was. She swore up and down they enabled my cheating and deceit. She swears they knew all along about the other women in my life but continued to smile on her face.

It is all water under the bridge now. We both have a chance at a fresh beginning leaving the negativity and destruction behind. Her having Debra and Karen help her put me out of my home is something I will never live down. No woman will ever do that to me again. Mya helped me select the home I'm about to purchase and is taking care of the entire interior decorating. My name will be the only name on the mortgage. Whether we marry one day or not, I plan to keep it that way.

I call Kim to see if she has received copies of the closing documents and ensure everything is in order. When she answers the phone, she sounds a bit out of sorts. "Yes, I just opened the envelope."

"Well, please go through everything, and make sure it's okay. I don't need any surprises next week." Kim is silent. "Are you still here? Please don't tell me you're having second thoughts."

"No, LaDamien, I'm not having second thoughts," she said in a harsh tone. "I just don't need you calling every five seconds, aggravating me about it. I've bought a house before, so I know what to look for." Kim was noticeably having a bad day, and I had called at the wrong time. My goodbye was barely complete when I realized she had disconnected the call.

Moving to Orlando has turned out to be quite profitable. I have flipped more properties in the short time I've been here than I had the six months prior. The most lucrative deal was a block of condos where the builder had filed bankruptcy. It was too good of a deal to pass up on that I had to breakdown, and call Mark, my former partner, to assist with funding the project. Not only will he double his investment, but I will walk away with enough to pay cash for my new house. The reward sounded good, but it took more than numbers to get Mark to agree. His first question pertained to my relationship with Mya. After filling him in on the details of my marriage's demise, Mark was ready to end the call. I begged and pleaded for several days before he relented and decided to get in on the deal.

Had I closed on the property already, I wouldn't need Kim to sign on my mortgage. I used every tactic I could think of to delay the house's closing, but the bank finally forced my hand and set a final date, one day before the divorce was finalized. Kim had yet to question why I couldn't just wait until after the procedure to buy a house. She probably has figured out that my income on paper wouldn't satisfy the bank, and she's just not saying anything.

Kim has been very accommodating, almost borderline arrogant. She acts as though getting rid of me is her only goal in life. My being in Orlando now probably has her jumping for joy. She no longer has to see my face or deal with my period if she doesn't want to, and I don't have to witness her new relationship with this Taj person. Kim deserves to be happy, but honestly, I don't think I could bear witness to it knowing that I was not the source.

The only thing that seems right in my life at this moment is my love for Mya. She's simply everything I ever hoped for and more. Getting my family to accept my marriage was over is more challenging than I thought it would be. Almost everyone took Kim's side, calling me selfish and egotistical. Pam and Lynn even went so far as to predict that my relationship with Mya would never work. It was as if no one could see my marriage's torment all these years and appreciate the fact that Kim and I are both free to find the happiness we deserve.

Dawn was the only one clearly in my corner. "I knew you were in love with that girl the first time I saw you with her," she said the day word reached her through the family grapevine. "You deserve to be happy, so screw what everybody has to say. They just mad because they're stuck in their lifeless marriages. Having Dawn on my side was good, but I needed my entire family to accept Mya.

I just knew for sure my mom would have been my biggest cheerleader, but she surprised me when she admonished my actions. We were having dinner at her home one evening when I told her my plans.

"Boy, there's a right and a wrong way to do things. You don't marry a woman when you are still looking for a wife. You have a child to consider in all this, but all you think about is yourself. LaDamien, this isn't good. Karma is going to come back and bite you hard for this. You need to get down on your knees and pray that God forgives you for these transgressions. Pray for forgiveness, baby, 'cause God isn't pleased with this at all."

I needed my mother's support. To hear her admonish me this way hurt the most. She has always been in my corner.

If it had not been for her words of encouragement the night, I put my fears aside and finally spoke to Mya; I would never have known her in the way I do now. "Mama, I thought this was what you wanted for me. I thought you knew I wasn't happy with Kim and wanted me to find someone who could make me happy." My mama looked at me, confused as I had imagined that whole conversation years ago.

"LaDamien, you weren't raised this way. If you didn't love Kim, you never should have married her. That was your first mistake. You are always acting on impulse and never thinking about how what you do affects other people. To make matters worse, you go out, have an affair, and then leave your wife for this woman. Now you have hurt Kim and damaged your daughter, and you know what not having your dad around did to you, so why would you do that to your child?"

"But mama…"

"Don't you but mama me. When do we get to meet this girl?" She asked, letting me know the lecture was over, and it was time for Mya to win her affection. The following weekend I drove over to St. Pete, and picked my mama up, and took her to Orlando to spend the weekend with us.

"Mya, have you ever been married before?" was my mom's first question. She gave our place a good-looking over, checking out

Mya's housekeeping skills before making her way into the kitchen to check out what was cooking. "Do you attend church?"

Mya was already prepared for the scrutiny she would receive. She was so happy and excited about meeting my mother that I don't think there was much she could have said or done to hurt Mya's feelings. "No, Mrs. Bryson, I have never been married before. As for the church, I do attend, but we haven't found a church home here in Orlando."

"You look awfully familiar to me. What church did you attend back in St. Petersburg?" Mya looked to me for direction. I jokingly grimaced before smiling to let her know it was okay to tell the truth.

"Bethel Inspirational," Mya stopped mid-sentence when my mother frowned incredulously.

"Lord Jesus, you two is something else. Well, ain't no need in me fretting over this mess. You're together now, I guess. So what does your family think of LaDamien, and the two of you being together although he's still married?" My mom wasn't holding any punches. She was going at Mya the same as she had me on the ride over. I walked behind Mya and placed my arms around her shoulders.

"My parents don't know. I mean, they don't know LaDamien is married or living here. My sister Sonja knows but not my parents." Mya was so tense now I could feel it as I pulled her closer. My mom asked her a few more questions, including why she kept me a secret from her parents. Mya stated I wasn't a secret. She just didn't feel the need to discuss my marital status yet. She then added that she wouldn't be surprised if they already knew. "My sister probably told them a long time ago, and they just aren't saying anything."

"So, mama, what do you think?" I asked my mom on the way back to St. Petersburg.

"She's a sweet girl, and I just hope you'll be happy. That's all I've ever wanted for you, baby, to be a good man, a good father, and to marry someone who makes you happy. Life can seem so much more challenging when you don't have someone helping you along the way. She approved of Mya, and that's what matters the most to me.

After dropping my mother off that Sunday afternoon, I went by Lynn's house to visit Ariel. Kim agreed on the visit after Lynn contacted her and assured her that Mya wouldn't be with me when I dropped mama off. Ariel was happy to see her old man, and that did my heart good. I missed my little girl and was anxious for things to settle down and her mother to start allowing her to visit in Orlando. Part of the divorce agreement had me paying Kim almost one thousand dollars a month in child support. The judge threatened family mediation if we didn't come to terms on visitation. This was a step in the right direction.

Mya and I discussed children. She was approaching forty, and time was running out for us to have a successful pregnancy. Mya was open to having our child but made it crystal clear that we would need to be married before she could consider starting a family. She also commented on her desire to build a good relationship with Ariel, and eventually Kim, before having a baby. Ariel probably wouldn't be a problem, but I pray my next child doesn't have to wait for Kim to come around, or Ariel may be an only child.

I left Lynn around seven p.m. and decided to go by Mya's old place to check on things. A vehicle was left at all times, so as I pulled into the driveway, I pressed the remote for the garage door but quickly stopped the action when another car pulled in behind me. Without hesitation, I reached under the seat for my gun. Whoever was behind me wasn't getting out, and this made me nervous. After a two-minute stand-off, the headlights on the vehicle behind me went out, and I was relieved, yet disappointed, to see that the car looked a great deal like Faye's. "What the hell does she want?" I asked out loud. Sliding the gun back into place, I open the door and got out.

Faye rolled down her window with a huge smile plastered across her face. "Hey, stranger, where have you been?" She was looking from the front door of the house to the passenger door of my vehicle. "Where's Mya?"

"What are you doing?" I asked. Faye and I hadn't been together since the day before Mya moved to Orlando, almost six months ago. She had called several times, sent sexy text messages, some even included provocative pictures, but I was through with Faye forever.

"I saw you turn the corner and decided to stop and say hello. I hear you've moved to Orlando, and you and Kim are getting a divorce." Wow, this woman must have a tracking device in my life.

"What do you want, Faye?" I ask, irritated that she's here.

"What do I always want, some of you. Is Mya here? How damn freaky would it be to fuck in her house." She opened the door and stepped out. My God, I don't need one of Mya's friends coming up and getting this all wrong.

"Get back in your car Faye. I'm not fucking you in Mya's house or anywhere else. I told you before. It's over between us."

"I mean, seriously, LaDamien, how many times have you said that only to be buried between my legs again and again?" Faye was now leaning on her car with her arms folded across her chest. "So if not here, then where?"

I take in a deep breath. A confrontation isn't what I need, so I decide to be smart. "Let me check on the house, and I'll meet you somewhere. You want to go ahead and get a room?" I reach into my pocket and pull out three twenties. With Faye's discount, this should more than cover the cost. Instead of taking the money, she burst out laughing.

"Do you think I'm that stupid? This is Faye, not Wanda. You're not going to have me sitting up in a hotel room waiting for you to show up, and your ass is halfway back to Orlando, and that big ass house I heard you bought for that bitch." Faye snatched the money from my hand and slid it into her back pocket.

How did she hear about my house, I wonder? Faye laughs again. "Why don't I just follow you back to Orlando, and we christen that new house."

"Faye, please, let's not make this harder than it has to be, I'm going inside to check on the house, and then I'm going home. Why don't you go home to your husband and forget about me?"

"Why don't you go to hell, LaDamien," she said a little bit louder than she had to.

"So what are we going to do, Faye? Just stand here going back and forth? Nothing is going to happen between us tonight or any other night. Now leave before I call the police." My threat of calling the police didn't sit well with her. Before I knew it, she had lounged towards me and slapped my face. I felt the sting of a thin scratch before her hand was back at her side.

At that moment, I had two choices, react or retreat. I saw the half-open garage door and chose to retreat. Quickly, I jetted inside, and closed the door then made my way inside the house. I peered into the mirror in the bathroom, and my reflection revealed a nasty welt with spots of blood jotting down its length. "Damn, what am I going to tell Mya?"

Minutes later, my cell phone started to buzz. Faye was calling me. "You ain't shit, LaDamien. That tramp is going to see for herself.

Take your weak ass on back to Orlando, and I hope I never see your ass again, you punk motherfucker."

Where was this coming from? What had I done to this woman to deserve the anger directed at me? It didn't matter. I thought as I looked out the window and didn't see her car. Faye was another part of my past that had to be discarded. One more transgression I would need to atone for to move forward in my new life.

Ten minutes later, I exited the house and headed back home. Home, the place where love resided, and peace reigned. Mya never brought drama to me like this. Thinking of Mya, I felt it would be best to call her now and tell her what Faye had done. No secrets, and no lies, it was my promise to her, and I planned on keeping it.

"Oh no," Mya moaned. "Do I need to have someone watch the house for a few days? What if she comes back and does something?" I assured Mya, Faye was not that stupid.

"She may want to hurt me, but she isn't going to do anything that would get her arrested or that will get back to her husband. Trust me, okay?" This must-have appeased Mya because she greeted me at the door wearing a sexy soft pink teddy when I arrived home.

"These tricks got me confused with Kim. I play for keeps." Closing the door behind me and walking into Mya's embrace, I felt as if I'd hit the lottery. To let her tell it, I had. After my third orgasm, she had finally convinced herself that no one had gotten what belonged to her. If I had any ideas of going back and getting something, I'd need to buy some stamina to help me maintain.

"Happy?" I asked after we showered and climbed into bed.

"Yes," was her only response. Minutes later, she had drifted off to sleep.

Life continued to improve. Everything was going as planned. I had no more drama in my life. My days flowed smoothly, and my nights were full of rest. No one was calling, no one begging, no one mad, and no one angry, especially me. A life free of lies, games, sneaking, and searching, was beautiful. Coming home to a woman I loved and who loved me was what heaven must be like for real. The last part of the puzzle was about to go into place. I met with Wanda to let her know that I was closing the St. Pete office and relocating everything to Orlando. It was a decision I had made long ago but delayed putting into action. Wanda and I were a team for a very long time. Even when Mark was there, it was all about Wanda and me. She asked me numerous times what my plans were for the future of LaDamien Bryson Enterprises. I stalled, skirted the issue, and on a couple of occasions lied, but that's all over now. Today I will let her know that our time as a team is over.

My visit with Wanda was awkward, to say the least. First, she was angry, yelling, and screaming that I had used her, built my company off her hard work and expertise. From there, she began to cry, begging me to leave the office open and promising to keep things together across county lines. "It won't be that difficult with today's technology, and when needed, I don't mind driving to Orlando. LaDamien, you can't be serious. What will you do without me?" she pleaded

Was she serious? Did she believe I could not function without her, that my business would fail if she weren't around? This only increased my resolve. LaDamien Bryson Enterprise was a success because I made it one. Wanda was a great employee, and I hate to let her go, but there are just as many talented people ready to take up the slack. What shocked me was her thinking she could offer me sex in exchange for my keeping her on. She even went so far as to suggest bringing Faye of all people back into my life.

"I'll do anything you ask LaDamien, anything, and I mean it." At first, I thought she was just expressing her commitment, and loyalty but when she stepped closer and placed her hand on my crotch, I felt repulsed.

"Come on, Wanda, let's not go there." Now I was pleading. I didn't want it to go down like this. The money I offered her to assist as I moved would keep her straight for at least six months.

Wanda was somewhere else, and I had to remove her hand. "Don't reject me like this, not after all I've done for you and us. What about Faye? We can have another night together."

"Night together, Wanda, no, there won't be another night together with you or Faye or anyone else except Mya. My visit today is about business and business only, so let's stay focused." My mind was scrambling, and I couldn't understand why everyone was trying to make this so difficult for me.

The whole scene caught me off guard. I didn't expect this from Wanda after all we'd been through together. The times when I went there with her were some of my lowest points. Afterward, I would stay gone from the office for days mulling over my regret.

I was hoping to have Wanda handle the office's transition from St. Pete to Orlando and was willing to pay her for her time. She pulled herself together and told me what I could do with my company. As Wanda gathered her personal effects, she wished me good luck with my transition. Of course, she didn't mean it because she threw my office keys at me and stormed out of the office.

A week passed, and she still had not called or returned any of my calls. Mya didn't understand my dismay. She didn't understand that years of company knowledge walked out the door with Wanda.

"Well, that's your fault, LaDamien. No one should have that much influence on your company. You're just going to have to chalk this up to a lesson learned. What can I do to help?"

"Quit your job, and run the administrative side of my, I mean our, business." Mya smiled, but I was serious. This union can't turn into what Kim and I had. She would have to play an active role in the business, no questions asked.

"Baby, I can't quit my job, but I will do everything I can to help until you hire someone locally. We can go look for office space, and get all the office equipment set up, and go from there, okay."

I would take that for now, but ultimately my goal is for Mya to run the office. Forcing the issue now won't get us anywhere, so I plan to ease her into the role without realizing that is what is happening. Once she sees how much easier it will be, she'll see things my way. She just has to.

LOVE...

- is patient
- is kind
- is not rude
- does not envy
- will not lie
- is not self-seeking
- is not proud
- is not quick to anger
- protects
- does not boast
- does not record wrongs
- trusts
- hopes
- perseveres
- finds no joy in evil but celebrates truth
- never fails

Kim

I held on to the news that TayJohn had a fiancé until I could learn if it was true or not. We were scheduled for a weekend outing, so I planned to ask him afterward if something he needed to share with me. The reason for the delay… I wasn't prepared to lose two men in one week.

Friday, I learned TayJohn had called out sick. Concerned about his wellbeing, I called to see if something was seriously wrong and if he needed anything. "Hey you, what's going on?" I asked when he answered the phone, sounding like his usual upbeat self.

"Kim, you busted me, huh?" he joked, bringing attention to my position as Director of Human Resources. "Please don't write me up, sweetheart." I laugh.

"So what's up with you? Why did you take off?" My curiosity is peaked. "Are we still on for this weekend?

TayJohn hesitates, and I feel as if the floor is about to open up beneath me. Then it does. "About this weekend, I'm going to have to cancel. "I know how much it meant to you for us to hang out, but a couple of friends flew in from B-more this morning, and I'm going to ride down to Miami with them. Kim, I promise to make it up to you, I promise."

Before TayJohn could say goodbye, I had my keys in hand and my Coach bag on my shoulder. "Melanie, I'm leaving for the day. I'll see you on Monday, okay." Melanie waved as she listened to a caller on the phone. Thankful that I wouldn't have to explain myself, I hastened my pace and hopped on the open elevator.

The first sign of trouble was the cramping in my stomach. The second was the reservation in the guards' demeanor when I stated I was here to see TayJohn Neilson. Reluctantly, he let me in. Passing through the gate, I peered into the rearview mirror to see him placing a call. This was the third sign and a clear indication that I needed to turn around and head back home. But I couldn't. My intuition was telling me to press forward. By the time I turned into the parking space, TayJohn was already standing at the end of his walkway. The first thing I noticed was his attire. He was dressed in a shirt and tie. Not like someone planning to ride down to Miami for a weekend of fun with his homies.

"Taj, I hope you don't mind, but I wanted to see you before you left." My tone was giving away how panicked I am.

"Why did you come all the way over here without asking?" He said more than asked.

"Without asking? Since when do I have to have permission to come over?" His tone startled me. "Can we go inside? I think we need to talk?"

"Yes, we do need to talk, but you can't come inside."

Fear rose to my throat, restricting my voice. TayJohn came towards me and grabbed my hand, leading me down the sidewalk towards a pergola located between the building that housed his townhouse and the building next to it. "Kim, there's something I need to tell you."

I did my best to brace myself, although I knew what he was about to say. I think the biggest challenge was having to hear that she was as close as his townhouse. I would be expected to leave without seeing what she looked like, what she had that I didn't have, besides the obvious...TayJohn. "Why did you lie to me?" I asked as if the answer made a difference. LaDamien had lied from day one, and I accepted it without question,

"I didn't lie. I never promised you anything. We were never a couple or in a committed relationship." TayJohn was standing before me, but LaDamien was speaking. How could I not see it? Why didn't I pick up on it after so many years of practice? The thought that I had made the same mistake three times in a row made me feel so dumb.

"Okay, Taj, let's play it your way. Why did you lie to her? What's her name, what does she know about me, what does she think you're doing right now?"

"Whoa, slow down, Kim. I didn't lie to anybody. Chyna and I were dating when I was forced to relocate or find another job." He was making light of the situation. No one forced him to do anything. "I tried to Kim, okay, I tried to give you an option, but you weren't interested at the time. Chyna started calling, and we eventually rekindled things. I know I should have talked to you about it, but things between you and LaDamien went south real fast, and I just didn't know what to do."

"But now you do. You chose her."

"It's not that simple, Kim."

"The hell it isn't. You just canceled our weekend getaway to be with her."

"She showed up late last night, unannounced, and I guess I need to figure things out." TayJohn didn't look like a man who needed to figure things out. He already knew what he wanted, and nothing I said was going to change his mind. This Chyna person had stolen his heart right from under me. Just like Mya stole LaDamien's. Why he couldn't be honest is what's pissing me off.

"Please be honest with me, TayJohn, don't try to sugar coat it. Someone told me you had a fiancé, but I didn't want to believe it." He stopped me.

"She isn't my fiancée, but we have been discussing the possibility of her moving here. Kim, you and I could have had something beautiful, but your situation was just too complex."

Again, it's my fault. The names change, but in the end, it's always the same. Kim, you didn't try hard enough, Kim, you don't know how to take care of my needs, Kim, you aren't giving enough, Kim, you have too much going on. Nobody wants to acknowledge that it's not me but for them.

"It's okay, TayJohn. I'm used to being the odd woman out. I just wish you could have recognized what I had already been dealing with and chose to be a real man and not dump any more bullshit on me. My God, I'm divorcing my husband and hoping we have a future together. Now, what am I supposed to do." I didn't want to admit it, but it came out. I would never have asked LaDamien for a divorce if I'd known TayJohn, and I never had a chance at a future together.

He stood in front of me and wiped my tears away, his touch as gentle as ever. I tilted my head into his palm, wistfully pleading for him to take me into his arms and tell me it had all been a colossal mistake. Still, the soft voice calling his name from behind me let me know it wasn't.

Chyna wasn't a full-figured woman, but she was light-skinned, with long silky hair, the kind that belonged to bi-racial women who spent lots of time and money keeping it bone straight. When she walked up, there was nothing left for me to do but leave. TayJohn stopped me.

"Kim, this is Chyna. Chyna, this is my friend Kim."

What was he expecting? Were we going to go inside and discuss things like mature adults? Was he going to get us to get along so he could continue seeing us both? It somehow worked for LaDamien. He was a pro at convincing women it was enough of him to go around.

Chyna and I looked each other over and then turned our attention to TayJohn. "Kim was just leaving. I told her that you and I would make a go of it, so our friendship has to end. She understands. Don't you, Kim?"

The fucking coward, how dare he. "Yes, better than you think I do. Good luck, Mr. Neilson, Chyna." Nervously, I walked away. I was wearing four-inch heels, and my stomach was quivering. The last thing I needed was to trip, stumble, or fall. Thank God, neither happened. I started my car and drove away. I was refusing to cry and refusing to be a victim again. I pulled myself together and headed home. I had a lot of soul-searching to do.

I still had two hours before Ariel was due to get out of school, so I treated myself to lunch at a downtown restaurant. My head was spinning, and I would have given anything to have my mother here to help me sort through this mess. LaDamien was gone, TayJohn was gone, and I had to figure out a way to recover. I called Debra to see if she could accompany me on the trip to Key West since it was paid for already.

"I'm watching Ariel, remember. But if you can get someone else, I would be happy to go with you." Debra said apologetically. "Where are you? I can meet you so we can talk. I'm so sorry this is happening to you."

As I listen to Debra, I see clearly why she chose to stay and save her marriage. It was easier. "You don't have to do that. I'm about to leave anyway. You know the Key West outing can be postponed to another time. It's probably best if I spend time with my daughter and stop pawning her off so I can traipse around with men who don't care anything about me."

"Kim, don't talk like that. You know it's not too late to work things out with LaDamien. The divorce isn't final yet. Maybe that's where you need to focus your energy." Debra had to be joking. Did she forget LaDamien had moved in with his mistress in another city?

"Hey Kim," I turned to find my soon-to-be ex-sister-in-law standing beside me. Pam was dressed in a tailored blue pantsuit, leading me to believe she had just left a hearing for one of her clients. She had been a Social Worker for the Department of Children and Families for nearly fifteen years. The suit was what we called her "going to meet the judge" attire.

"Debra, let me call you later. Pam is here." Folding my phone and placing it in my purse, I beckoned Pam to have a seat.

"I hear doomsday is next Friday," she began. "You know it's not too late to change your mind, Kim." Was there a conspiracy against me? Debra was just saying the same thing.

"No, I think it's Pam. Plus, your brother seems very happy with his little tramp." Pam frowned, I thought, because I referred to Mya as a tramp, but as we talked, I quickly learned she was disappointed that I would just give my husband to another woman.

"Marriage takes hard work, Kim, and if you had come to one of the sisters or me, we could have helped you with LaDamien. We knew things were strained between you two but had no idea it was this bad. Now I'm hearing all sorts of horrible tales about what he's been doing, and I'm just ashamed and hurt."

"So then you know I can't fix it. Our marriage is too broken."

"Kim, nothing is too broken for God to fix. LaDamien will be here Sunday. Why don't you join us for church, and afterward, we can have a family meeting to see what we can do to help you two save your marriage."

"Pam, it's too late for that, seriously. Plus, I'm sure Mya will be with him, and then what."

"And then we ask her to excuse herself. She doesn't count in all of this, Kim. In God's eye, you and my brother are husband and wife, and whatever you two ask him to do, he'll do it, including saving your marriage."

Pam made it all seem so easy. If God planned to save my marriage, he would have stopped my husband from cheating years ago. What would I do at this juncture in the game? Call LaDamien, and say I changed my mind.

"Just come to church Sunday. We'll do the rest. Promise?"

"Promise."

LaDamien

Sunday, Mya and I had plans to head over to St. Petersburg for the day. We hit the road at seven a.m. By eight-thirty, we were pulling into the driveway of Mya's parent's home. With my divorce a week away, we decided it was time to let them know about our future plans. Mya's mother greeted us at the door.

"Well, good morning, don't you two look spiffy." We enter the home after exchanging hugs and pleasantries. Mrs. Blake lets us know she has breakfast ready, and Mr. Blake will be joining us shortly.

"Daddy had to run out to the store for some orange juice, but we have apple and cranberry, as well as coffee. LaDamien, do you drink coffee?" She asks as she ushers us into the oversized kitchen.

"Ma, you didn't have to go to all this trouble. Who is going to eat all of this food?" A lot of food covered the large granite-topped island in the middle of the kitchen. It was a kitchen that looked perfect for family gatherings. I made a mental note to let Mya know we should have one installed in our kitchen at the new house.

As Mya and her mom chatted about the meal, I took in as much of the Blake's home as possible. It was apparent where Mya inherited her sharp eye for decorating. Hardwood floors were laid throughout, including the kitchen. Top of the line stainless steel appliances lined the walls. Multiple KitchenAid products in burgundy to match the décor lined the countertops. Although I had stopped by the Blake's home in the past, after seeing Mya's car parked outside, this was my first real invitation. Our other meetings had been at Mya's house.

"Have a seat LaDamien, or would you prefer to eat outside on the patio? It's nice enough out that we could move everything out there."

"Whatever is best for you, Mrs. Blake, I don't want to be any trouble." Mya is going to look a lot like her mother when she gets older. Mrs. Blake is wearing her age well and is in good physical shape, I think to myself.

Soon after we arrived, Mr. Blake returned with a gallon of orange juice and a loaf of bread. "Hey, you two, how fast were y'all driving along that interstate." Mya walked over and gave her dad a big hug.

"Not fast at all, daddy. I keep telling you Orlando isn't as far as you think it's."

"Regardless of how far it is, you shouldn't be able to get home as fast as you do. It takes us over two hours to get to your place." Mr. Blake placed his items on the table, turned back to face his daughter, and continued his lecture.

"Hush-up, you two, Bill, you know it takes us that long because we always stop for a meal on our way, plus the bathroom breaks you have to take," she joked.

"Uhn huh," Mya added with a smile. "Mom, and Dad, there's something I need to talk to you about, so can we go ahead, and get started with breakfast."

Both the Blake's looked at each other with concern before looking to Mya and then to me. "It's nothing bad, just something you should know." After we washed up, said grace, and fixed our plates, Mya got to the real reason behind our visit.

"LaDamien moved to Orlando. Well, he moved in with me a few months ago." She waited for a reaction, and when none came, she continued. "Mom, I'm sure Ms. Janice has already told you that LaDamien is married, so don't act like it's a surprise. Anyway, he and his wife are getting divorced, and it will be final next week. Afterward, we'll be moving into our new home, probably in a few weeks. We'll still be in Orlando but in one of the subdivisions near where I'm now."

"Mya Blake, you weren't raised like this," her dad began in a stern tone. "And you, young man, how long have you been running around with my daughter knowing you already had a wife. Or should I be asking my daughter how long she knew you had a wife?" Mya's mother was silent, but her fathers' disappointment came through fluently. He was not pleased.

"Daddy, what we did was wrong, and we know it, there's no plausible excuse, but we love each other and have since the day we met, and now we are together, and I'm happy. Doesn't that count for something?" Mya looked to me to add something, but I didn't know what to say. If Ariel were sitting at my table professing her love for a married man, I'd think she was crazy and would be ready to beat his ass. Mya's father hadn't looked my way.

"LaDamien, you're awfully quiet." Her baby girl was drowning in sin, and her mother needed me to save her and to prove I'm worthy of her love.

"Uhm, I can't say or do anything to change how we met, but I can tell you both that I love your daughter. Always have, and always will. I can tell you my entire life story. About my marriage, which I knew was a mistake the second I said I do, but what it boils down to is what I plan to do in the future, and that's love Mya and take care of her. Please give me the chance to show you that we are happy together and meant to be together." Mya reached for my hand and squeezed it, reassuring me that we were a team.

After several tense minutes, her father asked me what I thought about the Magic's chances at the playoffs this year after adding Vince Carter to the line-up. "We may have to catch some games. That's if you can get your hand on some good tickets."

I wasn't sure, but I think my future father-in-law was about to pimp me for season tickets. As if Mya and her mom read my mind, they both burst out laughing.

As we sat outside Bethel Inspirational, it dawned on us that attending church as a couple probably wouldn't look right, so we decided to worship elsewhere. "What about First Ebenezer?" I asked. Mya looked as though she was going to have a heart attack.

"You know we can't go there. Minister Epps would probably come down out of the pulpit and snatch us both up."

"Why would you say that?" I asked, confused.

"You know why. Remember, I know Pastor Epps wife. She counseled me on our situation."

Why she had to run all over town telling our business was a mystery to me. Instead of talking to Epps wife, she should have been talking to me. "So what do you suggest? Should we just go in? It's not like people aren't already talking, and they are going to know we are together soon enough. No sooner had the question left my mouth than I saw my sister Lynn and her family pull up to the church with my mom in the front seat. Turning back to Mya, I noticed Pam and Veronica's cars parked two rows over from us.

"Did you know your entire family was coming to church today?" Mya asked as she followed my line of sight.

"No, I just thought we were having dinner at Lynn's. Let me go see what's up." I exited my SUV and walked over to Lynn's Towne car. "Hey sis, what's going on?"

Lynn looked surprised to see me. "We didn't know you would be her little brother. Where's Mya?"

"In the car. You knew we were coming over. Why didn't you tell me everyone was coming to church? We could have planned to join you." Lynn looked over at the Escalade and then back to me. "Why don't you walk mama inside while I go park."

Minutes after we were seated, Kim, with Ariel in tow, made their way into the pew and sat next to me. My heart began to pound erratically. What was going on, and where was Mya? Nervously, I scanned the church for her presence. Kim looked at me and smile and then placed her left hand on my right knee, displaying the wedding band I placed on her finger the day we were married. Why was she still wearing the ring but more importantly, why was she here acting like we were one big happy family? I needed to find Mya and assure her that this was not my doing.

The choir went into the up-tempo gospel hit by Hezekiah Walker, *Souled Out*. I stood up with the vast majority of the congregation and used the opportunity to look around. To my left was Mya. Although she was doing her best to hide her hurt feelings, I knew she was not happy with how things were turning out. If things couldn't have gotten any worst, the sermon, which started out dealing with the greatest love, taken from I Corinthian 13, quickly turned to a sermon on adultery.

1 What if I could speak all languages of humans and of angels? If I didn't love others, I would be nothing more than a noisy gong or a clanging cymbal. 2 What if I could prophesy and understand all secrets and all knowledge?, and what if I had faith that moved mountains? I would be nothing unless I loved others. 3 What if I gave away all that I owned and let myself be burned alive? I would gain nothing unless I loved others. 4 Love is kind and patient, never jealous, boastful, proud, or 5 rude. Love isn't selfish or quick-tempered. It doesn't keep a record of wrongs that others do. 6Love rejoices in the truth, but not in evil. 7 Love is always supportive, loyal, hopeful, and trusting. 8 Love never fails! Everyone who prophesies will stop, and unknown languages will no longer be spoken. All that we know will be forgotten. 9 We don't know everything, and our prophecies aren't complete. 10 But what is perfect will someday appear, and what isn't perfect will then disappear. 11When we were children, we thought and reasoned as children do. But when we grew up, we quit our childish ways. 12 Now, all we can see of God is like a cloudy picture in a mirror. Later we will see him face to face. We don't know everything, but then we will, just as God completely understands us. 13 For now, there are faith, hope, and love. But of these three, the greatest is love.

Pastor Lawrence switched gears so fast many of the congregants seemed as lost as I was. My sister Pam sounded as if she was enjoying my torment. Her amens and hallelujahs were way louder than they needed to be. Mom was to my left moaning and groaning as if the agony of my sins were too much for her soul to bear, while Kim was to my right savoring every word as she kept a sharp eye on my future wife.

"Regardless of what you and your spouse are going through, you must be reminded that the answer can't be found outside the home," he stated to loud applauds.

"No matter what she or he's telling you, that outside person has not made a vow to you. They don't know your little bad habits. All they see is the good side, and if you spent as much time showing your wife or husband that good side, you might rekindle what you felt when you first decided to marry that person. Love, yes, love is a wonderful thing when all is well. The second things start going array you want to toss love aside and get a new model. Well, just remember the grass isn't always greener across the way. Sometimes it's just the time of day and the position of the sun." Pastor Lawrence spun around as the congregation, mostly women, including my wife, and sisters, stood to their feet. To my surprise, Mya was standing and clapping also.

At the end of the service, as I assisted my mom out of the pew, Kim reached for my hand. I turned to face her and let her know I didn't appreciate the game she was playing. She looked serious, and her words were the last thing I needed to hear.

"We need to talk. It's important. I've had a change of heart."

Mya

"*A change* of heart, is that what she said to you?" LaDamien and I are on our way back to Orlando. We had made plans to spend the day in St. Petersburg with family. The day started as planned, but it certainly didn't end that way.

We had breakfast at the home of my parents. While there, I told them that LaDamien was married, but he and his wife were getting a divorce. My mothers' reaction all but confirmed what I suspected all along. She knew LaDamien was already married and chose to keep it to herself. My mom has a friend who lives on the same street as LaDamien and Kim, making it inconceivable that my mom had never mentioned LaDamien to her. Janice, her friend, never mentioned he was her neighbor.

Although mom was reserved, my dad was not. He admonished me right there at the breakfast table like I was still his little girl, which I guess in his eyes, I still am. LaDamien finally came to my rescue and ended the lecture by promising to take my dad to a couple of Magic games.

From my parents' home, we headed to church, and that's where our plans got off track. As we sat in the parking lot debated if we should go inside, LaDamien's family began showing up. He left me to speak with his sister, Lynn. Shortly after, LaDamien assisted his mother out of the car and the two-headed inside. He nodded for me to come along, but I saw Kim and Ariel approaching the church when I exited the SUV. The whole scene came out of nowhere. One minute we were debating whether we should go to another church since he wasn't divorced yet. The next, his entire family had descended upon us and swooped him up. Leaving me feeling like the outsider I was. I know I could have made a scene and joined the family, but I chose to sit in another section. LaDamien looked so uncomfortable. At least I thought he did until Kim placed her hand on his knee, and he didn't move it away. On top of all that, Pastor Lawrence switched up his sermon midway through and started harping on infidelity and fornication.

LaDamien's entire family was against me. The way they were whooping and hollering and carrying on like this was the best sermon they had ever heard was obvious. It was funny how they were so pious when each had their marital discords they needed to be dealing with, according to their little brother.

"What does this mean? What is she having a change of heart about, the house, child support, the divorce, what?"

"Calm down, baby. This was all a shock to me as it's to you. I'm sorry you had to endure that, and trust me, I will be talking with my sisters."

"You still haven't answered my question?"

At the end of the church service, Kim informed LaDamien she needed to talk to him. He excused himself, came over to me, suggested that I take the SUV, and head over to Lynn's. He said Kim needed to talk to him. Of course, I wanted to know why I had to head over to Lynn's without him. He responded that he would talk with Kim and didn't want me to be uncomfortable. "I was uncomfortable for the past three hours, so a few more minutes won't hurt."

LaDamien knew me well enough to know I wasn't leaving without him. He walked back over to Kim, and the two huddled together for nearly a half-hour. The expression on his face was a mixture of confusion and anger. Whatever Kim was saying was not sitting well with him. I stood outside the Escalade, hoping I could pick up on a portion of their conversation. Pam walked past with her husband and two kids in tow. She barely spoke in an audible tone. Based on her body language, I knew she was already privy to the subject of conversation between LaDamien, and Kim. It also confirmed in my mind that we wouldn't be going to Lynn's for dinner.

"Let's go," LaDamien commanded as he stepped into the driver's side of the SUV. "I can't believe this shit."

We've been on the road for over a half-hour. I still have not gotten to the meat and potatoes of their conversation.

LaDamien pulled into the parking lot of *Boston Lobster* on International Drive. Once we were seated, he apologized again for what happened at church. "I had no idea, Mya. When I spoke to Kim the other day, everything was still on schedule. Now she's saying she doesn't want a divorce."

"How do you feel about it?" I knew I should have finished the sentence by asking him if he wanted to give their marriage another try, but the answer had the potential to kill me. Every day I have awakened expecting LaDamien to say he'd had a change of heart. The closer we got to the date of their final hearing, my anxiety grew.

He tells me, "I feel like a rug is being pulled from beneath me. I feel as if happiness isn't mine to have. Why would I want to go back to a marriage I didn't want to be in, in the first place.

"We're finally together and happy, and no one wants that; they want me to be miserable like they are." LaDamien was hyperventilating. I hated when he allowed himself to get worked up like this. He kept going on and on about "they this" and "they that," leaving me to believe he was referring to his sisters.

"Well, baby, just because she asked to try again doesn't mean you have to pack up your things and go back home. Unless, of course, that's what you want to do."

"Is that what you want me to do, Mya, because that's damn sure not what I want?"

He was becoming more and more agitated. "All I want, LaDamien, and all I have ever wanted is to be happy. You make me happy, and I want you here, but if a part of you that wants to be back with Kim, and Ariel then I need to know now, and not later."

LaDamien requested the check from the waitress. Upon paying the receipt, he stormed out of the restaurant. He was moving so fast I could hardly keep up.

"You have so little faith in me, Mya. You are so sure I'm going to leave you that you would rather just send me back."

"That's not true, LaDamien, and you know it."

"No, I don't know it, Mya. Why aren't you telling me how much you want this, how you won't let Kim come between us, or how much it will hurt if I went back?"

"Because you should already know all those things, I shouldn't have to say it," I scream, tears rolling down my face. "I don't know how to react in this kind of situation because I've never been in one before. I've never been married before, so I don't know if it's easier to stay or leave. I don't know what you're feeling or why, but I know I love you, LaDamien, and I know I'm scared I'm going to lose you."

He stopped at the back of the Escalade and turned to face me. "I'm scared too, Mya, but I'm not going to leave you and go back to Kim. If she stops the divorce or tries to make this harder, we've got to stick together and make this work. You need to understand it could get ugly and cost me a lot of money."

"I don't care about the money. I just need you here with me. Please promise me you won't go back because if you do, I will never forgive you." LaDamien pulled me into his arms, and we embraced until we both felt secure again.

"Promise." He declared as we parted, and he walked around to open the door for me.

"Baby, what's wrong?" LaDamien is asking as I sit up in bed. Sweat is pouring from my face, and my heart is beating ten times faster than normal. I peer around the room and rest my eyes on the green lights illuminating from the clock. It's three a.m.

"It's a dream I've been having for quite some time." I'm wiping tears from my eyes as I tell him about my recurring dream.

"Calm down, baby, and tell me why the dream has you so upset." LaDamien pulls me into his arms and tries to comfort me as I explain the dream to him in detail.

"It always ends the same. Mya admonishes me and then tells me that under no uncertain terms will God bless me with another woman's husband, not ever."

LaDamien exhales a deep sigh and holds me tighter. "No, he won't bless you with another woman's husband, but he will bless you with your own, and after Friday, I will be free to be that husband for you." I knew LaDamien believed what he was saying, but deep in my heart, I knew that would never happen.

LOVE...
- is patient
- is kind
- is not rude
- does not envy
- will not lie
- is not self-seeking
- is not proud
- is not quick to anger
- does not boast
- protects
- does not record wrongs
- trusts
- hopes
- perseveres
- finds no joy in evil but celebrates truth
- never fails

LaDamien

"Hey, do you think you can get off early today and go over to the house and meet with the guy about the paint colors? I have to go to St. Pete to meet with Mark." Mya cringed the moment I mentioned St. Petersburg. Since the incident Sunday where Kim asked if we could reconcile, Mya has been on edge.

"Why didn't you ask me to go with you?"

"Mya, I'm going to meet with Mark and finish packing up my office since we didn't get a chance to do it on Sunday. I'm not going to see Kim if that's what you're worried about." That's precisely what she was worried about, and I knew she had every right to be with my track record.

Kim had called me both Monday and Tuesday, and my answer was the same "no." I didn't tell Mya about the calls, but given the look of uncertainty that she's giving me now, I probably should have. "Baby, tomorrow I close on the house, and Friday we finalize the divorce. Okay?"

"Okay." Mya agreed as we walked into the garage and prepared to leave. She kissed me, and all her love came through. I was a lucky man, and I was going to make Mya a very happy woman.

My meeting with Mark lasted a little longer than anticipated. For some reason, I needed a male perspective on what was happening with Kim.

"It's normal, man, you two have history, you have a child together, and you've already found her replacement. It's only natural for her to feel this way. I'm surprised you don't have any doubts."

"Why would I have doubts? "I ask. "I love Mya and have already wasted too much time." Mark nodded his head in agreement as I spoke. He, of all people, should know how much Mya means to me. She's the reason our business relationship ended.

"Man, I'm not questioning your love for Mya. I'm just saying you must still have feelings for Kim, that's all. Have you truly dealt with that? Ask yourself, Dame, if you never found out Kim had another man, would you have begged your way back in the house by now, and it been business as usual. Man, if Mya hadn't let you come back you, and Kim would have worked this out."

All of what Mark was saying was true, but it didn't play itself out that way, which for me is a sign that Mya is who I'm meant to be with after all. "My life has been stress-free, and I'm a truly happy man, so I don't want to worry about the what-ifs."

Mark felt where I was coming from, knowing not everybody had what he and his wife had. All I was trying to do was get a little piece of that heaven. When I left Mark, I headed over to the office and began boxing up files and office equipment. The task would take longer than I had time, so it looked like Mya and I would have to come over and finish it up on the weekend. I took a seat at what was once Wanda's desk. She hadn't called to ask for her job back or to apologize since she stormed out on me. I was starting to feel a little melancholy and even considered giving her a call to apologize when I opened one of the drawers to her desk. One she always kept locked, and I never had a key to, until I found it in the set of keys she threw at me the day she quit.

Inside the drawer were some personal items like deodorant, lotion, tampons, and condoms. That made me laugh, and I wondered how long they had been here since we never used condoms. I pulled out some file folders and began to sort through the information. Wanda had personal bank statements, credit card statements, and other documents. "Horace had better watch out. His wife was building quite a nest egg."

I needed to box these items up and call Wanda to come to retrieve them. I'm surprised she hadn't missed them already. As I was placing the items in a box, I came across an envelope with pictures inside. Pictures of my wife and the same man whose place I followed her to in Lutz. Why would Wanda have these pictures? What had she been up to following Kim or even hiring someone else to follow her? In the midst of my wondering what she was doing with the pictures, a thought came to me. I could use the pictures as leverage in my divorce if Kim tried to back out. "Thanks, Wanda," I said out loud. "Even in your absence, you are still working things out for me."

My search of her "private" drawer unveiled another surprise. Months ago, Mya mentioned a letter that was supposedly faxed to her house. I didn't pay her any attention at the time because her story was so far-fetched but in my hands was a letter that could possibly be the letter Mya was talking about, and attached to it's a piece of paper with several phone numbers, including Mya's home number, and her email address. I sit back and take a pause. This is crazy. I read the letter in its entirety, and a chill comes over me. Wanda took our set-up way too seriously. She had a husband, and kids, so like Faye, I never thought I was a threat to her marriage. But reading this letter, I see she was willing and ready to give it all up. "Oh man, good thing things ended the way that they did."

My last stop before I headed back to Orlando was to visit my mother. I'm sure she has a mouthful waiting for me after Sunday's fiasco at church. When I pull into the parking lot, Pam's car is the first thing I see, so I take a deep breath and prepare to go in firing.

"Hey, baby brother," she greets me.

Smiling, I say hello, and walk past her to hug mama and give her a kiss. "Been conspiring with my soon-to-be ex-wife lately?"

Pam doesn't miss a beat. "She's still your wife, and you need to stop playing house with that girl and take your butt home."

Mama throws up her hand. "Stop it, both of you. Pam, tend to your own marriage and let LaDamien tend to his. I don't need to listen to this nonsense today. My soul is heavy today, and I just want to hear the good stuff."

Upsetting my mother is never on my agenda. I sit on the sofa adjacent to her favorite chair and begin to tell her how happy I've been lately.

Kim

LaDamien is visiting St. Petersburg. I saw him driving down thirty-fourth street. My first thought was to call and set up some time for us to get together. Then I glanced over at the closing papers still in my car and decided to make a trip over to Orlando to check out what could be our new home. I've done a lot of thinking and praying since running into Pam last Friday and hearing her say I need to reclaim my marriage. Debra agreed with everything Pam had said, and I began to feel hopeful. Even when Karen nixed the idea, my resolve was to move forward full steam ahead.

There was so much to consider if I, no, if we were going to make this work. LaDamien would be angry at first, but eventually, I think he would come around. I would go ahead and do the closing on the house but then refuse to sign the Quit Claim Deed relinquishing my rights. Afterward, I would let him know that the divorce petition was being withdrawn. The papers were being filed this evening. That way, his attorney wouldn't have a chance to notify him before my plan was fully activated.

My job was the next thing to consider. Would I be willing to relocate and take a lesser-paying position to save my marriage? The answer was yes. I had done it before and could do it again. But I wasn't sure if living in the same city as Mya was such a good idea. It may be best to force him to stay right here in St. Petersburg. I'd learned that Wanda quit upon learning he was moving the office to Orlando. It would require me swallowing my pride, but I'd beg her personally to come back and work for us.

The bottom line was I had to do whatever was required of me to save my marriage. Thinking another man was the answer to my problems was the biggest mistake I ever made. Talking to Pam made me realize this, although I didn't dare tell her I was as guilty as her brother, and when you got right down to the facts, I was. Thinking of Pam had me dialing her number. Her greeting was upbeat as usual.

"Hey Pam, are you busy?"

"No, just visiting mama. She says LaDamien is coming over later. Why don't you stop by?"

"Are you serious? I saw him not too long ago, so you think he will be in town most of the day?" I ask her.

"If you need him to be, why, what do you have in mind?"

"I have a couple of meetings today and won't be able to get away until about three. What time is he coming over to visit mama?" Pam muffled the receiver and began talking to someone else, I assumed is her mother.

"Mom says he was meeting with Mark for breakfast and then going over to clean out his office. She thinks he should be here by two. Should we look for you? I can cook a little extra for dinner?" Where were Pam and all her goodwill when my marriage was falling apart?

"I'll do my best to get there, but you don't have to worry about dinner. Pam, thanks so much for the guidance you're providing me. You are so right. My marriage is worth fighting for." Pam was happy to know I had not changed my mind. She promised to call and let me know when LaDamien arrived.

My mind was made up, I was going to see the house, and then I would find Mya and pay her a little visit to let her know that neither my marriage nor my husband was hers for the taking.

Mya

I am turning into the woman I don't want to be. LaDamien is probably tiring of my repeated phone calls. Each time, assuring me that he has not seen or talked to Kim, he has no intentions to do so. Still, knowing he has not left St. Pete yet worries me. It's two o'clock, and I'm leaving the office to head over to the house and meet with the painters. The owners of the property LaDamien was purchasing were anxious to unload the home so they could relocate back up to D.C. They were willing to accommodate many of the changes he was requesting. In true fashion, my baby was taking full advantage.

"Hi," the middle-aged Hispanic man greeted.

"Hi, I'm Mya. I'm here to go over the paint choices for the interior rooms." The man introduced himself as Jose and led me inside.

We went from room to room with me identifying which colors go in each room. About an hour into my visit, the doorbell rang. Jose' excused himself and went down to answer. I followed him as far as the top of the stairs. Jose' and the visitor talked for a brief moment before he looked at me and asked if I was the new owner's wife.

Making my way down the stairs, I advised him that we weren't married yet. I asked who was at the door.

"There's a lady here who says she's the owner of this house and that she and her husband is closing on the home tomorrow." He replied.

The confusion must have shown clearly on my face because Jose' seemed torn between allowing the visitor in or closing the door and locking it. I reached the door and pulled it open. In a stylish designer suit with a matching *Coach* bag, and looking like a million bucks, was Kim. Her professional demeanor quickly changed to a scowl and then a smile.

"Mya, nice meeting you here. It looks like I can kill two birds with one stone."

"Kim, what are you doing here?" I asked as if she had no right to be. She *was* about to place her name on the dotted line.

"I wanted to see what I was about to purchase. I don't want to have buyer's remorse. Do you know what I mean? Are you going to let me in?" Hesitantly, I stepped back and allowed her to enter.

"Nice, LaDamien does have rich taste. So what are you doing here?"

She had the nerve to ask me what I'm doing here. The question was why she was here and did LaDamien know she was coming. "LaDamien is in St. Petersburg. Do you want me to call him?"

"No. I came to see the house and was hoping to see you as well. God must be working on my behalf because what are the chances that you'd be here. Come show me around." Kim walked ahead of me, and past Jose' like she thought I would give her a tour.

Jose' looked from Kim back to me and then back to Kim. "Do you need me to call Mr. Bryson?" he whispered.

"There's no need for that," Kim answered for me. "Mya and I are going to have a little chat, and then I'm leaving."

I looked at Jose and instructed him to call LaDamien. Kim looked at me with displeasure.

"Kim, what do you want?' I ask as Jose' made his way out the door.

"My husband back, Mya. I'm not divorcing LaDamien. So you know, I rescinded the divorce petition before coming over here. I'm going to save my marriage, and I expect you to respect my decision."

"And what about LaDamien? Does he get a say-so in any of this?" Today Kim isn't the sorrowful-looking woman who always looked full of contempt but fearful of speaking the anger that raged within her. Today she's confident and direct, probably her boardroom guise.

"You know LaDamien as well I do, Mya. He's going to do what's best for him. When I tell him that I will not sign for this house or go through with the divorce, he'll realize this little fantasy world you two have been living in is about to end."

Kim's walking around the foyer, peering into entryways as if she needs permission to enter any of the rooms or walk up the stairs. If she were in charge, she'd look through the house on her.

The front door opens, and Jose' enters with a man from the security team. "Ms. Mya, I have spoken to Mr. Bryson, and he's on his way. This is Mr. Paul from security."

Jose' looked concerned, but Paul looked as if the last thing about to happen on his watch was two Black women acting a damn fool. "You ladies want to tell me what's going on here?"

This whole mess is so embarrassing, "Nothing, I came to discuss paint colors with Jose', and Mrs. Bryson stopped by to take a look at the house. I'm going to leave so she can finish her walk-though, and Jose' if it's okay with you, I'll come back later today when Mr. Bryson can join me." No need to hang around and escalate a confrontation with Kim. She had a plan, so I would let her and LaDamien deal with it. In my car, I pulled out my phone and saw I had eleven missed calls from him. They are all followed by a text asking me to PLEASE CALL.

"She said she doesn't want a divorce," I screamed after he repeatedly asked me what Kim was trying to prove. "She's your wife! Why don't you call her? I don't know if she's still there. Security showed up, and rather than make matters worse, I left. But LaDamien, you should know this; Kim said she isn't giving you a divorce, nor is she going to sign the house over to you after the closing. She wants you back. Now you need to decide what you're going to do."

I stopped at the four-way stop near my townhouse. I peered into the rearview mirror, and Kim was behind me. "Oh shit, she followed me."

"Where are you?" LaDamien asked, panicked.

"About a block away. You better get your wife LaDamien because I will not have this drama where I sleep." I turned into the drive, and Kim pulled in beside me. "Hurry up, LaDamien."

"I'm about thirty minutes away. Call the police if you have to. Mya, I love you, and I'm not going back to Kim. Okay?"

"Okay., and LaDamien, I love you too. I just need for the madness to stop." We ended our call, and I took a deep breath before stepping out of my car and addressing Kim. She had crossed the line. I never disrespected her home, and she wasn't about to disrespect mine.

"I just want to talk, Mya. Woman to woman, that's all I'm asking; no street scene, and no drama, just two women in love with the same man coming to a resolution."

"He's not going back to you, Kim. Do you want to come inside and wait for him to get here so he can tell you to your face? Is that what it's going to take for you to get it?" I say sarcastically.

"Yes, let's not do this outside, Mya."

"I don't want you in my home Kim." This woman was starting to work my nerves. LaDamien was calling again. Why was he calling me and not her? She was the one who was out of order and needed to get over it.

"Hello...yes, she's still here. Do you want to talk to her?" Of course, he didn't.

"Listen, Mya, just go inside, and I'll be there as quick as I can. I'll call Kim and tell her to leave."

"Good luck with that one." I turned and walked to the front door with Kim on my heels.

"Kim! Please don't make me call the police on you. LaDamien will be here in about twenty minutes. You need to go get in your car and wait for him." She wasn't taking no for an answer.

"Mya, please," she said, her tone much softer. "I just want to talk to you to understand why this happened."

"Why what happened, Kim, that you're supposed to be divorcing your husband, but now you're at my doorstep trying to engage me in some ghetto bullshit?"

Part of me wanted to talk to her, ask why she would stay with LaDamien as long as she had and put up with his mess. I also wanted to know what happened to the guy she was supposed to be seeing. It was starting to make sense now. He didn't want her, so she wanted LaDamien back. I unlocked the door and let her in as she ignored her ringing cell phone.

"This is nice," Kim said as she took in her surroundings and spied the pictures of LaDamien and me displayed around the room. "You two look like a happy couple." She said sarcastically. "I can't say that he and I have any pictures together, at least none like these."

I fain a nervous smile, already regretting my decision to allow Kim to come in. "Have a seat," I say, pointing to the living area.

Once Kim is seated, I choose a place opposite her but closer to the door. My cell phone in hand. "What do you want to talk about, Kim?"

She looked at me, her eyes now revealing the real hurt she must be feeling. "What is it about women like you that make a man leave his family?"

"Women like me...what is that supposed to mean? Kim, I'm no different than you or anyone else."

"No, Mya, you are very different than most women I know and me. Because unlike you, I would never try and steal another woman's husband."

Oh, this was going to be lovely, well let me burst her pious bubble right now. "I didn't try and steal your husband, Kim." I look around the room at the pictures of LaDamien and me. For effect, I pause at the ones we took at the park one afternoon. The ones I kept hidden in my bedroom until recently. Kim needed to get the full effect...I had her husband.

"For starters, your husband approached me. Your husband initiated the affair with me. On more occasions than I care to remember, he begged me to come back after things had ended between us." She looked as if she was regretting this conversation, so I decided to finish. "Do you know about Faye and his secretary? See, it's not women like me Kim, maybe it's women like you. Your husband was out running the streets in search of something, so maybe you should be asking yourself what you could have done to keep him home. Or, just maybe the two of you never should have gotten married in the first place."

"But we are together. He was my husband when you met him, and that should have been enough for you to turn down his advances."

"So he could just go on to the next woman and the next woman. You're right, Kim, and I was dead wrong for getting involved with LaDamien. Still, if I had it all to do over, I don't think I would have done anything differently because as wrong as we were, the love we share is real. The joy he brings to my life I can't compare to anything else. So if you think I'm going to feel sorry for you and say I'll walk away, well I can't, and I won't."

"Damn, Mya, he isn't all that. Don't you know that the second he gets tired of you, he's going to do the same thing to you he did to me? And how silly is it of you to throw Faye and Wanda in my face? It looks like you are fighting the same battle I did."

"Then why are you here fighting to get him back?" The room was silent for what felt like an eternity. I don't know if it was my words that stung or the key placed in the lock. Kim and I both turned at the same time to see the front door open and LaDamien walk in.

"Kim, why in the fuck are you here?" He demanded in an anger-laced voice.

I was frozen. The look in LaDamien's eyes screamed rage. The seriousness of the situation must have finally set in. He was two days away from being free, and here Kim sat before him, unwilling to let go. Suddenly, I wished I could go back to the moment my alarm clock went off this morning. I wished I could go back to the day I opened the door and told him he could come in. I wished I could go back to the first night he called me, and I agreed to this affair. No, I wished I could go back to that night we first met so I could skip all of my regrets.

"Kim, do you hear me talking to you?" He yelled.

"LaDamien, lower your voice before the neighbors hear you. She just wanted to talk." Something had pissed him off between our last conversation and his arrival.

Kim just sat there like a deer caught in headlights. She wouldn't say a word, just stared at him like he was crazy, and the way he was yelling, I thought he just might be.

"You just can't stand for me to be happy, can you? Why would you go behind my back and conspire with my sister to get me back? Don't you see I'm happy where I'm at, and why did you call Faye and Wanda's husbands and tell them I was sleeping with their wives? Why stir the pot, Kim? Did your boyfriend decide he didn't want you anymore? So you thought you'd come begging back to me?"

What in the world was he talking about? Kim was standing now, but LaDamien was in her face. This was going south real fast. I called his name, but he had zoned out. Kim looked terrified.

"I don't know what you're talking about," Kim stuttered as she stepped backward. "I haven't called anybody's husband. Now get out of my way so I can leave."

"Oh, you want to leave. You've created all this chaos, and now you want out? You rescinded the divorce decree. You claim you're not going to sign the house over to me. My former secretary called me hysterical because her husband thinks we're having an affair. Faye is blowing up my phone, so I can only assume that's what she wants to bitch about."

I felt he was seconds away from striking Kim. She kept insisting she hadn't called anyone and was promising to sign the divorce papers if he just got out of her way so she could leave.

Fear was rising inside me, and I was afraid of the man standing in between his wife and me. "Baby, let her leave." I pleaded, but he still didn't budge.

There was a knock at the door, barely audible over LaDamien's tirade and Kim insisting she hadn't done anything wrong. My thoughts are spinning because this day has turned into a nightmare. LaDamien finally heard the knocking, walked over to the door, and opened it with force. "My God, what are you doing here? How do you know where we live?"

This was not happening. Who was at my door? LaDamien ran his hand from his forehead over his bald head, stopping at his neck that was bulging from tension. I walked up behind him and was horrified to see Wanda standing at my door. Now I was asking what she was doing here and how she found my house.

LaDamien

When I overheard my sister Pam talking to Kim on the phone, I knew I had to get home quickly. Pam should have left well enough alone and allowed me to make my decisions. If being with Mya was a mistake, it was a mistake I needed to make. Regardless of how others felt, they chose to stay out of it, but Pam had made it her pet project. She fought to keep me there. Our arguing was upsetting mama, but Pam didn't care. She was preaching and spewing bible verses at me like I was demonically possessed. The tiny apartment was closing in on me, so I grabbed my keys and left.

I was almost past Lakeland when Jose' called to let me know Kim was at the house, and he had left her and Mya inside. How could she be in Orlando if she was on the phone with Pam plotting to corner me at mamas? Nothing was making sense. When I finally talked to Mya, she said she was leaving. We had come too far for this to be happening. Kim knew she didn't want me back. She was just mean and hateful. Now Mya is saying that Kim isn't going to go through with the divorce and won't give me the house as she promised. *Hell has no fury like a woman scorned.* The passage came to me out of nowhere. Yes, I had done Kim wrong, but we discussed this and decided it was best. I had Mya, and she had Taj or whatever his name was. We agreed it was time to move on. Now she was flipping the script.

As bad as I didn't want to consider it, I found myself wondering if I should give Kim another chance. Maybe our marriage deserved a second chance. If she had not asked for the divorce, would I have ever moved in with Mya? My head was spinning. I needed to think clearly. Today's events were starting to take a toll on me.

My phone is ringing, and I look to see if it's Mya, but it's not. It's Wanda. She's returning my phone call from earlier today. I decided to call and set up a time for her to get her things.

"Hello."

"Where is your wife?" she asked. I could tell she was crying.

"Why are you asking about Kim?"

"She called Horace and told him about us. He thinks we're having an affair." My heart stopped. Kim wouldn't do that. Then I remember the pictures. Maybe Kim knew about the pictures Wanda had of her and that guy and was seeking revenge by calling Horace.

"She told him everything LaDamien, even about you sleeping with Faye, and said she was calling her husband as well." Still, I didn't think Kim would do that.

"Why would Kim do something like that Wanda, it makes no sense." Hell, none of this made any sense. Mya was calling, and I had to go. I told Wanda I would call her back and clicked over.

My mind is spinning.

Kim had followed Mya home. She's acting so out of character. I told Mya to hang up, and I would call Kim. She isn't answering. I could end all of this by telling Mya I was sorry and going back to my wife. Kim must be having some sort of breakdown. Ariel, what must all of this be doing to her? Mya would be hurt, but she would understand. That is what I love so much about her. She analyzes everything and does what is best. Still, I deserve to be happy. I shouldn't forsake my happiness to appease Kim.

My mind is spinning.

Kim won't leave, Wanda is calling back, and now Faye is calling.

My mind is spinning.

I finally reach the townhouse, and Kim's Mercedes is still parked outside, forcing me to park on the street. My breathing is labored, so I try to relax. Resting my head on the steering wheel, I recall Mya's dream. Was it a premonition? Was God refusing to bless our relationship? Prayer, I need to pray.

"God, please give me the strength to get through this day. I'm sorry, Lord, for being weak, not being a man, and honoring my wedding vows. God remove me from this situation and allow your will to be done. Whatever you lead me to do, I will do. If it's staying with Kim, then please have Mya understand. If it's to be with Mya, oh Lord, help Kim accept this and bless her with someone who will love her completely. Amen."

Turning off the car, I open the door and step out. My mind isn't clear, but I have to go in and settle this. The second I opened the door, the tension between Mya and Kim filled the air. There was no way I could walk away from Mya and back to my marriage. Kim needed to understand we are done.

"LaDamien, LaDamien," I heard my name but couldn't decipher which one was calling me. My mind is spinning. The more I yelled at Kim, the more I felt myself losing control.

"LaDamien, LaDamien."

Kim denies any wrongdoing saying everything is my fault. "If you kept your ass at home, none of this would be happening. This was a huge mistake. She can have your trifling ass."

Mya was grabbing my arm when someone knocked at the door. I spun around and grabbed the knob. The last person on this earth that I needed to see was standing there.

Wanda must have followed me from St. Petersburg. She had been crying. I remembered our conversation and wondered if Horace had put her out. I looked beyond her as if I expected Faye to pull up next.

"Wanda, what are you doing here? How did you know where I lived?" The questions rolled out as Mya joined me at the door.

My mind stopped spinning. Now it was the room that had taken on a life and was spinning around me. An escape, I needed to make an escape. My focus went to Mya, from Mya to Kim, from Kim to Mya, and then to Wanda. How did I weave such a massive web of deceit? How could three beautiful women fall for someone like me?

Being at this pivotal crossroad frightened me. What would I do if I lost them both? What if I've cost Wanda her marriage? The possibilities seemed too real, and I knew what I had to do. I would decide how this story would end. I would end what I started, right here and right now. Abruptly, I walked past Wanda knocking her aside.

Mya is calling out to me, "Baby, where are you going? LaDamien, where are you going?" She's crying. I can hear it in her voice.

It was too late. My decision was made. I can't stop the tears from flowing. "God, I don't want to do this," I cried out.

Mya is crying. Our sobs are muffled into one. She's pleading for me to come back so we can work it out. Now Kim is screaming for her to lock the door and call the police.

As I make my way to the Escalade, I recall the day I asked Kim to marry me. It was a mistake from the start, but I tried to make the best of it. Deep inside, I knew I could be a good husband. Why couldn't I just be a man and stand on my two feet? Then my thoughts went to the first day I ever saw Mya. The day I finally spoke to her. "God, why did things have to turn out this way? Why couldn't I have a real chance at love?"

My mind is spinning again, and I need God to stop this madness and make us all whole again. "God, please let me get in my vehicle, and allow me to drive away, drive away from this situation, to make everything okay."

He isn't listening. My mind is taking me back to a morning breakfast with Mya. She's shaking her head as she watches a story on the local news where a man had killed his ex-wife, her lesbian lover, and their two children before turning the gun on himself. Her words are resonating in my head, "why do people do this? If you can't deal with what's happening, why not just kill yourself? Why do you have to kill other people?' Why be so selfish, selfish, selfish…"

I reach under the drivers' seat for my gun. It's gone. God has heard my prayers. "Thank you," I cry as I climb inside and start the engine. My heart yearns to take one final look, but my mind is telling me to drive off. As usual, I follow my heart. Mya is no longer crying, nor is Kim yelling. Coming towards my SUV is Wanda, and she has my nine-millimeter pointed directly at me. The window is down. Why is the window down? Wanda is pointing the extra car's remote may way to control the locks and windows.

Wanda

"*So sweetheart*, this is how it ends? I loved you with everything within me. I have forsaken all others for you. I stood by your side through thick and thin. I kept your business afloat when you were unable to. I watched you run from this woman to that woman and stay in your unfulfilling marriage. All while I looked forward to the day when you would finally wake up and see what was staring you in the face all along.

"But no, you had to go out and find that bitch. That bitch who never loved you, who never cared for you, and who never understood who you were or what you need. You lost your damn mind behind that bitch, but I was there to pick up the pieces and to cover your ass. So what do you do? You decide to move your business, to move away from me, to leave me behind all alone to go on without you. Did you think you could survive without me?" Despite my tears, I held the gun steady, pointed straight at his head. He was probably shitting in his pants right now.

"Focus, Wanda, focus." I willed myself to tune out Mya's irritating wailing. In the shiny reflection of the Escalade, I could see Kim peering out the window of the townhouse with the cordless phone pressed to her ear as her lips moved up and down. The sirens, although upon us, still seemed miles and miles away. I looked at LaDamien, the love of my life, the man I had given up the security of my marriage, to confront, and give an ultimatum, sat before me frightened. I looked at him as though it was the first time I had ever seen him. Gone was the tall, sexy, intelligent man who appeared to have it all together. Gone was the suave businessman who could charm a snake out of his skin. No longer did I see the bright smile—the unbendable spirit. The warrior I dreamed would one day rescue me from my monotonous life. The life I lived with a man I never loved but married because he loved me. I looked at LaDamien, and at that moment, questioned what I ever saw in him. I looked at this man I was obsessed with and wondered why he was sitting before me with fear-filled eyes, with empathy, disgust, and contempt.

Suddenly, it all made sense, but in the same instance, none of it made sense. He never loved me, he never wanted me, and he could never be what he was to Kim or Mya. He didn't love Kim. He married her for the same reason I married Horace. He stayed with Kim for the same reason I stayed with Horace. It was convenient, it was reliable, and it was the right thing to do. Divorce was hard, even when you didn't love the person you chose to marry. It was easier to stay than to leave. What we had was guaranteed. What we desired came with uncertainty, and Mya, he didn't love her either. It was a sick obsession. She was the forbidden fruit. She broke rule number one of Affairs 101. She fell in love with the married man and demanded what she knew she didn't deserve.

I had to pull the trigger and be the savior for all three of us. F for every woman who had loved a man who was unable to love her in return. I wanted to put a bullet in him for every woman he had been with since he met me. A bullet for every time he slid his dick in my mouth and then walked away after being satisfied, making me feel like a two-dollar whore. I wanted to kill him and leave him dead in the road like the dog he was. But it was too late for that. If I killed him, I had to kill everyone. The sirens were closer. I have to think fast. I have to make a decision. Do I kill LaDamien, and then Kim, and then Mya? No, they've probably locked the door by now. The sirens were too close. Horace, my children, and my family, will they ever forgive me? Tears streamed down my face. I hated LaDamien. He just sat there as if he was at peace with my decision. He was spineless and a coward, as always. He manipulated me into doing the dirty work to fix his mess. The sirens were blaring. They were around the corner. I have to decide.

Kim

I stared out the window as I rushed the 911 operator to hurry up. "She has a gun. She's going to kill my husband. Please, for God's sake, do something."

Mya is in the background mumbling something. What LaDamien ever saw in this silly bitch is beyond me. She didn't even see the gun in Wanda's hand. If it had not been for me, she would be locked outside with them instead of crouching on the floor, mumbling a bunch of gibberish.

"Shut the fuck up, will you! This is your fault. If you hadn't fucked my husband, we wouldn't be in this mess. No! I'm not talking to you. I'm talking to my husband's whore. Yes, my husband, whose secretary is holding a gun on him. No, I don't know why she would try to kill my husband. Well, yes, I guess she was fucking him too. I'm sorry, just please hurry up, what's taking so long. Mya! Please SHUT UP!"

Mya

I saw Wanda the second I stepped out the door behind LaDamien. I tried to warn him that she had a gun, but he kept walking. My worst nightmare was coming to fruition. Mrs. Epps, Angie, Aubrey, even my sister all told me that nothing good would come of this relationship with LaDamien. Still, I never thought it would end like this. Kim grabbed my arm, pulled me inside, and slammed the door. She was screaming about the key. She was going to lock the door. I just stared at her because I couldn't understand why Kim would lock her husband out with a woman who had a gun. Now she was on the phone with nine-one-one blaming me for this mess.

I was scared out of my wits, so I did the one thing I knew to do. I prayed. I grabbed my bible from the counter, and got down on my knees, and prayed. I prayed to God to intercede on all of our behalfs. I prayed to God to forgive us of our trespasses. I prayed to God to allow everyone to walk away from this day unscathed physically but trusting in him to heal all mental wounds. I prayed to God that there were no bullets in the gun. I prayed to God that Wanda would realize what she was doing, that she would think about all the lives that would be destroyed. I prayed, and I prayed, and I prayed until Kim's harsh words evaporated. Until the sirens outside stopped blaring in my ear. I prayed for forgiveness, for strength, for divine intervention. I prayed, and I cried, and I pleaded, and I begged until the sound of my voice was overshadowed by the sound of gunshots piercing my ears. Suddenly I knew that karma had arrived.

I sprung up and ran to the door. Kim had dropped the phone and was screaming for me to stop. "You can't go out there. Mya, stop!"

Maybe she didn't love LaDamien. Maybe she was just selfish, but I had to see. I had to have hope beyond all hope that he was okay.

"Maybe she missed, and the police shot her, maybe the gun misfired," I screamed as I fought Kim to get the door open.

"No!" I screamed. Blood was everywhere. Wanda lay on the ground. What was left of her head was now a mass of blood and matter. I was going to be sick. Police were surrounding LaDamien's vehicle, blocking my view. As I inched forward, they beckoned me to stop. "Miss, please don't come any further. You need to go back inside."

Go back inside. He said it with no emotion. As if it was just another patrol stop, and I was a nosey bystander. The officers stepped back, and I was able to see what my heart willed me not to. LaDamien was hunched over the steering wheel, blood gushing from his neck. Crimson flowed like a fountain. She had hit the carotid artery, he wouldn't be getting out, and we wouldn't have a future together. Still, I cried out for them to help him, to do something. An officer held me back, insisting I calm down and go back inside. At that moment, I wished Wanda had killed me also.

LaDamien

Death wasn't as quick as I hoped it would be. I should have been dead by the time Wanda placed the gun under her chin and pulled the trigger, but I wasn't. No, I had to watch the residuals of my indiscretions.

The gun fired, and blood spouted from the crown of her head like fruit punch in a champagne fountain. It was followed by fragments of tissue, most likely her brains. She didn't fall immediately. I willed her to drop so God could impose my sentence. My body was paralyzed as my head rested on the steering wheel.

The door opened, and Mya came running out. In that instant, I didn't want to die. Minutes earlier, I had, but now I wished I could live. I wanted to get out of the truck and run to Mya, letting her know everything would be okay. That I would be all I had promised her I would be. I wanted to see Ariel and be the father to her that mine wasn't to me. I wanted to see my mother and let her know that she had done a great job despite my faults. Kim, my God, I owed her an apology for all the hurt and pain I had caused her.

It was too late. I was choking on my blood, bleeding to death through wounds in my neck. The bullet entered through the left, and fire shot through my throat. I was dying. When Wanda approached me, I could have easily driven off like a coward. But Mya had followed me outside, and Kim was trying to get her back inside.

Kim saved Mya's life. Imagine that. Now the two women who had loved me in life would mourn me in death. They both lost, and in the end, I'm the winner. God, please forgive me. I cry in my mind, which has finally stopped spinning.

*Somethings happening to me...*It won't be long now...*The man I used to be is gone...*I wonder if Mya can hear Kem singing our song. Memories of Naples flash by...*He gave up his life so I could go on...*Is the song playing? If it is, and she can hear it, she knows it's okay...*Girl, on in heaven*...that I'm okay...*Where the love of a lifetime resides in you.*

Epilogue

Faye

I still can't believe LaDamien is gone. Who would have thought that scene would have gone down the way that it did? Wanda had to be out of her mind, and to think I could have been caught up in that drama paralyzes my mind.

Someone called my house and spoke to my husband. All I know to this day is that it was a female. She revealed to Luke everything that had transpired between me and LaDamien, which I didn't know anyone else knew. They told him about Wanda and Mya and how we had all disrespected Kim. They knew that Kim was having an affair and that she and LaDamien were divorcing.

LaDamien was in St. Petersburg, and I was making plans to see him on my lunch break. Luke called me at the office, upset and asking, no telling me, to come home immediately. Of course, I refused, but Luke said it was urgent that I could never return if I didn't come home at once. Something major was going on. Luke had never spoken to me in such a harsh and demanding tone. I looked at the clock and decided I could stop by the house, see what Luke wanted, and still have enough time to spring my surprise visit on LaDamien.

Luke pulled the door open before I could place the key in the lock. "It's over today," he began. "This thing with LaDamien Bryson, it ends today. You have brought enough shame on me, on our marriage, and it stops today!"

Was he serious? I could not believe he had me come home for this same tired speech, but today, there was more. Luke's entire appearance was different. He was not backing down. For once, I felt as if he meant what he was saying, even before he shared the phone conversation from an anonymous caller.

"I know everything, Faye. You and LaDamien, the dirty sex, you with that woman that works for him, all about the woman named Mya, everything, Faye, every nasty little detail.

"My God, how could you carry on that way? I'm active in the church, and my wife is out blatantly fucking another man, a married man at that, and the whole town knows about it. Faye, it's time for you to turn from your wickedness and seek God. He's the only thing that will save us. If you are to continue being my wife, this affair ends right now."

Luke was giving me an ultimatum, and I still was not taking him seriously. The only thing on my mind was contacting LaDamien, and telling him how low that skank bitch of his had sunk. How dare she call my husband and tell him anything about me. My husband was waiting for some sort of response from me, but I didn't have one.

"It's time for me to get back to work," I finally said and left the house. It was too late for me to see LaDamien as planned, so I prayed that he would still be around when I got off for the day. My ire was too much for me to concentrate, and two hours later, I told my manager that I needed to leave for the day. LaDamien was not answering the phone. I left my office and rode by his office. He wasn't there. Next, I drove by his house, and then Mya's, and each of his sister's houses. I was afraid he had returned to Orlando. My phone rang, and it was Luke.

"Come home now." He demanded.
"I'm at work," I countered.
"You left work an hour ago. Faye, come home now."

Luke was trying my patience. I didn't want to come home. I had to find LaDamien, and tell him what Mya had done. If she had cost me my marriage, there would be hell to pay. Luke was still babbling in my ear when it dawned on me how silly I was being. My husband wasn't going anywhere, and there would be time to deal with LaDamien, and Mya later. If I were smart, Wanda would probably be able to help me. "Shit, I wonder if that bitch called Wanda's husband too."

At Luke's insistence, or shall I say begging, I returned home. LaDamien still wasn't acknowledging my calls, so I decided to play wife and cook my husband dinner. Luke was watching the six o'clock news when he called my name, followed by, "Oh my God, No!" I rushed into the den to see what was wrong, and he simply pointed at the television.

That evening I accompanied Luke to Bible Study. Afterward, we met with his Pastor. I don't know if I was in shock or what, but I confessed my sin to this man. Tears flowed and in abundance, some for LaDamien, some for Wanda, but most for me in thanksgiving to God for saving me and giving me another chance.

That night I recommitted myself to my husband and God. Every day since I have given His name the praise. Things aren't perfect between Luke and me, but I recognize that I have to do my part in this marriage. I can't go looking outside to solve what is going on inside. We've been attending couples counseling and working hard to become united as one. Sometimes I think about Kim, and Ariel, and even Mya. I'm no longer resentful. Instead, I find myself praying for them as I pray for myself. Hoping that we will all one day know peace, and whatever lesson was to be learned, it will help us become better women in the future.

Kim

TayJohn was waiting when I returned home from LaDamien's funeral. Days following his death, I held a private ceremony in the chapel at *Smith Funeral Home.* It was a Sunday morning service that only included Ariel and me, along with LaDamien's immediate family. Anything else would have prolonged the agony. There was no announcement in the paper. I don't even know if Mya was aware, and I didn't care.

No one understands what I felt witnessing my husband's murder at the hands of one of his many mistresses. The embarrassment of it all was just too much, so the sooner I put it all behind me, the better. His family didn't understand, not even Pam. It's as if they can't comprehend the depth of LaDamien's deception. Right now, my only focus is on Ariel and returning to normalcy. I do miss LaDamien, but he did this to our family, not me.

The day before, the police had delivered the effects from LaDamien's SUV. I was surprised to find among them copies of the pictures of TayJohn and me. It also included pages and pages of some sort of letter detailing Wanda's obsession with him. Other items were bank statements and items he must have cleaned out of the office and prepared to give back to her. The more his deception unravels, the crazier it becomes. I have no more energy to give to it, so I removed the pictures and the letter from the box and delivered them to her home.

"Hey, Big Red," TayJohn said as I walked over to his car. He was leaning against it, wearing a pair of denim shorts and a white t-shirt.

"What are you doing here?" I asked, confused by his presence since I had not seen or spoken to him since the day I met Chyna.

"I'm sorry."

"For what?"

"For not seeing your beauty, for not feeling your strength, and for not recognizing what a gem you are." TayJohn was still leaning on the car. Ariel walked around and leaned her head into me. We both looked at this man before us and wondered if he could fill the void left in our lives.

"He canceled the insurance policies months ago, so there's no money," I said casually.

TayJohn laughed. "Then there won't be any doubt regarding my intentions. I love you, Kim. Please give me a chance to be the man you deserve." He stepped forward and kissed me on the forehead

That was two months ago. The wound is still fresh, but TayJohn has nursed my heart. He says when I'm ready, he wants to marry me. Right now, I'm enjoying getting to know him and being loved by him. Marriage might complicate things, so I will choose to take my time. Karen and Debra are worried that I'm having a nervous breakdown, but I swear I'm not. I've simply exhaled and learned to breathe with the flow of life.

Mya

I didn't get a chance to say goodbye to LaDamien. Kim had a private service a few days after his death, and only she and God know where he's buried, or maybe she had him cremated and dumped his ashes in the trash. She was detached during the whole ordeal, unlike a wife whose husband was just gunned down in cold blood. I still can't believe that she didn't do anything to stop Wanda. In the end, all I was left with was the nightmare we all lived the day Wanda murdered him.

My heart ached not only for my loss but also for Wanda's family, husband, and children. My parents begged me to move back to St. Petersburg, but I refused. I couldn't even return to my townhouse. Angie and the others helped find me a new place and moved me in while I took a much-needed vacation. Brigit and I drove to Savannah, Georgia. It was the one place I always wanted to visit, and LaDamien promised to take me. I decided to have my little private memorial and pay homage to the man I loved. No matter what Kim did, she could not wipe out what LaDamien, and I shared.

Brigit and I drove over to Tybee Island one day during our trip, and there we purchased balloons and roses. I wrote my favorite scriptures and poems on pieces of paper and then attached them to the balloons. I walked out into the water and said a silent prayer. After releasing the balloons, I took the roses, tossed them out into the beautiful blue waters, and watched as the waves carried them out.

Brigit consoled me, listened to me, and cried with and for me. Brigit also shared with me the conversation between her and LaDamien, the day she took him the key to my house in St. Pete.

Weeks earlier, I was so happy and my life so complete, but it all changed instantly. No matter how many times Brigit told me that LaDamien truly loved me, it didn't ease the pain. Nothing she shared from that night mattered because LaDamien was gone, and her words wouldn't bring him back. Still, she kept talking as if she had a burden that she needed to lay down.

The grief was devastating, and I was feeling so overwhelmed. "You're severely depressed," Beverly Epps said as she cradled me in her arms.

She had come to Orlando a few days after Brigit and I returned from Savannah. Mrs. Epps stated she had been so worried when she learned LaDamien and I was living together. She wished she had gone against her will and reached out to me to offer counsel.

I asked her if she believed this was karma coming back to punish us. My heart was made glad when she boldly stated, "no."

"Sweetheart, as sure as a man is born of a woman, he will one day die. Just as our date of birth is predestined, so is our date of death. LaDamien could have died in a car crash, of a stroke, in a robbery, or a plane crash. I think what you need to take from this is that there's a right and a wrong way to do everything. Was God pleased? No, but I don't believe he's a God that sends *karma* to those he loves. I believe he wants to use us even in our frailties and sin. It's so we can minister to others through our situations. God is a healer, and he will heal your heart and give you the strength to carry on."

"I don't know if I can," I say in a weak voice.

"You don't have a choice. Life goes on, and you have to move with it. Take time to mourn, and then put this behind you, and don't look back." Mrs. Epps advised.

Don't look back. It was all clear now. Rashad told me I was like Lot's wife, God blessed me to relocate and get a fresh start, but I looked back the moment I felt LaDamien's presence. Now I had lost LaDamien, and Rashad hadn't called since the day he left. I'm too much of a wreck even to consider giving him a call now. No, right now, I just need some me-time.

Two months to the day of LaDamien's death, I received a call from his old business partner, Mark. He said he needed to give me something. I had no idea what he had to give to me and based on how he treated me when we first met. I had my reservations. Mark never approved of me, but I was so desperate to feel some sort of connection to LaDamien, I agreed to meet him. Perhaps he had a funeral program or the location of his burial. Any crumb would have satisfied me.

"How are you doing?" he asked, void of emotion when I approached. He had come to my place of employment, and we were standing near his car in visitor parking.

Mark handed me an envelope and stated LaDamien had given it to him the morning he died. I gasped. "He talked to me that morning as if he knew what the future held," he began. "I don't know what to say to you, Mya. It's no secret that I wasn't cheering for you even when I saw how much he loved you. To be honest, I debated this visit over and over. I tried to ignore his instructions and give this to Kim."

He handed me a cashier's check. It was apparent he was waiting for me to react to the amount. Instead, I opened the envelope.

Dear Mya,

If you are reading this letter, my worst fear has probably come true. I pray that this letter comes after we have spent a lifetime loving each other, not a time shortly after it was written. Remember the book you told me about the night when you described your dream? "Something Wicked This Way Comes." That's what I feel as I write this letter. Something evil is over us. I don't know what the future holds for us, but I know that I love you right now as I'm writing this letter. If we have lived a long life together, I have probably said those three words a million times, but if I have left you sooner, I want you to know that I... truly... love... you. If Mark has given you this letter, he has proven to be a man of his word. The money he has given to you is from the condo project he signed on to assist me with a while back. The money is my profit. It's not much, Mya, but I wanted to leave you with something. As I write this letter to you, I already know our time together was short-lived. I apologize for allowing my desire for you to overwhelm me and disregard what was best for everyone else. I simply had to know what loving you would be like, and I must say the past few months have been worth more than all the years that preceded them. Do you remember that day at the park when you had me listen to Kem's song, "You Are?" I can't get that song out of my mind today. As I think about our love, I can say that you are everything that song describes. I want to write you a million letters over a million years to let you know what your love means to me. I love you, Mya, I do.

Please forgive me for not weighing the consequences of my actions, and please don't ever forget me or what we had together.
I love you.
LaDamien.

"Thank you," I say as I fold the check inside the letter and place it back inside the envelope. "Is Kim and Ariel okay? Financially, I mean." I ask this as I fight back the tears. LaDamien spoke of meeting with his broker to make changes to the policies, but I don't know what, if anything, he did.

Mark says he doesn't know. When he and LaDamien were in business together, he had life insurance policies. "If he kept them up, then Kim and Ariel will be just fine."

"Good," I say. "Thank you, Mark," I say this time, for LaDamien. He smiles at me for the first time and turns to walk away but stops and turns back.

"It wasn't that I didn't like you, Mya. It was that LaDamien loved you. He was a married man, and he broke rule number one of Affairs 101."

"What's that?" I ask, with a slight smile but a little confused.

He replied, "Never fall in love with the affair."

A READING GROUP GUIDE

Love...
Like Snow in Florida on a Hot Summer Day

Tracy L. Darity

About This Guide

The suggested questions are intended to enhance your groups reading of *Love...Like Snow in Florida on a Hot Summer Day* by Tracy L. Darity and only serve as a guide.

DISCUSSION QUESTIONS

1. Have you ever been cheated on by a spouse or significant other? If so, how did you handle the betrayal?

2. Have you ever been the "third" person in a relationship? If so, how do you think your actions affected the person's spouse or significant other?

3. Kim willingly married LaDamien knowing he was being unfaithful. Mya willing went into this relationship with LaDamien, knowing he was married. Do you believe women promote infidelity by accepting this type of behavior?

4. LaDamien revealed to Mya a secret he had held inside most of his life. Do you believe what happened to him as a child played a significant part in his inability to commit as an adult? If so, how?

5. Mya was smitten with LaDamien from the start and was willing to give him a chance despite him being married. Throughout the story, she battled with her immorality. Why was it so easy for her to enter into an adulterous affair and then stay in it despite LaDamien's actions?

6. Mya believed Pastor Epps showed a dismissive attitude when she met with him about her affair with LaDamien. Do you believe Pastor Epps handled things correctly, or should he have heard Mya out? Do you believe his approach led to her going back to LaDamien?

7. Kim blamed both Mya and LaDamien for her infidelity. Was it fair for her to do so? Could another person's actions force you to do something you normally wouldn't think of doing?

8. Friends played an instrumental part in the lives of Kim and Mya. Having close friends can be a blessing. Do you feel the friends in this story provided good advice? Was there advice given that should have been followed but wasn't, or shouldn't have been followed, but was?

9. Religion played a part in the story, with the characters knowing right from wrong and understanding that their actions were not Christ-like. Do you feel it's common for "church folk" to indulge in sinful activities? Do you believe they feel remorse afterward?

10. Ariel, Kim and LaDamien's daughter, is old enough to understand what is happening with her parents. How much, if any, damage do you believe was done to Ariel by her parents?

11. How hard is it for children to witness their parents' infidelities?

12. Both Wanda and Faye were married to men who appeared to be the complete opposite of LaDamien. How common do you think it's for a wife to cheat on a faithful husband?

13. HIV/AIDS is the fastest-growing cause of death for African-American women between 25 and 44. In the story, condoms were rarely, if ever, used. Could this type of behavior be at the root of the epidemic?

14. Throughout the story, LaDamien professed his love for Mya. Do you believe he truly loved her or was it all an obsession? Have you ever experienced a love like theirs?

15. In the story, both Kim and LaDamien professed to be the "marrying kind." Meaning they both wanted to be married and enjoyed the title of husband and wife. Do you think people can get too caught up in the titles that come with being married that they fail to do what is required to be married?

Made in the USA
Coppell, TX
04 August 2021